PRAISE FOR K⟨  E

"A haunting, unflinching portrait of ne⟨... ...⟨-chilling terror and staggering empathy. With nimble pacing, genuine scares, and a riveting central mystery, *Graveyard of Lost Children* is a bona fide page-tuner that will have your heart racing and breaking that will linger long after the final chapter. Magnificent."

—**RACHEL HARRISON**, author of *Such Sharp Teeth*, for *Graveyard of Lost Children*

"*They Drown Our Daughters* is the best kind of story—one that will both break your heart and scare the hell out of you."

—**JENNIFER McMAHON**, *New York Times* bestselling author of *The Invited* and *The Children on the Hill*, for *They Drown Our Daughters*

"*They Drown Our Daughters* is a stunner. Beautifully written, deeply creepy, and carefully plotted—but above all, a fantastic meditation on what it means to be a parent."

—**ROB HART**, author of *The Warehouse* and *The Paradox Hotel*, for *They Drown Our Daughters*

"An atmospheric, absorbing, multi-generational novel, which explores the way historical events can impact the present. I was at turns terrified by the air of ghostly myth and compelled by the excellent prose. A brilliant achievement!"

—**MELANIE GOLDING**, author of *The Hidden*, for *They Drown Our Daughters*

ALSO BY KATRINA MONROE

They Drown Our Daughters

GRAVEYARD OF LOST CHILDREN

KATRINA MONROE

Poisoned Pen
PRESS

Sourcebooks, Poisoned Pen Press, and the colophon are registered trademarks of Sourcebooks.

Published by Poisoned Pen Press, an imprint of Sourcebooks
P.O. Box 4410, Naperville, Illinois 60567-4410
(630) 961-3900
sourcebooks.com

Library of Congress Cataloging-in-Publication Data

Names: Monroe, Katrina, author.
Title: Graveyard of lost children / Katrina Monroe.
Description: Naperville, Illinois : Poisoned Pen Press, [2023]
Identifiers: LCCN 2022052128 (print) | LCCN 2022052129 (ebook) | (trade paperback) | (epub)
Classification: LCC PS3613.O53696 G73 2023 (print) | LCC PS3613.O53696
(ebook) | DDC 813/.6--dc23/eng/20220128
LC record available at https://lccn.loc.gov/2022052128
LC ebook record available at https://lccn.loc.gov/2022052129

Printed and bound in Canada.
MBP 10 9 8 7 6 5 4 3 2 1

To Abby and Dillan, my little changelings

AUTHOR'S NOTE:

This book contains themes of mental illness and postpartum depression, including thoughts of harm and suicide, as well as semi-graphic depictions of childbirth. Please exercise self-care during and after reading.

CHAPTER ONE

OLIVIA

Hours passed like seconds. Seconds like hours. Olivia's body twisted inside out, and waves of heat and cold rippled across her skin. She smelled blood and meat. Her mouth watered. She swallowed against the nausea only for it to come roaring back.

"Ready?"

She shook her head, worrying what would come out if she opened her mouth.

"It's okay, Liv. It'll be okay."

Something inside her ripped and she felt liquid seep down her legs, soaking the sheet beneath her. She shivered.

"Get ready, Olivia. We're almost there."

The room had taken on a smoky quality. She blinked and it cleared for a second. Long enough that she saw the bloody fabric by her feet. The murky puddle on the floor.

"Is she supposed to—there's a lot of—"

"It's fluid."

A giggle choked the back of her throat. Of course blood was *fluid*. No. Wrong word. *Viscous*.

Vicious.

Viscera.

Coppery and unnervingly cold.

"Up on your elbows, now."

Olivia didn't have elbows. Or arms. Or legs. She was on fire.

"Here we go, and—"

Push.

———

After it was all over, after they whisked the baby away, leaving Olivia spent and sweaty and broken in the middle of the bed with fresh stitches between her legs, a janitor mopped her fluids up off the floor while a ring of keys jangled merrily on his hip.

"Don't worry," he said, "I've seen worse."

———

The midwife popped up from between her legs, waving a white cloth like the last few hours had been some twisted magic trick. "There. You'll have to keep an eye on that for a few weeks. You'll want to avoid wiping while that heals. We'll send you home with some stool softeners and a fun little squeeze bottle. You'll be fine."

Olivia's midwife's name was Happy. She liked breathing exercises to the beat of "Another One Bites the Dust" and fun little squeeze bottles and tie-dyed hair wraps.

She patted Olivia's thigh before easing her leg down flat. The epidural had only worked on the left side of her body, so while her right side had been in agony, she'd screamed at the nurse to catch the left leg before it fell off the bed.

She still couldn't feel it and in her post-birth haze imagined herself a one-legged Barbie, hopping on tiptoe through her pink and purple dream house.

"You did good," Happy said. "Really good."

On the other side of the room, Olivia's baby shrieked. Her skull tingled with the force of it.

"Is she okay?"

"More than okay. The louder, the better."

Olivia's wife, Kris, didn't seem to think so. Kris leaned over the side of the bassinet where another nurse poked and prodded and cooed.

Kris frowned, deepening the lines around her soft gray eyes. At some point she'd sweated through her nice shirt—a navy button-down with faint pinstripes she'd insisted on wearing because this was the first time they were meeting their daughter and she'd wanted to make a good impression—and was now wearing a T-shirt Olivia didn't recognize. "She sounds scared."

Happy nodded. "She probably is."

"She sounds angry."

"She probably is." She winked. "She'll feel better once she's had a bath and something to eat."

"Sounds like someone else I know." Kris smiled at Olivia. "She's right, you know. You did good."

The baby shrieked again, a sharp yelp of pain.

It was like a needle to the pain center of Olivia's brain. "What are they doing to her?"

"Shots," Kris said. "It's okay."

"It's *not* okay. Are you listening? It sounds like they're *murdering* her." Olivia started to pull herself up, but her leg lay there useless, and any movement sent waves of pain up her middle. She felt a gush and, for a hot, humiliating second, thought she'd pissed herself. An excellent start to motherhood.

"Done," the nurse chirped.

But no amount of petting and shushing would calm the baby. Her screams were like ice water down Olivia's neck. Her heartbeat thumping in her ears, her temples, her throat, Olivia leaned as far over the side of the bed as she dared, but the nurse blocked her view of the bassinet.

Happy gently grabbed her shoulder, pulling her back against the pillows. "Better bring her over. Mom's getting antsy."

Mom.

The word startled Olivia. She was only brought back into herself when the nurse placed a bundle on her chest, a squirming, writhing thing wrapped tight in a thin blanket that smelled like lavender and laundry soap.

"Remember the latch," the nurse said.

The baby's mouth gaped wide, her tiny tongue trembling with the force of her cries. Her face was purple.

The nurse helped Olivia wrestle her breast free of the hospital gown and within a few seconds, the baby was latched. Her daughter made throaty *kah, kah, kah* sounds as she swallowed. The purple in her face faded to a soft pink.

Kris leaned over the both of them, kissing their heads. "My girls."

Olivia gently stroked the soft down of the baby's head. Her eyelashes were long and pale, and her fat cheeks trembled with the force of her swallows. Her eyelids fluttered over blue-gray eyes. Olivia searched for a piece of herself in her daughter's face, anxious to claim the curve of an earlobe or subtle swoop of the nose.

She didn't notice Happy and the nurses leaving, but when Olivia finally looked up, the three of them were alone.

Kris pulled a chair beside the bed and set a cup of coffee on the table, pushing aside the stack of books Olivia had brought, thinking there'd be time to read (because there was always, always time to read), and rested her head on Olivia's shoulder. "She's beautiful."

Olivia frowned, only to snatch it back. New mothers weren't supposed to frown. "She's a stranger."

"What do you mean?"

"I mean she doesn't look like me."

"Sure she does."

"I don't see it."

"She's a baby. Babies change, like, hourly. You'll see."

Olivia hoped so. They'd chosen artificial insemination over in vitro mainly because of the cost. Olivia was an adjunct English professor, and Kris worked in human resources for a tech firm that always seemed on the cusp of going out of business. They didn't have a ton of extra money and, thankfully, it only took two rounds for the pregnancy to take. But every day she was pregnant, Olivia couldn't help thinking that the baby growing inside her was half of someone she would never meet. She would look into her child's face and see someone she didn't know. Their biggest fight had been over whether to ask a friend to donate sperm. Kris had hated the idea, saying she didn't want to risk losing their daughter to a guilty conscience and biased court system. Olivia had wanted to tell her that their friends wouldn't do anything like that, but she couldn't. She hadn't realized until that moment, but she didn't know their friends all that well because, at the end of it, they were all Kris's friends.

"She's still going," Kris said, impressed, as she wiped some dribbled milk from the baby's cheek.

Olivia's back was starting to ache and the tug on her nipple had gotten sharp, but she didn't dare move.

A good eater, Olivia's aunt Erin would have called her. Olivia smiled, oddly proud at the thought.

My daughter, the good eater.

Olivia remained perfectly still, her lower half still throbbing with pain and her arm falling asleep. Soon, she thought. Soon she would feel that rush of warmth, of fierce protectiveness. Soon she would feel like a mother.

They named her Flora, after Kris's grandmother. Olivia signed the paperwork over Flora's head as she fed, the third time in an hour. Olivia, however, hadn't eaten in almost forty-eight hours, dreading that first trip to the toilet. Her insides felt wrung out and weak, and each time she felt her own diaper fill with blood, her stomach rolled. It didn't stop Kris from trying to ply her with vending machine chocolate, egg rolls from her favorite Chinese restaurant, and a slice of apple pie from the hospital cafeteria.

"You have to eat something," Kris said, holding the egg rolls under Olivia's nose. "You gotta be starving."

If Olivia was starving, she didn't feel it. Hours after giving birth, it was like she was a passenger in her own body, seeing through a thick pane of glass and going through the motions, detached. The pain was someone else's. The weight against the pillows was someone else's. The arms holding Flora were someone else's.

"What I need is a break." Olivia arched her back, only to quickly readjust when Flora lost her latch and immediately started to whimper.

"Already?" Kris said. "You just got her." Seeing Olivia's face, she added, "I'm kidding."

The barb had already hit home. Kris was right. Of course she was tired. Of course it was hard. That was what it meant to be a mom.

Better not to say it though. Not out loud.

She gently brushed the bridge of Flora's nose with her fingertip, and Flora's eyes fluttered open. She remembered their birthing class—the one they'd signed up for as a joke, two in the morning and laugh-drunk after Lamaze, breathing at each other for so long they almost passed out—and how they told her babies couldn't see more than a couple of inches in front of their faces. Olivia could swear Flora saw her just fine.

I'm your mama, Olivia thought. *I love you very much, and I would never do anything to hurt you.*

Flora's eyes fluttered closed, and her eating slowed. Soon she was asleep.

"There, see?" Kris said. "You're a pro."

"You'd sleep too, if you drank your weight in warm milk."

"No. It's you." Kris kissed her. "You're the best."

The room went briefly out of focus as Olivia heard a murmur in the back of her mind. It sounded like a rush of air, like hot, expended breath. It sounded like *lies.*

Olivia tried to sleep while Flora slept, but Kris's anxious puttering around the room—fixing pillows, unpacking and repacking Olivia's overnight bag, reading through their paperwork, messing with the television—jarred her awake every few minutes. Finally, when she was within grabbing distance, Olivia snatched Kris's sleeve and refused to let her go until she promised to sit down and be quiet.

It didn't matter.

The movement had disturbed Flora, and pained wails shuddered through her little body.

"What should I do?" Kris asked. "How can I help?"

Olivia shifted Flora to the other arm, careful not to disturb the intricate Jenga of pillows propping her arms up. Only when Flora was plugged in and eating happily did Olivia finally look up at her wife. "I love you. Please leave."

Kris pouted. "I don't want to."

"Well one of us has to go or I'm never going to sleep. And if I don't sleep, I can't promise either of us will survive."

"But, I mean, will you be okay?"

"Definitely."

"You're sure."

Olivia waved using Flora's tiny hand. "Bye, Mama."

Kris shook her head, but she was beaming. "Okay, okay. I'll go. But I'll be back first thing in the morning."

"We wait with bated breath."

Kris kissed Olivia's forehead. "Jerk."

"Love you."

"Love you more."

The second the door clicked behind Kris, Olivia felt a rush of panic. Her overtired imagination looped through a disjointed reel of images, flashing across her consciousness in bursts of red and shadow. Olivia leaving the hospital with Flora still attached at her breast, only to find themselves alone. Lost. She imagined walking the side of a highway, rocks in her shoes and dirt in her mouth. She imagined finally finding her house only to realize it was empty, that the phone wouldn't connect, that she was completely, utterly alone.

Olivia readjusted, earning a gargley squawk from Flora. She told herself that would never happen. She was being ridiculous. All she needed was a little sleep. Kris would be back in the morning, when they would take Flora home and they would be a family. Complete. Happy.

She kissed the top of Flora's fuzzy head, her heart fluttering at Flora's powdery scent.

Yes, she thought, gratefully. *We will be happy.*

Over the next several hours, it seemed every time Olivia fell asleep, a nurse knocked on the door. They needed to check her vitals, to have her take a short walk, to give Flora a once-over, like she'd spontaneously grown a tail. All of them asked about bowel movements—hers and Flora's—clearly the pinnacle of litmus tests for health, and encouraged Olivia to let Flora sleep in the plastic bassinet beside her bed.

"She'll be plenty warm," one nurse told her. "Don't worry about it."

Olivia didn't tell her that she'd tried, that the moment Flora was more than a few inches from her, the whimpering and writhing began—hers *and* Flora's.

Instead, Olivia thanked the nurse and promised to give it a shot.

Finally, around 10:00 p.m., the knocking stopped. Flora had been snoozing for several minutes and looked like she might finally be down for the count. It unnerved Olivia, how still Flora was as she slept. Her tiny chest barely rose and fell with each breath, and Olivia's eyes ached from not blinking as she watched, assuring herself that, yes, Flora *was* still breathing.

Olivia ordered herself to close her eyes. She was desperate for sleep, and something inside warned her that this would be her only chance. But every time her eyelids drooped, it was like something prodded her awake. A feeling of unease, like someone watching her, that she couldn't explain. She shouldn't have sent Kris away. Kris would have soothed her worries, would have promised to watch Flora throughout the night so Olivia could rest. Or, at minimum, she would have reminded Olivia that even if she hadn't just given birth, even if her hormones weren't spiraling and her body wasn't trying to find a way back to itself, she had never been able to sleep well in a place that wasn't home.

Sleep, she imagined Kris saying. *Sleep, sweetie.*

Though Olivia's back was twisted in a weird direction thanks to a few pillows that'd come untucked, and her bladder throbbed with the need to pee, she finally closed her eyes and sank quickly, deeply, asleep.

Until a sharp pinch yanked her back.

She had been dreaming of home, not their house, but the house she grew up in. The woods that butted up against their yard. She had been running between the trees, away from or to something, she wasn't sure. One of the trees had turned, its trunk twisted and seeping sap, and reached fingerlike branches toward her, only to scrape her chest as she twisted away.

She blinked hard, trying to clear the image of the nightmare. But the room was pitch black, save for the eerie green glow from the machines like nocturnal animal eyes peering through the brush. Her feet tingled, like she'd been running for hours, the dark of the dream lingering. In that place between asleep and awake, long-fingered shadows reached for the corners of her eyes and she bit her tongue to keep from shouting, remembering at the last second where she was. When she looked down to make sure Flora was still snuggled and asleep, she saw her hospital gown had been ripped open at the neck, exposing both her breasts. Flora had latched on to one, eyes wide and unblinking. Milk had spilled down both her cheeks, soaking the blanket beneath her head. Razor-sharp nails grazed Olivia's tender flesh as Flora clung to her, the throaty *kah, kah, kah* noise the only sound in the dark.

CHAPTER TWO

SHANNON

I never wanted to be a parent.

When I was young, most women wouldn't say that. Not out loud. Most women were cowards.

It wasn't that I didn't like children. I liked them just fine—helped my mom and aunts raise enough of them—but I didn't want to be stripped down and cracked in half in order to have my own. My mother used to say a woman forgot the pain of childbirth almost immediately. Had to, to convince her to do it all over again.

That's a lie.

A woman doesn't forget the feel of a vice squeezing her until she can't breathe. She doesn't forget the way her hips separate and split her in two. She doesn't forget the meaty, irony smell of herself, the hot drip of blood down her thighs. The fire between her legs. The tearing.

No. A woman is convinced to do it all over again because some things are worth the pain.

I never wanted to be a parent, until I saw your face. Those curious eyes, attentive and fixed on me. The curve of your chin, your patchy dark hair and pink lips.

It was like I'd made you on my own, with no trace of your father on your body. I knew then that you and I were meant for each other. You would understand me. You would love me.

Doesn't mean I don't have regrets. Can't get through life without them. Biggest of them all is having spent most of my life locked away from the world. The way I hear it, though, there's worse places, and I'm inclined to believe it. Jo told me about one hospital they slip tranquilizers in the milk to keep everyone nice and complacent, and Jo's no bullshitter. I don't mind sharing a room. Jo has her side, I have mine. Jo has her things, I have mine. I get three hot meals and snacks in between if it's been a good day, and I have more and more of those lately. Gained a good ten pounds in the last few months. Jo says they look good on me.

It's a strange thing knowing my meals come like clockwork, that I'll eat until I'm…not full, but satisfied. Growing up in a house of eight meant hoarding and scrounging, all of us little mice creeping into the kitchen in the middle of the night. One time my sister, Erin, snuck an entire jar of cake icing into the bedroom we shared, and we ate it with our fingers, unable to sleep with the sugar high. Most nights, though, all we wanted were a handful of saltines to bridge the gap.

You eat and be grateful.

I'm getting hungry just thinking about those days. Feels like I'm always hungry. Always trying to fill the empty space where you used to be. Lately, though, I am *ravenous*.

It's easier to go back to *that dinner* with the tang of tomato sauce on the back of my tongue. Spaghetti with jarred sauce. One of about three things Mom could fix for all of us without breaking the bank. Once in a while we got slices of bread with it, and we'd all pile the spaghetti into sandwiches, slurping noodles as marinara dripped down our chins. Can't stand the stuff now, but back then, it was my favorite. I suppose that should have been my first clue.

No sooner were my siblings at the table did they start chewing, making a limp sign of the cross when Dad gave them the look. I twirled noodles around and around on my fork, stomach sloshing.

"You're green," Erin said.

My older sister always had a way of pointing out exactly what you didn't want pointed out.

"I don't feel good," I said.

"Period?"

"Gross." John Jack, one of my brothers, mimed puking into the spaghetti.

He was seven, second youngest and none too happy about the way things turned out, birth-order-wise. Erin was the eldest, so she got the respect. At six, Patrick was the baby, so he got all the attention. Smack in the middle, John Jack and me got whatever was left. It wasn't much.

Mom eyed me from across the table and I couldn't help but squirm. Didn't matter that I was sixteen, a woman in my own mind. I could feel her probing around in my head looking for the thing I'd done wrong, or would do wrong in the future. She fancied herself some kind of behavior oracle—she could tell with one look whether you'd be getting into something you shouldn't, even before you did, and made sure the punishment was swift and fierce.

"If you're gonna be sick," Dad said, "leave the table."

"I'm fine," I said, feeling not fine at all.

I thought it was guilt. Growing up Catholic, I knew it had a way of eating a person inside out. I went to my first confession when I was nine years old and talked the poor priest's ear off about coveting my sister's new clothes and stealing food and lying to Mom about stealing food—little things that, looking back, didn't matter much. But this was something else.

His name was Matthew. He was eighteen. Mature. Even had a job. I figured I loved him well enough, and that he loved me well enough, so what was the harm in letting him do things to me? He'd liked it. Gave me long, sweet kisses and called me his girl after. It was all incredibly romantic, I thought.

"I just don't want spaghetti," I said when Mom wouldn't stop her eye probing. "We always have spaghetti."

Dad pointed at me with his fork, the tines bloody. "You eat and be grateful."

Around the table, my siblings stared at my plate, still full while most of their dinner was long gone. Seemed we were always leaving the table hungry. I knew I'd better eat up or I'd be sitting at the table staring down a plate of cold spaghetti all night—spaghetti any one of them would have gladly taken off my hands—so I set my jaw and twirled the noodles and shoved as much as I could into my mouth. My eyes watered as I started to choke, but Mom gave me that look again so I chewed and chewed and chewed until finally I swallowed.

I flashed Mom a weak smile, but it only hardened her expression. I could tell she was trying to dig into me, to see what I'd done. I silently begged John Jack to shove Patrick, or for Erin to say something obnoxious, anything to get her attention off me.

My throat felt tight. I coughed and a bit of spaghetti came up. I swallowed it before I could think, and then the acid started bubbling up and my face got hot and cold at the same time and Mom stared harder, leaning toward me, so I scooped up another bite thinking I could force my body to behave, but it was all too much.

I cupped my mouth and ran to the sink.

"Go lay down," Mom ordered once I'd finished gagging and rinsed the sink and my mouth.

I passed by the table where my plate sat empty and bloody. I caught John Jack's gaze and he shrugged. *Every man for himself.*

Later, Mom took my temperature—normal—and studied the back of my throat for those little white pustules that meant strep.

"You eat something funny?" she asked.

I shook my head.

"You been drinking?"

"No," I said.

She went into the bathroom to find the puke bucket to set by my bed, and when she came back, her face had twisted into something I didn't recognize: stony, with hair-thin cracks on the surface.

She held up the garbage bin from the bathroom. "You see this?"

I nodded.

"Should be full of sanitary napkins by now. You and Erin typically start your period within days of each other."

"So?"

"So, it's practically empty." She sat on the edge of my bed and looked me hard in the face. "I'm not going to ask you, because I know you'll just lie. So instead I want you to go in my bathroom and grab a test from the box under the sink."

I tried to argue, but Mom wouldn't let me. She frog-marched me into her bathroom and practically peed on the test stick for me. We sat in a heavy silence for ten minutes, until the little pink plus sign appeared.

I'd expected her to scream, to rip another slat out of the already broken cabinet door to spank me. She didn't do either of those things.

I suppose I should have been worried for myself. Frightened for my future, for what that little pink plus sign meant. But all I could do was stare at my mom, fascinated. Four children, two cars that never seemed to work, rowdy boys with broken bones and teeth too expensive to fix properly, an empty wallet and food stamps that always ran out the week before the end of the month, and *this* was the first time I had ever seen her cry.

———————

Doctor James Call-Me-Jim Tran spotted me writing yesterday and spent the rest of my leisure hour telling me how proud he was that I'd taken his advice. His tone changed lickety-split when he asked to read it and I refused, until I called it my confessional.

He smiled that crooked-tooth grin and said, "Writing our feelings is often the first step to properly processing them. We take them out of ourselves and analyze with detached rationality. Well done, Shannon."

It'd been a long time since I'd earned a *well done* from anyone, let alone the doctor, so I don't feel any shame in telling you I fluffed up and preened like a little bird.

This isn't a confession. Not exactly. But if I'm lucky, it might be the tool to my salvation.

I'm writing this from the leisure room, my third day in a row with my pen to paper in direct view of Doctor Call-Me-Jim and his cronies. They smile and nod, and every so often, Doctor Call-Me-Jim scribbles a note in my file.

It's all going to plan, my little girl.

I'll see you soon.

CHAPTER THREE

OLIVIA

For someone so tiny, Flora took up an incredible amount of space.

Their kitchen was small, with hardly enough counter space for the KitchenAid mixer Olivia had (guiltily) spent too much money on when she decided she would be the kind of woman who made her own bread. Stupid, because she'd hardly mastered scrambled eggs. Now every inch was covered in bottles (some still in the packaging), pacifiers, and teething toys she was pretty sure they wouldn't need for several months. The mixer was stuck in a cabinet, jammed Tetris-like behind the plastic take-out containers Kris insisted on keeping—*Cheaper than buying Tupperware.*

The living room was covered in boxes that'd trickled in over the last few days from her aunt and uncles. The biggest had come from Aunt Erin, full of hand-me-down onesies and toys she thought she recognized from her childhood. It'd been sitting next to the coffee table since they brought Flora home from the hospital; every time Olivia so much as looked at it, Flora wailed for Mommy's attention.

This time, though, Olivia managed to pull out a few rattles before Flora went off. Kris stood over Olivia, patting Flora's back.

When Olivia instinctively put her arms out, Kris nudged them away with her knee. "It's fine. I got it. Look." She turned around to show Olivia Flora's face. "We're alive. We're good."

"She's probably hungry," Olivia said.

"She just ate."

"Is she wet?"

Kris patted Flora's diaper. "Don't think so."

"Then she's hungry. Hand her over."

Kris swapped Flora to the other side. Flora hiccuped, paused, then started crying all over again. "I'm the last person to want to give our daughter a complex, but is it possible you're overfeeding her?"

At the sound of Flora's crying, Olivia's breasts ached. She glanced down at her shirt, expecting to see twin, damp circles. "I'm not overfeeding her."

"Let me try the pacifier."

Frustration bubbled under Olivia's skin. She knew what her daughter needed.

"It doesn't work." Olivia's arms started to hurt from holding them out. "Just give her." Kris's expression fell. Feeling guilty, Olivia added, "You're going to be late, anyway."

"I don't have to go."

"You do."

She sighed. "I do."

"It's okay."

"It's only a half day."

"I know."

"You're not mad?"

"Not yet." Olivia stood and pried Flora from Kris's arms. Flora was already rooting. Olivia couldn't get her shirt unbuttoned fast enough, and when Flora finally latched, Olivia winced at the force.

Sighing, Kris draped a cloth over Olivia's shoulder. "This goes on much longer, I might start to get jealous."

"Well we have her for another eighteen years, minimum. You're gonna have to get used to it."

"I know, babe. I was kidding." She gently squeezed Olivia's shoulder. "Are you okay?"

"Fine," Olivia lied.

She was running on only a few hours' sleep, most of it on the couch, drifting as Flora fed, perched on a pillow. Her bleeding hadn't slowed the way Happy explained it would, and eating had become a chore. The only thing carrying her through it all was the look on Flora's face when she'd finish nursing, her cheeks plump and rosy. Already her blue-gray eyes had begun to turn a deep brown similar to Olivia's, and it gave her comfort. Her nose might have been someone else's, but her eyes were Olivia's. And when they would drift closed after nursing, Olivia missed them.

Kris looked her hard in the face before planting a soft kiss on her forehead. "Call me, okay? Any reason. I'll come running back."

"You won't run."

"I'll walk very quickly." She smiled. "I love you. You did the most incredible thing, and I am in awe of you. You know that, right?"

Olivia blinked away tears, nuzzling her head into Kris's shoulder. She loved how her wife always smelled like the woods. Closing her eyes and breathing Kris in felt like an escape. Then a tug on her breast pulled her back again. She had to remind herself that she wasn't a wife anymore. She was a mother. "Love you too."

Flora fed for several minutes after Kris left, and it put her in the kind of sleep even jostling her into the bouncy seat didn't disturb, so Olivia didn't question it. A smarter woman would have laid down on the floor next to the bouncy seat and slept, but the boxes would be there when she woke up, and so would Flora's hunger.

With exaggeratedly slow movements, Olivia unfolded the box flaps and started pulling out the contents, cringing as a play mat with half a dozen noise-makers flopped over the side. She shot a glance at Flora. Her lips trembled for a brief second. Olivia held her breath until Flora resettled, a soft sigh escaping her lips.

Most of the clothes she pulled out she recognized from baby pictures of herself. During the first few months of her pregnancy, her grandmother and Aunt Erin must have flipped through a dozen photo albums, waxing poetic on what a good child Olivia was.

"Never really fussy," Aunt Erin said. "For a while I thought something was wrong with you."

Most of the clothes were in good condition, probably spent years folded between sheets of tissue paper in her grandmother's attic. Notes had been pinned to the clothing—*Erin's communion dress; Olivia's first birthday outfit.* Taking care of things had always been important to her grandmother. Growing up, Olivia only ever got in trouble if she stained her good clothes or didn't keep her shoes clean. It was a waste of money, her grandmother said, not taking care of things. Aunt Erin said it was a holdover from their childhood, with very little split between too many people.

"And then you were born," Aunt Erin had said, and then refused to elaborate.

Olivia separated the clothes, one pile for things she'd keep, another for things she'd pass on to Goodwill, but by the time she reached the bottom of the box, the only thing in the Goodwill pile was a yellow-stained onesie with a missing snap. The last thing she pulled out was a set of zippered, footy pajamas, a pink and brown plaid pattern with velvet paws stitched to the feet. On the hood were two fuzzy ears, the delicate fur still soft.

Her ears rang and a dull throb started at the base of her skull as she stroked the velvet. Unlike the other things in the box, this one didn't come with a note, but Olivia would know it anywhere.

The photo, an old Polaroid, was in an envelope stuffed way in the back of Olivia's underwear drawer. Once a year it came out just long enough for her to recommit it to memory, then back in the drawer it went. She closed her eyes and could see the image perfectly: Grandma's dining room table, a picked turkey carcass in the center, surrounded by abandoned plates. Aunt Erin, barely nineteen at the time, stood on a chair, hands up out of frame. In the chair in front of her, four-month-old Olivia was in the foot pajamas, the hood folded low over her face. The woman holding her had the same auburn hair Olivia had now, the same round face and slightly pointed nose. In the picture, her hair was wild, coming away from her ponytail in tight corkscrews. She looked somewhere past the camera, eyes sharp and bright, her lips pulled in a tight, forced smile.

A month after the photo was taken, Shannon MacArthur was locked away at Sleepy Eye State Hospital. Olivia never saw her again.

Until she was in middle school, Olivia had believed her mother was dead. The way Aunt Erin eulogized her every time they passed the one photo that hung in her grandmother's house—a school photo, tenth grade; how her grandmother had been her grandmother from the beginning, no trying to take her mother's place… There was a solemness that surrounded her mother's memory, a fog no amount of subtle questioning could penetrate.

Then, while she was away at college, she received an email from a reporter. He wrote that he was with the *Times*, one of the smaller papers from home, and asked if he could interview her for the twentieth anniversary of her rescue. At first, she wrote it off as a mistake. *Sorry, wrong person.* But that evening she got curious. A short internet search led her to a series of articles published in the *Times* twenty years prior.

New Mom Arrested for Attempted Murder

Well-Baby Alive and Healthy

Postpartum Depression to Blame for Infant's Near-Death

Olivia read every article she could find, equal parts disbelief and anger surging through her, but she didn't confront her family until she came home for Thanksgiving the following week. Her grandmother didn't want to talk about it, but Aunt Erin caved after several glasses of cheap wine. She gave Olivia the photograph.

"The thing you need to know," Aunt Erin said, "is that Shannon did love you. Too much, I think. But having a baby broke her in a way that can't be fixed."

But the more Olivia probed, the quicker Aunt Erin shut down.

Shortly after that, Olivia agreed to the interview, but only if he would answer a few questions of her own. They met the following day at a Starbucks, where the reporter told her her mother had been held at Sleepy Eye State Hospital, on and off, for twenty years. She'd been granted outpatient care twice, but each time she violated the perpetual restraining order put in place when Olivia was a baby.

"But don't worry," he'd said. "I doubt they'll make that mistake again."

"Tell me what happened." Olivia had read all the articles, some of them multiple times, but she needed someone to tell her. She needed to hear it. Out loud.

He told her that on the night of December 14, 1984, Shannon MacArthur, sixteen, took four-month-old Olivia into a small wooded area behind her parents' home. In the middle of it was an abandoned well that'd previously been protected by a wood plug. No one knew that Shannon had removed the plug the night before. Much of the local uproar had been over the hazard posed to other children in the area who might have gone into the woods to play and fallen down themselves.

"But why did she do it?" Olivia had asked. All of the articles mentioned postpartum depression, bipolar disorder, a handful of other proposed mental health conditions.

"Look," he'd said, "your mom wasn't all there. She told police she believed you had been replaced by a demon or something. She said the only way to get you back was to give *it* back to the women at the bottom of the well."

"By throwing me in."

"Not to put too fine a point on it, but yes." He'd paused, pen poised. "Lucky for you, Shannon's sister had followed her that night. If she hadn't..."

"I'd be dead."

Olivia ended the interview shortly after it started. There was no way he had the full story. The only person who would—Aunt Erin—wasn't interested in talking about it. So Olivia was left with more questions than answers.

Though she never lived more than an hour's drive from the place, she never tried to visit her mother. Apart from the restraining order that wouldn't allow it, Olivia wasn't sure she wanted to know what her mother would say when she saw her. What she would do.

Now, looking at Flora as she began to wake, her tiny hands curled into fists tucked under her chin, Olivia wondered if her mother had ever looked at her this way. If she'd looked for pieces of herself in Olivia, the way Olivia did with Flora.

"Little flower," Olivia murmured, gently stroking her daughter's hands.

She hesitated a beat, catching a flash of green in Flora's eyes. She looked closer, studying their shape, the way Flora squeezed them shut as she yawned. It hadn't occurred to her to wonder if Flora would look like Olivia's mother. Now she couldn't stop picking apart every fold, every angle of Flora's face, imagining she saw Shannon in every pore.

A noise at the window startled her. She jumped, making Flora flinch, then cry. Shushing her, Olivia looked up to see a shadow pass behind the blinds. Her gaze immediately shot to the door. Realizing Kris hadn't locked the door on her way out, Olivia crept toward it, listening for footsteps or voices. She imagined a hundred scenarios in an instant, all of them ending with Olivia dead and the house ransacked. Flora stolen or worse.

Stop it, she ordered herself. Her fear only intensified Flora's, her cries building to a crescendo. At best it was one of the two neighbors Olivia knew by name, coming by with a misdelivered package or halfhearted well wishes. At worst, it would be a kid looking to sell a magazine subscription or candy bars.

So why couldn't she shake the chill in her gut? It was like her body knew something her mind didn't.

Holding her breath, she peered out the peephole. The stoop was empty, but she slammed the deadbolt and slid the chain into place. A sound like wheezy laughter drifted through the gap under the door. *Kids*, she told herself, thoughts frantic. Still, Olivia snatched a blanket off the back of a chair and shoved it up against the gap.

"Go away," she hissed, lips pressed against the door. "Go *away*."

She was met with silence, but she felt something there, on the other side of the door. Felt its heat. Its presence.

Kris would call her paranoid, but it was like giving birth had opened a door in Olivia's mind. With every noise came a deluge of terrifying images, of all the terrible things that could possibly happen. A survival instinct, maybe, but only one of a thousand ways becoming a mother had altered her. Would *continue* to alter her, for better or worse.

When she finally worked up the nerve to look back through the peephole, nothing had changed. She stared, unblinking into the yard, the street, until a car drove past. Whatever—whoever—it was, was gone.

CHAPTER FOUR

SHANNON

O live Juice.

If you mouth it slowly, what does it look like?

Now imagine you're standing in line at a gas station, a few crumpled food stamps in your hand and a damp gallon of milk at your feet. You hear whispers somewhere behind you, and when you turn around, you see a group of guys, foreheads apexed over dirty concert T-shirts. You recognize one of them. He pretends not to recognize you, but over the others' heads, he mouths it. *Olive Juice.*

A childish code for childish feelings.

I fell for it every time, bitter and brine-soaked.

Matthew wasn't all bad. When I told him about you, he was upset at first, but warmed up to the idea after a day or two. He wanted to get married—which my mother pushed for, practically accepting on my behalf. In the end though, I told him no and kept his last name a secret from everyone. Yes, even you, because I had no doubt that once you were older, nothing would stop you from hunting him down.

"Tell her she'd be disappointed anyway."

Jo reads over my shoulder sometimes, but I don't much mind. She's always perched on my shoulder. Angel or devil or both.

I suppose I could tell you you'd be disappointed, that Matthew was so relieved at the thought of not having a family to weigh him down that he fucked off to the Ozarks where he started a band or a business or died.

I won't though.

The first promise I ever made to you was that I would never lie to you.

Doctor Call-Me-Jim likes affirmations.

I am here.

I am present.

I accept my illness and its consequences.

I am committed to creating a better life.

They change depending on the day, the weather, his mood. Today: my mind is a palace with doors at every turn.

"Behind door number one, a brand-new car!"

Jo likes to distract me. Doesn't like me spending too much time in my head. Says it's not good for me. I tell her it's my head, so I decide what's good and what isn't. That always sends her off in a huff.

Without Jo to distract me, I find myself getting lost in my mind palace, opening doors as I walk. I don't expect to find anything behind them. There are rooms though. Empty rooms, dark rooms, rooms with so much light I cover my eyes with my arm, groping for the handle. There are stairwells to nowhere and delicious smells emanating from around corners. There are shadows too. And as they move across the walls, they make a sound like iron nails on bricks. I ignore them as best I can, but I start to feel like a cow being corralled, and before I can snap myself out of it, I'm in front of a plain, laminate wood door with a wobbly brass handle.

A voice that sounds a lot like Jo whispers, "Open it."

The morning of Patrick's seventh birthday I was sick as a dog, the ends of my hair damp with toilet water. There was no one around to hold my hair back. Too much to do with streamers and balloons and a bright-red foil sign Dad suspended from hooks in the ceiling. Frozen pizzas and cake. There were gifts stacked on the dining room table, none of them hand-me-downs, no, because for the first time there would be guests that weren't blood related at the party.

When I finally came downstairs, my mother wiggled a plain gold band on my finger. "You don't get to keep it," she said. "Just for today."

It was too small, barely sliding over my finger. By the time the doorbell rang, my fingertip was purple.

Erin took one look at the thing and smirked. "Gonna have to cut it off, now."

I almost let her do it.

Only a few weeks along, I hadn't really had any cravings, but once the charred, tomato-y scent of near-burnt pizza hit my nose it was like you could fill a bath with how much I salivated. Before the cardboard serving platters hit the table, I'd swiped several slices, which I hid wrapped in paper towels like garbage. My mother would have beat my ass—pregnant or not—if she caught me stealing food from the party, so I couldn't risk eating it in the house. I went out into the backyard, hopping across the patches of yellow grass to keep my shoes from getting muddy. I paused by the rusty swing set and started to open the paper towels when I heard voices at the back door.

Still too close to the house.

So even as the cheese congealed against the greasy paper, I climbed through the broken section of fence that separated our property from the woods.

At one time or another, the woods had been a kind of haven for me and my siblings, together and separately. You couldn't pay my father to cross the tree line, and my mother often pretended the woods weren't even there, so if it was escape or solitude we needed, we knew we could count on the woods.

I barely crossed the tree line before tearing the paper away and devouring the first slice. The cheese was still too hot and burned the roof of my mouth, but I inhaled the second slice just as quickly. My jaw ached as I chewed, but I held the bulging mass of crust and sauce in with my hand, even as my eyes watered. I wouldn't waste a single crumb.

I know how it sounds. Selfish. Gluttonous. But I had you to think about.

I continued to walk as I shoved more and more food down my throat, not paying attention to which direction my feet took me. I tried to slow down, to savor the taste, knowing when I returned to the party there would be questions I couldn't answer, but it was like something primal had taken over. Sweat beaded on my forehead despite the slight chill in the air, and when I ran out of pizza, I started to lick the grease from the paper towels, swallowing bits of paper in the process.

By the time I stopped to look around, it'd gotten darker, and as I turned in a circle on the spot, all I could see were trees.

I wasn't scared. Not really. I'd been up, in, and around and through those woods a hundred or more times. It wasn't a big place. Maybe ten minutes walking in one direction you'd be out the other side, no problem.

Except I'd been walking for at least that while I'd been eating and I couldn't even hear the main road from where I stood. In fact, the only sound that punctuated the thick silence was my own heavy breath. The ground was covered in leaves, but as I started to walk in the direction I thought I'd come from, the sound of them beneath my feet was muffled. Wind rustled the canopy, but I could only feel dead, acrid air. It was like a bubble had formed around me; I could smell my breath—greasy and stale—like it was being blown back in my face. My stomach twisted, like even you, all fishy and barely alive, knew something was wrong.

And the eyes. I felt them on the back of my head, sliding down my neck and spine, poking like needles between my ribs. I wanted to turn around, but my body wouldn't listen, my feet frozen in place.

"This isn't funny," I said, my voice scorched and raspy.

Shadows flickered in and out of the corners of my eyes. I didn't dare blink.

"Erin? Patrick?"

It sounded like my voice carried no more than a couple of feet, the dense, stuffy bubble closing in. I rested my hands on my belly—on you—and tried to focus on breathing, on finding a sliver of reality I could use to pull myself back into the world. That's when I saw the well.

It came up to my hips, the old stones covered in slick, gray-green moss.

I'd been through those woods a hundred, a million, times, and I'd never seen anything like it. The stones were cracked and crumbling in places, and prickly vines clung to the base. Anyone else would have said it was ancient, abandoned.

Now I know better.

The well was old, all right, older than anything else in the woods. But it was hardly abandoned. You think of a well, you think of a hole. But a well isn't just a hole.

Sometimes a well is a door.

CHAPTER FIVE

OLIVIA

For the third night in a row, Olivia was in bed by 7:30. Every night when Flora fell asleep, Olivia told herself she would get back to the book she'd been reading the week she went into labor, that she would do the New York Times crossword even though every time she looked at it, her eyes crossed. Seemed like a million years ago that she would be up until the early morning hours reading some thriller her ridiculous colleagues didn't think was *literary* enough or hunting down a quote to make sure she got it right for the next day's lesson. Sleep was for other people. Olivia had Things To Do.

Now, sleep was all her body craved. Sleep and peanut butter and jelly sandwiches—the only meal she could prepare herself without breaking down because she couldn't find where the pots were anymore.

Sitting up in bed, she listened to Kris laugh from the living room. The glow of the television drifted under the bedroom door. Probably something stupid like *Trailer Park Boys* or *The Office* reruns, shows Olivia always said she hated, but ended up watching anyway because it meant she and Kris had time together, time not complaining about work or Kris's parents or worrying about whether the leak under the sink would get any worse.

Olivia started to climb out from under the covers but couldn't make herself stand.

Was this all she was now?

All the books told her this part wouldn't last forever, that she'd start to feel like herself again in no time. She had to admit, she wasn't hopeful. She hadn't imagined the bulk of her maternity leave being a desperate claw for sleep between nursing Flora and feeding herself. She thought she'd be tired, sure, but the sweet sort of tired, the bedroom-eyes and fluffy robe in a comfy chair with her daughter in one arm and a book in the other tired. She thought she'd be content.

Another laugh from the living room. The sound of the microwave door slamming.

Kris was digging into the popcorn; she'd be up a few hours yet.

Get up, Olivia told herself. *Get up and eat some popcorn and make fun of your wife for the way her eyes sort of look like* Trailer Park Boys' *Bubbles when she's had a few.*

But she didn't get up. Instead, she laid back down and pulled the covers over her face. She'd get some sleep. Try again tomorrow. And the next day. And the next. Until she could look in the mirror and recognize herself. Until she was finally whole again.

The next morning, Kris was supposed to go with Olivia to Flora's first well-baby visit. At five days old, Flora was already a handful and Olivia skirted the edges of sleep deprivation. But, again, work got in the way.

"You can tell them no, can't you?" Olivia asked. "Or did that even cross your mind?" It was getting harder not to resent her wife. She told herself it wasn't even because of the baby. Of course Olivia had to be the one to get up and do the feedings. Of course Olivia would change her while she was up. Yes, it would have been nice if Kris had offered to wake up with them both, a show of solidarity, that they were in this together come hell or high water or projectile spit-up. Olivia wanted that small bit of freedom Kris had, to go to work, be miserable, come home and complain, and then do it all over again.

As a community college adjunct, Olivia had only just started inching her way toward a full class load when they found out she was pregnant. Now, she was worried whatever headway she'd made was gone forever.

Kris poked through her computer bag, avoiding Olivia's gaze. "When corporate America decides to start paying parental leave for people like me, then I'll start telling them to fuck off." She shifted the bag to her other shoulder and sighed. "I'm sorry, okay? I know this is important. Don't you think I'd rather be with you two?"

"Would you?"

Kris's face crumpled. "That's not fair."

A tirade brewed in Olivia's belly, but she quashed it before it could reach her mouth. *Fair.* Flora burbled on her shoulder, and she felt spit drip down the back of her shirt. "I just don't want to do this alone."

"You're not alone, Liv. I promise." She kissed Flora's back and pressed her forehead to Olivia's. "I'll figure it out, okay? I'll do better."

Flora writhed on Olivia's shoulder, a whimper building into a full-blown cry.

"You'd better go," Olivia said, turning away to hide the hurt. "You'll be late."

———

It was impossible to carry Flora's car seat, the diaper bag, Olivia's bag, and the folder of paperwork they sent with her home from the hospital that she may or may not have neglected to look at once in the few days she'd been home, all the way to the car at the same time. She tried leaving Flora in the house—buckled safely in her car seat, right by the window where Olivia could see her—but the minute Flora was out of her sight, it was like a switch had been thrown in her body, all hyperaware and terrified. In the end, Olivia made three trips, hauling Flora's car seat along each time, until finally, the bags were in the car, Flora's car seat was clicked into the base, and Olivia buckled her seat belt only to realize she'd left the keys in the front door.

Biting back frustrated tears, she started to climb out of the car, but a voice in the back of her head yanked her back.

Someone will take Flora.

Their street was quiet, most of the driveways empty. Her neighbors had a tall hedge that made it difficult to see anything past the bend in the street, but if Olivia locked Flora in, she'd be back in time before—

They'll see her alone in the car. Suffocating.

Olivia's skin crawled.

No. There was no one in the neighborhood over fifty; everyone was too self-absorbed to give a shit about anyone else's business, and if she locked her daughter in the car so she could get the keys so they could go to the doctor it was all because she was a good mother, damn it.

She was gone only five seconds—she'd counted under her breath—and when she climbed back into the car, Flora hardly noticed, eyelids drooping and drool pooling in the corner of her mouth.

There, she thought. *See? Everything's fine.*

She turned the key, but the car struggled to turn over. The engine coughed like there was something caught in it, and then a high-pitched shriek vibrated the windows as the engine finally sputtered to life. An animal, she thought, horrified. But it was too early in the season for stray cats to be looking for warmth under the car, and there were plenty of trees around for the birds. A squirrel, maybe?

More than anything she didn't want to get out and look, but the thought of the carcass jamming up the belts while her daughter was in the car turned her stomach. She shut off the engine and watched the hood for smoke or something worse, distracted by a *clink, clink, clink* sound. She caught a glimpse of something in her rearview mirror, and when she turned around, she saw a long, brown nail tap, tap, tapping her back window, the body attached to it hidden on the roof of the car.

Olivia's mouth went dry. In the car seat, Flora started to whimper.

The edges of Olivia's vision went fuzzy, until all she could see was the nail. She was hallucinating. Had to be. Exhaustion made the mind play tricks, made her see things that weren't there, or twisted the ordinary into nightmares. She told herself it was a thin branch knocking against her window in the wind, even though she knew with frightening clarity that there was no tree that close to her driveway.

Shushing Flora as quietly as she could, Olivia reached for the automatic lock on her door. She pressed the button and the locks engaged like a shot. The hand in her window snapped back, but she didn't hear any other movement.

This is Kris's fault.

I told her I couldn't do this alone. I told her I couldn't—

Movement on the roof of the car made Olivia jump. *The branch broke. It's just a branch. Just a tree.* There *had* to be a tree, she just couldn't remember. She was tired. So, so tired.

She started the car again and, before the thing on the roof (*a branch, just a branch*) had a chance to climb down and do God knew what, she threw the gear into reverse and bolted down the driveway without looking. Heart pounding, she slammed on the brakes and waited for the thing (*the branch!*) to fly off the back of the car, but when she got the nerve to look behind her, all she saw was an empty road.

The entire drive to the doctor's office, Olivia had to remind herself to slow down. The needle edged past sixty, seventy miles per hour on the winding roads, and every time she thought she heard something hit the road behind her, she couldn't tear her eyes away from the mirror. By the time she parked, her nerves were fried. They were inching close to being late for the appointment, but she refused to even unlock the doors until there were other people around. Finally out of the car, she braced herself to confront the thing, only to find the roof empty, streaked with dirt and leaves. A long scratch marred the paint.

See? Only a branch, just like you thought. You're fine. Flora's fine. Everything is fine.

Had it rained last night? She tried to picture the ground outside their house—had it been damp? Had there been leaves and twigs littering the driveway? And if so, from where?

She didn't have time to think about it. Slinging the diaper bag over her shoulder, Olivia hooked her arms through the car seat and waddled the bulk of them inside.

The waiting room was nearly full. The receptionist waved Olivia over, her smile dipping slightly when Olivia rested the bulging diaper bag on the counter.

"You alright, hon?" the receptionist asked.

Olivia opened her mouth to answer, pausing as she looked down at herself. She'd been wearing the same yoga pants for three days, the same mesh underwear to hold the diaper-like pad in place. She was pretty sure she wasn't supposed to still be bleeding as much as she was, but she was too worried to ask. She could feel her hair coming out of her ponytail, brushing the stray hairs behind her ears. She'd remembered deodorant, at least. She was pretty sure.

"I'm fine," Olivia said. "Just tired."

The receptionist nodded. Olivia caught a glimpse of the photos on the desk, cheap black frames holding half a dozen pictures of gap-toothed kids.

"It gets better, darlin'. Just hang in there." The receptionist smiled again, all teeth, and turned to her computer to get Olivia checked in. "Have a seat. We'll call you back shortly."

Olivia sat in the only empty seat, between a cloudy fish tank and a table full of wrinkled magazines. She sat Flora in front of her, toe nudging the car seat so it gently rocked. At some point in the drive, Flora had fallen asleep. Spit bubbled in the corner of her mouth.

"How old?"

The woman two seats over smiled, deep-red lipstick making her lips look bloody.

"Five days," Olivia said.

"Bless 'er, she's a cute one." The woman straightened blankets over what Olivia assumed was a baby but was too buried in cotton and soft toys for her to see. "We just crossed the two-week mark."

Olivia took in the woman's skintight jeans and expensive-looking sweater, her low-heeled boots and smooth makeup, her hair in soft, beachy curls, the kind that took hours, and felt only defeat. Two weeks. That was eleven days away. How could anyone expect her to look like this woman in eleven days?

"Congratulations," Olivia said, turning away.

A nurse propped open a door, clipboard in hand. "Flora?"

Olivia snatched up her daughter and practically ran for the door.

After taking Flora's temperature and weight, the pediatrician slipped Flora out of her onesie and laid her out on the table, one hand pinning her down while the other probed her ribs and neck and mouth. She examined the umbilical cord, still a stump of black in the middle of Flora's belly, and nodded.

"Looks like she's a little jaundiced," the pediatrician finally said, readjusting the tabs on Flora's diaper. "See how there's some yellow in her eyes there? Usually means she's not getting enough to eat."

Olivia's stomach fell. Not enough? "She eats every two hours. Sometimes more."

The pediatrician frowned. "A full feed?"

"Yes—I mean, I guess? She eats until she stops. I'm all…" She gestured to her chest. "Torn up."

"May I have a look?"

Before Olivia could answer, the pediatrician slapped on a pair of gloves and helped ease Olivia out of her shirt before unclipping the cup on her nursing bra. The scrape of the fabric over Olivia's sore nipples made her wince. The pediatrician's hands, even through the gloves, were like ice as she probed Olivia's nipple, chapped and flecked with dried blood.

Eyebrows knotted with concern, she moved Flora from the table to Olivia's arms. "We should take a look at your latch. If it's too shallow, those little gums'll tear you to hell."

Olivia barely had ahold of her before Flora began to root, mouth wide and searching. Her fists dug into her throat and her legs twitched, eyes wide and desperate. Holding her breath, Olivia lifted Flora's head and when Flora latched, the pain was extraordinary. Her eyes stung and she sat ramrod straight against the twitch in her spine. Her toes curled in her shoes and her arms shook until the pediatrician finally slid a flimsy pillow beneath them.

"Good latch," the pediatrician said. "It's important to swap sides. If you don't, that could be causing the bleeding."

Olivia was in too much pain to tell her the other side was worse.

The pediatrician sent her home with a jar of petroleum jelly to help with healing. "But don't worry, it won't bother the baby." She also recommended Olivia start pumping, saying it would help with milk production and keep Flora on breast milk while Olivia healed a little. "And if it comes down to it," the pediatrician continued, "there's nothing wrong with formula feeding. Calories are calories. Making sure she eats and grows is what matters."

All those *breast is best* moms had been harping in her head for her entire pregnancy—blog posts and newsreels and toothy smiles in the birthing classes... Formula? You might as well kill her yourself. But it felt like the pediatrician had thrown her a life jacket. Maybe it *was* okay to be a little selfish.

Olivia thanked her and stopped at the grocery store on the way home, smuggling the bag with the formula beneath her sweater, the receipt crumpled in her pocket. She'd felt the judgment radiating off the woman in line behind her, the woman's apple-cheeked toddler banging his sippy cup on the handle of the cart like a gavel.

But the moment she reached her car, all she felt was quiet relief. She wouldn't stop nursing Flora, not completely, but they both needed this change. Calories for Flora, like the nurse said, and a chance for sleep for Olivia. She and Kris could switch off for night feedings. Olivia's mind would get the recharge it desperately needed, and she could put incidents like this morning, the branch on the window, behind her.

The formula sitting on the passenger seat was like a talisman to sanity. Olivia realized how ridiculous she'd been. She even laughed, earning a gurgle from Flora.

"Mommy's silly." Olivia reached back and tickled Flora's belly, giddy. "Silly, silly mommy."

But her relief was short-lived.

Shortly after getting home, Olivia prepared a bottle with the formula, making sure to sterilize the bottle and nipple before mixing the stale-smelling powder with warm, distilled water. She sat on the kitchen floor, Flora snuggled in the crook of her elbow. As Flora excitedly took to the bottle, Olivia suppressed an excited laugh. This would work. There was light at the end of the tunnel.

But when Flora finished and Olivia lifted Flora to her shoulder for a burp, Flora spit up something thicker, more foul-smelling than she'd ever done before. Olivia suppressed a gag, even as panic surged through her. Something was *wrong*.

Poisoned, a voice murmured in the back of her mind.

Had she bothered to check the expiration date? No, because she'd been too excited about the prospect of a nap—too *selfish*—to worry about something like that.

She's not poisoned, Olivia thought as she fought her way to standing, Flora pinned to her shoulder, smearing spit-up.

Still, she couldn't contain the tremor in her voice as she called the pediatrician's office.

"She might be lactose sensitive," the nurse told her. "You've done nothing wrong. Next time, buy the sensitive stomach formula. It'll help."

Olivia nodded through the nurse's assurances and promises, feeling the burn of judgment all over again.

That night, after her shower, Olivia slathered her nipples in the jelly, cringing when her T-shirt stuck to them, leaving twin damp spots in the fabric. It looked ridiculous. Porny. But for the first time in days, it didn't feel like her skin was on fire.

She found Kris in the kitchen preparing a bottle with Flora beside her, content in her papasan swing. Olivia had pumped between feedings the entire afternoon, the thought of a few hours rest that night the only motivation she needed to push through the pain. Another of the nurse's suggestions, when Olivia had broken down at the end of their phone call. *I'm just so tired.*

Kris plunged the full bottle into a pot of simmering water to warm the milk, testing it on her wrist every few minutes. "I'm excited."

"You say that now."

Kris chuckled. "I'm surprised you're not already in bed."

She'd tried, but the moment she'd laid down she heard Flora's whimper in the other room and her body went on high alert.

Olivia yawned, barely able to keep her eyes open. "I'm fine."

But Kris wasn't having it. She shooed Olivia to the couch. "I got this. Lavender bath. Baby massage. Comfy jammies. No problem."

Olivia didn't argue. She curled up in the corner of the couch and covered herself with a blanket. She drifted in and out of sleep, eyelids fluttering open with each splash or burble from the kitchen. Somewhere in that place between sleep and awake, she heard a *tap, tap, tap,* and when she opened her eyes, she saw a shadow lingering outside the window.

Adrenaline pulsed through her body, chasing away the last vestiges of sleep as she stared at the shadow, willing her eyes to adjust, to make it take shape.

Tap. Tap. Tap.

Just like on her car window.

No, she reminded herself. *That wasn't real.* Or it was real, but it wasn't what she'd thought it was.

How long had she been asleep? Minutes? Hours? Not long enough for her mind to rest. It was fighting her again. She was frustrated, exhausted, *angry.*

She hated when Kris left a gap in the curtains at night. With their lights on, everyone could see in, but they couldn't see out. Her skin crawled imagining hundreds of eyes on her; she could feel the jelly of them on her skin. She tried to ignore it, to tell herself this was just like the branch on her car. But she was too tired to fight even herself. The fear she kept tamped down with assurances and logic threatened to overwhelm her. She leaned slowly toward the lamp, struggling to keep her hand still. She was an intelligent, educated woman, for God's sake. She would look, and she would see that there was nothing there. She would go back to sleep, and then, in the morning when she was rested and she could think clearly, she would talk to Kris about keeping the curtains closed at night.

She clicked the button and the light went out, bathing the room in darkness.

In the window was the shape of a person with wild hair, their nails tap, tap, tapping on the glass.

Olivia went cold. She screamed.

Kris ran into the living room, a damp, naked Flora on her shoulder. "What happened? Are you okay?"

"There's someone outside!" Wasn't there? "They were looking in the window!"

Without a word, Kris handed Flora to Olivia, and grabbing the small pink bat they kept in the closet, she opened the front door and stuck her head out. "I don't see anyone."

"Check the neighbor's hedge. I think that's where they were earlier."

"Earlier?"

"By my car. There was someone—I don't know. Just look, okay?"

Kris shut the door behind her, and Olivia followed her shadow as it crossed the yard. In her lap, Flora flopped, fishlike, rooting for Olivia's breast, but before Olivia could get her situated, Kris was back, shaking her head.

"There's no one," Kris said. "If there was, they're long gone."

"Lock the door," Olivia said. "And shut the fucking curtain."

Kris obeyed, then scooped up Flora. "Come on, little flower. Mommy needs some sleep."

"No. I'm awake now." Olivia took a deep breath to calm the tremble in her voice. "It's fine."

"Sleep, babe. We got this handled, don't we?"

Kris nibbled Flora's neck, making her fists curl and a gurgle bubble from her throat.

There was no one there.

Olivia repeated it in her mind until the muscles in her shoulders and legs loosened. She knew sleep deprivation could cause hallucinations, but how much sleep had to be lost until the mind started to unravel? She tried to count the number of hours she'd slept since Flora's birth but *thinking* at all was like trying to catch smoke with her hands.

"Okay," Olivia said finally. She remembered how the shadows from her nightmare at the hospital had bled into her waking mind. That was all this was. A nightmare. "Check the locks though, okay?"

Kris promised she would, and when Olivia finally climbed into bed, she felt every muscle in her body melt. Kris could handle Flora. Tonight, Olivia would sleep. But as she drifted off, just before everything went black, she heard it again, faint, almost inaudible.

Tap, tap, tap.

CHAPTER SIX

SHANNON

J o tried to kill herself last night. It was all very dramatic, a long speech delivered as she knelt on her bed, the covers bunched around her legs, before brandishing a pair of contraband nail scissors. She didn't mean it, of course. Not really. The marks on her wrists were only scratches; if Jo'd meant to do it, there would have been blood. Lots and lots of it.

Doctor Call-Me-Jim asked me afterward if I knew where she'd gotten the scissors. Being her roommate, he figured I knew all her secrets. I do, but I'm no rat. See, Jo's sister visits pretty regular and always brings presents. Usually it's an off-brand package of cookies or one of those romance paperbacks with Fabio on the cover. To hear her sister tell it, Jo used to be quite the romantic, always looking for her knight in shining armor. I don't go for that stuff, me. Can't get through life hoping someone will rescue you; you gotta do it yourself. Anyway, this time her sister brought a manicure kit. I was grateful on Jo's behalf—I cringe every time she sticks one of those broken, dirty nails in her mouth. On account of her sister being a regular visitor, the on-duty nurse must not have taken the proper glance through her things before letting her in. Jo took one look at those tiny scissors and had her mind made up. I pretended not to see her slip them out of the kit and beneath her pillow.

At first, Doctor Call-Me-Jim didn't want to let me in to see her. Said rewarding Jo's bad behavior would only lead to more of it.

Pardon my French, but that's bullshit.

You would think Doctor Call-Me-Jim would know better. Jo has been in Sleepy Eye as long as me—to the day, as a matter of fact—which is to say many, many years. A lot of time to learn the heartbeat of this place, to know what we can get away with and what's not worth the bother. Sometimes a scratch on the wrist is a cry for help or attention. Sometimes it's cowardice. And sometimes, it's punishment.

I asked Doctor Call-Me-Jim if I could speak to him in confidence, which he enthusiastically agreed to. (Doctors are just like people, really. All they want is to feel needed.) I told him Jo wouldn't want me saying it, especially not to him, but she has begun to feel a long-buried remorse for the actions that'd landed her here, for the people she'd hurt. I explained he wouldn't know this because he's not as close to her as I am, but Jo is a very eye-for-an-eye kind of gal. Her actions weren't attention-seeking. They were retribution.

I won't lie and tell you he bought it, hook, line, and sinker. That would be giving him too much credit. Underneath the lab coat and tie, he was still a man, and men are suspicious of women with too-big feelings. I brought him around in the end though. I think Doctor Call-Me-Jim is starting to believe he can see to the heart of me, or, at least somewhere close to it.

I'm not a bad person, Olivia. Whatever else you think, whatever else they tell you, I hope you know at least that.

Part of the reason Jo did it might have been remorse, but the bigger part, I suspected, was so she'd have a reason to sleep in the clinic for a night, where the beds were softer and the blankets warmer. There were three beds in total, and Jo pretended to snooze in the middle one, her wrists wrapped in a thin layer of gauze.

We didn't have a library at Sleepy Eye, but we did have a book cart that a few of the dewy-eyed volunteers swapped out every once in a while with secondhand paperbacks or books they'd picked up at garage sales. All of the romances had been taken (and though I've got nothing against Fabio, I wasn't looking forward to reading heaving bosoms and throbbing members aloud), so I took a book of poems instead. Emily Dickinson. I imagine she's the kind of poet you might like. You were prone to these thoughtful expressions. Calm. What Erin called *pensive*. But I'm getting ahead of myself.

I laid in bed with her, the book tucked under one arm, and snuck a peek beneath her bandages. Deep, but not life-threatening. I checked to see if the nurse was looking, and prodded the cut, sucking in a breath when a few drops of blood pooled. It was probably painful, but Jo was too gilled-up to tell the difference. I didn't want to hurt her, mind, I just needed to see.

I waited till her breathing settled a bit before opening the book. It was old, the pages yellow, and smelled a little like feet. I flipped through until a poem about a well and neighbors from other worlds caught my eye. I started to read.

I came home from that first visit to the well what felt like hours later, but Erin figured I'd only been gone a few minutes. It was impossible, I knew, but the party had barely started and the remainder of the pizza was still warm from the oven. I'd lost time before—I'm a bit of a dreamer, you see—but not like this. Still, it wasn't the bounce in and out of time that'd disturbed me. I couldn't remember walking back, like muscle memory through a thin veil of fog, until I was in the shadow of my house, and even then thinking of the well was like remembering a dream.

By the time the party ended, I'd all but forgotten about it.

That night, I woke up, jarred out of sleep by a sharp pain in my arms, like someone digging their nails into my skin. I probed my shoulders and could feel the indentations, ice cold and tender. I was too angry to be scared; uninterrupted sleep was a luxury in a house of six, especially with Erin snoring like a strangled hippo not four feet away. I figured it was one of my brothers getting their kicks in while they still could. Once I started to show, Dad would likely wallop them if they so much as lay a finger on me.

Worse, now I had to pee.

There were two toilets in the house, but only one we were allowed to use at night: the basement, because Mom said the upstairs toilet was too loud. Most nights I could hold it, but with you swimming around in there, as small as you were, my body wouldn't have it. I was halfway to the basement stairs when a soft light through the sheer curtains made me stop.

Everything else fell out of my head. All I could think of was the well.

I needed to get back to it. Don't ask me why. There was a voice in the back of my head ordering me to do it, that there would be consequences if I didn't.

I wore no shoes, no pants, only an oversized T-shirt that barely covered my thighs.

I don't remember the walk. I remember buzzing in my ears and fog in the corners of my eyes.

"Like the second before you pass out," Jo says. "But you don't. You just keep walking."

She's right. It's like that moment before the blackness, but it never comes, so you just keep walking because your brain tells you the blackness is coming and your feet figure the blackness is somewhere up ahead.

So I walked and walked, and there, at the edge of the blackness, was the well.

You know the feeling. A big, empty space and then all of a sudden you can feel it fill up even though there's nothing there. The woods weren't all that dense, but it was like I couldn't breathe. Eyes on me from every angle. I could feel them there in the darkness, watching me, and with each step closer to the well—I couldn't stay away, I couldn't—a collective breath in.

You'll think I'm crazy.

They all thought I was crazy, in the end.

I leaned over the side of the well, my belly brushing against the damp stone. I don't know why I thought I'd see anything. The night was black as anything, and the well was no different. It seemed to go on for miles, though I could smell the fetid, moldy water somewhere below. I wondered what would happen if I fell in.

The longer I stared down the well and my eyes adjusted to the dark, the more I could make out—scratches on the walls, patches of moss and mud. Something that might have been a snake wriggled beneath it all. I leaned further in to get a better look, so far my toes barely grazed the ground. A flicker of light caught my attention, like a bright-orange eye midblink, and it spooked me so much that my grip on the stone slipped and there was a moment of confusion as my feet lifted off the ground, followed by heart-banging terror as my entire body tipped over the side.

I fell for less than a second, but I hit the water hard enough to knock the wind out of me.

Treading water and gasping for breath, I looked up, but there was no opening. No moonlight. My eyes ached with the effort of trying to see through all the black.

"I don't like the dark," Jo says, pulling me out of my memory just before the hands circle my belly. Before the hot breath touches my ear. Before sharp teeth graze my earlobe. Before they take a bite.

CHAPTER SEVEN

OLIVIA

There was a moment where Olivia struggled to climb out of her dream. All she remembered when she finally woke up was blackness, heavy and sap-sticky and clinging to her skin. More disturbing was that the entire front of her T-shirt was soaked, which immediately conjured images of drowning somewhere dark. Claustrophobic. She kicked the blankets away and sat up, taking deep, measured breaths. It was hard to orient herself; the light coming from between the curtains was too bright. Pain throbbed behind her eyes and her breasts ached and she couldn't remember if it was yesterday or today, what time she'd gone to bed, or where her wife was.

The dampness on her front smelled faintly musty, and she realized she'd leaked. The pressure from sleeping on her stomach all night, uninterrupted by midnight feedings, had forced the milk to express. She checked the sheet and was grateful to see it was only her side of the bed that'd been soaked. Still, the embarrassment burned. It was like her body wasn't her own anymore. A liquid bag with holes poked in. Blood and piss and milk. Any relief she felt from having a full night's rest was pushed away thinking of how she'd have to strip the bed, do laundry. It brought her back to a childhood plagued by nightmares, hiding in the bathroom while her grandmother yanked the sheets off her bed, both of them pretending nothing happened.

As she let her thoughts fester, the shame in her belly evolved.

How many YouTube videos had she and Kris watched together during those last months of pregnancy, the bright, glowing faces of new mothers taking center stage as the pain was left behind and their children placed in their arms? Where was that bliss? That wonder? Did all those women go home to wake up each morning only because there was the promise of sleep at the other end of it? Did they complain and resent what their days had become the way Olivia did?

No, she thought. It was just her.

She didn't *glow*.

Maybe it was her fault Flora wasn't eating properly. Maybe poison laced her milk. She needed to do better. To *be* better.

She stood to strip out of her wet T-shirt, and it was when her hip didn't bump the bassinet that she realized—Flora was gone. Not just Flora, the whole bassinet. She ran around the other side of the bed thinking Kris had moved her sometime in the night. No bassinet. No Flora. Olivia started for the door—*please be in the living room, please be feeding our daughter, please, please*—when she heard the screams.

Every nerve on fire, she fumbled with the doorknob before finally getting the door open and followed Flora's screams across the hall to the second bedroom. The bassinet sat in the middle of the mostly empty room, shaking with the force of Flora's flailing body. Olivia moved to pick her up, a small sliver of relief that Flora was here, she was safe, but stopped when she saw Flora's face. Her skin was sallow and dry, the whites of her eyes a pale yellow, and her wide-open mouth was cottony, her tongue spotted white and subtly pointed. Olivia's shirt dampened with new milk, but she couldn't make herself reach into the bassinet. She shivered, and in the corner of her eye noticed the open window. Her gaze dragged along the windowsill, where streaks of mud ended at the latch.

She took a step toward the window, but Flora screamed at a new pitch, freezing her to the spot.

Something was wrong with her daughter.

Except, her daughter's eyes were brown, not the strange green she saw now, weren't they?

Kids change, Kris had said.

Footsteps pounded down the hall. Kris appeared in the doorway, visibly shaken. "Jesus Christ. I thought someone was killing her in here."

Olivia couldn't move. Each time she thought of taking a step toward Kris, Flora's livid eyes fell on her and they were like nails through her feet.

Kris shot her a look she couldn't quite interpret before scooping Flora out of the bassinet. She rocked, patting Flora's back. "Did you feed her?" Kris asked.

"No," Olivia said.

Kris frowned.

Olivia continued. "Why is the bassinet in here?"

Kris shifted Flora to her other shoulder. The back of her head was red from screaming. It looked hot to the touch. "I wanted you to sleep. Every time she sighed you jumped, like she'd poked you." She started toward the hallway with Olivia following behind. "I just went to the gas station. I was gone fifteen minutes."

Flora sounded like she'd been screaming for hours. Her voice was hoarse, and she'd started to hiccup.

Had an animal gotten in, maybe, and scared Flora? Had she scared it back out to where it came from with her cries? Olivia glanced up at the window, guessing what could have slipped through and out again without breaking the glass. She squinted at the streaks of mud. But then, they weren't mud, were they? The streaks weren't nearly as dark as they had appeared earlier. In fact, they didn't look like mud at all. Dust, maybe. Thick dust. They almost never used this room— when was the last time she'd cleaned the floors, let alone a forgotten windowsill?

But if nothing had gotten through, what was wrong with Flora? Why did she look so... "She's starving," Olivia said, distressed. How many feedings had she missed? How long had Flora been crying desperately for food? Hours? Was this an effect of the jaundice? Olivia's gut instinct was to call the pediatrician, but a voice inside her cautioned against it. *It's your fault*, the voice said. *They'll take her from you if they find out.*

"She's not starving," Kris said, but she sounded unsure.

Had Kris even looked at their daughter's face?

In the kitchen, Kris struggled to balance warming a bottle under the hot tap water and the flailing Flora. Olivia was rooted to the spot by Flora's sunken cheeks and spindly limbs. Something was wrong. Olivia couldn't stop thinking about the open window. The mud that wasn't mud. What had happened to their little girl last night?

"Liv," Kris said, "little help?"

Jaundice, she decided. *That's what the doctor said. That's all. She just needs to eat.*

She took Flora, who immediately began rooting. Something sharp nicked Olivia and she jumped.

"I got her," Kris said after testing the bottle. But the moment she tried to take Flora out of Olivia's arms, Flora let out a scream that vibrated Olivia's entire body. It was like she was dying.

Kris tried to hand Olivia the bottle, but Olivia shook her head. The bottle wouldn't be good enough. Flora wanted her.

Olivia wriggled out of her damp shirt and helped Flora latch. The pinch of Flora's mouth was so tight that it sent little jabs of pain up Olivia's chest and into the back of her head. She bit back a wince, knowing Kris was watching them carefully.

Kris rubbed Olivia's shoulder. "Do you want to sit down?"

Olivia didn't answer.

"Babe?"

"I'm fine," Olivia whispered, afraid to break the fragile calm, of disturbing Flora, whose eyes were closed and whose fists bunched on either side of Olivia's breast. Olivia could see Flora's veins beneath her skin. Could see them pulsing.

Then she looked again. Soft, pale skin. Fat, cherubic cheeks. Flora was here. She was fine. What she'd seen had been a nightmare, Olivia thought, bleeding into the daylight.

"You're beautiful," Kris said.

Out of the corner of her eye, Olivia saw Kris take her phone out of her pocket and snap a picture.

"The most beautiful thing I've ever seen," Kris murmured. "Truly."

Yes, Olivia thought. *I am a mom. I am beautiful. I am glowing.*

Flora's eyes flickered open, and her gaze locked on Olivia's.

Lies, the baby seemed to say.

Flora fed for a long time, her strangled cries filling the house as Olivia swapped her from one side to the other and back again. She lost track of time and how often she switched. One of their friends had given her a thin, beaded bracelet that was meant to help remind her—switching the bracelet when she switched the baby—but she'd never worn it and couldn't imagine remembering to use it anyway. She could barely keep a shirt on, let alone jewelry.

She wouldn't have been able to remember her own name, watching Flora's face. Gone was the sallow yellow, the protruding veins, the old paper texture of her skin. When Flora finally sighed, sated, her cheeks were fat and pink. Olivia just caught a glimpse of the dark brown of Flora's eyes, the green long gone, as they fluttered shut.

I'm losing it, she thought, then banished the thought just as quickly. No, she absolutely, one hundred percent, was not losing it. She would not fall down that hole. She refused.

At some point, Kris had wrapped a blanket around Olivia's shoulders and guided her to the couch, but Olivia couldn't remember it happening. Despite the blanket, she shivered. She spotted the papasan swing and desperately wanted to lay Flora in it to give her body a break, but her arms wouldn't move. An ache traveled down from her shoulders, touching every nerve, every muscle. She couldn't even unfold her legs without whimpering. And why was she suddenly so tired? She'd slept all night. The adrenaline, maybe, from earlier. A surge and crash.

Kris sat next to her on the couch, a steaming mug in her hands. "Coffee?"

As much as she craved the caffeine, Olivia's stomach turned. She couldn't remember the last time she'd eaten or had anything to drink other than water.

"Take her," Olivia said. "I need to pee. And get dressed." And be human for two seconds.

With Flora safely in her papasan, still sleeping, Olivia went into the bathroom with the blanket still wrapped around her shoulders. She locked the door behind her, and the moment she caught her reflection, her breath caught.

That's not me, she thought.

Her skin was sallow and yellow, like old paper. The veins in her chest and neck protruded, blue and ropey. Her cheeks were sunken, and her lips were pale and chapped.

A knock on the door made her flinch. A small dribble of urine dripped down her thigh. She barely noticed. Her pelvic floor was shot, so even the smallest sneeze had her peeing herself.

"Liv?" Kris knocked again. "You okay in there?"

"Fine," Olivia croaked, unable to look away from the mirror. She touched her face, bordering on disbelief as her reflection followed suit. *This isn't real,* she thought.

"I forgot to mention—to ask, really—I invited Edie and Mark over for dinner."

Edie. Mark. Dinner. Words that passed over her consciousness without sticking.

"From the birthing class. You remember? Edie always had that stuffed elephant and Mark was—Mark—but you and Edie seemed to get on and she gave birth about a week before us." She paused. "Liv? Are you mad? I thought it might be nice to know some parents our age. Maybe Flora makes a friend. I don't know."

A small laugh escaped Olivia's lips, even as tears burned her eyes. Her wife was talking about dinner, while she stood mostly naked in the bathroom with piss on her leg. And her face—God, she looked like death. She tried to convince herself this was like the shadow in the window, like the branch on her car. Another trick from an overtired mind. But this was too real. This was her *face*. Her *body*. She touched the veins in her neck and pulled at the loose skin under her eyes. She looked deflated. Drained of energy, of blood, of *life*.

"It'll be fun. You'll see," Kris continued. "You can get back to being Liv. Right?"

Could she? There seemed to be so little left of herself in her reflection.

"Right." Her voice sounded like she was gargling gravel. "Be right out."

It took monumental effort to turn away from the mirror, to ignore the image in her peripheral. She turned on the shower and stepped in, the water scalding. If she stood here long enough, maybe she could burn these new, dangerous thoughts out of her head.

Olivia was dying from the inside out.

Flora was killing her.

CHAPTER EIGHT

SHANNON

There's a scar on my left earlobe, a half-moon shape about as wide as my pinky nail. Raised and rigid, I've never been able to wear earrings because of it. Jo likes to touch it sometimes, when it's after lights-out but neither of us can sleep, so we sit up next to each other on my bed and talk about the Before Times. Jo tells me I'm not remembering right, but I know that can't be true. My mind, despite what Doctor Call-Me-Jim might say, is a steel trap.

So you can imagine how upset I was to find myself in my bed, again, when I'd closed my eyes at the bottom of that rancid well, and no memory of how I'd gotten home. Wasn't a dream though. I knew that much. The T-shirt I wore to bed was stiff in places with mud, and there were small twigs tangled in my hair. The skin on the sides of my arms was scraped up good. Bruises on my thigh shot lightning pain up my hip when I touched them. Seemed I'd put up a fight. A good one, likely, but I knew my own strength. It wasn't good enough to climb out of that well on my own. I had to know what had happened to me.

Given the chance to raise you, this would be one of those *do as I say, not as I do* situations. If you escape with your life, you don't tap on the bear's nose to ask why he chose not to maul you today.

The only benefit to being one of a brood is the anonymity. While everyone else piled into the kitchen to snatch up the last of the cereal, I slipped out the back door. I figured no one would care.

I should have known Erin would follow.

I didn't notice her until I reached the tree line, when a sound behind me all but sent me running. When I turned and saw her—not the thing from the bottom of the well—fear turned into anger.

"Go away," I said.

Erin smirked. She figured she'd caught me in something. Having something over one of our siblings was better than money in those days. "Where are you going?"

"Nowhere."

"Liar." When I didn't budge, "I'll tell Mom."

You would think we would have been too old for vague threats like that— Erin being nineteen, and me, sixteen—especially given my current condition. I doubted there was much Erin could tell her that would trump *Mom, I'm pregnant,* but I didn't want to risk it. My mother could level a forest with a look.

"I just want to be alone," I said, absently rubbing my belly.

"Alone to what? *Take care of things?*"

The accusation hung in the air, and I could tell the moment it left her mouth Erin regretted it, but I'd be lying if, in that moment, I didn't want to wrap my hands around her neck and squeeze.

Rather than take it back though, Erin doubled down. "I heard you last night."

Heard, not saw. We slept in the same room. If she saw me leave or come back, she would have said so.

"You can't hear nothin' over that snore," I said.

Erin rolled her eyes. Then, all the taunt out of her voice, "You're not planning anything stupid, right?"

I didn't bother answering. Nothing I said would make a difference.

"Can I come with you?"

If I told her no, she would follow anyway. I figured, let her come. We'll have a wander, she'll get bored, then I can find my answers.

"Fine," I said.

But the second we entered the woods, I knew I wouldn't have found anything, with or without Erin tagging along. The thin canopy let in too much light, and the bubble that'd closed in around me the night before was gone, replaced by crisp, sweet-smelling air.

"Are you okay?" Erin finally said. "Like, really and actually?"

I stopped and turned to look at her. Her fingers were knotted in front of her stomach, and her eyebrows were crunched in a deep V.

"Why?" I asked.

"Why?" Erin laughed. "Because if I were you, I'd be a total fucking mess, that's why."

"Well, you're not me."

Her expression changed into something I couldn't decipher. Looking back, I'd call it intrigue. "No. I guess I'm not." She sighed. "I'll leave you to…whatever it is you're doing, but I just wanted to let you know that I'm here for you. Okay? You can be Madame Brass Balls in front of Mom if that makes you feel better, but don't hide shit from me. You make me crazy, but you're my sister and I love you."

It took me a second to register her words. I'm sure we all felt it, but none of us would actually say to each other that we cared. That while we were holding each other in a headlock over some petty slight, we made sure we didn't cause any actual damage. Call it love if you want, but we sure didn't. Not out loud.

"Thanks," I said finally.

Erin waited a beat before turning back to the house. I stood in the same spot for a long time after she left, waiting for the air to turn acrid, to close in around me and guide me back to the well, but nothing happened. Part of me believed it'd all been a dream. The other part, the louder part, worried it wasn't.

A few weeks into my pregnancy, my mother started to pick at me.

You're lazy.

Why aren't you helping your sister with dinner?

Why is your laundry still in the basket?

"No reason for you to be loafing around the house all day," my mother said. "Just because you're pregnant doesn't mean you get to be useless to the rest of the world."

"I'm not loafing," I said.

"That television's been on all day."

"Blame the boys."

"You can't keep blaming other people for your problems, Shannon."

I had a feeling this wasn't about the television.

I would have been in school, but the Monday after finding out about you, my mother pulled me out, citing my health. I'm glad I wasn't there to see the looks on the office ladies' faces. To hear their snide comments. I wasn't the first girl at my high school to get pregnant young and out of wedlock and wouldn't be the last, but that didn't make it any less a scandal. It would have been worse had my parents been anybody. As it was, they kept to themselves, kept their business their business, and expected others to do the same.

"You didn't have to pull me out so soon," I said. "I could have gone to class. Worn sweaters."

"Sweaters don't fool nobody."

"I'm not even showing yet."

"Yet."

"What do you want me to do, then? Clean everything?"

"As tempting as that offer is, that leaves nothing for your brothers to do. No, I have a better idea. Get ready and meet me at the car. Five minutes."

I was never a fan of my mother's "better ideas," and when we pulled up to an old brick building after what felt like a million-year drive, my heart sank into my stomach.

"Go on in," she said. "Tell 'em your name. They know you're coming."

I climbed out of the car but lingered by the open passenger window. I became immediately suspicious when she stayed put. "Why can't you come in with me?"

"You're a grown woman now, right? Making big, grown-up decisions. You don't need me to walk you into every building you go into from now until eternity, do you?"

"What if I do?"

She raised her eyebrow. "Then you're worse off than I thought." She shook her head. "I'll pick you up in a couple of hours."

"Hours? But—"

She took off before I could finish my question.

I could have done the cowardly thing and looked for a bench or somewhere to pass the time until (if) my mother came back. Sometimes I wonder how things might have changed if I had. If it would have made a difference.

Instead, I went inside like a good girl.

You could tell right away the place used to be someone's home. Or several someones' homes. The front room had a vaulted ceiling, with an open door directly to my left—a closet, where a ragged brown coat hung from a cracked wooden hanger. The hallway directly ahead was empty and smelled like a combination of antiseptic and the rose petal perfume my grandmother used to wear.

I waited for someone to pop out of an alcove and notice me, but it was eerily quiet. I took a few steps into the hallway and peered around the corner into another room, empty except for a television and a couch with a plastic cover. The tiled floor was stained, and the corners of the ceiling were mottled with what looked like mold.

"TV time isn't for another hour, you know that."

I turned and the woman who'd appeared in the hallway frowned. She looked barely older than me, her hair a soft blond and pulled in a tight bun at the back of her head. She looked me up and down before fixing her face into something less pleasant.

"Thought you were someone else," she said. Then, "How did you get in here?"

"Front door," I said.

She rolled her eyes. "I meant who let you in?"

"No one. There wasn't anyone around."

"Figures. No one gives a shit around here anymore." She hesitated, her cheeks flushed. "Sorry. Do you have someone here or something?"

"I don't even know where here is."

"Tina!" A voice echoed down the hall, followed by sharp heel clicks.

The blond woman, Tina, gritted her teeth. "Here, miss."

It took a minute to place the woman who approached, all legs in a pantsuit with shoulder pads too thick for her frame. She smiled, but it didn't reach her eyes. "Glad you could make it, Shannon."

Mrs. Something-or-other. Her name floated around my head without ever getting stuck. She'd taught Sunday school at church when I was nine or ten. I remembered she always placed a cream-colored ceramic statue of the Virgin Mary on the corner of the desk and made all us kids stand in line to kiss it before she would start the lesson. Jesus may have healed the world, she'd said, but it was Mary who gave birth to it.

She must have seen the struggle on my face.

"You can call me Marcia," she said. "Seeing as we're all adults here now."

"Okay," I said.

"We'll get you started in the cafeteria. Some of them can be a little...stand-offish. Having a counter between you might help get you acclimated."

I nodded, even though I had no idea what she was talking about.

"You'll need an apron. Tina can grab that for you, can't you, Tina?"

"Sure," Tina said, but her hands had balled into fists in her pockets.

"Excellent." Marcia gestured for me to follow. "No time like the present. Let's go meet the mothers."

Jo's out of the clinic now, still half-drugged on the tranquilizers they're feeding her because she can't stop picking at her scabs. She leaves a trail of them on the floor on her way to bed, and by the time she wakes up, there's blood on the sheets. I told her if she didn't cut it out, there was no chance she was getting out of here. Ever.

"So?" she said.

If I didn't like her so much, I'd have slapped her. "So you want to spend the rest of your life doing arts and crafts with the safety scissors and hoarding tranqs for that one night you get just weepy enough to end it all?"

Jo guffawed. "Don't threaten me with a good time."

Used to be me and Jo were of one mind. All we wanted was to get out of here, to get back to living our lives and see the people we love and hope they could love us back. Now it's like Jo is determined to sabotage all the hard work we've done. We're not young women. I refuse to waste what time I have left. If that means she rots in here alone, so be it.

CHAPTER NINE

OLIVIA

N othing fit, apart from her maternity clothes, and putting them on felt like a time warp. Olivia hid her belly—still loose and bloated—beneath a sweater too hot for the season, but thick enough to hide any leakage that managed to penetrate the two nursing pads tucked awkwardly in her bra. Any attempt at makeup was undone by the tears that streamed down her face every time she looked in the mirror, and she hadn't brushed her hair in days, so the only thing she could do was throw it in a ponytail.

She didn't notice the coffee stain on her sleeve until the doorbell rang.

In their birthing class, Edie had been the outspoken one, cracking off-color jokes about episiotomies that had endeared most of the other women to her, Kris included, but only managed to make Olivia more anxious about childbirth. She'd had nightmares about getting sliced in half for weeks.

Now, Edie stood in Olivia's doorway with her arm linked through Mark's, the same *wouldn't you like to know* grin on her face. Kris said she'd given birth a week before Olivia, yet Edie had the audacity to look well rested, doe-eyed, with perfectly applied mascara and lipstick.

Edie locked eyes with Olivia and shrugged out of Mark's grip to pull her into a crushing hug. "We did it, Mama!"

Olivia bit back a groan. Edie had called every woman in their birthing class *Mama*, including the instructor.

Mark cradled a bottle, offering it to Kris. "Sparkling grape juice. Edie's nursing."

"Thanks. So is Liv. She's a pro." Kris squeezed Olivia's shoulder, then accepted the grape juice and ushered them in. "Dinner's almost ready."

Mark followed Kris into the kitchen, leaving Edie and Olivia in the foyer, Edie's arm still awkwardly draped around Olivia's shoulders.

"So." Edie made a show of looking behind the coat rack and under the end table. "Where's the little one?"

"Sleeping." Finally, thankfully, after another marathon feeding.

Edie pouted. "I wanted to bring Mason with us, but Mark insisted on a night out alone. We'll have to get the kids together for a play date soon though."

Olivia's sleep-deprived brain struggled to keep up. Play dates? The concept seemed ridiculous. Olivia could barely see to the next feeding. "Uh, sure. Yeah. That sounds fun." Looking for an escape, she added, "I should see if Kris needs help in the kitchen."

Edie grabbed her arm before she could slink off. "She's fine. And if she isn't, Mark is in there. Between the two of them, they can't screw it up too badly, right?"

"You would think."

Edie wandered a few steps further into the living room. Olivia spotted a pair of her underwear on the floor next to the couch, a leftover from the pile she'd moved from the living room floor to the bedroom floor, and hurried over to kick it under the couch. She turned and caught Edie looking.

Olivia's face burned. "I, uh—"

"Oh, stop," Edie said, putting her hand up. "Do you have any idea how much laundry is in my basement right now? It looks like a Goodwill donation room down there. This"—she gestured to her clothes—"I bought today so I wouldn't have to do a load. Mark's wearing his brother's shirt and day-old underwear."

Edie was clearly lying to make Olivia feel better. Though part of her appreciated the effort, the rest of her resented it.

Forcing a smile, Olivia told Edie to sit while she got them a drink.

She couldn't help glancing up at the mirror in the dining room as she passed. Her eyes were bloodshot and her lips were a little dry, but otherwise she looked okay. Tired. Worn out, but alive. But even this close to the kitchen, where there was enough garlic in the air to make her eyes water, Olivia could smell herself, all sour milk and old fruit. The baby monitor crackled from the counter. Flora had been asleep for almost an hour. Olivia was jealous. All she wanted was to crawl into bed and maybe never get back out.

Later, at the table, Edie took the chair beside Olivia, too close, her elbow constantly brushing Olivia's while she shot winks across the table at her husband. It all felt very conspiratorial—moms versus dads—and Olivia seemed to be the only one not in on the joke. She pushed her food around her plate while Edie chirped about Mason. He was so sweet. Such a good sleeper. Already babbling and smiling. Each comment felt more pointed. *I am a success; you are a failure.* Olivia tried to catch Kris's eye, to ask in that unspoken language of married couples—*Are you hearing this? Am I crazy?* But Kris's gaze seemed to purposefully drift over Olivia without pausing. Either she was ignoring Olivia, or her distress didn't matter. Olivia didn't know which was worse.

Despite her growling stomach, Olivia couldn't swallow more than a few small bites. Her jaw ached as she chewed, and the first crunch of garlic bread sent a sharp shard of pain through her mouth. When she managed to swallow, she tongued her back teeth to find one of them slightly loose.

Kris finally looked at her from across the small table. "You okay?"

Olivia fought the urge to stick her finger in her mouth and prod the loose tooth. "Just not hungry, I guess."

"Eat," Edie urged, lips glistening with garlic oil. "The better you eat, the better baby eats."

Almost on cue, Flora's cry exploded through the baby monitor.

"Lungs on that one," Mark said.

"Babe?" Kris pushed her plate away. "You want me to—"

"What's the point?" Olivia snapped. She started to backpedal, but something had broken loose inside her. It was like Kris was putting on a show for Edie and Mark—Kris, the helpful, doting spouse—while Olivia was left to flounder, uncertain and afraid. Her voice dropped. "You know she won't take the bottle. You know she'll scream until she drains me dry."

Edie patted her shoulder. "Sweetie, it's okay to be tired."

Tired? What Olivia felt was beyond tired. Tired was days ago, when it was only the edges of her mind that were clouded. Tired was a mindless trudge between feedings and diaper changes and rocking. Something else was happening to her, something only she could see.

"Don't touch me." Olivia's voice caught as she stood on shaky legs, knocking her chair backward. As Flora cried, her voice twisted and deepened. It sounded like wood dragged on stone. Beneath her screams, that *tap, tap, tapping* on glass. Olivia rounded the table and grabbed the baby monitor off the counter. "Do you hear that?"

"I'll get her." Kris started to stand, but Olivia shushed her.

"No! Listen." She held out the monitor. The tapping got louder, practically drowning out Flora's cries. "You hear it?"

"Hear what?" Edie asked.

Olivia scowled, ignoring her. She walked the monitor over to Kris. "Do you hear it?" Before Kris could answer, Olivia continued, "I heard it last night. On the window. Tap, tap, tap. Nails on glass. And then the window was open. I saw—there was something there. And Flora—" A sick feeling moved through her. She had been right, hadn't she? It wasn't dust on the windowsill. It was mud. There had been something—*someone*—there in the dark. And before, the shadow in the window...had that been real too? Was it the same someone?

The baby went suddenly silent. Olivia's skin crawled as she realized—the baby was listening.

A familiar, eerie feeling crept up through Olivia's body where it settled like a spider in her chest, legs twitching between her nerves. This was how she'd felt at the hospital, that first night when the shadows from her nightmares had slipped through the dark and into her waking world.

"Must've been a nightmare," Mark said. His face was pale.

"Poor thing." Edie reached out to touch Olivia's hand, frowning when Olivia pulled away. "Best to just leave her, I think."

Olivia had no intention of going in that room.

"I'll just check on her," Kris said.

Olivia pushed her back in her chair. "No. Edie's right."

"She could have choked or something. I just want to make sure."

"She's *fine.*"

Kris removed Olivia's hand from her shoulder and stood, but didn't wipe the worry from her face quick enough. Olivia felt it in her guts. *She sees it now,* Olivia thought. *There's something wrong with me, and she sees it.*

"Sit. I'll be right back," Kris said.

Olivia obeyed, and the three of them sat in silence, listening to Kris's gentle coos through the baby monitor.

When Kris returned, she sat, casting apologetic smiles at Edie and Mark, but avoiding Olivia altogether. "Where were we?"

"Maybe we should go," Mark said. "We didn't mean to impose—"

"No. Please." Kris leaned over the table, pouring more of the sparkling grape juice. "We all deserve the adult time. Flora is already back to sleep. Please. Stay."

Edie tucked back into her salad, probably pleased to be invited to witness Olivia's further breakdown.

Olivia tried to catch Kris's eyes. What had she seen in the bedroom? Had she heard the nails on the glass? But Kris made it through the rest of the meal—including dessert—without so much as looking in Olivia's direction.

Finally, more than an hour later, Olivia followed behind Kris as they walked Edie and Mark to the door.

"Well, that was—er, thanks." Mark shook Kris's hand and shot Olivia a wary smile over Kris's shoulder.

"We should do this again," Kris said.

Mark's smile didn't falter, but Olivia could see in his eyes he wouldn't be back anytime soon.

Edie hugged Kris, then moved toward Olivia with her arms out. Olivia had no choice but to be squished against Edie. She prayed her nursing pads held up. It'd been more than two hours since she'd last fed Flora; much longer and she'd need to pump. Edie kissed her cheek, barely missing her mouth, and set her chin on Olivia's shoulder. "Don't worry too much. I've read it's normal to be...off. It was probably just the baby monitor ticking. Mine does it sometimes. Scares the crap out of me if I'm half asleep." She pulled away. Smiled. "Everything will be fine. You'll see."

So Edie *had* heard it. That meant Kris had to have heard it too. But why didn't she say anything? Why did she leave Olivia sitting there feeling like she was crazy?

Olivia could feel Kris's eyes on her, so she forced a smile. "Thanks."

"And, listen. I meant to mention earlier. A few of us have been meeting on Wednesdays. The moms. Just to chat and be away from everything, you know?"

"A mommy group."

Edie smiled. "If you like. Anyway, you should come. I think it'd do you some good."

"That sounds good," Kris said, overenthused. "Liv would love it, I bet."

"Sure." *Never.* "Sounds great."

"Kris and I were talking about postpartum, how—" Edie stopped, gaze somewhere over Olivia's shoulder. Olivia turned, but only saw Kris, her lips set in a tight line.

"How what?" Olivia prompted.

"That—uh, that you've been cooped up since the baby came. That you were hoping for some girl time." She flashed a bright, fake smile.

"I see."

"So we'll see you Wednesday?"

Olivia nodded, if only to push Edie the rest of the way out the door.

With Edie and Mark finally gone, Kris and Olivia stood in silence until their car pulled out of the driveway. Olivia released a breath she hadn't realized she was holding. Kris brushed past her and started clearing the table.

"What was that?" Olivia rounded the table, trying to catch Kris's eye.

"What was what?"

"You made me feel—"

"How? How did I make you feel, Liv?" Kris stacked plates, slapping silverware on the stack hard enough to crack the ceramic. "This whole thing—the dinner, inviting them over—was for you. Or did that not occur to you?"

The baby monitor came to life as Flora sighed and blankets rustled.

They both dropped their voices.

"You know how exhausted I am," Olivia said. "How could that possibly have been for me?"

"You need friends, Liv. We both do." Kris lugged the pile of plates into the kitchen, where she set them on the counter with exaggerated care. "My parents live in Florida, and your family…" She shook her head.

Olivia didn't need her to say it. It was like her grandmother's house had a springboard in the doorway, launching everyone out the moment they turned eighteen. Aunt Erin was the only one who'd stayed local, but even she was hard to track down lately. Olivia couldn't count on her grandparents either. Both of them had survived one form of cancer or another and spent most of their time moving as little as possible. They'd done their job by taking care of Olivia when her mother couldn't. Once she'd put her own two feet on the ground, they were off the clock.

"I have friends," Olivia said.

"Who? Simone?"

Simone was the other adjunct in her department at the community college. They had lunch together every Monday and spent more than one evening over glasses of cheap red wine commiserating about the unfairness of tenure. No doubt she'd taken on what would have been Olivia's classes by now. And, now that she thought about it, she hadn't heard from Simone—or anyone from the college—since her maternity leave began.

Loading the dishwasher, Kris continued, "I'm not trying to be an asshole, okay? I'm being proactive. When we got pregnant, the first thing you told me was that you were scared of losing yourself. You didn't want to be just someone's mom."

It was the way she said it, the words dripping with disdain, that made the tears come. She furiously blinked them away—not that Kris would have noticed. She strode past Olivia back to the table, retrieved the empty service bowls, and went back to cleaning, all without looking at Olivia.

"I'm just worried that—" Kris bit off the last of the sentence. Swallowed it.

It was like someone had poured cold water under her skin. "Worried that what?"

"Nothing."

This was all wrong. Why were they fighting? They were supposed to be a team. Always on each other's side. Every time. "Tell me."

"Gonna have to let this soak," Kris muttered. Then, sighing, "I just want us to be happy."

The bottom dropped out of Olivia's stomach. "I didn't realize we weren't."

Before Kris could say anything else, Flora's gentle whine came through the baby monitor.

"Better get that," Kris said, "before she really gets going."

She must have read the hesitation on Olivia's face.

"Never mind. Finish this. I'll get her."

Panicked, Olivia moved to block her. "No, I—" but Kris brushed past her without effort.

The right thing to do would have been to follow her. To tell her everything, the things she saw and heard. To tell Kris that she was afraid, and not just of the tapping noises. But she couldn't make herself take that first step. The pettier, stubborn part of her thought Kris should have already realized, and the fact that she didn't meant that she wasn't paying attention because she didn't care. Flora was the child, which meant, Kris likely believed, her needs superseded Olivia. She was right, of course.

She stood next to the sink, water running, and listened, straining to hear what Kris was whispering to Flora. Was she telling her she was sorry that she ended up with such a terrible mother? Was she telling Flora they'd be their own family one day?

A weight settled on Olivia's chest and nothing she did would budge it. She could barely breathe. Cotton filled her head, and through it, she heard the soft *thump, thump, thump* of her heart.

No.

Not her heart. It was coming from the window above the sink.

She couldn't see anything out of the corner of her eye, but didn't dare turn toward the tapping. Part of her clung to what Edie had said—she couldn't blame this on the baby monitor, but Olivia was exhausted and upset. Her mind was in overdrive, conjuring all the horrible things that could happen to Flora, to her, to her marriage... It made sense that she'd start to hear things. But as she set her hand on the edge of the sink, she could feel the vibration of the thumps on the window.

Holding her breath, she forced herself to look at the window, but there were too many lights on in here, making the dark outside impossible to see through. The sheer curtains hid whatever the dark might have given up anyway. But at the very center of the window, through the tiniest sliver of an opening, she spotted a streak of steam. It faded and shot across the window, and then faded again. Someone's breath.

She started to call for Kris—her wife needed to see this, to know Olivia wasn't making it up—but her voice was trapped in her throat. When she looked back, the breath had stopped.

Without thinking about it, she turned off the kitchen lights and threw open the curtains. In the dregs of the faint light coming from her neighbor's garage, she saw someone running across her yard—a woman, maybe, with long gnarled hair that dragged in the dirt.

It's her, Olivia thought. The face in the shadows. The nails on her windows.

She started to call for Kris again, but she knew if she waited for Kris to come, hoping to prove her fear was justified not just to Kris, but to herself, the woman would be gone and Kris would look at Olivia the way she'd looked at her at dinner. Olivia didn't know if she could handle another look like that.

If the woman was real, then whoever she was, she had *done* something to Olivia. To Flora. And Olivia wouldn't let her get away with it.

She ran to the back door and clipped her hip on the corner of the counter, but she barely registered the pain. She struggled with the chain—installed a month before she gave birth in a frenzy to make the house as safe as possible—and finally made it into the yard. The cold hit her like a wall. She hadn't been outside since Flora's doctor's appointment, and the sudden change in temperature threw her off.

A tall wood fence surrounded their yard. The woman couldn't have gotten far.

Olivia walked slowly in the direction she'd seen the woman run, jumping at the slightest sound. Next door, her neighbors spoke in hushed voices. A noise like a gunshot made her stop midstep. *Planks*, she told herself. *They're building a deck. They told you all about it.*

Her neighbors' garage light went out, bathing her in darkness.

Fuck.

She blinked until her eyes adjusted, but even then she couldn't see into the corners of the fence where shadows were dense. There was only one way the woman could have gone. Olivia ran for the gate only to find the lock intact. The woman would have needed a key to open it, and even if she'd had it—Olivia's mind flashed through images of the woman creeping through her house, touching them, touching Flora, taking their things—there's no way she would have gotten out without Olivia seeing her.

Either the woman had jumped the fence—unlikely—or there was a break in it somewhere. The fence had come with the house when they bought it five years ago, and Olivia couldn't remember ever taking a close look at it.

Body trembling with the feeling of eyes probing the back of her head, she went to the shed—*we really need to start locking this*—and found a flashlight hanging next to the door.

Starting back at the gate, she walked the perimeter, dragging the light over each board, looking for cracks, testing for loose nails, digging around at the base to feel for holes, anything that would tell her where the woman went.

If it even was a woman.

The longer she walked, the harder she had to try to convince herself about what she'd seen. If there were footprints in the dirt, Olivia had already trampled them, and the fence, while a little wobbly in places, was intact.

"I saw her," she mumbled, a mantra to sanity. "I saw her."

Hadn't she? Coming down from the adrenaline spike made her woozy, head foggy. It shook her confidence.

In the kitchen, the water was still running. Olivia rinsed the dirt off her hands as she studied the window. Any sign of the woman's breath, of her hands on the glass, was gone.

"Liv?"

Kris stood in the doorway, a burp towel draped over her shoulder.

Olivia took a subtle breath to calm her hammering heart. How long had Kris been standing there? "How's Flora?"

"Fine."

Olivia nodded, following Kris's gaze toward the sink, the open dishwasher. Her fingers were pruned, and the sink had begun to clog with mud.

Kris moved next to her, saw the mud and frowned. She shut off the water, and they stood in silence for what felt like a long time before tears burned Olivia's eyes.

"I'm not crazy," Olivia said.

"No one said—"

"Stop. Just—I need to know something."

"Okay."

"When you look at Flora, what do you see?"

Kris crossed her arms, a confused look on her face. "Is this a trick question?"

Olivia shook her head. "Never mind."

"No. Wait. Okay. I want to help; I just don't know what you mean."

"How about when you look at me?" Olivia turned and forced herself to look her wife in the eye. "What do you see?"

"I see you." Kris shrugged. "I don't know what you want me to say."

"How do my eyes look to you?" She took a step closer, only for Kris to take a half step away. "What about my skin? It's dry, right? And my lips—" She bit her bottom lip, dragging her teeth over chapped skin until it peeled away.

"Everyone gets chapped lips."

"No, but *look*. I look—" Olivia shook her head. How could she not see it?

Except, maybe she *did* see. The way Kris couldn't look at her for more than a second, the concern in her expression—Kris saw the sallow skin and protruding bones, even if she didn't want to admit it. She could see what was happening to her, but she wouldn't even acknowledge it.

Olivia wanted to tell her that she'd read all those books Kris took out from the library. She knew what postpartum depression was. She knew the symptoms by heart, and every morning since the birth, she'd run them through her head, checking them against herself. The way she'd done with the signs of alcoholism, obsession, any and all mental illnesses she figured she could self-diagnose. If she was going to inherit something from her mother, some genetic abnormality, she was going to catch it before it did any real damage.

Part of her *wanted* this to be depression. At least then she would know what to do. There would be treatment, and she would get better.

But this was different. Worse, her wife, her other half, didn't believe her.

Kris kissed her, a chaste peck on the lips. "I'm sorry for not seeing how tired you were right out of the gate. That's my fault. I'll fix it, okay?"

Olivia nodded, not believing her.

"Flora and I will sleep in the guest room. You catch up on sleep while you can, and we'll go from there. Deal?"

Kris didn't wait for an answer before leaving the kitchen.

Olivia kept it together long enough to hear the soft click of the guest room door being shut.

Covering her face with a towel, she sank to the floor, streaking mud on the tile, and cried.

CHAPTER TEN

SHANNON

Got any eights?"

"Go fish."

Jo may not be a bullshitter, but she's an excellent liar. We're more than halfway down the deck now, and I've been hanging onto this eight of hearts the whole time. Part of me thinks Jo's hanging onto all three of them just to spite me, but that's not her style.

The cards are brand new, a gift from Doctor Call-Me-Jim's daughter, Angela. She's a good kid. I took to her immediately the first time I met her. This was, oh, a decade or more back, when Angela was barely twelve years old, a big spirit in a little body. No mother, poor thing. She reminded me of you—all big brown eyes and expressive mouth. How could I not be drawn in? I think Doctor Call-Me-Jim was unsettled by my closeness with his daughter, but she soon put that to rights. She's got her daddy wrapped around her little finger. That hold only got tighter once she decided to follow in his footsteps. She'll make a wonderful psychiatrist one day.

Don't be jealous, Olive Juice. She may have brought a ray of sunshine into this otherwise dowdy place, but you are my whole sun.

Jo doesn't like Angela.

"A user's what she is," Jo says.

"You got no problem using her presents," I say.

"Nothin' wrong with using a user."

There's no point in arguing with Jo when she gets like this. Ever since her "accident," she's been moody.

Jo snorts. "That's, uh, wassa-word? Deflection." She nods. "Textbook deflection, alright."

Jo wouldn't know textbook deflection if it hit her in the mouth.

"I dare you," Jo says.

"Got any threes?"

Jo shrugs. "Go fish."

It's been over a week since I last wrote here. Don't tell her, but Jo was right, in a way. I hate this part. Hate thinking about it. Now I have the pen in my hand and the thought of committing it to paper, making it real…my insides are tangled in knots and my throat burns with bile.

"There's no point in clinging to our actions," Angela told me once. "We can't take them back. All we can do is move forward with the truth in our hearts."

Forgive me, Olivia. This is my truth.

"Though I've only been here for twelve years, Bethany Home has served as a sanctuary for women since the 1870s," Marcia explained as she gave me a brief tour of the main floor. A wide hallway led from the front room to the common areas—the cafeteria, the lounge, the large room where families of the mothers could visit on their birthdays and Christmas. Narrow hallways branched off to the resident wings. Marcia made a point to ignore them as she spoke. "As you may be able to imagine, benefactors aren't exactly drooling at the idea of support- ing unwed mothers and other...delicate women. No profit in philanthropy, I'm afraid. We depend largely on the work of volunteers like yourself."

Marcia may have called it volunteer work, but really it was indentured ser- vitude. Twenty minutes of scooping crusty-edged mashed potatoes onto paper plates and I saw this for what it was—punishment. And, maybe, a warning.

The cafeteria looked like it'd been carved from the bones of the house, the marrow used to shape small chairs and tables with rubber stoppers affixed to the corners. The ceiling was low and the lighting too bright. It cast a harsh white glow on everything, including the mothers. As they entered through the only door in groups of two or three, from a distance, they looked ethereal—all long hair and loose clothes like robes. Up close, though, the brightness faded from their faces. Shadows caved in their cheeks and sank their eyes. I couldn't look at them for longer than a few seconds without chills snaking down my back.

They weren't shy about looking at me though. As I handed each mother a paper plate half-filled with food, they met my gaze and held it, the corners of their mouths bending upward, satisfied, when I looked away first.

About halfway through, I spotted a few strands of hair next to the mashed potato pan. One hard puff of air and it would have ended up on the food. Swallowing against a gag, I reached a plastic-gloved hand toward the hair, intend- ing to brush it onto the ground, when one of the mothers slapped her hand over mine, trapping it.

I tried to pull away, but she was surprisingly strong. She barely flinched as I panicked, looking around for Tina or Marcia or someone to help me. Finally, she let go and I snatched my hand away like it'd been burned. The two hairs sat unbothered on the stainless steel. The mother—stark blond hair hanging in ragged wisps around her face—carefully brushed the hairs into her palm and stuck them in her pocket.

All I could do was stare, dumb and wide-eyed.

"Those aren't yours," she said. Her voice was soft. I found myself leaning closer to hear her.

"Not yours either," I said, surprising both of us.

"Keep moving, Iris," Marcia interrupted, setting a fresh pan of potatoes on the counter. "Don't want to keep our friends from a hot lunch because we're too busy chitchatting."

"Not chitchatting," Iris mumbled. "She was trying to steal."

Marcia raised an eyebrow. My stomach flipped. I wouldn't exactly have minded being asked to leave, but I could only imagine the hell my mother would raise if she thought I was stealing, especially from a place like this.

"Is that true, Shannon?" Marcia asked.

I shook my head.

"Thank you." She turned to Iris. "I'd like you to apologize to Shannon. She's here to help you. It wouldn't do to run her off with your lies."

"I'm not lying." Iris's cheeks bloomed and a purple vein started to bulge in her forehead. "I don't lie."

Instead of fighting her, Marcia sighed, gesturing toward the end of the aisle where a girl in an apron impatiently held a carton of milk. "We'll talk about this later."

After lunch, Marcia left to attend to some business, putting me in Tina's hands. I wanted to ask how much longer I was expected to stay, if the volunteer schtick had been some elaborate scheme to ease me into confinement. It didn't take a genius to see the mothers weren't at ease here, no matter how much Marcia prattled on about activities and enrichment. But Tina wasn't interested in talking unless it was about the mothers.

With her long legs, each step was like two of mine. I practically had to jog to keep up with her.

"Can't leave them alone for longer than a few minutes," Tina said. "Especially Iris."

My ears perked up at the name. "Why?"

"She likes to piss me off." Tina paused at the doorway to the lounge. "Couple of weeks ago I was supposed to leave an hour early so I could meet a friend. Jessie." The way Tina blushed at the name made me think Jessie was more than a friend. "I was all set to go when I see one of the hallways flooded. The smell was awful. An actual turd floated by my new shoes." She grimaced. "Didn't take long to find out what'd happened. Iris had stopped up the toilets with her ripped up bedsheet."

"Why?" I asked.

"Because she's nuts, that's why."

I spotted Iris on the far side of the lounge. She stood with her back to the corner, twirling something around her fingers.

"Marcia keeps calling them the mothers," I said. "Why? Where are their kids?"

Tina turned and looked at me, eyebrows all scrunched up. "You serious?" When I didn't answer, she crossed her arms and leaned against the doorway. "She told you about it being a sanctuary for women or whatever, right?"

I nodded.

"That's not actually what Bethany Home is. She likes to say it is because it makes her feel better about herself." Tina sniffed. "Up until the fifties it was a home for unwed mothers. Uppity families would send their knocked-up daughters here until they gave birth. If they had a husband waiting on the other side of those doors, great. If not, the baby disappeared into the night and the girl went home to live like nothing happened."

"And now?" I asked, making every conscious effort not to touch my belly.

"Girls still come here sometimes, even before they're showing. It's not like they're that young. Sixteen, seventeen. Old enough to know better, but too young to try to make a go of it as a single parent. You should see the way these parents waltz their daughters in her, yoked with shame. Stupid. I mean, it's the eighties, right? My aunt's generation didn't burn their bras just so their daughters could get stuck in a place like this because some asshole boyfriend didn't wear a condom. Mostly, though, the women who come here are mothers, or used to be mothers. Sometimes it's because they hurt their kids. Sometimes they hurt themselves. Sometimes both."

I glanced toward Iris, who'd stopped playing with the thing in her hands and was now staring at me. Her eyes drifted toward my belly and back again. The corner of her mouth lifted, a half-hidden grin.

A bang on the other side of the room made me jump.

"Shit." Tina started toward the commotion—a woman reached across a small card table, aiming for another woman's hair. Tina paused, looked back at me. "Just…don't move, I guess."

She didn't have to tell me twice.

I didn't realize Iris had started walking toward me until she was inches from me, close enough I could smell her—stale and a little like baby powder. I was frozen to the spot. I glanced in Tina's direction hoping she would notice Iris and come to my rescue, but she was too busy trying to pry a woman's fingers out of another woman's hair. A chunk of it had already come away and drifted across the tile like a tumbleweed.

"You dropped this," Iris said.

She held out her hand. In the middle of her palm was a tiny sliver of skin. I looked at the side of my thumb where a bit of blood had already begun to dry. To this day, when I'm nervous, I pick and bite at myself, tearing away long swaths of dead skin from around my cuticles. I hardly feel it.

She kept her hand there until I finally took the piece of skin. I pinched and rolled it between my fingers.

"You need to be more careful," she said.

"It's dead," I said. "I'm fine. It hardly bled."

She shook her head. Her fingertips brushed my belly, there and gone so quick I hardly felt it.

"She likes dead things. Things she can use."

I sucked in a breath as her hand moved toward my belly again. "Who?"

"The black-haired woman. Buried and broken and dead."

Her fingertips grazed my belly. I held my breath.

"She'll come for you," Iris said, "She comes for all of us, eventually."

"No one's coming for me," I said, my voice shaky.

Iris smiled sadly. Kissed my cheek. "Not yet."

"Got any queens?"

"Go fish."

It's more fun to play Go Fish with Angela than it is with Jo. Angela, for one, don't cheat. For two, she has a tell. If she picks up a card and it's the one I'd just asked her for, the corner of her mouth twitches and she bites the inside of her cheek to keep from smiling. Most times I don't take advantage. You should see the way she lights up on her next turn, knowing she's got me right where she wants me.

"Got any...queens?"

"Gah!" I playfully fling the card across the table, and Angela does a little dance in the chair as she sets down the pair: hearts and diamonds.

I hesitate before taking my turn. "Can I ask you a question?"

"Of course." A little of the playfulness dims in her face.

"Do you think I'm crazy?"

Angela frowns. "You know how I feel about that word."

I wink. "Humor a crazy lady."

A thin smile. "That's probably a question for my dad."

"I value your opinion."

She sits up straighter at that. Probably the first time she's heard it. "I'm not a professional. Not yet. I mean, I've gone to school, and I've applied to some of the best residencies—"

"Oh, pish. You're going to run circles around everyone and you know it. Just as soon as they let you loose."

Her face flushes a delicate pink. "Thank you."

"So?"

"So." She sets her cards facedown on the table and folds her arms. She leans back, those scrutinizing eyes running up and down my face. Finally, she shakes her head. Faintly, and just the once. "No, Shannon. I don't think you're crazy at all."

CHAPTER ELEVEN

OLIVIA

I t'd taken ages to fall asleep, and when she finally did, it didn't last. Nightmares carried out of the dream world and into Olivia's reality— shadows twisting in the corners of the dark room and voices whispering from under her pillow. Around 2:00 a.m., she turned on the television and watched old PBS programming until she fell asleep, only to wake again an hour later to complete darkness. The remote that she'd left on Kris's side of the bed was on the floor. Olivia tried to convince herself she'd kicked it in her sleep, that the impact had somehow triggered the power button, but the air in the room had changed. She laid, unmoving, barely breathing for fear of disturbing the fragile silence. Finally, exhausted, she slept.

The sound of her neighbor's lawn mower jarred her out of sleep sometime around 9:00. The sun poked sharply through the blinds. Blinking hard against the pounding in her head, she leaned over and pulled the cord, letting the full force of the sunlight break up the lingering shadows. Sitting up, she massaged her temples and cheeks. Her face was puffy and achy, like she'd been crying in her sleep.

"Just nightmares," she murmured. "You're a grown-up. Get a grip."

Her shirt was damp, but significantly less so than before. Flora had fed only once in thirty-six hours and already Olivia's milk was leaving. Part of her was pleased. Whatever was wrong with Flora, that thing inside her that made each feed drain Olivia of more than just milk, would starve. But then, so might her daughter. The jaundice could get worse. Could kill her if nothing was done.

God, what was she even thinking? There was nothing wrong with Flora. She was a baby who needed her mother. Olivia was just tired. Wrung out. That was normal. It had to be. She thought of Edie last night, how put-together she looked, how chipper she sounded when she talked about her son. All lies, obviously. She bet that if she went over to Edie's this morning, she'd find Edie hunched over and haggard, tits swinging like empty balloons and spit-up on her neck.

Olivia was becoming a completely different person, a person who shrank under the gaze of others and spent too long in her own head. Kris was right. All Olivia needed was some sleep to get her head on straight. She wasn't exactly rested, but that would come with time. She saw that now. She also saw how awful she'd been. Her only saving grace was that Flora was too young to store any long-term memories. She could already imagine the therapy sessions twenty, thirty years from now: *My mother starved me because she thought I was eating her soul.*

The house sounded quiet; she figured Flora and Kris were still asleep. Olivia would get up and shower, put herself together, and then pump like a madwoman until her milk came back in full force. She would spend the entire day with Flora, getting to know her the way she should have been doing from the beginning. Thinking of it, Olivia was pleased to realize she missed her daughter. Her fingers traced the outline of Flora's head against her chest, and she smiled. Everything would be okay now.

Finally climbing out of bed, she turned to straighten the duvet before heading to the shower. She froze when her gaze fell on Kris's pillow. There was a fresh dent in the middle of it. Maybe Kris came to bed after all, she thought. But before the thought could comfort her, she spotted a long black hair on the pillow, too long and too dark to belong to either of them.

I'm hallucinating, she thought, even as she picked up the hair and wound it around her finger.

The woman had been here. Had laid in her bed.

No. Olivia couldn't believe it. She refused.

It was all meant to be in her head. But how could it be if she had the evidence in her hands?

She ran to the bathroom, tossed the hair into the toilet, and flushed.

A scalding shower left Olivia feeling light-headed and no more clean than when she went in. Every time she blinked, her mind conjured snapshots of the woman from the backyard breathing down her neck, touching her hair and face. She needed to tell Kris. Olivia had listened to too many true-crime podcasts in her life; these kinds of things escalated. The logical part of her rationalized that she had a stalker. Maybe someone from the hospital. How many babies were stolen from new mothers by women who wanted them for their own? She didn't want to think about it, but now it was the only thing in her head. The smart thing would have been to call the police, file a report, but she couldn't. There was the chance Kris wouldn't believe her and, worse, might mention something to the police about last night. There'd be a record of mental instability. Who was she kidding—there already was. Her genes were tainted. It was why adoption went off the table immediately. No one would give a baby to Olivia, not after what her mother did.

Maybe they had good reason.

She dressed—properly this time, in her favorite maternity jeans (because her pre-pregnancy jeans still didn't fit) and a sweater—and yanked a brush through her hair before leaving the room. She smelled bacon and followed the scent to the kitchen where she found Kris in the kitchen, munching a slice of toast over the sink.

Kris wiped her mouth and smiled. "She lives."

"Barely." She swallowed the panic in her throat. "Where's Flora?"

"Back porch."

"Alone?"

Before Kris could answer, Olivia brushed past her through the kitchen and out the back door to the porch. A woman sat in a chair, black hair piled on top of her head and water dripping down her back. She cooed at Flora, asleep in her arms, and it sounded like gravel.

Olivia blinked and the image changed.

The woman's black hair was now rust red with thick swatches of gray, clipped into an intricate pattern with what looked like a hundred bobby pins. Freckles dotted the back of her pale neck, made paler by the deep purple of her shawl.

"Aunt Erin?"

She turned, giving Olivia the full force of her very expensive veneers. Her lipstick, the same shade of purple as her shawl, made her mouth look like a bruise. Lines crinkled around her eyes as she smiled. Her cheeks were dotted with flecks of dry mascara. A retired cruise ship performer, Olivia had never known her aunt to leave her home without a full face of makeup.

"I was starting to think you'd never get up," Aunt Erin said. "How you can stand to be away from this darling face for more than five minutes astounds me."

Flora laid in the crook of Aunt Erin's elbow, wrapped in a thin yellow blanket.

As quickly as the jaundice seemed to have disappeared, it'd come back just as fast, the tinge of her face and the whites of her eyes a sickly yellow. Her gaze eventually found Olivia's, and she stared hard at her.

"I called her," Kris said from behind Olivia, offering a cup of coffee. Olivia took it just to have something to hold.

"Gave me an earful," Aunt Erin said, then stuck her tongue out at Kris. "She was right though. I should have come sooner, and I'm sorry. I've been sort of tied up at home."

Knowing Aunt Erin, tied up at home could have meant anything from a flooded basement to a surprise visit from European royalty. Olivia decided not to ask.

"To make it up," Aunt Erin continued, "I want to take you to lunch. Both of you." She nuzzled Flora's neck, sparking a rare giggle from the baby. She flashed Kris a smile. "Sorry. Girl time. You know."

"Far be it from me to infringe on the sacredness of girl time." Kris smiled at Aunt Erin, then rolled her eyes toward Olivia, flashing her the kind of *can you believe this* grin that had made Olivia fall for her in the beginning.

Olivia felt her insides loosen. The rock in her gut became a little more dislodged. Her wife loved her, she knew that, but sometimes she needed to be reminded.

The longer Flora laid in Aunt Erin's arms, the more she fidgeted, until finally her pacifier popped loose, releasing a hitching cry.

"I got her," Kris said.

"No." Olivia handed her the untouched coffee. "I got her." Then, before Kris could protest, "Hand her over, Erin."

Holding Flora was like holding a bundle of loosely wrapped twigs. Too light. Too fragile. Olivia sat cross-legged on the floor and lifted her shirt. Flora began rooting immediately, her sunken cheeks and chapped lips twitching. Olivia hesitated for the briefest second, the words ordering Kris to take Flora instead on the tip of her tongue. But she felt Kris's eyes on her, could see Erin holding her breath out of the corner of her eye. Flora latched and it was like nails being driven through Olivia's breast. She bit back a gasp, hunched over to hide the pain on her face.

It only took a few seconds for her arms to start trembling, to feel cold and weak.

"Beautiful," Aunt Erin said. "Just beautiful."

Aunt Erin insisted on bringing them to a tapas restaurant downtown, despite Olivia's insistence she'd be happy with a fast-food sandwich.

"Nonsense," Aunt Erin said. "One of my girls told me about it. Supposed to be the best thing you've ever put in your mouth." She bounced her eyebrows. "She would know, of course. Little tramp."

Aunt Erin had several *girls*, all of them cruise-line performers she'd taken under her wing, for better or worse. It was no secret she'd been pushed into retirement. Keeping tabs on her replacements was either an exercise in masochism or revenge. Either way, it kept her busy. *Idle hands do the devil's work*, as her grandmother was fond of saying.

The hostess led them through the restaurant, past wrought-iron candelabras covered in dripping wax, colorful *luchador* posters, and oil lamp light fixtures that gave off more heat than light. Olivia struggled to move through the densely packed high-top tables with Flora's carrier, nearly knocking over every chair she bumped. Her face burned, keenly aware of people staring, rolling their eyes, and sighing. The restaurant was in the heart of the business district— one of those trendy places people brought clients or potential investors they wanted to impress. None of them had counted on a baby disrupting their Very Important Lunch.

Though Flora managed to sleep through most of the bumping, when they finally reached the table, Olivia realized there was nowhere to put the carrier. The booth was too narrow, and if they put a chair at the end, it would trip every server coming out of the kitchen.

"Let's go somewhere else," Olivia said, but Aunt Erin was already in the booth.

The hostess paused, menus hovering over the table.

Aunt Erin ignored her. "Margarita for me, please. Lime, no salt, on the rocks."

Olivia fought with the carrier, finally forcing it between the table and the booth as the hostess trotted across the restaurant to hunt down a server.

"She's not the server," Olivia said, flashing the hostess an apologetic smile.

Aunt Erin shrugged. "You should have one too."

"I'm breastfeeding."

"You never were any fun."

Olivia grinned. She'd almost missed the poking. When Olivia was a teenager, Aunt Erin proclaimed herself to be the sharp stick everyone needed in their lives. *Otherwise we get too soft.*

Aunt Erin's margarita arrived, and she sucked half of it down before ordering seven different tacos because she couldn't make up her mind. Olivia ordered soup—her stomach still didn't feel right after feeding Flora. She drank two glasses of water trying to get the coppery bile taste out of her mouth.

She started on her third just after the food arrived. The soup looked sad: reddish brown water with unidentifiable bits in it. She ate it anyway, spilling an embarrassing amount of it down her chin thanks to a shaky grip on the spoon.

Aunt Erin finally looked at her in only the way Aunt Erin could, like there was a spider crawling beneath Olivia's skin and she was the only one who could see it. "You okay, Livvy?"

It was the *Livvy* that broke her.

Olivia squeezed her eyes shut, pressing a napkin to her face to hide the tears dripping down her cheeks.

"Shit. Oh, Livvy, I'm sorry." Aunt Erin moved to the other side of the booth, squishing Olivia between her ample body and Flora's carrier. "I promise to never torment another food service worker. Scout's honor."

Olivia snorted through her tears.

"Now you've got snot on the table."

"Erin—"

"On the baby too. Poor thing looks like she's back in the womb."

"Stop, okay?" She wiped her face with a napkin, only to realize she'd used it earlier to wipe soup dribble off the table and now there was a smear of tomato on her cheek, which only made her cry harder.

Aunt Erin grabbed her hands and forced them onto the table, then dabbed a clean napkin in her water glass to clean the tomato off her face.

"Thanks," Olivia muttered.

"You going to tell me or do I have to drag it out of you?"

Movement in the carrier made Olivia look at Flora. She stopped kicking the second Olivia's eyes were on her, her face slack and gaze bright. *Don't you dare,* she seemed to say.

"I need to pee," Olivia said.

Sighing, Aunt Erin climbed out of the booth, trying to catch Olivia's gaze as she made a beeline for the bathroom, but Olivia kept her eyes on her feet. She just needed to pee. Splash some water on her face. Someone bumped into her on the way inside. She looked up to apologize, but the black-haired woman was already halfway through the restaurant.

In her wrung out state, it took a beat for Olivia's brain to catch up. Was that *her*? The woman who'd been sneaking through Olivia's house, tormenting her? It seemed ridiculous that she would be here, hiding in a restaurant bathroom, but what if she'd followed Olivia? What if she was stalking her now, intent on causing more harm? What if she was here to take Flora?

Olivia started toward the front of the restaurant, already having lost sight of the woman, but there was only one exit. If she was fast enough—

Their server cut her off, heading for one of the terminals lining the wall beside the bathrooms. She spotted Olivia and offered a weak smile.

"Everything okay?" she asked.

Why was she looking at Olivia like that? Like she pitied her? Olivia looked past her, hoping to glimpse the woman before she left, but the door was too far away, too many people blocking her line of sight. She might still have been able to catch her, but something in the server's expression kept Olivia rooted.

"Fine," Olivia said, pointing to the bathroom. "Just freshening up."

The server nodded, unconvinced. "Okay. Well, let me know if you need anything."

"Mmhmm." Olivia turned, regretfully, back toward the bathroom.

In the stall, she stared at the gap beneath the door, heart hammering, wondering if the woman would come back. A million years seemed to pass before her legs fell asleep and she was forced to stand. Sharp tingles ran down her legs and as she bent over to massage some life back into her thighs, pain shot through her breast. She felt her nipple peel away from the nursing pad, which was strange. If she was leaking, it'd only get damp. She looked inside her bra and her stomach turned.

Blood had congealed in the nursing pad, two almost perfectly round dots, rust-brown, like she'd been bitten.

Back at the table, Aunt Erin held Flora, rocking her almost frantically with her pinky stuck in Flora's mouth.

"Thank God," Aunt Erin said. "Poor thing's famished." She stood and handed Flora to her. "Let's head back to the car. I've already paid."

The moment Aunt Erin extracted her pinky, Flora started to cry. Somewhere behind Olivia, a group of women clucked disapprovingly. Olivia shot them a look like fire as they passed. *Say something,* she thought. *I dare you.*

In the car, Olivia fed Flora, her latch harder, sharper, than it'd been this morning. She thought of the blood in her nursing pad and suppressed a shudder.

She caught Aunt Erin watching and forced a smile, all teeth.

"I know it's rough, kid," Aunt Erin said, "but you'll get through it. They're just shitting, eating machines at this point—cute or not—but once they get a little older and become people… that's when the fun starts." She smiled encouragingly. "I remember when you were about eighteen months old, crawling all over the place. I left you on the couch so I could run upstairs. I came back and you were in the middle of the dining room table. You saw me and busted up laughing like even you couldn't believe you'd done it." She sighed. "I can't wait to see what mischief Flora gets into."

"There's something wrong with her."

The words were out before Olivia could stop them.

"She looks fine to me."

"Does she, though?" Olivia shook her head, tears biting her eyes. "Her face is all wrong. It's like she was here, and then she wasn't, and now there's this baby in my arms and I don't know who she belongs to."

"Livvy, what do you want me to say? She's a beautiful little girl. Spitting image of her mommy."

Olivia stroked Flora's face, praying to feel that smooth, soft skin she'd had at birth, but all she felt was old paper. She could almost believe she was hallucinating Flora's yellow skin and penetrating green eyes, but touch was tangible. You couldn't hallucinate touch, could you?

"Have you talked to anyone about this?" Aunt Erin asked, all warmth gone from her voice. "Said anything to the doctors? To Kris?"

Olivia shook her head.

"Good. Don't."

Olivia frowned. "Why?"

"They won't believe you. They look at you and Flora, and they'll see—" Aunt Erin's voice caught. "Just, if you want to talk, talk to me, okay?"

"But you don't believe me either."

"Livvy, please. I'm trying to help."

"You can't help though, can you?" Olivia hissed as Flora's latch tightened. Was that blood in the corner of her mouth?

Aunt Erin rubbed her face, smearing her drawn-on eyebrows. She looked at her hands and shook her head, a wry smile on her lips. "The worst sort of déjà vu. You sound just like her." She added, "I think she's done."

Olivia looked down. Flora had settled, a dribble of milk in the corner of her mouth. Olivia put herself together, but hesitated before moving Flora to her carrier. There was a faint flush of pink on her cheeks, but the veins in Olivia's hands stood out, little blue ropes beneath her skin, and her nails had turned slightly yellow. It was like a pendulum between them. How long before the swing stopped?

"Sound like who?" Olivia finally asked.

"It's my fault. Part of it, anyway," Aunt Erin said. "I think if we were closer, if she could confide in me, it might have all turned out differently." She turned, finally looking Olivia full in the face. "I fucked up with Shannon. I will not fuck up with you. Promise me you'll talk it out with me. Call me. I don't care if it's two in the morning, just call me and we'll talk and we'll figure it out." She stroked Flora's cheek and Olivia held her breath, waiting for the realization that never came. "You know what will happen if you say anything to them doctors." When Olivia didn't answer: "They'll take her. I've seen it happen. It's ugly and you can't fix it once it's done. Promise me we'll work this out together. We're family. Family sticks together, right? You and me, yeah?"

Olivia nodded, but only to stop Aunt Erin from shaking, to wipe the fear off her face.

But she knew now, without doubt, what she'd already suspected. Olivia was on her own. There was no one she could talk to, no one who would understand what was happening.

Almost no one.

CHAPTER TWELVE

SHANNON

I f I'd had the chance to go to college, I would have studied math, a fact that tickles Angela when I tell her.

"Why math?" she asks.

"Why not?" I say.

"Most people hate math."

Usually we have to have our visits in the recreation room, surrounded by eavesdroppers and distractions. This time, though, we're in Angela's new office. She's interning with her dad while she finishes her dissertation. When I asked her what she was writing on, she wouldn't tell me, but promised she would lend me a copy once it's finished.

Her office is the opposite of her dad's—bright colors and soft furniture. She has pictures on her desk, mostly of friends, but in an ornate silver frame is one of her mother. She's just the kind of woman I would have pictured for Doctor Call-Me-Jim—collar buttoned up her throat, no makeup on a plain face. But Angela clearly adores her, so I say nothing but nice things. I ask polite questions about the kinds of books she read to Angela before bed, and nod and smile all sweet and wistful. I don't ever tell her how the old nurses talk like us patients aren't breathing, walking humans who can hear and think and speak. I don't tell her how I know her link to this place isn't just through her dad, that her mother's file isn't all that different to mine.

"Stupid to hate something that can't hate you back," I say, earning a smile. "Math doesn't care who you are or what you've done. It doesn't care that maybe you smell a little or that you put your foot in your mouth again. It's black and white, no gray area. It either works, or it doesn't, and nothing you can say will change it."

"You don't like gray areas," Angela says.

"Hate 'em."

"Why's that?"

"There's too much room to mess up."

"Some people think the gray area is where you can't possibly mess up. It's the essence of the gray area. No failure, only interpretation."

"Then some people have never been lost in it. They wouldn't know."

"But you have," Angela says.

"Yes," I say. "More than once."

———

I spent three days a week at Bethany Home but didn't see Iris again for months. I assumed she'd gone home—wherever that was—but Tina, as much as she loved to complain about her charges, wasn't giving up anything.

"Not my problem," she said the couple of times I tried to nonchalantly bring Iris up. "Don't know, and don't care."

Late June brought sweltering heat the building's air-conditioning system could barely compete with. I was showing by then and had started wearing my dad's T-shirts, hoping it would hide the bump. It didn't help. Even though I was on the same side of the cafeteria counter, the same side of the meds distribution window, the nurses, orderlies, and a smattering of volunteers that cycled through all looked at me the way they looked at the mothers—small smirks perched over thinly veiled disdain.

The work was hard, but I'd started to enjoy my time at Bethany Home, if only because it kept me out of my mother's way and away from my siblings. For once, I felt like an actual, capable grown-up. Someone who could take care of herself. But each time they looked at me like I didn't belong, like it was only a matter of time before I stood on the other side, wearing my own Bethany Home–issued lavender day clothes, the capable, grown-up feeling crumpled at the edges.

Summer meant fewer volunteers, more nurses taking off early or coming in late to squeeze in a few precious hours of sunlight. Before you knew it, it'd be September and the leaves would change and the snow would fall, and it would feel like the sun had disappeared for the next six months. I told Marcia I didn't mind picking up the slack, but I'd often linger by the windows of the lounge, the curtains pulled back, and close my eyes and just feel the warmth on my skin. You seemed to enjoy it too. I felt you move for the first time in front of a sun-soaked window at Bethany Home.

―――――――――

One Friday in late June, Marcia came running into the cafeteria. There was a stain on the sleeve of her blouse. She tucked her hands behind her back when she caught me looking.

"Come with me," she said.

One of the managers, a dark-haired woman with thin lips and a thinner temper, scoffed. "She's still got hot food pans to prep and apples to cut."

"That doesn't sound difficult," Marcia said. "I'm sure you can manage." She turned to me. "Now, please."

I followed after her, still wearing the cafeteria apron stained with this morning's oatmeal. I'd squished against a carton of raspberries and the bloody remains of it streaked across my middle, a gruesome wound. Marcia—prim and proper and (usually) not a hair out of place—didn't notice. I figured I'd done something wrong, that I was on my way to a scolding, but I couldn't think of anything I'd done to set Marcia off.

Had Tina said something? One of the other girls? Was it because I was showing now?

Halfway down the main hall, Marcia cut down one of the residence halls. I followed, thinking about Tina's toilet story all those weeks ago, and cringed. I'd been lucky—my bout of morning sickness was mild and quick, but the thought of cleaning up a grown person's shit was enough to get my stomach rolling.

Finally, Marcia stopped in front of a door, composed herself, and knocked.

I heard shuffling footsteps on the other side, then the door opened. One of the orderlies—Chloe or Cathy, I couldn't remember her name in the moment—stood in the doorway, her expression haggard.

"Is she still asleep?" Marcia asked.

Chloe or Cathy nodded. "Probably be out for a while. The dose was…high."

"Maybe. Still, to be on the safe side…" Marcia finally looked at me. "You'll step in for Carrie." *Oh right*, I thought. *Carrie.* "I don't have to tell you we're spread thin these days, and Carrie's time is better spent elsewhere."

"Doing what?" I asked, anxious but afraid to peer over Carrie's shoulder into the room.

"Babysitting," Carrie said. To Marcia: "I put the straps on."

Marcia sighed. "She'll hate that."

Carrie shrugged. "Maybe it'll make her think before she gets bitey."

Bitey.

Part of me wanted to run. The other part—the bigger, stronger part—was curious.

"Hush." Marcia glanced past Carrie into the room. Seemingly satisfied, she looked to me. "All you need to do is sit quietly until she wakes up. She's on a heavy tranquilizer so it's possible she won't even wake up before I send someone else in to relieve you."

"If she's knocked out and…strapped…why do I need to be in there at all?" I asked.

Marcia raised an eyebrow. I'd never questioned her directions before. "We don't like to unnecessarily drug the mothers. It breeds distrust. Having a kind face there when she wakes up will soften the edges of what she will surely see as a betrayal."

Behind her, Carrie rolled her eyes.

"What do I do if she wakes up?" I asked.

"Find me," Marcia said.

Sure, I thought. *Simple.*

Carrie left the second Marcia gave her the go-ahead, then Marcia patted my shoulder. "I want you to know how pleased I am, Shannon. Despite—well, everything, you're turning into quite the respectable young woman."

I'm sure she meant it as a compliment, but it only felt sour. I thanked her and she nudged me into the room, shutting the door behind me.

The only light came from the small window too high to be opened without a stepladder. I spotted a chair on one side of the room, a magazine draped over the arm to bookmark it.

On the small bed, ankles and wrists bound with thick fabric cuffs, was Iris.

I sat in the chair because I didn't know what else to do, if I should check that she was breathing or if she'd hurt herself somehow. From the vantage point of the chair, I could just see the rise and fall of her belly as she breathed, slow and deep. I decided she was probably fine and occupied myself by studying her room.

It was private—rare at Bethany Home, from the way Tina talks—and small, almost a half room, with just enough space for the bed, the chair I sat in, and a table barely two feet wide. There were sheets of paper spread across the table and a few on the floor around it. They were drawings, mostly scribbles, some clear and surprisingly good—a hand on one page, a sharp-lined eye on another.

"There's something behind you."

Her voice made me jump, knocking the magazine off the arm of the chair. Iris peered at me through the space between her feet. Wiggled her toes.

I turned around knowing there was nothing there, but fear prickled my skin anyway.

"There's a wall behind me," I said.

"Someone."

"They said you'd be asleep for hours."

She scowled. "I hate sleeping." Then her eyes went bright. "My bag. Did they take my bag? I can't feel it."

I stood but didn't move any closer. "What bag?"

She writhed on the bed, tugging at the cuffs. I heard the Velcro start to give and took a step toward the door. I needed to get Marcia.

"No! Wait!" She sank against the pillow. "I'll be good. I'm sorry. I'll be good. I just need—can you look? Under my pillow. My bag."

I told myself it was fine, that the cuffs would hold, that Iris didn't care about hurting me. A flutter rushed up from my belly—you or my own fear or both. I inched closer to her, careful to keep my head angled away. I'd seen too many nurses get their hair snatched and knew better. Leaning back, I eased my hand beneath her pillow, feeling around until my fingers touched plastic. I pulled the sandwich bag out and held it up for her to see.

Every muscle in her body relaxed. "Okay. Good."

Relief was the last thing I felt. The contents of the bag were foggy and damp—snarls of blond hair, dirty nail clippings, shards of what was probably skin, like the kind she'd handed to me the last time we saw each other. My stomach rolled as I slid it back beneath the pillow.

"Have to keep it safe," Iris muttered. "Have to keep me safe."

"You are safe," I said, unconvincingly. "No one's going to hurt you."

I felt the pity in her eyes all the way to my marrow.

"You don't know 'cause you don't look. You don't see. It's like you're coming apart and the pieces of you are standing over your shoulder licking their pointed teeth."

A chill snaked down my body.

"I need to get Marcia," I said.

"Go, then. Get mummy Marcy and the others. They don't care because they don't see. They haven't heard them whispering in the pipes, in the walls."

I moved backward until my back was pressed against the door. I groped for the handle. "Who?"

Iris whispered so low I had to strain to hear her. "I told you."

"The dead women," I said.

Iris nodded. "They're listening and waiting, and it's only a matter of time. They're coming for you. The black-haired woman's coming for you."

"I've got good news and bad news," Angela says.

You get used to bad news in this place. Doesn't mean I'm not immediately on my guard. Angela's the kind of woman who will make up some small piece of good news to ease the blow of the bad.

Doctor Call-Me-Jim doesn't like that we've been chatting. Angela believes in openness between doctor and patient—*Yes, but we're also friends*, I argued, earning one of her rare side-smiles—but Doctor Call-Me-Jim is from the school of *Great Wall of China between doctor and patient*. They would never argue in front of me—both of them too professional for that sort of thing—but the tension between them over the last few days has been thick as molasses.

"Like my mom said," I tell her, "'You eat your frog first thing in the morning.' Bad news first."

"We haven't talked about your mom much."

"Put it on the list."

She mimes scribbling in the air. "Okay. The bad news is that there's an issue with the heating in the Bethany Wing, so it's a little chilly."

The Bethany Wing, named for Bethany Home, which stood on this very spot until it was demolished in the nineties. It was a modern world, they said. Gone was the time when young women, young mothers, distressed mothers would be locked away, treated as though they never existed.

Now it houses what Jo calls the Sads. They're not insane the same way the good doctors at Sleepy Eye believe the rest of us are—mostly they're self-admits. Life got too hard, so they took a time-out. Low security. Better food. Day trips.

"Okay," I say, confused.

"But the good news is the repairs are expected to be quick, so the chill won't linger for longer than a day or two."

If Angela were anything like her dad, I would assume this is a test. She isn't, so it's not.

"Good for them."

"Oh! Also—" Her grin widens, until it takes up her whole face. "More good news. I asked maintenance to have your room ready within the hour. I doubt you'll need that long to pack up."

"My room?" And then it hits me. "Wait. I'm moving? To the Bethany Wing?"

The way she nods, it's like she's ten years old and she's just handed me a wonky clay mug she made in art class. "I mean, only if you want to, of course. If you'd prefer to stay here—"

"Prefer nothin'. Out of my way, Angela." I nudge her with my hip, and she chuckles. "I'm not even going to ask what Daddy said."

"Technically, he is your doctor. He had to sign off."

"But he didn't want to."

She hesitated before answering. "No, he didn't."

"But you talked him around."

"Something like that."

I wink. "Good girl."

"You put your stuff together, and I'll see if I can find some extra blankets." Her smile dips, but only slightly. "This is going to be good for you, I think."

"Me too," I say. "Me too."

It'll almost be like going home.

Back in my room, Jo is nowhere to be found. Probably off somewhere pouting. It's not unusual for her to eavesdrop on my chats with Angela. If she wasn't jealous before, she will be now. For a solid year before her "accident," the Bethany Wing was all she could talk about. I'm sure they'll let her visit though. Angela will arrange it. It'll take a few days, maybe even weeks, but I will miss her.

There isn't much to pack—my clothes (barely three full outfits, along with underthings), a few family photographs, and books. I don't have a suitcase or a box—no sharp corners outside of the Bethany Wing—so I strip the pillowcase off my pillow and start shoving what I can inside. I don't notice the long black hair on my pillow until the pillowcase is stuffed to capacity.

"Won't miss that," I mutter, flinging Jo's hair onto the floor.

CHAPTER THIRTEEN

OLIVIA

Surprising, how it easy it became to pretend that everything was fine.

Easy, when Flora woke in the middle of the night and Olivia, half asleep, climbed out of bed to nurse, to pretend she didn't hear the crinkle of her paper-thin skin, that she didn't feel the harsh brush of the sheets over the rough surface of her legs. Easy to pretend she didn't feel a jolt of extraordinary pain each time Flora latched, drawing blood that dribbled down her chin. Easy, with the shine of Kris's wide-open eyes reflected in the window, to pretend her whole body wasn't trembling with the effort to sit upright, to hold Flora in her arms.

After a long time she drifted, her body becoming less and less able to stay awake for longer than a few minutes at a time, only to be jolted back to consciousness by a *scritch-scritch-scritch* on the window.

She didn't dare get up to look.

———

Clumps of Olivia's hair fell out in the shower, clogging the drain. She probed her head with shaky fingers, looking for a bald spot, sucking in a breath when she found it at the edge of her crown.

"Stress," she muttered, a throwback from college when she would rather have sewn her own arm back on than go to the emergency room only to come out with a bill that would rival her student loans and no arm. It'd become a mantra for her. Missed period? Stress. Clicking knee? Stress. Daylong vomiting? Stress.

As she rinsed the shampoo out of her hair, her fingers caught on small sharp objects. Finally grabbing hold of one, she squinted through the steam to get a closer look. It was a shard of fingernail. She studied her hands. Her nails were brittle and broken—on a couple of fingers midway down the nail. She felt a sharp sting as the water hit exposed skin. Biting back a whimper, she gently pressed her remaining nails, which bent easily.

Stress, she thought, biting off the shards and spitting them down the drain.

Kris was in the kitchen, standing over a pan of spitting bacon. She'd unexpectedly taken the day off, and Olivia was determined Kris wouldn't find a reason to extend what she'd called a "self-imposed parental leave." Whatever was happening with Olivia, she couldn't figure it out with Kris watching her. There would have been questions if she emerged from the bathroom with Band-Aids around her fingers and a patch of hair missing from the back of her head, so Olivia tied her hair in a ponytail and painstakingly painted her nails, and the thin strips of skin where her nails had broken off, a deep blue. The sting of the paint left her fingertips numb.

Flora lay in her swing, one fist expertly stuffed in her mouth. She caught Olivia's gaze and slowly extracted her fist.

"I didn't think you were ever coming out of there," Kris joked.

Between her shower, painting her nails, and glopping enough makeup on her face to hide the yellow tinge to her skin, Olivia had been in the bathroom for more than an hour.

"You think this just happens?" Olivia struck a pose, hoping Kris wouldn't notice the tremble in her voice.

Kris smiled. "You look beautiful."

Olivia studied Kris's expression for the lie. Olivia could feel the cavernous lines that'd carved into her forehead and under her eyes, wincing every time she smiled or frowned too hard, because the tug on her dry skin was so tight it felt like it would split. She felt the difference in her face, her body, but second glances in the mirror told a different story. In the mirror, she was Olivia. Normal, tired, frustrated Olivia. But as soon as she looked away, she felt it again. The wrongness.

"Hungry?" Kris asked.

Olivia hadn't been eating much lately. It wasn't that she didn't want to, but anything she put in her mouth tasted like dirt and ash. In twenty-four hours she'd only been able to choke down a few crackers and carrot sticks.

"Starving," Olivia said.

"That's my girl."

Kris plated up eggs, bacon, and toast, and they ate standing side by side at the counter. When they first moved in together, most meals were eaten at the counter, at first because they didn't have a proper place to sit, and then because they rarely made it through a meal without their hands all over each other. They'd disappear into the bedroom—if they made it that far—only to find the remains of their dinner on the counter the following morning, which they'd heat up and eat with their fingers because new love was beautiful and disgusting in equal measure.

Kris started to eat, pausing and glancing expectantly at Olivia when she didn't.

"Everything okay?" Kris asked.

"Yeah. Fine. Great." Olivia shoveled a large forkful of greasy eggs into her mouth and chewed. She closed her eyes to keep the tears at bay, her gag reflex fighting for control.

Finally, she swallowed and Kris patted her ass. For every bite Olivia swallowed, Kris either patted her ass again or squeezed her thigh, like a reward.

Olivia managed most of the eggs and one slice of bacon before Kris (mercifully) took both plates away. "I'll stick yours in the fridge for later, if you want," she said. "We should probably head out anyway. We'll be late for Flora's appointment."

"You're coming?" Olivia asked.

"Of course." Kris grinned. "Need to make sure my girls are well taken care of."

On the surface, Olivia was grateful. Kris carried the car seat and diaper bag, held open doors, gave Olivia a little cuddle when she shivered as a cold breeze ripped through the hospital parking lot. Deeper, though, she was terrified of what Kris might mention during the appointment. Would she bring up the outburst at dinner? The way Olivia inwardly cringed each time Flora cried, a Pavlovian response to the incoming pain?

In the waiting room, Olivia focused on her facial expression, offering a small smile every time Kris looked at her. She rocked the carrier with her foot, adjusting Flora's blankets, stroking her cheek when she fussed. Flora responded to Olivia's touch in a way she didn't with Kris—leaning into it like a kitten butting her head. It was easy, in these brief moments, to pretend there was nothing wrong, that she was a normal baby and Olivia was a normal mother, and an ember of warmth stoked in her chest.

Kris was already on her feet when Olivia looked up to see the nurse smiling at her from the doorway. She was young, couldn't have been older than twenty-two, with long black hair sleek as a seal. Olivia half stood, gripping the handle to Flora's carrier, trying to place her. To make her familiar. That hair.

"You okay?" Kris asked.

Like a switch turning off, Olivia smiled and nodded. "Of course."

It couldn't have been her. The nurse was too tall—the woman she'd seen following her at the restaurant was much shorter, her shoulders broader. Besides, she had a hard time imagining someone who wore Winnie the Pooh scrubs and pink plastic rings as capable of stalking.

You need to tell your wife, a voice insisted.

You can't, another countered.

Because what if it was all in her head? She couldn't risk it. Aunt Erin was right. She could lose everything. With new resolve, Olivia looped her arm through the carrier and walked toward the nurse, blasting her with the full force of her proud-mama smile.

"Six pounds, eleven ounces." The nurse squinted at the scale, nodded, then scribbled in the chart.

"That's it?" Kris asked.

"Doesn't seem like much, I know. But it's good! Looks like she's gained almost a full pound since the last time she was here."

"And she's not yellow," Olivia pointed out.

The nurse shot her a pitying look. "Nope. She's not yellow."

Olivia frowned. "That's...good though."

"Oh, definitely." She glanced back at the chart. "I'll just go grab the doctor and we'll be back."

As soon as the nurse shut the door, Olivia turned to Kris. "Do you know her?"

"No. Why?"

Kris was careful not to look at Olivia when she spoke, focusing on adjusting Flora's onesie, which had ridden up while she was on the scale.

"She doesn't look familiar? At all?"

That made her turn. "What do you mean?"

"What do you mean what do I mean? I asked if she looked familiar."

"And I said no." Confusion settled on Kris's face. "What is this about?"

Olivia hadn't liked the way the nurse had looked at her, like she knew more than she was letting on. She caught subtle glances at Kris, like the nurse had been seeking Kris's approval. The air between them felt too familiar. And now that she thought about it, Olivia was almost positive the appointment had been made for yesterday—had even gotten up expecting to have to go through this whole charade only to find a note on the calendar for today, which was odd because they never put appointment information on the wall calendar. They both lived and died by their phones. Had Kris rescheduled? If so, why? Did this nurse have something to do with it? Had they talked about her?

"Nothing," Olivia said. "Never mind."

"If you think I—"

"Knock, knock." The doctor peered in, pinched smile between fat cheeks. "Are we ready?"

Olivia nodded, still feeling Kris's eyes on her. "All set."

The doctor went to work on Flora, peering in her ears and eyes and prodding her umbilical stump. "Keeping it clean?"

"Yes," Kris said. "Shouldn't it have fallen off by now?"

"On average, yes, but all babies are different. No need to worry." He smiled, but it was clear to Olivia he was bothered. "I see the jaundice has subsided." He looked at Olivia. "Nursing going well?"

She nodded.

"There's a note here from your last visit about a questionable latch. Still painful?" She must have hesitated a beat too long. He continued, "I'd like to take a look. Just to be sure."

"No," Olivia said. "Everything's fine."

"Liv," Kris said, "You should let him. Just in case."

"I said I'm fine."

"Still." The doctor gave her the same pitying smile the nurse had. "It would make me feel better. Baby is gaining weight, but she's still not back to her birth weight. We want to make sure baby's getting enough nutrition, don't we?"

It was clear she wasn't going to win. She tried catching Kris's eye, to make her see how uncomfortable this was making her, but Kris had been sucked in by Flora gurgles and fist-munching.

Seeing the acquiescence in her face, the doctor and nurse turned away while Olivia took off her sweater. She leaned over the table to scoop up Flora before unclipping the cover of her nursing bra.

The nurse turned and her expression fell. "Oh my word."

Kris looked at the nurse, puzzled, before finally looking at Olivia. Her mouth fell open just as the doctor turned.

"Jesus," he said.

Dried blood and flaked skin—it was like her nipple had been gnawed on by something with sharp teeth.

"She puts that in her mouth?" Kris asked, aghast.

"It won't hurt her," the doctor said, getting so close to Olivia she could smell the tuna he'd had for lunch. "It's the latch. If it's too shallow—"

"The latch is fine," Olivia said through clenched teeth. "Look."

Flora was practically seizing with the desire to eat, but the doctor pulled her away, passing her off to Kris. Face burning, Olivia tried to shrug herself back into her nursing bra, but the doctor's cold hands were on her, probing and poking the sorest areas of her.

"Marissa, can you hand me the—yes—"

The nurse handed him tweezers, which he used to peel the flaked skin away. He pinched the skin and Olivia jumped.

"Sorry," the doctor muttered.

"Can you please stop," Olivia said. "Kris, tell him—"

"Hush, Liv. It'll be over in a second." Kris said, "You're upsetting Flora."

"—worried about infection—"

Olivia was trapped between the doctor and the wall, the nurse on one side and Kris on the other. It was hard to breathe. The doctor shone a light in her eyes and down to her breast, his tweezers plucking and jabbing. She bit her lip to keep from crying out, her half-shorn nails digging into the plastic chair.

"Did you have any piercings here?" the doctor asked.

Olivia shook her head, too afraid she'd start screaming if she opened her mouth.

"You're sure?"

"Why?" Kris asked, peering over his shoulder.

Please, Olivia silently begged. *Make him stop.*

"Pinholes," he said, bending her nipple to make them wider. Olivia choked.

"She's never had piercings," Kris said, unsure.

No. She hadn't. But there were pinholes in her skin that bled as he tugged.

Pinholes or teeth marks? a voice asked.

Finally, mercifully, the doctor released her, and she shamefully tucked her breast back into her bra.

He wrote her a prescription for ointment and recommended a hold on breastfeeding.

"I can't," she argued.

"Why?"

But she didn't have an answer. Not one he'd believe.

Once the doctor and nurse left them alone, Flora started to cry. Her wails shook her little body, and she kicked her legs so hard Kris almost lost her grip. She was going to drop her. Olivia could almost see it happening in slow motion, could feel the vibration of the impact in her feet.

"Give," Olivia said, holding out her arms.

"I got it," Kris said.

"She doesn't want you," Olivia said through clenched teeth.

Taken aback, Kris didn't fight when Olivia pulled Flora away.

Flora nuzzled Olivia's chest. Not rooting, exactly. Comforting. Apologetic, almost. Olivia held her close and smelled her head, for the first time taking pleasure in the heady, dirt smell of it. They were in this together, *just* the two of them. Whatever *this* was…

Back at home, Olivia and Kris moved around each other like planets trapped in their own orbits, gravity repelling them the moment they got too close.

Olivia couldn't understand what'd happened. Couldn't understand why her wife had sat there while the doctor picked her apart and just…let it happen. And each time she got herself worked up enough she was going to confront her, to demand an explanation and an apology, Flora needed her attention more. After a while, she was too tired to be angry, so she settled for apathy. So her body was failing her. So her wife didn't seem to notice or care. So the world looked at her differently now that she was a mother, the critical eye turned sharper, the accusatory finger prodding harder. It was one thing to be an inferior woman. Another thing entirely to be an inferior mother.

It felt like Kris lived in the kitchen now, her head perpetually buried in the refrigerator.

Olivia leaned against the counter. Kris didn't look up.

"What do you want to do for dinner?" Olivia asked. *See? Everything's normal. Everything's fine.*

"I'll probably just scrounge some Chinese leftovers or something."

"What do you mean?"

"There's a ton here. Not much point in ordering in or cooking something if it's just going to be me." She finally pulled her head out of the refrigerator. When she saw Olivia's confused expression, she frowned. "It's Wednesday."

So? Olivia started to say, when it dawned on her. The mommy group.

"You didn't think I was actually going," Olivia said. "Did you?"

Kris's expression hardened. "Edie already offered to drive you. I said yes."

"And when were either of you going to discuss it with me?"

"I just figured—"

"You'd just figured it didn't matter, right? Just like today, it didn't matter that I was in pain. That I was begging you—"

Flora's cry came through the baby monitor, cutting her off.

Kris brushed past her, heading for the bedroom. "You're upsetting her."

"So when Flora cries, the world stops. If I cry, I should just get over it, yeah? That's how this works?"

Kris stopped. Turned. "You sound like you're jealous of your own daughter."

Olivia's face burned. "I'm not jealous."

"You've been stuck in this house for weeks. I'd be going stir crazy right now."

"I'm not you."

Kris sighed. "I know you like to put up this tough exterior. Nothing happens that Olivia can't handle. Olivia is a badass. Olivia takes no shit from no one. But it's okay to be a little weak sometimes. It's okay to need things."

"What I need is my wife to listen when I talk to her. To discuss things with me before shipping me off somewhere."

"No one's shipping you off anywhere, Liv. I just know it'll make you feel better. More you."

There was nothing that would make Olivia feel less like herself than going to a mommy group. She swore when she got pregnant she wasn't going to turn into one of those women, with their yoga pants and wine o'clock obsession. She loved books and teaching and taking the afternoon off to drive until she found something interesting. She loved her independence.

But she also loved her wife.

And Kris wasn't completely wrong. Olivia looked at the walls sometimes and imagined they'd moved an inch closer, the ceiling a bit lower. But Flora needed her. The idea of leaving her daughter behind was like a barb in her ribs.

"I'll go on one condition," Olivia said.

"Name it."

"We find another doctor." Kris started to protest, but Olivia cut her off. "Yes, it will be a pain, and yes we'll have to go through the process of explaining medical histories and all that, but those are my terms. Take them or leave them."

Kris was smiling before Olivia finished. "That's my girl." She planted a rough kiss on Olivia's forehead. "Better get dressed. Edie will be here soon."

She left Olivia standing in the hallway. From the bedroom, she heard Kris say, "Mommy's going to make some new friends. Isn't that exciting?"

Kill me, Olivia thought, and went into the bathroom where, she hoped, she'd find the part of herself that knew how to be a person *and* a mother.

CHAPTER FOURTEEN

SHANNON

The Bethany Wing is almost nothing like Bethany Home. Sure, they scavenged a few valuable bits here and there—an original Victorian archway ornately decorated and nailed above the front hall; stately wingback chairs scattered about the lounge, though the cushions are flat and the once vivid maroons and hunter greens are now dusty and faded; and a small, cloudy mirror, the frame gilded and covered in cherubs.

The rooms are better though. Not bigger, but brighter.

What I appreciate most about my new digs isn't the plush baby-pink carpet or the sunset-facing window (bars or no bars, after years without a window I all but cried at the sight of it)—though I do love both of those things—it's that, in the Bethany Wing, the orderlies don't pry open your mouth to make sure you've swallowed your medicine. Instead, a soft-faced woman named Jenny hands me my plastic cup of pills and a glass of water, and then hums "A Spoonful of Sugar" until I hand both cups back, the Tinas of the world left back in medium security.

I embarrassed myself the first morning, sticking my tongue out as far as it could go to give her a good view of my throat. She'd gently squeezed my hand—though it was pretty clear the sight of my tonsils didn't do much for putting her at ease—and said, "Don't worry, darlin.' I believe you."

I believe you.

How ridiculous that at these three little words, I damn near collapsed at her feet.

No one believes me.

Oh, Angela does her best. She thinks well of me, which is all I can ask for. Doesn't mean she believes everything I tell her. She's too smart for that.

Even in the Bethany Wing, we don't get much more than basic cable. The only thing on worth a damn is the Discovery Channel. I especially like the programs that show you the ugly side of nature. It isn't all big blue water and sprawling forest and mothers cleaning their young. I've learned more about the mating rituals of deer than I ever needed to know. A pair of bucks, when they're trying to impress a female, will fight until their antlers are locked. If both of them agreed it was a terrible idea, they could easily untangle themselves, walk away. Instead they starve to death, their antlers hopelessly tangled.

My mom and I were like that.

Tears and skin and hair and nails and angry, crumpled-up letters and pills flushed down the toilet and chicken bones. Banana peels and used tissues.

"Trash," Iris said that day. "That's how all of them see us. And we're thrown away, little by little. You try to save yourself. Break apart so the pieces are harder to find. The you that wears your face and the you that carries your heart. Your thoughts. But it doesn't matter. Enough of you gets thrown away, you end up like them."

"Them," I said. "The dead women."

Iris nodded. "Buried, most of them. Thrown away. That's what makes their skin crumple and their nails brown and their hair black with mud." Her voice softened. "I don't want to go down there. It's dark and cold and loud and angry."

I thought of the well in the woods behind my parents' house. Of the thick, heady silence that seemed to notice me when I was there. The voices I thought I heard echoing up from below.

"It's okay," I said, trying to keep her calm. Keep me calm. "They can't hurt you."

She laughed, low and rough. "Sometimes it's worse than the dark and cold and loud and angry. Sometimes they bind it all up and breathe life into it. They trick us. Make us love it like our own." Her gaze wandered down to my belly.

Her stare felt like pins. "Why?"

"Because there's nothing left but anger and need and hunger. All they want is to see you suffer." Tears welled in her eyes. "So you suffer until you can't anymore. Until you forget which reflection in the mirror is yours. That's when they get you. When you give in to it."

———

Marcia didn't want to tell me anything about Iris. *A lady's past is her business,* she said. But I pushed. When I told her what Iris had said, when I couldn't hide my worry, she caved.

"Like you," Marcia said, "Iris was young when she became pregnant. She finished high school during her third trimester and married her boyfriend shortly after. A week or two before she was due, Iris stopped feeling her baby kick. She had no one to talk to about it—her husband was already drifting and her mother refused to see her, would only speak to her on the phone, and even then would hang up if Iris mentioned the baby."

"But she got married," I said. "She fixed it. Didn't she?"

Marcia smiled sadly. "She did, as you say, fix it, but I suppose once the baby was born, her mother could pretend it appeared out of nowhere, that her daughter hadn't been defiled at all." Her lip curled. "So Iris had no choice but to sit and worry until finally her body went into labor.

"The baby was stillborn. A girl. Iris was devastated. I think she believed her baby would fill the void carved out by hateful parents and a husband with more sawdust in his head than sense. I spoke with her brother during the admissions process, and he told me it was like Iris was only half alive during those days after leaving the hospital without her daughter. Like pieces of her had broken away."

They take the pieces and they bind them.

Marcia continued, "About a week after the stillbirth, Iris started waking up in the middle of the night to sounds of a baby crying."

I bit my lip to keep from shivering.

"She dismissed it at first—they lived in an apartment building with lots of people. Thin walls. But the more it happened, the more she started to believe it was her daughter. She claimed to hear whispers in her walls and under her floor—women, she said, who'd taken her child and left a dead thing in her place." Marcia shook her head. "Horrifying for anyone, but for someone like Iris, delicate at the best of times, it broke her."

I wouldn't exactly have described Iris as delicate, but I understood what she meant. Love makes you brittle. Makes you breakable.

"She left her apartment one night without telling her husband and drove to the cemetery where her daughter was buried. She dug her baby up and brought her home and when her husband woke up, the baby was there in bed between them."

"Jesus," I muttered.

Marcia nodded. "She told him she was too late. That their baby had suffocated before she could find her." She pinched the bridge of her nose. Took a breath. "She blames herself for her daughter's death. Her stillbirth. To protect herself, she manifested this delusion, this belief that she can't seem to stop carrying. I can see the kindness in you, that you have begun to care for the mothers here. I'm grateful, but I need to caution you too. Don't let them pull you out of your sanity. Don't allow them to show you things that aren't there. Your baby is going to be born, and your life is going to change forever. Only you can determine what that life will be after."

Sometimes when I'm laying in bed and can't sleep—which is often—I close my eyes and remember labor pain. Jo says I'm a sadist, but it's not the pain I want to remember, it's the anticipation. It's one thing feeling the flutters of movement in your belly, of being told how much your life is going to change, but nothing compares to that time just before birth, when there's just you and the pain.

Erin insisted on going in the delivery room with me when my mother refused. It surprised me, given Erin's squeamishness around blood, or anything medical, but then I remembered her promise in the woods and was grateful she was there to hold my hand and feed me ice and tell me I was good.

You came out screaming, harsh and wild, and I smiled despite the doctor's hand deep inside me, fishing out the placenta that wouldn't release. Your face was swollen, dark eyes pinched between fat cheeks and furrowed brows. A tiny thing, but with a kick that gave one of the judgmental nurses a fat lip.

You and me, I thought. *We'll be just fine.*

When my mother found out I was serious about letting Matthew off the hook—her words—she gave me (and you) our marching orders.

I'd be lying if I said I wasn't expecting it, and at the same time, I wasn't as upset as I thought I'd be. I'm the kind of woman Eleanor Roosevelt was talking about when she said that thing about tea. Didn't blame my mother either. She figured she was teaching me a lesson, probably something about putting me in my place. Or maybe she resented the idea that she would be back at changing diapers and midnight crying while Matthew moved on with his life. Maybe got a good job and a house and waited for marriage to knock up some other girl.

A job and a house and a wife were all well and good, but I got something he didn't. I got you.

"It's 'cause you didn't let nobody hold her," Jo says, her chin perched on my shoulder. She's taken to visiting me in the Bethany Wing. Jo doesn't like to be left behind. I can smell her rotting tooth, the one she's always tonguing. "Your mama cri-ied."

If I was selfish, it was out of love. Out of protection.

"It's not the fifties," Erin tried to tell me. "It's not like they're gonna hide you in a convent or something."

Maybe if Erin had been to Bethany Home, if she'd seen the women there, the hurt in their eyes, she might have fought a little harder against my mother.

She hadn't seen the way the nurses turned up their noses. Didn't hear one turn to the other to make a remark about "the baby" and the other reply, "Which one?"

Slut. Easy. Jailbait.

Stupid. Trashy.

Probably grew up in Bogdanoff.

Where's that?

Just outside of wedlock!

Har-har.

If I held you too tight and for too long, if I didn't give you up, even to my mother, it was to keep you shielded from the hate and vitriol. You didn't hear it because it was my hands covering your ears.

I told Erin I had somewhere to stay. A lie, but a necessary one. Better for her not to worry. My dad slipped me a hundred dollars on my way out the door, but backed away when I leaned in for a hug. Mom was watching. Didn't want her to think he'd gone soft.

I spent a good chunk of the money on an extra-thick blanket, diapers, a gallon of water, and enough crackers and beef jerky to get me through a couple of days, just until I could figure out my next step. And then I went into the woods.

It was a mild night with a clear sky and enough moonlight to see decent by. Too chilly for bugs, and all the nighttime critters kept well away, distracted by each other and fireworks somewhere down the block. The new blanket was plenty warm, and you were content to curl up in my lap and make bubbles with your lips. Only a few days old, but there was a brightness in your eyes that told me you noticed everything. The books like to say a newborn can't see more than a few inches in front of their noses. Might have been true for other babies, but you were special.

Maybe that's why they wanted you.

I saw the well in my dreams. It looked the same as the first time, but the woods around it were different. Thicker. Darker. The tree trunks were coated in black muck that, when I touched it, felt damp and scummy, like algae or mold. The air was dense and humid; breathing in felt like breathing water. Each step was a slog, the pressure on my bones like being deep under water. The ground was littered with coins and debris—pieces of wet fabric, tangles of hair, a clutch of cracked, yellow teeth. I wondered if this was what lived at the bottom of the well I'd fallen into. Like the bottom wasn't actually a bottom, but a door. And everyone knows doors open both ways. I strained to hear something, anything, but the place was dead silent. It was the kind of quiet that made me question my hearing.

I opened my mouth to speak, but movement above the lip of the well made me stop. Bony, sticklike fingers emerged from the blackness, making the air above it ripple and distort. Wrapped around the fingers was a ragged strip of cloth, and when I looked down I realized the bottom of my shirt had been torn. The debris surrounding me trembled, and as a scream filled my throat, something grabbed my ankle, jarring me awake.

It took a minute to shake the last of the nightmare out of my head, to see what was in front of me. My dad, bent over with his hands on his knees, his face all scrunched up in something like confusion or fear.

"Shanny," he said, shaking me like I was still sleeping. "Shanny, what the hell happened?"

I was still trying to figure out where I was and started to ask if he'd followed me out to the woods when I saw Patrick's bike tipped over next to a baseball bat and mitt. No trees, only a patchy yellow lawn. I was in my parents' backyard.

Erin stood behind Dad, wringing her hands. I looked up at her and she flinched.

"Shanny." Dad squatted down next to me and wiped a thumb across my cheek. He wiped my blood on his pajamas. "Shanny, what happened to Olivia?"

I frowned. "Olivia?"

"The baby." He struggled to keep the desperation out of his voice. "Where's the baby?"

Behind him, Erin rubbed tears out of her eyes. "What did you do?"

I figured they'd all lost their minds, that this was punishment for lying about having somewhere to stay. They'd followed me and dragged me back to the house.

I looked down into my lap, expecting to find you there, curled in your little kitten ball, bubbles on your lips.

My jeans were torn and covered in dirt, the exposed skin mottled with dried blood.

You were gone.

CHAPTER FIFTEEN

OLIVIA

Edie showed up in a sundress and cardigan, all expectant smiles and nervous fidgets like this was a first date. Olivia had squeezed into a vintage blouse she used to wear to her classes on test days. Then, it'd made her look and feel more in charge. More adult. Now, with the buttons straining against her chest and belly, she felt foolish.

I will never be that woman again, she thought sadly.

Rather than change—there wasn't time—she threw a sweater over top, which bunched uncomfortably in her back. At least she could breathe; she couldn't imagine ever wearing anything other than her maternity jeans. That women's pants hadn't always come with a soft, stretchy band around the middle was proof alone that women's clothing was made for men's eyes, not women's comfort.

"Ready?" Edie asked, pointedly not looking at Olivia's hair, which she'd wrestled into submission with too much dry shampoo and hair spray.

"Have fun!" Kris called from the couch. Flora draped languidly across her lap, one fist stuffed whole in her mouth.

She's going to choke.

"Maybe I should stay," Olivia said.

Edie looked from Olivia to Kris and back again. Her smile only brightened. "Everything will be fine. Trust me."

"You didn't have to do this. I have a car. I can drive."

"She's already here, Liv," Kris said.

"It's no trouble," Edie said. "Really."

They weren't going to let her out of this. Better to go, get it over with. She'd make up a million reasons why she could never go again, and Kris couldn't tell her it was because she hadn't tried.

"Okay," she said finally. "Let's go."

———————

Edie's house looked exactly as Olivia imagined it would. The lawn was a perfect carpet of green, the yew shrubs along the house trimmed and shaped until they were smooth and plump. Flower boxes sat beneath each window, except for the large bay window in the front. The drapes—because Edie wouldn't have something as horribly typical as curtains—were pulled aside, allowing a soft white glow to drift from inside.

"Looks like the girls are already here," Edie said as she pulled into the garage, nodding at the cars parked in the street.

"And they just let themselves in?"

"Monica has a key."

Olivia nodded like she should know who Monica was. Part of her was jealous. She'd never had a friendship so solid she handed over a key to her home.

She followed Edie inside, through the mudroom and kitchen—recently renovated, it looked like, with white cabinets and stainless-steel appliances—into the living room where a group of women spoke animatedly from the couch and chairs. One woman sat on the floor with her legs stretched out in front of her, a bowl of pretzels perched in her lap.

"Edie, thank goodness," the woman on the floor said when she saw them. "Tell Nadiya that just because she's going the bottle route doesn't mean she can drink wine while the rest of us sit here tragically sober."

Nadiya—the oldest-looking of the bunch, with lines around her mouth and eyes and gray streaks in her messy bun—rolled her eyes. "You made a choice. I made a choice. Who cares?"

"You could always pump and dump," another woman said. She wore bright-pink lipstick, but little other makeup. She looked effortlessly beautiful in a way that made Olivia's stomach ache. She couldn't help staring. The woman noticed and raised her eyebrow. "Olivia, right?"

Edie nudged Olivia forward. "Olivia, you remember Monica? She was my birthing partner a few times during class."

Olivia could feel the sweat start to bead under her arms. The room was too full. Too hot. The sweater itched in places she didn't know she could itch. She looked down, away from Monica's expectant stare and met the gaze of the woman on the floor. The woman studied her, jaw clenched.

Finally, the woman broke away. To Monica, she said, "Look, I don't buy into that whole wasting milk thing, but if I'm going to strap my tits into that torture device, you'd best believe I'm not dumping it just to have to do it all over again."

Monica shrugged. "Just an idea."

"Here's an idea," Edie cut in. "Let's not talk about the kids for once. I mean, that's what we're all here for, right?"

Nadiya raised her wineglass and winked at the woman on the floor. "Hear, hear."

"Bite me," the woman on the floor said.

Monica cackled.

"Charlie isn't normally like this," Edie said, apologetic.

"Yes, she is," Nadiya said.

"But we love her anyway," Monica added sweetly.

The woman on the floor—Charlie—rolled her eyes, but her lips turned up in a genuine grin. "I hate y'all."

"It's what you get for ditching us," Monica said. "It's been, what, a month since you've joined us?"

"I got busy."

"A month?" Olivia blurted, unable to stop herself. She looked at Edie. "But your son is barely a few weeks old, right?"

Edie looked at her the way a kindergarten teacher looked at a kid who wouldn't stop asking why B came after A. "True. We used to be a book club."

"We needed a change," Nadiya said.

"No one read the books," Monica said.

"What's a book?" Charlie added.

Edie smirked. "There was something in the water, obviously. Charlie has two older kids, and Monica had a boy before we all got pregnant within a few weeks of each other."

Charlie eyed Nadiya's wineglass hungrily while snatching up a bottle of water from the table. "Our husbands figured we'd planned it."

"Did you?" Olivia asked. When they all looked at her, equal parts concern and distaste, she said, "I'm joking."

"I told you guys she was funny," Edie said.

Olivia didn't know whether that was meant to be a joke. She laughed too loudly—a giant squawk of a laugh that threatened to bring up the leftover dumplings she'd wolfed down before Edie picked her up. Monica looked at her uneasily.

"Here." Edie pushed Olivia toward a plush chair beside the couch. "Sit. I'll get you something to drink."

As soon as Edie shuffled out of the room, her presence was replaced with a thick silence. Olivia could almost hear their minds buzzing, judging her, mentally composing the texts they'd all send to each other after she left. Only Charlie seemed to be able to stand to look at her, but even she stared too hard and too deeply, like she was trying to see inside Olivia's head.

Finally, mercifully, Edie returned with a glass bottle of sparkling water, which she handed to Olivia. "Let me know if you'd like anything else. We've got some diet soda and coffee. Tea."

"This is fine," Olivia said. "Thanks."

Edie smiled. "I know you're worried about Flora. It's normal."

Olivia bristled. Who was Edie to tell her what was normal? She'd been a mother all of a week longer than Olivia.

"Flora? That's lovely," Monica said.

"I thought we weren't going to talk about the kids," Charlie said.

"She's new," Nadiya said. "She gets a pass."

"Tell us about her," Monica said. "What's she like?"

Charlie crunched down on a pretzel. "They're infants. Pooping, eating machines. They aren't like anything yet."

Olivia didn't like the way they'd latched on to the thought of Flora, like hyenas circling, hungry. Her belly ached for the weight of her. She had to sit on her hands to keep from touching it.

Monica threw a pillow, barely missing Charlie's head. "Speak for yourself. Malachi is already starting to hold his head up."

Charlie launched the pillow back. "I didn't realize a stiff neck was a personality trait."

Edie sank onto the couch between Nadiya and Monica, grabbing all the pillows within arm's reach—too many, if you asked Olivia—and dropped them behind the couch. "You're worse than your kids," she said to Charlie.

"And you wonder why I stopped coming to these things."

"Why did you stop?"

"It's that podcast, isn't it?" Nadiya asked. "You're obsessed."

"I'm not obsessed—"

"No. Of course not. The women who run it put out a book and you bought three copies the day it released because, what, you needed one for each hand?"

"And a foot," Monica added.

Charlie scowled. "You know my kids destroy my stuff. It was a precaution."

Nadiya's eyes glittered. "Uh huh."

"It's called *Let's Talk Murder*," Edie said to Olivia, the gracious hostess attempting to bring the newbie into the conversation. "Gruesome, right?"

Olivia had heard of it. She'd listened to true-crime podcasts in her past life— loved them, in fact—but after getting pregnant she couldn't stand the idea of listening to them. Couldn't hear the details of brutal killings and rape without seeing her daughter in the victims' places.

"Judge all you want," Charlie said, "but when some psycho comes murdering, you can bet I'll see him coming before you three bitches."

"If he's handsome like that Joe Goldberg character, I say let him come," Monica said. "Let *me* come."

Nadiya snorted.

"I'm telling your husband you said that," Edie said.

"I dare you."

Olivia sank in her chair, cradling the unopened bottle of water. Except for Charlie glancing up at her every few seconds, it was like Olivia was invisible. She didn't belong here with these women and their sitcom lives and their effortless ease with one another. Even stiff-upper-lipped Edie, who'd tried to get the others to behave like grown women, had given up the pretense, taking sneaky sips of Nadiya's wine while she wasn't looking. How was it that they didn't feel what Olivia felt? Every second away from Flora was a failure. And in those brief moments when a smile cracked on her face, or relief at being able to sit unburdened by someone else's need, guilt threatened to swallow her whole.

The room went quiet, and Olivia looked up to see them all staring at her with expectant expressions.

She knew that look. It was the look her students gave when she asked a question, knowing they weren't paying attention.

"Sorry," Olivia said, offering an awkward chuckle. "Mom brain. What did you say?"

"I said, 'Tell us about yourself,'" Charlie said. "These cows are all up in each other's business, not caring about the new person in the room."

Edie colored.

"Oh." Olivia twisted the lid off the sparkling water and sipped to give her brain a chance to work. The bubbles burned her throat. "Uh, what do you want to know?"

"Anything. Everything. Job. Family."

"Yes," Nadiya added. "Please tell me what it's like to have a wife. I bet it's so much better than having a husband."

"You don't have either," Monica said.

Nadiya shrugged. "Keeping my options open."

"Kris is good. Great," Olivia said.

"She's very doting on Flora," Edie added. "It's lovely."

"Yes. Lovely."

In the moment of silence that followed, Olivia's imagination flashed to a scene—their living room, Olivia walking through the door to find Kris passed out and Flora suffocating on her own fist or the blanket or a bottle left propped on a pillow. Or worse, the black-haired woman standing over them both, all rancid breath and teeth and blood—

"I need to go," she said suddenly.

Edie leaned forward, but didn't stand. "What's wrong?"

"I just—sorry, I just need to go home."

Nadiya and Monica looked at each other, but Olivia couldn't read their expressions. Didn't care. She felt in her marrow that Flora was in danger.

Edie started to protest, but Charlie stood, sliding the bowl of pretzels on the coffee table, cutting her off. "I can take you," she said.

Edie flashed her a defeated look.

"Thank you," Olivia said, already on her feet. "Thanks, Edie. I just—I'm sorry. I can't—" She bit off the last of her sentence before she said too much. Before she started sounding crazy again.

"Are you coming back?" Edie asked Charlie.

"Sure."

"Means no," Nadiya said. To Olivia, "I hope we didn't scare you off."

Olivia tried to smile, but it was all teeth. "Yes. I mean no. It was nice meeting you all."

She started for the door with Charlie hot on her heels. "Let's go," Charlie whispered, "before they try to walk us to the car."

Charlie drove an ancient-looking jeep with fuzzy dice hanging from the mirror and floodlights perched on the roof.

"My husband's," Charlie said as she climbed into the driver's seat. "He's a walking innuendo, but I love him anyway."

"That's nice," Olivia said before anxiously giving directions.

Charlie drove too slow and stopped too completely at stop signs. Every second that passed felt like an eternity, that scene playing over and over in Olivia's mind. Charlie asked questions—Olivia could tell by the way her voice lifted between pauses—but Olivia didn't hear any of the words, so she nodded, made noncommittal noises.

"—because of you."

Olivia frowned, finally looking at Charlie for the first time since getting in the car. "What did you say?"

Charlie swallowed. Kept her eyes firmly fixed on the road. "I said I hate going to those things. All they want to do is talk about their kids and their husbands or lack of husband, and I get enough of that from my mother, you know?"

Olivia waited.

Charlie continued, "I said I only went this time because of you. Because Edie told me you'd be there."

Olivia was suddenly aware of the moving car, the location of the lock on the door. "Why would you care? You don't even know me."

"No, see, I do! Sort of. I know about you." She paused. "About your mom."

"Stop the car. I want to get out."

"No. Please. Just hear me out, okay? Look—they talked about that podcast, right? That's how I know you. Of you. There's a whole episode dedicated to Shannon and the black-haired woman."

It was like the blood in her veins turned to ice. "What do you know about the black-haired woman?" It occurred to Olivia she'd gotten in a car with a perfect stranger. Didn't ask questions because a woman trusts other women not to murder them. And this perfect stranger just admitted to what sounded to Olivia like stalker behavior. What if Charlie had been the one staring in and tapping on her windows? What if Charlie had been the presence on the other side of the door, terrifying her?

"Nothing. I mean, not a lot? She's mentioned a few times in the police files."

How did Charlie—and these podcast people—get her mother's police files? What did they say?

Did she even want to know?

Yes. Part of her very much did. Because it wasn't a coincidence that Charlie would mention the black-haired woman. Olivia didn't know who or what the woman was, but the fact that she was tormenting Olivia, had maybe tormented her mother the same way, meant something. Good or bad, she *needed* to know. But if it *was* bad, if she discovered some sort of shared genetic psychosis, what would that mean for Olivia? For her family? Would she end up locked away the way her mother was? Would she, in a moment of insanity, do something to hurt Flora?

No, she vehemently decided. She would *not*.

Today.

But what about tomorrow?

"You said you came to Edie's because of me. Why?"

"I don't know. To talk to you? Maybe learn a few things about Shannon."

"I probably know less than you do."

"Oh." Charlie didn't bother hiding her disappointment. Then, "Do you want to? Know more, I mean."

They pulled up to Olivia's house before she could answer. Lights were on in the living room. All she wanted was to run inside and make sure Flora was safe.

"No," Olivia said finally. "I don't ever want to talk about her."

She slammed the car door behind her. Charlie didn't drive away until Olivia was inside, the door shut and locked.

Shaking off the conversation, Olivia went into the living room where the television was on mute. One of those low-budget true-crime shows. She wondered if they'd ever mentioned her or her mother. How many people thought they knew her. What she'd gone through. Was still going through.

Kris was asleep on the couch, with Flora tucked beside her, pillows spread out on the floor.

Safe.

Still, she needed to touch her daughter. To hold her and know for sure. She scooped Flora up, not caring whether she disturbed Kris, and sank onto the floor in the middle of the room. Flora drifted easily back to sleep, but Olivia was still unsettled.

If her mother had seen the black-haired woman, what did that mean for Olivia? What else would Olivia see? What else would she *do*?

CHAPTER SIXTEEN

SHANNON

Y ou know you don't belong here, right?"

"Of course," I say. "It's only a matter of time now before they let me go."

Jo shakes her head. "That's not what I meant."

I know that. She knows I know that—we practically share a brain these days—but I refuse to let her negative attitude get in the way of my not-so-small success. I've been doing the math. Patients in the Bethany Wing stay, on average, three months before they're either released to outpatient care or sent back to the jungle of medium security. Tomorrow, I will have been here for two months and seven days.

I've been a good girl. Early to every session with Angela, lingering when it's clear there are wells she wants to keep plumbing. I clear my plate, three meals a day, even when I'm not hungry. Most importantly though, I've made a friend.

Her name's Jennifer. She's new and most of the others haven't made the effort to remember her name, so mostly people just call her Mommy.

"Mommie Dearest," Jo says, "Now that was a good book."

"I haven't read it," I say.

"Yes you have," Jo says, smiling. *"Long time ago."*

Jennifer showed up in the activity room a little over a week ago, tiny feet curled beneath her tiny body on the couch, eyes glued to the television. She couldn't have been older than twenty—you can tell by the hands, hands are everything—but the skin on her face seemed to hang off her bones, and her hair looked like it hadn't been properly washed in days. She reminded me a little of Iris. I probably wouldn't have noticed her, if not for the life-size baby doll she cradled in her arms. It clearly wasn't a toy. Not to her. She absently rocked, stroking the doll's forehead and tucking the blanket around its feet when it came undone. I didn't know why she was here, but I could guess.

I still had half an hour to kill before my session with Angela, so I sat next to Jennifer and, for a few minutes, quietly watched *The Young and the Restless.* I felt her looking at me, little glances between breathy swoons, but I left her be until a commercial break when I stretched, yawned, and pretended to notice the doll for the first time.

"Is she yours?" I asked, sweet as you like.

For a long time she wouldn't answer, her hair like a curtain over her and the doll's faces.

"He," she croaked. "He's a boy."

I shrugged. "Boy, girl, they're all blessings."

She brushed a bit of hair behind her ear, and I barely caught a smile.

"What's his name?" I asked.

"Michael."

"Well, it looks like Michael is a very lucky boy for having such a loving mom."

That earned a genuine smile. "Do you want to hold him?"

"Please."

I took special care with the doll's head, laying it gently in the crook of my elbow and then readjusting the blanket around his body. I bounced and baby-talked until Jennifer all but exploded with the need to have him back, her hands shaking and teeth tearing at her bottom lip until there was blood.

"Uh oh," I said, "Looks like someone needs their mommy back."

Jennifer nodded, nearly snatching the doll out of my arms. I tried to ask her questions about Michael, how old he was, if he looked like his dad, but *The Young and the Restless* was back and it was like she'd slipped into some sort of trance. Her lips moved but no sound came out. She didn't blink.

After that, she saved a spot for me during *The Young and the Restless,* and I held Michael for a couple of minutes during the commercial breaks. We don't talk much, but I don't think we have to. When you have that much in common with someone, when you share an ache that lives so viscerally in your guts that words don't do it justice, words aren't necessary.

I think that's what's got Jo all riled up. She's jealous. Bitter. It was always Jo whispering in my ear, sweet nothings and heartbreak in equal measure. She knows me better than anyone. Longer than anyone. What would happen if I stopped listening, I wonder.

The first thing they did was call the police. I sat in the kitchen, still in my muddy pajamas. My dad tried to feed me, tried to stuff me full of coffee and assurances.

"You tell them everything, understand?" he said. "We'll find her. Don't you worry."

Then he left to pace the porch. Mom came into the kitchen, face and hair done up nice. Using a dish rag that smelled a little like mold, she scrubbed my face and neck and hissed in my ear, "Don't you say a word. You keep quiet, understand?"

Erin watched from a safe place on the stairs, too far to be any help but close enough to keep an eye. Of all the people who'd come after and try to pick apart my story, it was Erin that'd hurt me the most.

It seemed to take hours before the police finally arrived, but it was probably more like ten minutes. Dad led them into the kitchen, offered coffee and a slice of the Entenmann's Mom bought as a treat for herself and Dad once a month, voice all high and anxious and looking to anyone with a brain like he was guilty of something. He could have told them, flat out, he'd taken you, stuffed you in a bag and buried you under the house, and they wouldn't have blinked an eye. Those cops had it in for me from the moment they walked in the door.

On my police report, in bold pen strokes like the cop had gone over it to make sure it stood out is this: *Subject appears nervous but not at all concerned for the welfare of her missing baby.*

I was more than nervous. The last time a police officer had been to our house he was following up on a lead. Someone had broken into our neighbors' garage and stolen a couple thousand dollars' worth of stuff. He took one look at our cramped house with its peeling wallpaper and cheap, sparse furniture and decided we were exactly the type. Dad had been taken in for questioning twice.

As for concern, I imagine they wanted me to be on the floor, bawling and ripping my hair out and *where's my baby*-ing until I lost my voice. Further down on the same police report (and, later, in court records), they called me cold.

I say rip their babies out of their hands and see how they act.

The crying, the dread, the anger came later. At that moment I was struggling to wrap my head around what I was being told. I understood the bare minimum—you were in my arms, and then you weren't. I was in the woods, and then I wasn't. It was like being told the sky was red. I understood the words, but my brain rejected them because I refused to look up, knowing that when I finally did, the clouds would be on fire.

One cop sat at the table with me, notebook out, while the other chewed coffee cake over his shoulder. I couldn't stop watching the crumbs fall.

"Tell me what happened," he said.

So I told him about getting kicked out, about the trip to the gas station for food and finding the perfect spot in the woods to sleep until I could figure something else out.

"You didn't think to go to a shelter?" he asked.

"She's sixteen," Dad said, as though it were the answer to any number of why's. In some ways, probably it was.

"I didn't think she'd actually leave," Mom said. An effort to save her own skin. Child Services was the boogeyman in our house. *Get them dishes done right, or I'll be on the horn to Child Services, and they'll stick you in a home somewhere you have to share shoes with seven other kids, and all of them got athlete's foot.* Didn't mean it wasn't real. She had the littles to think of.

"I thought it was safe," I said.

"What happened?" the cop said. He repeated himself a lot.

"I fed Olivia. I ate. She slept, so I slept. When I woke up I was—"

"I saw her out front," Dad said. "When I walked up to her she looked—" He swallowed. "I thought something bad had happened, the way she was all scratched up."

As if on cue, both cops looked at my exposed arms. They didn't hurt, so I hadn't noticed either—four long, angry red scratches the length of my forearm, like someone had dragged their nails down my skin. It wasn't until I looked at them that they started to sting.

"It's the damndest thing," the cop said. "Babies got nails like razor blades. They get spooked and they're like cats."

Dad, bless him, moved between me and the cop. "What are you saying?"

Finally, the cop stuffing his face chimed in. "We're not saying anything,

Mr. MacArthur. We're just here to get a statement while we wait on the cavalry to arrive."

The sound of crunching gravel wafted in from outside, flashing red and blue lights painting the walls.

"That'll be the cavalry, then," Mom said. She pulled a cigarette from a crumpled pack and lit it with trembling hands.

"What time did you get to the woods when you came back from the gas station?"

"I don't know."

"If I showed you a map of the woods, could you point out where you and the baby were sleeping?"

"I don't know."

"Did you hear or see anything strange?"

"I don't remember."

The questioning went on and on, and the more they threw at me the harder it was to remember anything about the woods. Slowly, the reality of the situation came over me in waves—the police were here. My daughter was gone. They were questioning me. My daughter was gone. I couldn't remember anything after waking up in the front yard. My daughter was gone.

You did it. You did something to her.

The words flew to the front of my mind, and it was like they were all I could hear.

But the police only kept repeating their questions, and no one was out looking for you.

I stood—too quickly, because the cop questioning me put an automatic hand on his hip, fingertips grazing the gun there. Dad paled.

"Miss, I'm going to need you to—"

"If you want to sit in here and drink coffee and eat cake, fine. I'm going to find my daughter."

I only made it as far as the door before I collapsed.

Within an hour, most of the Carver County police were scattered on our front lawn, listening to one of their own talk about the woods. It wasn't a big place, but their first search hadn't turned you up.

"Anything that don't look right," he said, "you call it in."

Dad paced the living room while Mom chain-smoked in the kitchen, half sitting on the sink and blowing the smoke out the window.

"They're looking for a body now," Patrick whispered.

I pretended like I didn't hear.

Erin reached across my lap and slapped him, hard. Before he could even open his mouth, she raised her hand again, shutting him up. "Don't you dare say that again."

I didn't care that Erin was trying to be protective, that she stroked my arm and whispered sugarcoated assurances in my ear. I could feel the suspicion in her fingertips. *What did you do?* She thought—like the cops thought, like my own mother thought—that I'd done something to hurt you. More than that, Iris had planted this idea in my head and now it was growing thick black roots that dug into every inch of my body.

What if the dead women were real? What if they'd taken you? Would I ever see you again?

I traced the scratches down my arm, shivering as I imagined breath on the back of my neck.

Hours passed. Everyone else tried to keep themselves busy—Mom cleaned, Dad mowed the lawn, twice, and clipped a hedge that'd already been clipped to within an inch of its life. My brothers kept mostly to themselves, occasionally pausing at the window to looky-loo (much like our neighbors), until Dad shooed them up to their room. I sat by the window and watched the tree line. Each time someone emerged empty-handed, I found you and lost you all over again.

Erin tried to feed me, but it all sat untouched.

"Starving yourself won't bring her back," she said.

But it made me feel better. I wouldn't eat until you ate. That was what a good mother would do.

Still, I couldn't stand just sitting there and watching and hoping. My body ached with the need to do something. Before I could change my mind, I jumped out of my seat and ran for the door. Erin tried to grab me, but I easily slipped out of her grasp. I heard her yelling for my dad as I reached the lawn, but by the time he looked up, I was halfway to the tree line. A few cops looked up, registered my presence, but were too slow to react. Behind me, someone yelled, "Grab her!" I might have made it to the center of the woods, away from everyone, if I hadn't felt it.

The second I crossed the tree line my ears started to ring. It was still early afternoon, but the sky went a shade of dark blue-green and the air grew dense and hot. I was back inside the bubble. If you were here—if the dead woman, the woman in the well had taken you—this might have been my one chance to find you.

I hunted for footprints—mine and the woman's—drag marks, the things I'd brought with us, anything that might lead me in the right direction. After a long time circling the same patch of woods, I realized I'd been trapped somehow. I didn't know if they wanted you or me or both, but there was no way in hell I was going to let them win. I screamed until my voice broke. I grabbed whatever was lying around—broken tree limbs and rocks—and scratched and pummeled the trees. I hoped they felt it. I hoped they bled.

Someone grabbed me from behind—the scent of Old Spice strong enough to bring on a migraine—and dragged me away from the woods, cursing in my ear as I tried to fend off their grip.

"Calm down! Just—ugh, just hold still." He set me on my feet but didn't let go.

I bit his hand hard enough to draw blood. He shoved me pretty hard—I wore the bruises for a couple of days—but at least he'd let me go. I stumbled back the other way only to be stopped by another cop. He shoved me onto the ground. Grabbed my shoulders and made me face him.

"Shannon."

I bared my teeth. I'd bite him too, if he wanted. I'd rip his skin off.

Frowning, he glanced somewhere behind me, then slapped me hard enough to make my ears ring. I was too dazed to retaliate.

"Shut up," he said through clenched teeth. "Just calm down. We found her."

———————————————

"—half buried near a thorny bush. Couple of scratches on her face the EMTs are checking out, but otherwise she looks okay."

I was only half listening as they walked me to the ambulance where the cop said you were being looked over. I didn't get my hopes up. I refused to believe anything they told me until I saw you with my own two eyes. Still, my hands itched to hold you and I licked my lips thinking of how I would cover your bald head with kisses. From that moment, I would never sleep, never let you out of my sight again.

After a few wordless conversations passed between the EMTs and the cops, one of the medics finally scooped a bundle from inside the ambulance and carefully carried it out. I chewed the insides of my cheeks to keep from demanding she hand you over. But finally, finally, you were in my arms again and in that moment it was like I weighed nothing. I could barely feel my feet on the ground. I anxiously peeled the blankets away from your face, ignoring the cops—*Where were you heading? Why were you destroying the property?*—until I saw the perfect pink of your face.

Except it wasn't your face at all.

They were your brown eyes and your dimpled chin and cheeks with just a touch of eczema. You in parts, but put together wrong.

I could feel eyes on me from every direction, waiting, picking apart my reaction. I buried my face in your belly and breathed in deep, suppressing a shudder. Your smell was all wrong.

I thanked the police and the medics and went back into the house where my parents cried and cooed and their tears mingled on my face so that by the end of it, it looked like I'd been sobbing.

"Thank God she's back," Erin said.

"Thank God," I said.

"Uh oh." Jo leans against the doorway of my room, picking her nails bloody and looking at something down the hall. "Mommy's *raging.*"

"I just saw Jennifer this morning," I say. "She was fine."

Jo snorts. "Her too."

Before I can ask what she's talking about, Jo slips out of the doorway, the opposite direction she was looking. Angela appears seconds later, her mouth screwed up tighter than Doctor Call-Me-Jim's asshole and her arms stiff at her sides. I don't see Angela upset often, but I know to tread lightly. No matter how bad I want to ask, I have to wait for her to talk first.

"I know I'm your doctor," Angela says, "but you'd say we were friends too, right, Shannon?"

Worse than I thought, then. An old tack when it comes to handling people—use their names to keep their focus where you want it.

"Of course," I say.

"And as your friend, I would expect you to know that you can tell me anything, right?"

I nod, not totally sure where this is going.

"Good. I'm going to ask you something, and I need you to tell me the truth."

I don't appreciate her tone. She's right—we are friends—so she shouldn't be speaking to me like I'm a toddler. Still, friends or not, Angela is the one thing standing in the way of me and freedom. She knows it but has been kind enough never to bring it up. Yet.

"I can do that," I say.

She takes a step further into my room but doesn't shut the door. "There was a fire in the kitchen."

I can honestly say I'm surprised—and relieved. "Was anyone hurt?"

"No, thankfully."

"What happened?"

If Angela has one skill, it's a poker face. It's impossible to study her reactions while she's studying mine. "Why don't you tell me?"

"Because I have no idea," I say slowly. I set my journal aside, sticking the pen in the middle to keep the place. "You said we're friends, yeah? A friend would get to the point and not try to catch them in a lie."

"Fair enough." She clears her throat. "Jennifer is in the clinic recovering from second degree burns on her hands and forearms. She broke into the kitchen and cranked the oven as high as it would go, with her comfort doll inside."

"Michael?" I ask.

The corners of Angela's mouth tweak down, sharp as nails in my coffin.

"As the plastic burned it made a noise. She said she heard him screaming and reached inside to pull him out, burning the hell out of her arms."

"I'm very sorry to hear that," I say. "She's a sweet girl. But I don't get what this has to do with me."

"She said you told her to do it, that it would bring Michael back."

"I would never—"

"It can't be a coincidence, Shannon. Who else would say something like to her?"

Jo, I think, but don't dare say it.

"I don't know, but I didn't tell her to do anything."

"Jennifer told me the black-haired woman made her do it. That she promised her son would come back if she did what she was told."

I crossed my arms to hide the hair standing on end. "Jennifer's a liar." Even I flinch at the anger in my voice.

"I see," Angela says in a way that means she doesn't see at all. "Why would she lie about something like that?"

The same reason any of us will lie in here.

"I don't know," I say.

Angela watches me for a long time before nodding. "Okay. Thank you, Shannon."

Suspicious, I ask, "For what?"

Rather than answer, she takes a long look around my room before her gaze settles on me again. There's suspicion on her face, sure, but there's also disappointment, like I'd let her down in exactly the way she'd been expecting. I wait for her to shut the door before I throw my journal and pen across the room. The pen splits against the wall, spilling ink like blood.

CHAPTER SEVENTEEN

OLIVIA

You know how to reach me if anything happens, right? If I don't answer my cell, call—"

"Call Megan," Olivia finished, the last of her patience caught somewhere in her back teeth.

Megan, Kris's perpetually chipper intern, always answered on the first ring. It wasn't her job to field calls for Kris, but she was always too happy to help.

"Right." Kris probed Olivia's expression, no doubt looking for weakness.

Olivia hadn't slept all night, the slightest noise jolting her awake. Not that it would have mattered if the room was dead silent. Every time she closed her eyes, she saw the black-haired woman standing beside her mother, Charlie's voice echoing around her.

Kris tried to move Flora to the second bedroom—*she's going to have to sleep there eventually*—but Olivia put her foot down. Something primal had taken over inside her. She couldn't have Flora out of her sight for more than a few minutes without feeling that ache.

"Would it help if I gave you a rundown of our schedule today?" Olivia snipped. "As soon as you leave, we're busting out the cocaine—only the pure shit for my girl—then it's keg stands and edibles for the rest of the day. Don't want to do too much too fast, you know."

"Liv—"

"No, you're right. The edibles should come first. Slow rise, slow fall. Good thinking."

Kris had one hand on the door, the other death-gripped her laptop bag. "Okay. Fine. I get it."

"No, actually. I don't think you do." She took two steps into the living room where Flora was quietly revolting against tummy time. She picked Flora up and carried her, sack-like, over her forearm. Drool dripped down her skin. "You have no idea what giving birth does to someone. You couldn't possibly fathom the trauma my body has gone through over the last few weeks. I've been ripped apart from the inside out."

"If you regret—"

"No." Olivia put her hand up. "Don't you dare finish that sentence."

After a long moment, Kris nodded.

Guilt was Kris's kryptonite, the only thing that would distract her from the way Olivia's eyes twitched and her hands trembled. Growing up Catholic, Olivia knew guilt was a weapon. She didn't use it lightly.

"Go to work," Olivia continued, "then come home and be with us. But don't think that we can't function without you here, because we can. I can."

"Of course," Kris muttered. "I'm sorry."

Olivia let Kris pull them into a tight hug despite the sharp pain running through her skin, all pins and needles.

"I love you," Kris said.

Olivia shut the door behind her.

She opened her laptop even as she told herself she wasn't going to do it. Wasn't going to open that door. She would put it all out of her head—Charlie, the black-haired woman, the fucking *podcast*. All of it. She was clearly ill and needed help.

But they'll take her, a voice whispered. A voice growing louder by the day.

She found the web page for the podcast easily enough. She found herself clicking through the episodes, cursor hovering over the "Save for Later" option. It was like slipping on an old skin, too small, too tight. She'd liked listening to podcasts like this because, though the stories were awful, they felt like preparation. The more she listened, the more she learned. The more she learned, the better she could protect herself. Now she knew that was ridiculous. There was nothing that could protect you from the world. Nothing that could prepare you for the ways the world, and your own body, would betray you.

Still, she scrolled and scrolled until, finally, she found it.

Well, Baby, I Guess This Is Goodbye

This week, Corrinne and Dakota discuss attempted child killer, Shannon MacArthur.

The episode was almost three years old. Three years! Olivia would have put the episode out of her head, having already moved on to the next gruesome tale. What had made Charlie cling to it for so long? Was there something she knew, something that made her need to meet Olivia, something other than morbid curiosity?

She checked that Flora was still sleeping in her bouncy seat and then dug her headphones out of her work bag. She plugged them in, braced herself, and clicked Play.

The first ten minutes were filled with chitchat. Nothing that had anything to do with her mother's case. But Olivia resisted the urge to skip ahead. She didn't want to miss a single detail.

Now, for the reason you're all here.

Olivia held her breath.

Today, we're talking about Shannon MacArthur.

Look, I know we're not supposed to feel for the baddies, but her story makes me sad.

Oh, totally. And her daughter too.

Yes! Poor Olivia.

Olivia pressed the headphones hard down on her ears to block out the sound of her blood pumping. She tried to swallow, but her mouth was dry.

But we're getting ahead of ourselves! Let's start with Shannon.

Right. So, Shannon was born in a small town in Minnesota, the middle child of four. Her dad was a plumber, and her mother was a housewife. All told, she had a pretty normal childhood. A couple of friends, did okay in school.

And to tell us more about that—

Olivia froze. Her eyes stung from not blinking.

—we have a surprise guest! Please welcome Patrick MacArthur to the studio. Patrick, we can't tell you how grateful we are you agreed to talk with us.

Motherfucker, Olivia thought. *Motherfucker.*

Yes, it's always a treat to get the story straight from the horse's mouth.

Patrick chuckled. Though she hadn't spoken to her uncle Patrick in years, she'd know his laugh anywhere. A short, hitching neigh of a laugh.

She wondered if her grandmother knew about this. If that was why he hadn't been at Christmas dinner in a few years.

Well, I'm a real fan of the show, Patrick said. *When your producer reached out to me, my instinct was to just turn him down. Because, like, this is my family, right? What business does anyone have digging into my family? But then I figured, you know, Shannon was sick. And what happened could have been worse. If I can, you know, give some context or help anyone who might be going through the same, well, I figured I should.*

And we appreciate it.

And our listeners appreciate it.

It's my pleasure, Patrick said.

So. Tell us about Shannon. What was she like when she lived with you?

Patrick cleared his throat. Olivia could almost see him stretching back in the chair, stupid face fixed in an expression meant to look pensive. *I was a kid when she got sent away. Second grade, maybe. To me, she was my big sister, you know? Me and my brother, John Jack, tormented her when we could, mostly because our oldest sister, Erin, wasn't any fun anymore.* They all laughed. *But I loved her. She was nice to me.*

But then she got pregnant, Corrine or Dakota prompted.

Mmhmm. Things got...weird after that.

Weird how?

Mostly, she got quieter.

She was sixteen when she got pregnant, right? That had to have been scary.

Yeah, but it was more than that, Patrick said. *It was like she thought someone was after her. She was always looking over her shoulder. Listening at windows. I remember waking up one time to go to the bathroom, middle of the night, and I saw a light on downstairs. I went down to look—and maybe grab a snack while I was at it—and I saw Shannon sitting on the kitchen floor, back to the cabinets, a flashlight aimed at the cellar door.*

What was she waiting for?

The black-haired woman.

I don't know. I never asked her about it.

Tell us what happened after Olivia was born.

Olivia sucked in a breath. Held it.

Patrick sighed. *Well, my mom kicked her out.*

Jesus.

Oh my god.

Yeah, Patrick said. *My dad was pissed.*

It was like being pricked with a needle. She'd loved her grandfather. Had dipped into a dark place for a while when he died. It'd often seemed like he was the only person who hadn't seen her presence in their lives as a burden. She missed him.

Patrick continued, *She came back, but when she did, Olivia had disappeared.*

Did anyone ever think Shannon had done anything to her?

I think my mother suspected, but she never said. Hindsight's twenty-twenty, right?

You mean because of what happened after? At the well?

Because I wasn't a great sleeper when I was little. I got up a lot. Snuck around the house seeing what I could smuggle back to my room. It wasn't just Shannon I saw in the kitchen some nights. My mother did it too.

She stared at the cellar door?

Mmhmm. Sometimes the kitchen window or the back door. Just standing there, staring. When I was little I just figured it was a woman thing. He chuckled. *But like I said. Hindsight.*

You think your mother knew something but never said.

I don't know. I think maybe she knew more than she thought she did.

Olivia hit pause, taking deep, measured breaths to keep herself from throwing up. This was too much. This was her life laid bare for everyone—strangers—to do with what they wanted. And worse, it'd been there for years. Who knew how many of her colleagues and friends had heard it? She started running through every awkward interaction she'd ever had at work, every side eye cast her way during birthing classes or at her prenatal appointments. Had they known? Had they seen into her future before she did?

She thought of Simone, how she would have called this some kind of self-fulfilling prophecy, and all Olivia wanted to do was to pick up the phone and call her, but a petty need to ignore the friend who'd ignored her first made her stop. God, Olivia was so lonely.

Her finger started toward the track pad to restart the podcast when movement in the corner of her eye made her pause. She glanced at the time on the computer screen. It was too early for Kris to be home. The ceiling creaked, like footsteps, except her house only had the one level. Settling, she told herself. Except a house didn't settle that way. The sound traveled from one side to the other, as though pacing.

She's coming.

Olivia slipped off her headphones with shaky hands and bent down to grab Flora, still asleep in her bouncy chair. It took three tries to get a decent grip on her as the muscles in Olivia's body stiffened and twitched, adrenaline surging. Flora started whining the second Olivia had her arms around her, but they needed to get out of there.

But go where? Kris's office? As tempted as she was, Olivia knew she'd only earn that pitying look again, that look that said Olivia was weak and paranoid. Each moment she hesitated was a moment wasted. *Just get out*, she told herself. *Get out* now.

She clung too tight to Flora, arms locked, but her legs trembled and her mouth had gone dry. Every sound was like a sharp yellow fingernail scraping down the back of her neck.

She dug her keys out of her bag—there was no time to get anything else—and ran for the door. She threw it open and screamed when she saw the woman.

"Whoa! Okay, got you. You're okay."

Charlie had Olivia by the elbow with Flora squeezed between them as she helped Olivia get her footing. Olivia started to say *thank you*. Her grip on Flora was too loose—if Charlie hadn't been there, she would have dropped her. But then, Olivia thought once her head had cleared, if Charlie hadn't been there, she wouldn't have been startled in the first place.

"What are you doing here?" Olivia backed into the house and gripped the door, ready to slam it shut.

Charlie's face reddened. "I'm sorry. I just—I felt bad about last night. I didn't have your number, but I felt like I needed to explain myself." She glanced down at Flora. "Is that your little one?"

Flora yipped. Olivia realized her grip was digging into her daughter's thigh and backed further into the house, heading for the bouncy chair. When she looked back, Charlie had let herself inside by one tentative step.

Back in the bouncy chair, Flora's face twisted and turned red as she worked up a real good wail. She was probably starving. Olivia started to lift her shirt, but Charlie's presence made her stop. She went into the kitchen looking for a clean bottle, but the dishes she was supposed to have done this morning were still in the sink and the bottles were somewhere near the bottom, covered in God knew what. She could wash one, but what about the bacteria? Did she have to boil it too? As she dug through the sink, all she could think about were all the potential diseases Flora might contract from a bottle that hadn't been properly cleaned. She thought of the bacteria buildup in the nipples, fungus and mold, and what would happen when her daughter took it all in. Olivia's eyes stung as tears dripped down her cheeks, chapped from all the crying she'd done over the last few weeks.

She was a failure.

The water was scalding hot, but she held her hands under it, almost as punishment. She glanced up at the window over the sink and the reflection staring back made her stop breathing. Long black hair and bruise-like circles under the eyes. Lips peeling and bloodred. The reflection seemed to lean forward out of the glass. She could almost smell it—all moss and peat and sour milk.

She no longer felt the water. She barely felt her feet on the ground, like she was being lifted up to meet the black-haired woman, to be devoured.

"Olivia! What are you—?"

Charlie yanked Olivia's hands out of the stream and pulled her toward the refrigerator, where she sandwiched Olivia's hands between two bags of frozen vegetables. Olivia shot a panicked look over her shoulder, but the reflection was gone. Outside, the wind rustled the bushes softly, and the sun shone bright and hot.

"Flora—" Olivia tried to pull away, but Charlie's grip on her hands was tight. "She needs to eat."

"Flora's fine. Look."

Olivia followed Charlie's gaze to Flora, asleep in the bouncy seat, her pacifier dangling from her mouth by a string of drool.

"I think she was just tired," Charlie said. "Are you okay?"

The pain crept through her hands slowly, then all at once. Condensation from the bags dripped down her arms, making her shiver. When she finally extracted her hands, they were red but otherwise looked okay.

"You might blister," Charlie said.

Olivia tucked her hands under her arms, away from Charlie's inquisitive gaze. "I'm fine."

"You're sure?"

She nodded once.

"Okay."

They stood there in awkward silence for several seconds before Charlie spotted the laptop, open to the podcast. "You listened to it?" she asked.

"Some of it."

"What did you think?"

"I think the next time I see Patrick I might stab him."

Charlie laughed nervously. "Oh. Yeah. They don't usually have guests on, so it was kind of a big deal. People loved it."

"Good for them," she spat. "What do you want?"

"Like I said, I wanted to explain—"

"No." Olivia cut her off. "Don't bother. What do you *really* want?"

Charlie crossed her arms. Shifted her weight. She glanced from the laptop back to Olivia, but couldn't quite meet her eyes. "At first, yeah, it was pretty much just morbid curiosity. It sucks, but the shit that happened to you made you a kind of celebrity. Like Baby Jessica. Toward the end of the episode there's a lot of speculation about mental illness and genetics. They're not doctors, obviously. They just talk. But it made me curious."

"You wanted to see if I was just as fucked up as Shannon."

Charlie's face reddened. "More or less."

"And?"

She didn't respond.

Olivia continued, "You said *at first*. What changed?"

"Now I just want to help."

"Help?"

"Flora's your first kid, right?"

Olivia nodded.

"Brent's my third. He's been the easiest of them all—hardly cries except when he's hungry, sleeps well, hitting all those milestones like clockwork. Same with my first. My middle one though, Jemma, was a whole different story. She cried until she turned purple. Refused to eat sometimes. Everything I did was wrong, and she made sure I knew it. But I was lucky because my mom came over without me even having to ask. We took shifts so I could get a few hours' sleep. She helped keep my oldest occupied while I dealt with Jemma. She was a lifesaver." She paused. "I can't imagine being in your shoes. Not having my mom. Worse, wondering—"

"Wondering if I might fall down the same hole."

Charlie hesitated, then nodded. "Look, I know we just met. Your life is none of my business. I also know you have no reason to trust my intentions given that." She nodded at the laptop. "But I hope I can convince you that I do understand."

Olivia shook her head. "No one understands. No one sees—" She stopped. *They'll take her.* The voice was louder now, more insistent. "I don't need your help."

"Fair enough. But, before I leave, can I show you something?" She pulled out her phone before Olivia could protest. She held it out to her, but Olivia didn't take it. Whatever other twisted information she had for her about Shannon, she didn't want to know.

"Please," Charlie said. "Just look. Then I'll go."

Knowing Charlie wouldn't give up, Olivia took the phone. It was open to an article only a few lines long, about a woman named Iris Ficke. An obituary. Barely twenty-three when she died, there wasn't much written about her except that she'd been a longtime resident of a care facility for women called Bethany Home.

Sad, but Olivia couldn't see what it had to do with anything.

"And?" she asked.

"I did some digging. Bethany Home is what they called Sleepy Eye back in the day."

"Okay."

"Shannon volunteered there when she was pregnant with you. For a while after you were born too, I think. There's a picture in an old microfilm I found at the library. A group shot—some activity for the women—and your mom's there front and center with a baby in her arms." Charlie tapped and scrolled through her phone for another second before shoving it back in Olivia's hands. "Iris is second from the left, I'm pretty sure."

The photo was a little grainy. Olivia could just make out most of the details of her mother's face—a soft smile with a dimple on one side, dark hair lightly teased and framing her face—but she, if it was her in her mother's arms, was too wrapped up to be anything more than a bundle. The woman Charlie pointed out—Iris— stood toward the back of the group, second from the left. Her body was turned partly away from the camera, but her face looked dead on, as though someone had just called her name before the photo was taken. Her lips were set in a tight line and her eyebrows furrowed. There was a thick, gray haze around her, like smoke, pulling ever so slightly away from her head and shoulders, obscuring the women around her. The longer Olivia looked at the picture, the more the gray haze began to take shape. Dips and juts became the gentle round of a forehead, the sharp point of a nose. Long wisps became a slender neck and long black hair.

"You see it, right?" Charlie asked. "You see how she's looking at Shannon?"

At first, Olivia thought she was talking about Iris, but then she realized. The black-haired woman, hidden in plain sight. In the gray smoke around Iris's head.

Numb, Olivia nodded.

"There's something to it," Charlie said, excited now. "I don't know what and there's pretty much no information about Iris anywhere. Depending on who her parents were, they might have spent a pretty penny burying anything and every- thing that could tarnish their reputation. Iris might not even be the woman's real name. I've tried contacting the old director there, Marcia Donato, but she's protective. Told me off real good in an email, threatening me with a lawsuit if I kept digging. I figured she was the kind of woman who meant what she said, so I stopped." She paused. "This thing that exists between Iris and Shannon might be the thing that made her do…what she did. And maybe if we—if you—figure out what that is, maybe you can—"

"Stop it from happening again." Olivia finally looked up at Charlie. "I would never hurt Flora."

"I know."

But she needed to know what really happened. If this Iris woman—if she had known what would happen, if she knew anything about the black-haired woman, would she have told Olivia's mother? Would it have made a difference?

In her darkest moments, in the middle of the night when Kris slept peacefully on one side of her and Flora breathed gently on the other, Olivia believed she'd lost her mind. That, in the hours between pregnancy and birth, something had snapped inside her, terrifying and irreparable.

But what if it was something more than that? Something bigger. Scarier.

What if she wasn't crazy? What if it was all real?

There was only one way to know.

Am I broken? Is there something inside me I can't change, that will one day make me do something horrible?

She needed to talk to Shannon. She needed to talk to her mother.

CHAPTER EIGHTEEN

SHANNON

Word spreads like wildfire that I'm the one to blame for what Jennifer did, for what happened to her after. Without her comfort doll, she shut down. All progress she made toward recovery, gone. No one will look at me and though I've never developed any kind of relationship with any of these women, their hatred hits hard. I've only ever had Jo, who has also made herself scarce.

I know Angela wants to believe me. Does believe me. But she can't admit it, to herself or anyone else. So she's pulling away too.

I'm alone and lonely.

That's when they come, Iris used to say. When you're alone and lonely and no one else understands, they can see it and they follow it, like a light.

It used to scare me, looking over my shoulder for the black-haired woman, all despair and hunger for suffering. I used to feel her teeth on my neck. Used to hear her voice in my sleep.

I'm not afraid anymore. Hard to be afraid of something that's already here, already has its teeth in your chest and its nails in your eyes.

I see what she wants me to see. I feel what she wants me to feel.

Iris told me she shows us the truth, hidden like a fly among spiders. When Jo's not around, I can hear the truth buzzing, somewhere close.

She won't stay gone for long. Jealousy makes a person cling, makes them do ugly things. They don't think for a second someone could get ugly back.

"The baby isn't moving."

"She's boring."

"She's not boring, she's a baby."

"Boring."

I couldn't get five seconds to myself after you were lost. If my mother wasn't hovering at my shoulder spitting insults disguised as advice, or my father wasn't lingering silent in the doorway, it was the boys wanting to know when they could play with the baby, or Erin offering to hold you, change you, feed you... I needed to look at you, to really look at you, to figure out if what I'd seen with the EMTs was real.

I finally got my chance near midnight. I couldn't make you eat to save my life—I blame the commotion—but once my parents went to bed and my siblings drifted into their own hard-won corners of the house, you chewed your fists like you were starving.

I didn't want to feed you in my bedroom. Erin was there, probably waiting for me to bring you up, those laser eyes zeroed in on my movements, my expressions. So I locked us in the bathroom and sat on the edge of the tub.

Breastfeeding was awkward. I had barely gotten to know my body before I had to share it. I don't regret it, but at the time it felt wrong. My heart and mind were open and ready, but my body shrank back from what I was asking it to do. My mother encouraged breastfeeding—it was cheaper, for one—but the nurses looked at her sideways the more she pushed it. I was a child to them. What could my body possibly have to offer?

Still.

There was only one way to convince myself, to know for sure.

Cringing, I opened my blouse and lifted you up to nurse. At the hospital, you'd taken to nursing immediately. Now, it was like you'd forgotten what to do. Your eyes got wide and your mouth gaped over and over, a little fish out of water, even as I pressed your face against my skin. You kicked your legs and arms, a too-big thing inside a too small body. You didn't stop twitching until I closed my blouse again. Then you laid perfectly still, barely breathing, eyes fixed on a point on the ceiling, blank.

This isn't right, a voice whispered.

She's upset, I thought. *That's all.*

Babies take comfort in food, the voice countered. *Olivia would eat. Olivia would need you.*

That was when I knew. The baby they'd returned to me wasn't you at all.

I spent the rest of the night pacing the tree line, the baby sleeping in your carrier, waiting, hoping for that bubble to come over me, to let me back into the world where I felt in my bones you were still lost. Asleep, I could almost convince myself it was you laying there, wrapped in the first blanket I ever bought. I touched the baby's cheeks and they felt like your cheeks. The baby's nose was your upturned nose. But I smelled her head and instead of that sour-sweet baby scent, I smelled dirt and moss.

For days I walked the tree line. When my mother asked me about it, not bothering to hide her suspicion, I told her you like it outside, that you fell asleep easier when I was walking and that I didn't want to disturb anyone in the house with my pacing. It was good enough for Mom, but Erin wasn't as easy to fool.

One morning she followed me. "I'll come with you. Keep you company," she said.

I told her I was fine, but ever since that night, Erin didn't believe a word that came out of my mouth. I could've told her the sky was blue, the grass was green, and the sun shone over us all, but she'd still find a way to argue the point.

"Where's Olivia?" she asked.

"Upstairs," I said. "Sleeping."

While my father was delighted at how calm and quiet the baby was, it spooked my mother. *Babies should cry*, she'd told me.

Maybe I should have said something then. Maybe it would have all turned out different.

But I doubt it.

It wasn't just that the baby slept more than any newborn had any right to, it was that, when she was awake, she didn't make any of those soft gurgling, cooing noises babies make when they're trying to find their voice. Sometimes I would be folding laundry or looking through ads for hire in the newspaper Mom stuck under my nose every morning, and I would forget she was there. Then I would look up and those bright eyes would be staring straight through me. It was like I could feel her poking around inside my head. It disturbed me so much that I started to avoid being in the same room with her. If I needed to make dinner, I'd lock her in the bedroom. If I was doing laundry, I left her downstairs. The only time I couldn't escape was at night.

"You look like shit," Erin said, shoveling egg in her mouth with a wedge of toast. Then, when I didn't answer, "I saw you up again last night."

"So?"

"So, I'm just saying."

Just saying she was watching me.

"Can't be Olivia keeping you up," Erin continued. "She don't cry or anything."

Babies should cry.

No, the baby didn't cry. But every time I opened my eyes, jarred out of a dead sleep by the sensation of someone else coming into the room, I'd see her there, in your crib, gaze fixed on mine. I could never go back to sleep after that.

"If you're accusing me of something," I finally said, "just come out with it already."

"Not accusing you of nothing." She finished her eggs. Licked the butter off her fingers. "I'm just saying."

Once she finished *saying,* I figured she'd head back to the house, but Erin followed me all the way to the tree line.

"Were you really sleeping in the woods?" she asked.

I nodded.

"Why?"

"S'good a place as any," I said. "I wasn't planning on staying there forever. Just the night. I had a plan."

"Oh?" A beat of panic beneath the false curiosity.

"A shelter or something. I was gonna get a job. Take care of us."

"You know Mom didn't mean it, right? Two minutes after you left she was bordering on hysteric."

I didn't believe her but wasn't in any mood to fight about it.

We stood in awkward silence for too long—me waiting for her to take the hint and leave, her probably waiting for me to do the same.

"You're not alone though. You know that, right?" she said.

"I should go check on the baby," I said.

Mom jumped when I opened the door, clutching her chest. "Jesus Christ, Shan. Don't scare me like that." She took a settling breath. "I thought you were upstairs."

"I was outside."

"I see that. Must've been Erin up in the bedroom, then."

I raised my eyebrow.

"Kind of sweet, actually." Mom picked up the dish towel she'd dropped when I came in. Hummed a couple of bars of what I recognized as "Baby, Mine." "I never would have guessed Erin could sing. She's button-lipped during the hymnal."

My heart started to race. "What do you mean?"

"I was clearing out the boys' hamper. Came out in the hallway and heard someone singing a lullaby in your bedroom. I thought it was you, but it must've been Erin. I guess she's shy. Must've seen my feet under the door. She stopped the second I got too close."

I'm not crazy, but I didn't trust my mind then, same as I don't trust it now. I looked out the window hoping, praying, I'd imagined her. But Erin still stood at the tree line, holding a paper plate at her side. And if Erin was outside, who had been singing to the baby?

The thing about Jo is, she's a creature of habit. She's predictable, especially when she's trying not to be. She expected me to read her the riot act after that little stunt with Jennifer. She feeds on that kind of thing. Without a reaction, she's starving. Any other time I might have been content to let her stew and simmer and devour herself, but that kind of thing takes time, something I don't have. I can't afford to risk Jo getting bigger, more damaging ideas. Can't afford the way Angela looks at me now, still with a smile but eyes that linger too long on mine.

A full week goes by after Angela scolded me before I see Jo sitting at a card table in the recreation room, shuffling a deck of Uno cards. Every few times she splits the deck, she slips one of the cards in her shirt—a juvenile stab at small chaos. There hasn't been a complete deck of cards at Sleepy Eye in years. She doesn't look up, but the tension in her jaw, the slight pause before the next shuffle, means she saw me. It's hard not to smile as I realize—she's scared of me.

Good. It'll make the next bit easier.

Because when Jo is scared, she doesn't walk away. She runs toward the danger. And today, that's me.

Moving to the Bethany Wing gave me the freedom to move around this side of the hospital without special permission. Being Angela's favorite meant the orderlies didn't ask questions when I wandered one hallway outside the wing or I found my way into the cafeteria between mealtimes. There was at least another two hours before dinner, which meant the kitchen staff wouldn't be in for an hour or so. It's easy to slip past the guard on duty—he's mostly absorbed by his phone—and through the double doors that lead to the main hall. The cafeteria is at the end, the only door in the hallway that should be locked but isn't. I can smell the ghost of lunch lingering in the hall—ground beef and ketchup and cabbage.

Inside, the stench is worse. Minimum-wage kitchen workers can't be bothered to clean out sink traps. It's almost bad enough to make me turn around, but just under the steady hum of the ancient heating ducts I hear soft shuffle-steps behind me.

I pause in front of the bank of ovens. One of them has scorch marks toward the bottom, probably from where Michael caught fire.

"Good, right?"

I don't turn to face her. Don't acknowledge her. There's already an edge to her voice; I want to sharpen it.

Jo continues, "I get it. You're upset. Jennifer's your little pet and making her mad made Mommy mad. You see why I had to do it though, right? You know it's for our own good." She pauses. Clears her throat. "Besides, you got to appreciate the…what's the word…finesse. Almost like poetry, if you think about it."

"You wouldn't know poetry if it bit you on the ass," I say.

"'But soft, what light through yonder window breaks...'" Jo laughs, low and gravelly. "Never fancied myself a Romeo—more of a Tybalt myself." She takes a step closer, taps a metal table. "You and I both know you're gonna forgive me eventually. Might as well skip over all this and get to the end. Save us both a headache."

Jo's a talker. Likes the sound of her own voice so much she doesn't notice much else when she's doing it. It's why there's no lag time between the thoughts in her head and the words coming out of her mouth, why she doesn't notice how quickly, how smoothly, I slip a paring knife from the sink—left behind by those minimum-wage workers too anxious for a smoke break to double-check that all the sharp things are locked up tight.

Finally, I turn to face her, and the look on her face says she won.

"You're right," I say. "I'm done. Time to get to the end of this."

"Glad you see it my—oh."

We both look down to see the handle of the paring knife sticking out of her belly. The blade isn't long, so I doubt it damaged much, but it's enough that her knees give out and she falls, dragging me down with her. I scramble for the knife handle, but it's already in her hand. Blood pools between us, soaking the front of my shirt. She raises the knife and I put my arm up, bracing myself to take the blow, but the knife clatters somewhere behind me and when I finally look at her, she's smiling.

"Does this mean you forgive me?" she asks through clenched teeth.

It takes too long for her to finally pass out. She's not dead, but will be soon. Not soon enough though.

I drag her toward one of the pantries, grateful to find it mostly empty. She's just small enough I can fold her into the bottom shelf and shut the door, but it won't stay closed. Slipping in the blood trail from in front of the ovens to the pantry, I go through every drawer looking for a lock or string…something I can use to keep the pantry closed. In one of the last drawers I find a couple of zip ties, which I thread through the handles of the pantry and pull them tight. Either someone will assume it was meant to be locked up, or they won't care.

I use kitchen towels to clean up the blood as best I can, but there's nothing I can do about my shirt. I bury it in the bottom of the garbage beneath stinking leftovers and a bunch of gray expired meat, and put on a dirty chef's coat from the laundry bin.

If I'm lucky, they won't find her before I have the chance to undo all the damage she's done.

If I'm lucky, by the time someone thinks to open that pantry, I'll be long gone, and you, Olivia, will be in my arms.

CHAPTER NINETEEN

OLIVIA

W hen Kris left for work the next morning, Olivia took her time getting Flora ready for the drive. After her morning feed, when milk—pink with blood—collected in the folds of chub in Flora's neck, Olivia stripped her and gave her a bath in the sink even though a diaper wipe would have done the job. She packed and repacked the diaper bag with extra clothes and bottles and the copy of *Goodnight Moon* she was always meaning to read to Flora at bedtime but never did, because by the time Flora was calm enough to lay in her bassinet, Olivia could hardly keep her eyes open. It was 9:30 by the time Olivia finished packing the bag for the last time, and then 10:00 before she finished worrying whether there'd be enough time to drive the two hours to Sleepy Eye, somehow get up the nerve to see her mother, and then drive the two hours back without killing herself and Flora in a fiery wreck because her nerves had gone haywire. Pushing 11:00, when she stood in front of the bathroom mirror studying the new lines in her face, the burst blood vessels in her eyes, and the bony protrusions in her clavicle and shoulders and scared herself by knowing she was dying.

Flora was hungry and crabby, and with each wary glance at the clock, Olivia worried there wouldn't be enough time. Part of her was relieved—it was a terrible idea. She shouldn't go.

Flora gripped Olivia's thumb and her nail cracked down the middle.

She had to go, but she didn't have to do it alone.

Charlie was at the door in ten minutes, practically vibrating. "I promise I'll be good," she said, earning a rare smile from Olivia. She glanced over Olivia's shoulder. "I could just stay here with Flora, if you want."

Flora was bundled up in the car seat, bulging diaper bag next to her. Olivia knew she'd overpacked for an afternoon car ride, but every time she took something out of the bag, a voice inside told her it was vital. That Flora's happiness and health depended on it.

Don't leave her with Charlie. You don't know her. She'll take her and they'll disappear forever, and it'll be your fault. You'll never see her again. Kris will blame you. How could you even consider it? You should never have become a mother. You should never—

Olivia squeezed her hands over her ears, but the voice got louder. Filled her head until it was pressing against her skull and the pain was extraordinary. She blinked, but all she could see was fog.

"Stop," she muttered. "Please, stop."

"Olivia? Are you okay?"

Charlie's voice sounded far away. She grabbed Olivia's hands and pulled them away from her ears, holding them tight between them. She didn't let go until Olivia made eye contact, until the fog faded and the voice quieted, curling up somewhere in the corner of her head.

"What's wrong?" Charlie asked.

"Nothing," Olivia said. "Headache."

"Do you need to take something?" She didn't wait to be told, starting toward the kitchen. "I'll get you some water. I have meds in my bag."

She returned with a glass of tap water and rifled through her purse until she found an unlabeled bottle. She shook a couple of pills into Olivia's palm and waited.

Olivia studied the pills.

The shape looks wrong. She's trying to drug you. Take Flora.

The voice in her head got more agitated the longer she looked at the pills.

"Tylenol," Charlie said. "Extra strength. It'll knock any headache on its ass, guaranteed."

"Tylenol," Olivia said to herself. "Just Tylenol."

She threw the pills back and chased them with the water before the voice could interrupt. "Thanks," she said, adding, "Sorry."

"It's a lot," Charlie said. "Anyone who would blame you for going a little nuts isn't anyone I want to know."

Olivia snorted. "Yeah. Thanks."

"No problem." She cleared her throat. "So..."

"Flora comes with me," Olivia said, a little too forcefully. "We'll all go. It'll be fine."

Olivia would have been content to make the trip in silence, but Charlie was determined to fill the car with small talk.

Lived here all my life and never driven out this way.

My husband's from Duluth so we're always going up north. You ever been to the shore?

I grew up in Kansas. Being landlocked, I appreciate the big lakes.

Nodding along, Olivia glanced frequently into the rearview mirror, checking on Flora, who fell asleep shortly after they hit the highway.

"So you've really never met her?" Charlie asked.

"Hmm?"

"Shannon. You don't live that far away."

"Never wanted to," Olivia said.

It was an obvious lie, but Charlie was kind enough to swallow it.

"I get it," Charlie said. She sighed. Picked at a crusty bit on her jeans. "Actually, no, I don't. I mean, I do, kind of. But I can't imagine you wouldn't have been curious."

"Of course I was curious," Olivia snapped. After a beat, she lowered her voice. "I just couldn't. The way my grandparents talked about her—warning me off without warning me off. I was married before I realized I was an adult and could make my own decision about whether to see her or not, but by then I figured it didn't matter. Whatever I thought I wanted from her she wouldn't be able to give me."

"What did you want from her?"

Olivia thought for a moment, eyes fixed on the road. "I don't know." Then, "I talked to a reporter once. He told me she'd been released twice before I was eighteen, but she violated the protection order, so they sent her back."

"Wow. What happened? I mean, do you remember it happening? Did she try to see you?"

"No idea."

"Your grandparents didn't say anything?"

"My grandpa meant well, but he was a head-in-the-sand kind of guy. He believed good things and pretended bad things didn't exist." Olivia glanced in the rearview mirror, thinking she'd seen Flora move, but she was still asleep. "If my grandmother and I talked, it was never about my mother."

Olivia loved her grandmother, but they were never close. Even when she was little, she could sense this transparent wall between them. Olivia felt like she was being watched, not cared for. Observed through a lens of suspicion and worry. Aunt Erin made up for it where she could, but once she started working for the cruise line, Olivia saw her less and less. Though her grandmother never expressly said anything, when Olivia came out, the tension tightened, a string ready to snap. What little physical affection there was between them fizzled, and by the time Olivia graduated from high school, they were like ghosts haunting the same house, moving through and around each other, unseen and unheard.

"When I was in college," Olivia continued, "my grandmother made me promise I wouldn't try to see her."

"She wanted to protect you," Charlie said.

Olivia thought of the podcast, how Patrick speculated her grandmother knew more than she let on. What was it Olivia needed protecting from?

Halfway through the drive, her hands started to cramp, and her ankle ached from pressing the pedals. She hated how her body was failing her. Where was all that mom strength people liked to talk about? She didn't feel like she could lift a car or outrun someone, even if it meant saving Flora. She could barely keep herself upright.

Failure, the voice whispered. *Selfish. Getting pregnant to make your wife happy when you knew what would happen. You knew you weren't good enough.*

Tears stung her eyes, but she blinked them back before they could fall.

Didn't stop Charlie from noticing. "You okay?"

There was a moment when Olivia considered unburdening herself. She could tell Charlie everything—the way her body was breaking, how Flora seemed to be devouring her from the inside out—and Charlie would understand. Charlie, with her kindness and curiosity, would help.

Then she caught a glimpse of herself in the rearview mirror and the words died in her throat.

The shadow of the black-haired woman, all fog and faint lines pulling away from Olivia's mouth and chin, lifted a finger to her lips.

Don't you dare, the voice whispered.

Olivia squeezed her eyes shut, hoping, willing the vision to leave, but it was getting harder and harder to fight. If she focused too closely on her skin, she noticed how detached it felt from the rest of her, like there was someone inside her body, *wearing* her. No amount of gum could chase away the mossy taste in her mouth. And it seemed every time she blinked she saw an image of a black hole, heard whispers from somewhere deep within it. It was like she was losing herself, one breath at a time. What would happen when her body finally *gave*? Would the black-haired woman reassemble Olivia, puppet her around, a twisted marionette of herself?

Pushing away thoughts like this was like treading water with her feet encased in cement. Every pathetic mantra, every reassurance, was a gasping breath.

It's not real, she told herself now, but didn't dare look back at the mirror.

Flora was still asleep when they pulled into Sleepy Eye's parking lot. The building itself looked more like an office complex or a school than a hospital—clean red brick surrounded by a carefully manicured garden with young maple trees planted every few yards. Olivia didn't know what she'd been expecting. Institutional gray cinder blocks and cracked sidewalks and barbed wire, maybe. She didn't know whether to be relieved or disappointed.

"Wow," Charlie said. "There it is."

"There it is," Olivia echoed.

A pair of women walked, arms interlinked, along the sidewalk, taking a sharp turn at the edge of the building where a worn path lay in the grass. Olivia's stomach flipped. What if that was Shannon? Or someone who knew her? Had spoken to her?

It was becoming too real too quickly.

"Do you want me to come with you?" Charlie asked.

Olivia shook her head even as her body screamed yes.

"No problem. I can stay here with Flora. Keep each other company."

No.

"No," Olivia said. "I'll take her with me. She might get hungry."

"Are you sure?"

Olivia was already out of the car and opening the back door. Flora burbled complaints as she unclipped the car seat.

She was winded by the time she got the stroller out of the trunk and Flora's car seat hooked in. Her arms trembled with the effort of pushing the stroller up a low incline toward the building. She shouldn't have skipped breakfast this morning. And it looked like she would likely miss lunch too. She needed to take care of herself the way Edie and the others did, but it was like any self-preservation instinct had been switched off. She'd starve to death washing onesies.

The reception area was small, only a couple of chairs behind a coffee table strewn with old magazines. A bin of mostly broken toys sat in the corner beneath a television stuck on the Home Shopping Network. Before the receptionist could look up from her computer, Olivia spotted the bathroom and made a beeline for it. She peed while Flora stared from her stroller, fascinated, and when she stood, she noticed her urine was a stale color, rusty, like there was blood in it.

This is stupid, she thought. *See a doctor.*

But then she remembered the way the doctor at the children's hospital had twisted and probed her, not caring how much pain she was in. How he looked at her when he saw the pin pricks. He hadn't needed to say it; he figured she was doing it to herself.

No. She had to do this her way.

Back in the reception area, the receptionist was already watching her, a tight, bland smile on her face that didn't quite reach her eyes. Olivia tried to match it, tooth for tooth, but all she managed was a small grimace. In her stroller, Flora burbled.

"Cutie," the receptionist said. "What's her name?"

"Flora," Olivia said.

"Pretty. What can I do for you?"

"I'm not even sure I'm in the right place. Or if this is allowed? I should have called first, probably, or just taken five seconds to Google it. But we were in the car already and I just thought—" *Shut up, shut up, shut up.* "I'm here to see my— er—if I can, I'd like to see Shannon MacArthur. If possible." Olivia flashed a smile she hoped was charming, but the way the receptionist's eyes had glazed over meant she'd probably stopped listening.

"You know what," Olivia said, "never mind. This was dumb. I'll just—"

The receptionist cut in, "No, it's okay. Normally visiting times are structured—you need an appointment for most of our patients—but they do make exceptions. Why don't you have a seat and let me see what I can find out?"

Olivia obeyed. She picked at the hem of Flora's blanket to give her hands something to do, all the while not-so-subtly staring over the top of the stroller at the receptionist who got on the phone, frowned, then hung up and got on the phone again, only to frown deeper. Olivia strained to hear what she was saying, but her voice had dipped to barely a whisper. The receptionist caught her staring and flashed a smile that was half panic.

I should leave, Olivia thought.

But her legs wouldn't obey.

Several minutes later, the door behind the receptionist opened, and a man with too much face and too little hair stepped through. He wore a white lab coat, his shit-brown tie just visible over the collar. His glasses were too small for his face, but somehow managed to slide down his nose when he looked down at the receptionist.

"Miss, um—" The receptionist faltered, probably realizing she'd never asked for Olivia's name. "This is Doctor Tran. He'll be happy to help you."

Except Dr. Tran didn't look like he was happy to be in the room, let alone help Olivia. It took the entire time it took him to maneuver around the desk, cross the small reception area, and take Olivia's offered hand for her to make the connection.

Dr. James Tran. She remembered her grandmother mentioning him once, in passing, not meant for her ears.

Her mother's doctor.

She straightened, realizing how tightly he gripped her hand. She didn't like how deeply he looked into her face. Was it practice or habit to probe the expressions of everyone he met for signs of madness?

"I'm staring," he said finally. "Apologies. Usually it's reporters looking to speak with Ms. MacArthur, though that dropped off quite some time ago. I wasn't expecting..." He gestured to the stroller. "Unless that's a new journalistic tactic I'm not aware of."

Olivia shook her head. "My daughter. Flora."

"Lovely," he said. It sounded like *get to the point.*

From her interactions with male colleagues at the community college, Olivia knew prefacing a request with an apology was an easy way to garner...not favor, but something closer to pity, which made them more malleable to her requests. She smiled with what she hoped was naive charm, but probably looked desperate, then immediately abandoned the idea altogether.

"I know I should have called," she said, "or made an appointment. I was a little out of my head, I guess." She forced a laugh.

He raised an eyebrow.

"Right. Sorry. My name's Olivia Dahl. Well, MacArthur. Was MacArthur. I got married. Shannon was—is—my mother." It was the first time she'd said it out loud to another human being, apart from Kris. She half expected him to call her a liar. When he didn't, she continued. "I don't know what the rules are. I know there's this order in place, but I need to speak to her. I'd settle for a phone call at this point."

"Why?" he asked.

Olivia frowned. "Excuse me?"

"It's a fair question, I think. I'm not questioning who you say you are—that would be easy enough to verify—but you say you *need* to speak to her. *Need* is the kind of word that gets thrown around a lot in here, so I'm more familiar than most with its nuances. I'm also intimately familiar with the details regarding how and why Shannon MacArthur came to be in my care, so my first question for her daughter, who tells me she *needs* to speak to her, is, naturally, why?"

"With all due respect, I don't think it's any of your business."

"She's right."

Olivia and Dr. Tran looked up to see a woman—another doctor, judging by the lab coat and ID badge clipped carefully to her pocket—striding toward them. The receptionist, blatantly staring, grabbed her cell phone and started furiously tapping.

"Angela, I don't think—" Dr. Tran started, only to be cut off by the woman's hand.

"As of three months ago, Shannon MacArthur became my patient," the woman, Angela, said. "And I don't appreciate you circumventing my care this way."

"Rebecca called me."

"She was mistaken. It happens."

"Perhaps we should discuss this somewhere privately." He shot a glance at Olivia, who somehow managed to keep her mouth from hanging open.

"No need. I can handle it." She flashed a bright, pointed smile. "Thank you."

Angela watched the back of Dr. Tran's head until it disappeared behind the door. The receptionist—Rebecca, presumably—was bright red and squinting at her computer screen.

Finally, Angela turned back to Olivia and flashed the kind of smile that would have made Olivia weak in the knees under any other circumstances. "This room is way too small for a good talk. Walk with me."

Without waiting for Olivia to say anything, she started for the door, holding it open. Olivia followed, wrestling the stroller over the too-high doorstop. They walked in silence along the sidewalk, around the side of the building where an orderly was smoking and scrolling through his phone. When he looked up and saw Angela, he cursed under his breath, stubbed the cigarette, and stuck the nub in his pocket as he headed for a side entrance.

Angela ignored him, leading Olivia to a bench nestled cozily beneath a mature maple. Olivia sat, grateful, struggling to hide the fact that she couldn't seem to catch her breath. She had a feeling Angela was not the kind of woman you exposed your weaknesses to.

Angela sat beside her. Too closely, in Olivia's opinion.

"Are you okay? You look pale," she said.

"I'm fine," Olivia said, almost convincing herself. Then, "It's Angela, right?"

"Dr. Tran, technically, but Angela seems to work better around here."

"Oh. Are you two…married?"

Angela laughed. "Absolutely not. He's my father."

"I would hate that."

"It's not the best of circumstances. I was offered my choice of residencies, more prestige, better hours, but if I'd taken any of them, I wouldn't have met Shannon."

At the sound of her mother's name, Olivia stopped breathing.

"What do you know about her?" Angela continued. "Apart from the obvious?"

"Nothing, really," she lied. "My grandmother was always very tight-lipped."

"I imagine it's hard facing motherhood without your own mother around."

Olivia didn't know what to say without sounding insane, so she just nodded.

"Even one who tried to hurt you?"

Olivia should have known it was a trap. This false empathy. The toothy smile. It crossed her mind—a fleeting, horrible thought—that Kris had tracked her somehow, had deduced what she'd planned and called Sleepy Eye. Was this some kind of evaluation? She glanced over her shoulder, half expecting to see a pair of orderlies walking up with a straitjacket. She started to stand, bracing herself on the stroller. "I should go. This was a mistake."

"No. Wait," Angela said, too fast. She glanced down at the sidewalk, lips pursed, but when she looked up again that charming smile was back. "I thought you needed to speak to her?"

"What I need is to get my daughter home. She's exhausted. I'm exhausted. Just forget it."

Olivia tried to navigate the stroller away, but she missed the sidewalk and hit grass. The wheels dragged and when she tried to shove it free, something vital-sounding in her arm popped. She bit her lip until she tasted blood.

Angela moved in front of her, those eyes—yes, Olivia could see it now, the same probing eyes as Dr. Tran—digging trenches in Olivia's head.

"I'm sorry," Angela said. "I didn't mean to upset you."

Olivia scoffed.

"Honestly. I'm…protective of Shannon."

"Of—" Olivia frowned. Shook her head. "Okay."

"Would you like to sit back down?"

It felt like a test. Olivia glanced at the bench. Nodded. She sat with the stroller in front of her, a barricade, with one hand on Flora's belly.

"Okay." Angela flashed another smile. "So, you're right. There was a protective order in place, but it expired when you were eighteen. I assume your grandmother didn't tell you to, or how to, petition for renewal."

"She didn't."

"Well, that is an option. Rebecca can get you the paperwork if you like."

"I don't understand. Am I going to be allowed to talk to her or not?"

"That's not up to me."

"Who is it up to?"

"Shannon."

"What do you mean?"

"Shannon is no longer in inpatient care. She doesn't live here. What she does with her free time—when she's not in sessions with me—isn't my business, so long as it doesn't impede her progress."

Olivia's brain struggled to catch up. She wished Angela would sit or at least take a step back. The way the woman towered over her was distracting. Intimidating. "She was released?"

Angela nodded. "Three months ago."

"Where did she go?"

"I can't tell you that."

"But I'm her daughter."

"So you say. And I'm not saying I don't believe you. But Shannon's my patient. Her welfare is my first concern."

Olivia bit back her anger. She glanced down at Flora, who stared up expectantly. She couldn't give up. "Is there anything you can tell me?"

Angela considered her for what felt like a long time. "Would you say your life has been good? All things considered?"

"I don't see what that has to do with—"

"It's only a question."

"Do I have to answer it?"

"You don't *have* to do anything." Angela smiled, but it didn't reach her eyes. "Forgive me. I'm not very good at small talk and subtlety. My work requires me to be direct and succinct, and that can bleed into other conversations where it is usually construed as impolite. Trust that I don't intend to make you uncomfortable."

Olivia glanced at Flora, who raised her tiny fist, breathed a shuddering yawn, and settled, the tip of her tongue poking at her lip.

"Tell me," Angela urged. When Olivia only shook her head, Angela continued. "I can help, you know. With whatever it is."

That made Olivia finally look at her. "You don't even know me."

"I could. If you let me."

Olivia shook her head. "No. I don't need *help*. I just need to speak with my mother."

Angela placed a careful hand on Olivia's shoulder. "Sometimes we need someone to tell us what we need before we see it for ourselves."

A shiver raked down Olivia's back. "Please don't touch me."

Angela obeyed, smile unwavering. "I apologize. You're right. I don't know you, but I've been doing this job quite a while. As women, we're told to keep our issues to ourselves. Don't be too emotional or too hard. Be nurturing, but don't nurture yourself. It's hard getting up every day and just *being*. When I tell you I understand how hard it is to get up, unable to face yourself, and still have to give time and energy and your body to someone else, it can hurt. Physically and mentally."

Olivia blinked back tears. "My mother. How do I get in touch with her?"

"As her doctor, I would ask that you don't."

"Why?"

"Leave it be. Leave *her* be."

On your head be it.

The words were out before she could stop them. "And if I don't?"

Angela straightened. "Shannon's not a bad woman. I care about her very much. But what she did left a black mark inside her. You can't be near her and not get some on you." She glanced at Flora and grinned sadly before turning back to Olivia. "Or maybe that's it. Maybe you already have it in you. Either way, talking with Shannon won't help."

Tears bit the corners of Olivia's eyes. "You don't know that."

"Oh," Angela said, "but I do." She handed Olivia a business card. "Call me. Any time."

Olivia took it, if only to end the conversation. She dumped it in the first garbage can she passed. If Olivia needed help, it wasn't the kind Dr. Angela Tran could provide.

CHAPTER TWENTY

OLIVIA

Olivia trembled as she tried to hook Flora's car seat into the base. The plastic latches kept slipping out of the hooks and when she tried to steady it with her hand too close to the mechanism, she pinched her finger in the metal bit and shouted, spooking Flora.

Charlie appeared behind her, gently moving Olivia out of the way. "Hate these things…" she murmured. Then, soothing Flora with her pacifier, Charlie slipped the car seat into the base with a click.

Olivia nodded thanks, then shakily climbed into the driver's seat. Charlie climbed in a second later, and for a long moment, they sat there in heavy silence.

Released. Olivia couldn't wrap her head around it, but couldn't imagine why that Angela person would lie. Did that mean her mother was…cured?

"You were barely gone twenty minutes, so it either went very well or very badly," Charlie said. "I'm assuming badly, judging by the way that muscle in your forearm is dancing."

"She's not here," Olivia said.

Charlie frowned. "What do you mean?"

"I mean exactly what I said." Olivia took a breath. In through the nose, out through the mouth, just like in birthing class. "She was released."

"When?"

"Months ago."

"And they didn't think that was something you needed to know?"

Olivia shook her head.

"Well do you know where she went?"

"No," Olivia lied. "I have no idea."

———————————

It was impossible to find parking in front of Aunt Erin's apartment building. She lived in one of the oldest parts of the city where buildings butted up against each other for warmth, and the streets were just wide enough for a horse and buggy. There was a small parking lot beside the building—residents only. Olivia drove slowly past it, nodding to herself when she spotted Aunt Erin's blue Corolla. She circled the block twice, one arm stretched into the backseat as she tried to calm Flora's pretantrum whimper. On the third go-around, she spotted a car pulling off the curb. Another car coming the other direction must have seen it too, but Olivia was faster, sliding into the empty spot with the practiced ease of a Tokyo drifter.

She ignored the other driver flipping her off as he drove past, then wrestled Flora's car seat out of the back. She was running out of time. After leaving Sleepy Eye, Olivia offered to take Charlie home, only to remember she'd left her car at Olivia's place. There, Olivia made a big show of needing to get Flora down for a nap and to clean, and no she didn't want to talk about where Shannon might be, but yes she would call her later, until finally Charlie left.

She didn't have long until Kris called to check up on them. She'd already texted once to let Olivia know she'd be working a little late, but Olivia's terse

Okay reply wouldn't go unchecked for long. If Olivia took much longer getting home, she might have to come up with some elaborate lie about where they'd been and what they'd done because it was easier than telling her the truth.

Now, before Olivia could make it up the curb, her left knee gave out. She barely caught the trunk in time to keep them both upright. She was so *tired*. Tears stung her eyes. "God damn it. God fucking—" She lurched upright, panting as she wriggled the car seat back into the car. Her heart felt like it was going to pound out of her chest and her arms had begun to tingle. She couldn't carry the car seat up the stairs to Aunt Erin's second-floor apartment, and it wasn't like she could just leave Flora in the car.

Just call her, a voice in her head whispered.

The coward in her wanted to agree, but phone calls could be avoided. If Olivia didn't confront her in person, now, while she still had the fire burning in her belly, she doubted she ever would.

She scooped Flora out of the car seat, cradling her against her shoulder. If her knee gave out again and they both went down, Flora wasn't as safe without the car seat, but with the car seat she was too heavy. Flora molded herself against Olivia's shoulder, resting her head in the crook of her neck, like she was made to fit there. The tingle in her arms worsened, but Olivia steeled herself and started for the stairs, trying not to picture Flora's head cracked open like a melon on the stone steps.

The security door was (thankfully) unlocked, so she let herself in and started up another set of stairs to the second floor. The building was old and not well-maintained, so the metal railing wobbled as Olivia leaned on it for support.

Flora coughed into her neck and, for the millionth time today, Olivia felt the pinch of her bad mothering.

In for a penny, she thought.

It was only October, but hanging on Aunt Erin's door was a Christmas wreath, the artificial cinnamon scent mingling with the pot stink from someone's apartment. Olivia pinched the bridge of her nose against the impending headache. Someone had impaled a note on a holly stem: *For the last time please turn your TV down!!!*

Olivia leaned in toward the door, listening. It was possible Aunt Erin was out with one of her girls, but she also knew Erin had a thing about driving herself.

"Always have an out," she told Olivia once.

She knocked on the door and heard footsteps pause on the other side, probably Aunt Erin peering through the peephole. Olivia stood to one side, leaving only her shoulder visible, just in case. The chain came off and the door opened.

Aunt Erin's face fell just long enough for Olivia to catch the drop, then lifted into a toothy smile. "Livvy! What are you doing here?"

"Can I come in?" Olivia asked.

Aunt Erin hesitated, only for a second, but it was long enough for Olivia to know she was in the right place.

"For a few minutes, I suppose," Aunt Erin said, "since you're already here." She opened the door wider and shepherded Olivia to the living room, shutting one of the bedroom doors as they passed. "I have plans though, so it'll have to be a short visit." She smiled. "Kris and I talked about me coming by more often. To help. I know everything is overwhelming right now, but I think with some extra hands on the laundry and dishes you'll feel right as rain in no time."

She was talking too fast, messing with the clasp on her bracelet.

Olivia laid Flora on the couch—a floral number that always smelled like bourbon and lilac—and sat, opening and closing her hands to get some feeling back into them. Flora caught hold of a loose thread and shoved it into her mouth. Olivia only just grabbed it as Flora was starting to gag.

Aunt Erin watched from the other side of the room, one arm braced on the wall, the other angled back, hand itchy for the door. She glanced once, twice, three times up at the clock in a matter of seconds.

"Where are you going?" Olivia asked.

"What?" Aunt Erin snapped back to attention.

"You said you have plans. Where are you going? Somewhere fun?"

"Just dinner, dear. Nothing exciting."

"A date?"

"A friend."

The back of Olivia's mouth burned with bile. She swallowed. "Anyone I know?"

Aunt Erin forced a laugh. "Chatty today, eh? I get it. I don't know what I'd do if I had to be stuck in this place all day. You could have called though. I said you could call any time."

Olivia nodded. "I know."

She fiddled with one of the snaps on Flora's onesie and it slipped beneath her thumbnail, prying it up from the skin. A wave of nausea washed over her as she eased it back down. She could feel the sweat on her forehead, a sickly sheen she never seemed to be able to wash away. She wanted Aunt Erin to read her mind, to explain before Olivia needed to ask.

"So," Aunt Erin said, "what's new?"

Olivia looked up suddenly, startling her. "I went to Sleepy Eye today."

Had to give Aunt Erin credit. She didn't bat an eyelash. She'd clearly missed her calling as a daytime actress. "Oh? What for?"

"Cut the shit, Aunty. Please. I'm too tired. It was a long drive." When Aunt Erin didn't respond, Olivia bit the inside of her cheek to keep from screaming. "I'm not twelve anymore, okay? I know that's where my mother has been, just like I know now that she's been released. Where is she?"

"News to me," Aunt Erin said, eyes darting up to the clock. "But it doesn't matter, does it? Because there's that order in place. You and Flora are safe. I promise."

"The order expired when I was eighteen, but I guess no one told you that either." Aunt Erin blanched.

"Feels shitty, right? People not telling you important things." Flora started to whine, so Olivia scooped her onto her shoulder, patting her back. It wouldn't help for long. It'd been hours since Flora ate. She was probably starving. "I just want to know where she is."

"I told you, you're—"

"Safe?" Olivia laughed, absently tugging on the loose nail, relishing the pain a little. "I just want to talk to her."

Aunt Erin held her hands out, supplicant. "I get it. I do. You want to understand, but trust me, doctors have tried, I have tried; no one will ever understand what made her do what she did."

Olivia shook her head. "Just tell me where to find her, okay? Does she have an apartment or something?" She looked around, studying the walls, the floor, for answers. She spotted a couple of boxes in the corner, official-looking white labels affixed to the corners she couldn't quite read. Moving boxes. Aunt Erin knew exactly where Olivia's mother lived because she was living *here*.

"If they didn't tell you anything at the hospital, then they probably don't want me saying anything either," Aunt Erin said, but Olivia was only half listening.

Why had Aunt Erin shut the bedroom door when she came in?

Still holding Flora, Olivia lurched off the couch and went to the bedroom door with Aunt Erin on her heels.

What if she's in there? Hiding?

Olivia's arm seemed to move without her permission. She opened the door, holding her breath.

The bed was made, an old pink and lilac quilt draped neatly over the twin-sized mattress. The only other furniture was a cheap end table, the legs scuffed and chipped. An empty mug sat next to a notebook, pen poking out from the middle.

Clothes littered the floor. A framed print of some anonymous landscape had been hung on the wall, slightly crooked. The room looked lived in, but smelled stale. Olivia locked her knees to keep from running across the room and opening the window.

"She lives with you," Olivia said, giving voice to her suspicions.

Aunt Erin sighed. "I'm sorry, Liv. Truly. I wanted to tell you—"

Olivia put her hand up, then stepped into the room and shut the door behind her. Her arms shook with the effort of holding Flora, but she didn't dare put her on the bed. How long ago had Olivia's mother been in that bed? Was it still warm? She resisted the urge to climb beneath the covers, to cocoon herself in the sheets and smother herself in the pillow.

A soft knock on the door made her jump.

"Liv?" Aunt Erin said. "You okay?"

Olivia didn't answer. She eyed the closet, her stomach in knots. Her skin felt hot and cold at the same time, unable to shake the feeling of eyes on her.

"Liv?"

There was no lock on the door, so Olivia had to hope Aunt Erin wouldn't bust in and drag her out. Swallowing the lump in her throat, she crossed the room and threw open the closet door only to find it mostly empty—a few hangers, one or two sweaters, and a coat that looked new.

"She's with her doctor," Aunt Erin said through the door. "I have to get her soon. Please, Liv."

Olivia frowned. Angela said she was her mother's doctor. Surely Aunt Erin wouldn't drive two hours one way to take her mother to an appointment.

"Liv?"

She couldn't think. There was too much and not enough in her head and Aunt Erin kept knocking and Flora was crying and she could feel her breasts starting to leak despite the rest of her body going numb. She couldn't stay here.

Her gaze flicked to the nightstand. The notebook.

She had to see.

Checking once over her shoulder to make sure the door was still shut, Olivia flipped to a random page. The handwriting was small and slanted, hurried in some places and slow and deliberate in others. Near the top of the page, her gaze zeroed in on her name:

God help me, Olivia, this is my truth.

Without thinking, Olivia shut the notebook and shoved it down the side of her pants, half hidden beneath her sweater. The spine dug painfully into her ribs. Heart hammering and head aching with the force of Flora's cries, she finally opened the door and breezed past Aunt Erin, ignoring her pleas for forgiveness and understanding. She slammed the apartment door behind her.

The adrenaline didn't peter out until they were almost home, and by the time she pulled into the driveway, she barely had the energy to shove the gearshift into park. Flora hadn't stopped crying the entire drive—her face red and blotchy, foam collecting in the corners of her mouth. Kris would be home any minute. If she came in and heard Flora screaming, she'd insist on taking more time off, on keeping watch on Olivia. She could feel the notebook, still hidden under her sweater, hot and pounding like a heartbeat against her skin.

Rather than try and get them both inside, Olivia climbed into the back seat, unclipped Flora from the car seat and nursed her there. She barely registered the pain as Flora latched, but watched, equal parts fascinated and horrified as Flora dug her nails into Olivia's breast. The skin gave easily, like the skin of an overripe peach, and drops of blood trickled between Flora's fingers.

The black-haired woman watched from the rearview mirror. *Bad mommy.* Olivia was being punished.

Kris came home just as Olivia laid Flora down in the bedroom. She frantically wiped the blood from Flora's fingers, only to look back and see that they were clean. She inspected her skin, expecting to find raw, scabbed skin. There wasn't even a scratch.

She shoved the notebook in her top drawer, took one look in the mirror and cringed. She looked like hell. The skin under her eyes looked bruised, and her hair hung limp and damp with sweat.

"Babe?" Kris called from the front of the house. "Are you here?"

Olivia bolted for the bathroom, shedding clothes as she went. She turned on the shower and stepped in, flinching at the cold. "In here!"

Footsteps echoed down the hallway as the water finally started to heat up. Olivia frantically squirted shampoo into her hair and started to scrub just as Kris peered around the curtain.

"Hey," she said.

Olivia kept her back to her, still scrubbing. "Hey yourself."

"Everything okay?"

"Yeah," Olivia said, too quickly. "Why wouldn't it be?"

"Did you go anywhere?"

"No."

Kris paused a beat. "Not even to, like, the store or something?"

"Nope." She hesitated before adding, "Why?"

Olivia felt Kris looking at her. Before Flora, Olivia had never felt self-conscious about her wife looking at her body, but now she felt exposed, like she'd been cut open, her insides bared for Kris to examine. A chill snaked down her back and she realized she'd been standing there too long, fingers tangled in soapy hair, not moving. Rather than turn around, she stepped into the stream face-first, soap streaming down her face and burning her eyes.

"No reason," Kris said. "Where's Flora?"

Olivia moved out of the water and wiped her face. Clumps of hair remained tangled around her fingers and clung to her body as she stood under the stream. Why wouldn't Kris leave? "Sleeping."

"She doesn't normally sleep right now."

"Late lunch. She ate and passed out."

"Why late?"

"I don't know," Olivia snapped. "Why don't you ask her?"

Kris softened. "I'm only asking about your day."

"Can it wait until I'm out of the shower?"

Kris didn't answer. By the time Olivia got up the nerve to turn and look at her, Kris was gone. The door closed with a soft click.

Out of the shower, she was relieved to see her clothes still on the floor, but her dresser drawer, the one where she'd stashed the notebook, was slightly open, as if someone had rummaged around inside but didn't bother to check that they'd closed it all the way. She heard Kris in the kitchen. Had she found the notebook? Was she reading it?

No, thank God. Olivia found it buried beneath the pile of lacy underwear she never wore. She needed to hide it somewhere else, somewhere Kris had no reason to look. Judging by Kris's anxious cabinet-slamming, Olivia didn't have long. But everywhere she thought to shove it, she imagined a hundred ways Kris would happen upon it. Olivia hadn't even fully committed to the idea of reading it herself; if Kris got to it first, she wouldn't have a choice. Finally, she settled on the garment bag that held her wedding dress. Hanging in the back of their closet, untouched for close to four years, it was probably the last place Kris would think to look. Olivia hid the notebook in the folds of the train before zipping the bag and moving more clothes in front of it.

After checking that Flora was still asleep, Olivia went into the kitchen. Kris was on her cell phone, leaning on the counter, forehead resting in her hand, voice too low for Olivia to make out what she was saying. She stood at the other end of the counter, straining to hear. Kris must have sensed her though. She muttered, "Gotta go," before sticking her phone in her pocket. When she looked up, her smile was all teeth.

"Feel better?" Kris asked.

"Who was that?" Olivia asked, trying and failing at nonchalance.

"No one. Work." Kris lifted her eyebrow, as though daring Olivia to challenge her.

It was like a line had been drawn and both of them had crossed it without realizing. They didn't lie to each other, not about anything that mattered. It was new territory, an almost out-of-body experience, but Olivia still had a choice. Backtrack, tell Kris the truth about where she'd been and what she found and hope she wouldn't sound as insane as she felt. Kris might not understand at first, or ever, but she had to give Olivia credit, right? This was what she wanted— honesty and vulnerability. She wanted Olivia to trust her, to depend on her, and for the whole of their marriage, Olivia had been happy to.

Now?

Olivia strode past her toward the fridge, opening the door and staring in, stomach turning with the smell of ancient leftovers. "Any disasters?"

Kris almost sounded disappointed. "Nope. Everything's fine."

"Good." Olivia wiped the corner of her eye with her shoulder. "I'm glad."

The rest of the night, there was a wall between them—Olivia and her mother's notebook on one side, Kris and her secrets on the other. Every time Olivia was tempted to scale it, a voice whispered to her that it was that doctor on the phone, that one wrong move stood between Olivia and a hospital. So she stayed put, silently nursing Flora and then passing her off to Kris for bath and bedtime.

"Tuckered out," Kris said after laying Flora down. "I didn't think she'd sleep with the late nap."

"Must have been tired," Olivia said.

"Must have been."

Olivia could have filled a mountain with everything they didn't say to each other. They tried to watch a movie, but all Olivia could think about was the notebook, and Kris kept fiddling with her phone, angling her body away when Olivia tried to get a look. Ten o'clock came and went, and Olivia expected Kris to go to bed—she wasn't a night person and usually went to sleep early, conking out before her head even hit the pillow. But tonight she was fighting it. Was she waiting for Olivia to go to bed first?

By midnight, Olivia was exhausted. Kris squinted at the television. More than once, Olivia caught her pinching her thigh to keep herself awake.

This was insane. She should stop it.

"Tea?" Olivia asked.

Kris shrugged.

In the kitchen, Olivia filled the electric kettle and pulled down two mugs.

Later, she would tell herself she hadn't intended to go into the junk drawer and root around until she found the sleep-aid samples Kris's doctor gave her last year when work stress translated into horrible insomnia. But once it was in her hand, she stopped thinking. She crushed the pills beneath one of the mugs, and then scraped the remains into it. She let it dissolve in the hot water before adding a tea bag and a glob of honey, hoping it would mask the bitter taste.

Even as she handed her wife the tea, she knew she wouldn't get away with it.

It only took a few minutes for the drugs to work. Kris fell quickly and easily asleep on the couch. Olivia eased her back and covered her with a blanket, already rehearsing the conversation for the next day: *You fell asleep. You were so tired, I didn't want to move you.*

Olivia went straight to the bedroom and shut the door, leaving the light off. Using her phone as a flashlight, she unzipped the garment bag and pulled out the notebook, which she set gingerly in her lap. She didn't doubt her mother knew it was missing, but she wondered if she would say anything to Aunt Erin or if Aunt Erin would put two and two together and tell her.

She opened to the first page.

I never wanted to be a parent.

"No."

Olivia slapped it shut again, her eyes burning. She couldn't do this.

She shut off the phone's flashlight, but instead of putting it away, she scrolled until she found Aunt Erin's number. Hit the Send button before she could stop herself.

"Hello?"

It was a stranger's voice. Too supine to be Aunt Erin's. Too timid.

There was only one person it could be.

Olivia clutched the phone with both hands, holding her breath, praying Flora didn't pick now to wake up.

"Is anyone there?"

She tried to lock the sound of her mother's voice away in a box in her mind, to memorize the exact tone and cadence and pitch.

"Olivia?"

Her breath caught.

"Olivia. Oh, God, is it really—"

A strangled noise came out of Olivia's throat as she smashed the icons, trying to hang up. She turned it off and shoved it into the garment bag beside the notebook before crawling into bed and covering her head with the blanket.

CHAPTER TWENTY-ONE

SHANNON

I t's been eight days since the kitchen. I have to stop myself from going back down there and looking in the pantry because every night just before I'm about to fall asleep, I hear her whispering in my ear.

Nightmares, probably. I want to tell Angela about them. Make her put me on those heavy-duty tranquilizers they gave me in the beginning that made the night like a big pool of pudding I could just sink into. I can't though. Not when I've come this far.

It took some begging, but I got Angela to agree to a joint session with me and Jennifer.

"I want to apologize," I said. "I still don't know quite what happened, but I want to make things right with her."

Thirty minutes to go.

I was looking forward to my next shift at Bethany Home until I realized I wouldn't be alone.

"Get used to it," my mother said. "Where you go, Olivia goes."

Of course I wanted you to go with me. I never wanted you to leave my side, but there was something about the way you looked at me—through me—from my mother's arms that made the back of my head buzz.

"We never went anywhere you went," I said.

My mother smiled, like she'd won. "I had your father." Then, "It's not too late, you know. We could have dinner with Matthew, let him know what kind of compensation we think is fair—"

I cut her off. "No. It's fine." I glanced at the baby—so much like you, and so much not you. "She can come."

———

Marcia met me at the front door, hands already outstretched and aiming for the stroller. Once she had the baby in her arms, it was like a switch had flipped—gone was the hard face and stiff back. She buried her face in the blanket and made a sound of pure pleasure.

"I know I'm being ridiculous," she said, "and normally I wouldn't be. I like babies just fine, but goodness, Shannon, she is just beautiful."

I offered a small smile. "Thank you."

"I don't know how your mother can stand to let her out of the house. I remember when your brothers were born—John Jack, especially. Those eyelashes. She'd show them to anyone who could stand to listen." She gently tapped the baby's nose with the tip of her finger. "Don't tell her I said this, but this little one outshines even him."

It was hard not to feel a bubble of pride, even as I doubted you. Maybe I was wrong, I thought. I'd let Iris get in my head and twist my mind around her finger, just how Marcia warned me she would. But even as my muscles loosened and the grip on my heart faded and a genuine smile spread across my face, I heard Iris in my head—*they breathe life into it and make you love it.*

The longer I watched Marcia fawn over you, the more unusual it looked. Like there was some kind of spell cast over her.

Finally, Marcia set you back in the stroller and sighed as she looked at me. "You're sure you can do this?"

I didn't know whether she was referring to you or the work at Bethany Home. Either way, I nodded.

She grinned. "Good to see a young woman with some gumption. Maybe seeing you and Olivia, seeing you carrying on despite it all, will be good for the mothers. Inspiring."

"Sure," I said. "Sounds great."

Until we could work out a more permanent arrangement, Marcia sent me into the rec room. During recreation time, the mothers were watched over by no less than two orderlies and a handful of volunteers. The orderlies' job was to take a measure of the room, defuse any arguments or fights. No one ever said it out loud (except Tina, during one memorable tirade), but the volunteers' only purpose was to keep watch on the orderlies. Marcia didn't trust them not to manhandle the mothers, especially the mouthy ones, when there weren't witnesses around.

All I needed to do was hang out in the corner, keep you happy, and maybe walk one of the mothers to the bathroom if there was no one else around.

Easy.

Except the second I wheeled the stroller into the rec room, it was like someone had hit me with a spotlight. Every eye in the room was on me, boring so hard I could practically feel them on my skin.

"Is she serious?" someone muttered.

"Gonna be a fuckin' brawl," someone else said.

I pretended not to hear, settling in one of the corner chairs with the stroller parked in front of me, the wheels locked and my feet tucked behind them as an extra precaution.

The mothers wouldn't have hurt you. Even if I'd begged, if they had no one to help, Marcia wouldn't have allowed it if she thought for a second you were in danger. But that didn't mean they wouldn't want a look. Wouldn't try to wander off with you if they thought they could get away with it.

Within seconds, one of them—a stocky woman with a soft face and hair they kept buzzed because she couldn't stop pulling it out—started toward me. I made eye contact with one of the orderlies, who looked too ready to tackle her, and shook my head.

The stocky woman—Laura—paused a foot away from the stroller, arching her neck hard enough it popped. "Can I see?" she asked.

I tucked my feet further behind the wheels and nodded.

Wringing her hands, she stepped closer and peered into the stroller. Her expression fell—hope turned to disappointment. She shook her head. "No. That's not right. That's not her."

My stomach did a flip.

Laura hugged herself, digging her fingers into her ribs until it looked painful. "Liars. Liars. She's supposed to come back, they promised she would come back, but it's not her. You lied to me, you *liars!*"

Her shout startled you, and when you cried, it was like a bomb had gone off.

Before the mothers reacted, the orderlies started shouting, which made the mothers go into panic mode. The other volunteers sneered at me—*look what you've done*—before attempting to get between the orderlies and the mothers, both bent on doing as much damage to the other as possible.

I quickly kicked the locks up on the stroller wheels, but when I tried to push the stroller back, it wouldn't budge. Laura had her foot lodged behind one of the wheels.

"Move," I said.

But it was like she didn't hear me. She kept shaking her head, lips moving, but no sound came out.

Finally, she looked at me and it was like her face had aged a hundred years. The corners of her mouth turned deeply down, and the blue of her eyes had faded to a dirty mop-water gray.

"They took her from me," Laura said, barely loud enough to be heard over the others shouting. "She was in my arms and then they took her. They told me if I was good and did what I was told and got better, they'd bring her back. They promised." She glanced in the stroller again. Studied your red face. "They're never going to bring her back, are they?"

"I don't know," I said.

"She said they wouldn't, and I didn't believe her. She said I'd have to find her and take her back."

I couldn't stop looking at her hands, how close they were to the stroller, how they opened and closed, limbering up. I tried to stand, but I was trapped between the stroller and Laura.

"I'm sure she didn't mean it," I said, not knowing who she was. "I'm sure if you just—"

"The black-haired woman doesn't lie."

I stilled. "You know her? You've met her?" I tried to shove the stroller back so I could stand, but Laura was stronger. Inside, you wailed. "Who is she?"

Laura smiled, all teeth. "You know her. You've met her."

My whole body went cold. I couldn't stop myself from looking at you.

"Who is she?" I asked again. "Tell me."

"Enough." One of the orderlies grabbed Laura by the arm and twisted, yanking her back. "Leave the kid alone."

Laura's face twisted in pain.

"Stop," I said. "She's fine. It's fine."

"S'not fine and you know it," the orderly snapped. "Marcia ought to know better, bringing a baby in here." He looked me up and down, and the annoyance on his face morphed into something else. Something hungry. I could *feel* the shift. I noticed how much taller than me he was, remembered how easily he'd tossed Laura around. When he smiled, it made my stomach clench.

"Sorry," he said, not sounding sorry at all. "Long day, y'know? I don't mean to yell like that, especially to a young lady. How about I make it up to you? Lunch? My treat."

I wish I could say I told him to fuck off, that I kneed him in the balls and rolled over his feet with the stroller and kicked him in the shins as I passed. I didn't do any of those things, even though I knew what he was proposing didn't stop at a sandwich.

A voice in the back of my head told me to get used to it. That this was all I was good for now that I'd ruined myself. *You'll need to feed her*, the voice said. *You'll need money. You think your mother will keep a roof over your head forever? What kind of job are you going to get with no high school diploma, no experience, and a screaming baby pulling you away every other day? Tell him you'll put it in your mouth for ten dollars.*

The voice was so loud I couldn't hear anything else, not even you. Shaking my head, I finally wrangled the stroller free and practically ran from the rec room, not paying attention to where I was going. I needed to get out of there, needed to get somewhere I could think, somewhere I could clear my mind.

I didn't realize I'd run toward Iris's room until I saw the door standing ajar. I started to turn away, but something on the floor, barely visible from the hallway, made me stop. I scooped you out of the stroller—I couldn't let you sit there, and I wasn't going to try to maneuver the stroller into the small room, especially if it meant getting cornered again—and your wailing softened into hiccups. I patted your back, whether to comfort you or me I didn't know, and eased the door the rest of the way open with my foot.

No Iris, but the room looked like a tornado had gone through it. The bed covers were thrown aside, the mattress teetering on the edge of falling off the frame. The fabric of the chair I'd sat in weeks ago was torn. Drawings littered the floor, most of them crumpled. A few looked like the corners had been bitten off, the edges of the tear still damp.

I righted the mattress and laid you on the bed, tucking a pillow beside you in case you decided to roll, then kneeled beside the drawings. They were all of the same woman, hair drawn so black and with such force the pencil dragged holes in the page. In some images, the woman's eyes were cast somewhere in the distance, like she was looking over my shoulder. In others, it was like she was real, like she could see all the way through to the heart of me.

As I gathered the pages and flipped through, the woman's face slowly changed. Her chin softened and her eyes turned downward at the corners. Her cheeks sank in. It took a moment for me to realize Iris had drawn herself, her short blond hair replaced with long black snarls.

Me, she'd written beneath the picture.

Then the woman's face changed again. Small, light eyes became larger, darker. The lips filled out and the nose shortened. I was looking at my face, surrounded by thick black hair.

Beneath the drawing: *You.*

Hands shaking, I flipped the page again and the face staring back had been smeared like a picture taken at the moment the woman moved, her features blurring across the page.

Us.

Movement in the corner of my eye made me look up. I froze.

The woman hovered over the bed, practically horizontal, black-dirty toes grazing the mattress. Her hair fell like a curtain, covering her face, covering you. Under the mud and peat, her clothes looked eerily familiar. It took too long to realize they were mine. And when she finally turned to face me—each movement so slow it seemed to last a million years—with black eyes and yellow, rotten teeth, it was my face she wore. My smile that split it.

I could swear my heart stopped. Time stopped. But the woman moved through it like a fly through honey, leaning slowly, carefully down until her face was inches from yours.

No, a voice whispered in the back of my head. It isn't you on the bed. *This isn't my baby. It's hers. See the way she looks at her? How she reaches out when she should be afraid?*

I found myself nodding.

The black-haired woman may have been wearing my face, but *you* would know better. *You* would know to be afraid.

She leaned down and kissed the baby's forehead, and I felt the pressure on my own lips. Could taste the mud on them. I held my breath, but it didn't stop her putrid breath from invading my lungs. My whole body tingled, like ants were crawling beneath my skin. I could feel them biting at my muscles and scratching my bones. Like they were tunneling. Like they were making room. She caressed the baby with a hideous brown nail and then she began to turn her head, eyes moving slowly toward me.

A bang behind me made me jump.

"Oh, thank goodness." Marcia strode into the room, nodding. "I was hoping you two were alright. They told me—" She paused. "Are you okay?"

"The woman—" I started, but the black-haired woman was gone. I swallowed the bile in the back of my throat, still tasting dirt.

The baby's burble seemed to bring Marcia back into herself. Made her realize where we were. "Where's Iris?"

"I don't know," I said. "The door was open. I saw—" I shook my head. "She wasn't here."

"Get Olivia and go to my office," Maria ordered.

"Is something—?"

Her expression could have melted ice. "Now."

With the baby in the stroller, I all but ran in the direction I thought Marcia's office was in, but I was all turned around inside. Nothing looked right and each time I passed an open doorway, I saw the black-haired woman, still wearing my face. There and gone again with a blink.

I could still hear the chaos in the rec room. Two orderlies were nothing against nine or ten mothers, especially when they got in their heads they'd been wronged (and they'd been wronged a lot). I felt like I was going in circles, and the stroller seemed to get heavier, like the wheels were caught in concrete. Finally I spotted a hallway I thought looked familiar and ducked down it, away from the noise and doorways and big black eyes.

It was a wide hallway, different from the rest of the building. An add-on, judging by the cement block and plaster. A cheap add-on, my dad would have said. I smelled bleach and antiseptic, strong enough it made my eyes water.

This was the wrong way, I knew that, but something pulled me deeper down the hall, my head swimming and nose running. In the stroller, the baby gagged. The last door on the left was cracked open, the one with a bright-red sign that read *Staff Only*. A harsh yellow light dripped into the hall from the other side.

I should have turned back.

Instead, I nudged the door open wider and saw Iris standing in the middle of the room, surrounded by metal shelves of neon-colored cleaning supplies and towels. She was soaked, her hair dripping and her clothes sticking to her skin. I covered my nose and mouth—the bleach and ammonia miasma so strong it burned my throat and made my skin itch.

It was Iris. She was covered in it.

When she looked up at me, her eyes were solid black.

"It was my fault," she said. "I lost my baby because I wasn't looking. I wasn't listening. At first, she only came in the night, when it was too long between the baby's kicks, and I laid there, pretending everything was fine. She stood over me, pinning me to the bed with her big black eyes."

My body went cold as hot breath brushed the back of my neck.

"I saw her in the mirror," Iris said, "every time I looked into it and told myself I would be a good mother." She took a step toward me. "You can't lie to her, Shannon. She sees everything you feel. Everything you think. She knows you." Tears ran down her cheeks. "Don't let her get inside you."

I shrank back against the wall, wishing, begging it to split open, to let me crawl inside.

Iris's neck bent with an audible snap, and her voice twisted like metal. "She's a beautiful baby. Looks just like her mommy."

I glanced toward the stroller where the baby's face was just visible. Her eyes were twin black coals.

I screamed loud enough I didn't hear the click of the lighter, didn't hear the whoosh of Iris's body catch. But I felt the heat, like being thrown head-first into an oven. The hair on my arms singed as I struggled to claw my way along the wall, away from the room, away from Iris's black eyes, bubbling as the fire ate her.

————————

Jennifer won't look at me. Won't talk to me. But she hasn't asked to leave, so it's a start.

"I won't make excuses," I begin, getting a nod of approval from Angela. "In the past, my behavior has been…erratic, and hurt people I care about. I want you to know that I would never do anything to intentionally hurt you."

Jennifer buries her face deeper in her hair.

"I want us to be friends," I say. "If you don't want that, I understand." I pause, weighing my words carefully. "Being here as long as I have, I know it's hard to get to know people because you're too busy trying to relearn yourself. But I think you and I have too much in common to not give this another try."

I wait for a response, but none comes. I look at Angela and shrug.

"You don't have to give forgiveness," Angela says to Jennifer, "but it can go a long way toward healing."

I can see from the small glimpses of her face I get through her hair, Jennifer doesn't want anything to do with forgiving me. I don't blame her, but if she keeps refusing, it could ruin everything. I can't have that. I need to get out of here. To see you. Hold you. No matter what it takes. I think Jennifer would understand.

In my room after, I stretch out on my bed, digging my hands beneath the pillow where it gets cool from being against the wall, and my fingers brush against paper. At first I think it's a tag from the pillowcase, but when I sit up and pull, the paper slides free.

It's a note, written in pencil on the back of a canned tomato sauce label.

Ain't dead.

CHAPTER TWENTY-TWO

OLIVIA

S he thought it was Kris.

Bleary-eyed, the edges of her mind still clinging to the nightmare world where she hung from a tree, branches impaling her by her arms and hips, Olivia saw the figure in the doorway and was relieved to see her wife. Except in the dark, she didn't look right.

Honey, what big eyes you have.

The only light came from behind her, and Olivia's eyes took too long to adjust. By the time the figure came into focus, it was too late. Olivia froze as the black-haired woman inched into her bedroom, her shuffle-steps like electric shocks to Olivia's nerves. The woman had barely moved, but the door closed behind her, bathing them both in blackness. Olivia strained to see through the dark, barely glimpsing the shadows of the woman's movements. She could smell her—peat and dirt and something sickly sweet—and it turned her stomach.

Olivia tried to scream. All that came out was a pathetic gasp.

"I want her back," the woman said.

Olivia's arms and legs were stiff as boards. Flora slept in her bassinet only a foot away, but it might as well have been miles.

"Who?" Olivia's voice was barely above a whisper.

The woman's teeth flashed. "My little girl."

Wake up, wake up, wake up. Why didn't Kris wake up?

Because you drugged her. You're a horrible wife and mother and now you're going to die and it's all your fault.

"Stay away from her," Olivia growled.

The woman leaned in close to Olivia, so close she could feel the woman's breath on her face. "Oh," she whispered. "Mommy's mad."

"Stay away from her!"

The woman giggled. "Almost ready." She cast one last look at Flora, then at Olivia, lingering on her a beat too long, before finally turning back toward the door. Her hair dragged on the corner of the bed, close to Olivia's feet. Waves of revulsion washed over her. Her head swam with it.

Finally, the woman opened the bedroom door and left, closing it behind her.

At the click of the door, it was like a spell broke. Olivia scrambled out of bed and to Flora's bassinet. Her little belly rose and fell with the rhythmic breath of deep sleep. To doubly assure herself, she gently placed the back of her hand beneath Flora's nose. Frowning, she licked her skin and tried again. No. She still didn't feel anything. But Flora was clearly breathing. She was alive. She was safe.

For now.

It took ages to get up the nerve to walk into the living room. Kris was still on the couch, in the exact position Olivia had left her in. It was hard not to resent her—wife and child in danger, and she snoozes soundly, none the wiser. Was it her fault? No. But that didn't change how little she seemed to care about how Olivia was struggling.

The start of their marriage had been a sort of *fuck you* to the rest of the world. It'd only been legal for a few months in the United States, so obtaining a marriage certificate felt almost illicit, especially to Olivia. Being a woman married to another woman had put her into a box, separating her from family and acquaintances. She didn't mind though, because Kris was in the box with her. Getting married was supposed to mean that she would always have someone in her corner, someone to be on her side, no questions asked. Except now, Olivia had never felt more isolated.

She spotted Kris's phone on the floor, having fallen out of Kris's hand when she passed out. The blue notification light blinked.

They didn't hide things from each other. They didn't used to, anyway, and before this moment, Olivia wouldn't have thought twice about turning around and leaving the phone where it was.

She picked it up and entered Kris's pin before she could change her mind.

A new email. Work. Nothing special. She almost put the phone back, but she couldn't shake the feeling in the pit of her stomach, that deep wrongness she couldn't put a name to. She scrolled through Kris's text messages and social media—nothing stood out. She pulled up her search history and had to bite her lip to keep from crying.

Postpartum depression

Baby blues

Mother psychiatric care

When are baby blues dangerous

Sleepy Eye Hospital

Kris might have been her wife, but she wasn't on her side.

Olivia didn't sleep the rest of the night, pinching herself awake when she started to nod off. Fingertip bruises dotted her arm by the time the first rays of morning peeked through the blinds. At 6:00 a.m., Kris's phone alarm went off. Olivia sank low under the blankets and closed her eyes, struggling to pretend to be asleep without actually falling asleep.

The alarm continued, cycling through various pitches and volumes. Olivia buried her head in the pillow to try and drown out the sound. She heard a thump and a groan and then finally the alarm stopped.

"Babe?" Kris called groggily from the living room.

Olivia shut her eyes tight. Focused on keeping her breath slow and regular.

"Liv?"

She heard Kris trudge through the hall, and then the bedroom door creaked open. Olivia could feel Kris watching her. Could feel her face getting hot. Did she know what Olivia had done to her? A small, petty part of Olivia hoped she did. After seeing Kris's search history, she was itching for a fight.

"Why didn't you wake me up?" Kris asked.

Olivia was tempted to continuing feigning sleep, but what was the point? She couldn't avoid her wife forever. She opened her eyes and sat up, tucking the blankets around her middle. "I didn't realize I had to."

Kris frowned. "Did something happen?"

"I don't know, Kris. Did something happen?"

Frozen in the doorway, Kris looked like hell. A cushion scar marred her cheek, and her eyes were red, the skin under them bluish and swollen. Olivia felt a fleeting moment of guilt—had she overdone it with the sleeping pills?—but it passed just as quickly.

Kris absently patted her pocket. Grabbing for her phone, maybe. Her expression went blank, like she was trying to hide her thoughts, but they'd been together too long for Olivia not to know what she was thinking.

Olivia's only regret was not looking through the call history. She'd have bet everything she owned that Kris had made a call to Sleepy Eye. Maybe she'd even talked to Angela. Was that why Angela had been pushing so hard when Olivia wouldn't talk about herself?

She studied Kris's face, but the blank expression remained.

Say something, Olivia silently begged. *Tell me I'm wrong.*

"You should have woken me up," Kris said. "You know I can't sleep on that couch. My back kills."

It was like someone had died. Olivia felt the ache all the way to her bones.

"I didn't because, frankly, I was pissed at you." She made a show of checking Flora, adjusting her blanket, and then lowered her voice. "You're gonna be late."

Olivia felt Kris looking hard at her and struggled not to cringe under the weight of it.

"I'm gonna stay home today, I think," Kris said.

"Why?"

"I don't feel good."

Olivia worked her jaw. "Okay."

A stalemate, then. Fine. Olivia could work with that.

"Actually, that'll be good. I could use some time to myself." She climbed out of bed, wincing as her nightshirt rubbed the bruises. "Maybe get a coffee. Work on proposals for next year."

"That's...good." Was that relief in Kris's voice? "I'm gonna shower, then."

"I'll make breakfast."

She waited until she heard the water come on before bolting to the closet. She fished the journal out of the garment bag and shoved it into her backpack, empty from when she purged it at the end of last term. Then she went into the kitchen and made a plate of runny scrambled eggs and toast for Kris. The sight of food still turned Olivia's stomach, but she forced herself to eat a banana. By the time Kris emerged from the shower, a wall of steam following her into the bedroom, Olivia was dressed, her hair up to hide a growing bald spot. She even threw on some concealer and mascara and, she had to admit, it didn't make her look all that much better, but the routine of it helped.

"Coffee," Kris said.

Olivia shrugged. "To start."

"Okay."

Flora still slept. Now, Olivia could see the faint shudder of blanket fuzz by her face. Healthy lungs. She was fine. But part of Olivia knew she shouldn't leave. If the black-haired woman came back, would Kris be able to keep Flora safe? Olivia had to trust that she could, and if the black-haired woman came, maybe it would mean Kris would finally see that something was wrong.

Either way, Olivia needed time with her mother's journal. There were answers in it. She could feel it.

Kris followed her into the kitchen, where she picked at the eggs but didn't eat them. She'd throw them out as soon as Olivia left.

"Anything I need to know?" Kris asked.

"Like?"

"Tummy time, feeding time...that stuff."

"Use your best judgment."

Kris raised an eyebrow. "Aren't babies supposed to stick to a routine?"

Olivia laughed. "You try telling her that." She cleared her throat, anxious. "Call me if...anything happens."

"I will."

Olivia started for the door when Kris grabbed her elbow, gently, and pulled her back. She kissed her, and when she pulled away, her eyes were glassy. "I love you."

Startled, Olivia looked away. "Love you too." She looked back, forcing a smile. "Be good."

Kris smiled, but it didn't reach her eyes. "You too."

Walking into the coffee shop, the deep aroma saturating the air, should have been a balm. When she was teaching, she woke up an hour early to stop here and sit with her first cup of coffee by the fire, watching people. She'd felt anonymous, a voyeur into the lives of Important People who did Important Things and therefore needed their coffee as strong and as fast as possible. She'd written proposals here, graded papers here, started a still-in-progress novel here—for a long time, it'd felt like home. Now, though, she felt eyes on her the moment she walked in. None of the people behind the counter looked familiar, so she stumbled over her simple coffee order as they looked her up and down.

The comfy chair by the fire was gone, replaced with an out-of-season Adirondack. She took a seat at a table in the corner and had barely settled when a guy crawled beneath it, charge cord extended like the Olympic torch. Too stunned to say anything, she sat stiffly, thighs pinched tight together and arms wrapped around her middle, until he finally came out. He flashed a smile she supposed was meant to be charming. She scowled and, when he'd taken his seat a table over, she nudged the plug out of the outlet with her heel.

She pulled the journal out of her backpack and angled her body away from the rest of the room to stave off curious eyes. The window behind her could have been a problem, so she slid the journal down the side of the table, blocking it with her body. Though she desperately needed to know what was in the journal, she avoided reading by studying her mother's handwriting. Most of it was clear, each stroke intentional. In other places it was harried, barely legible. The pencil had smeared across several of the pages, leaving the words hanging in a cloud of gray. There were no dates anywhere, and the entries seemed to jump back and forth in time.

When Olivia did finally bring herself to read the first entry, she had to pause every few lines to catch her breath. It was like it was written for her—addressing Olivia directly and giving answers to questions she didn't know she had. She'd known her father—had reached out to him when she was in college at her grandmother's insistence. She was short on tuition and hated asking him for it. At the time, she suspected he only sent a check out of guilt. He had to have known what'd happened, why her mother had been locked up, but she'd never asked. Would he have stepped in if her mother hadn't pushed him away so quickly? Would Olivia's life have been different?

By the third entry her coffee had gone cold. She'd grown up in the same house as her mother, wandered the same woods, but she'd never seen a well. Granted, she didn't spend much time out there—between school and chores and work, she didn't have a ton of free time. Idle hands do the devil's work. Had it been out there all this time? Had her grandmother been hiding it from her? If so, why?

As she read an entry describing how her grandparents kicked them out, how Olivia went missing, her whole body went cold. She'd never heard this story.

When her mother started to write about Iris, Olivia had to close the journal. Catch her breath.

Her phone vibrating in her back made her jump. Kris, she assumed, probably begging her to come back.

But it was a text from Charlie: You at home?

Out, Olivia answered.

Meet you? I have something I want to show you.

Olivia took another long look at the journal. Okay.

Charlie ordered a black coffee and brought it to the table. She sat across from Olivia, a sheaf of papers tucked into a book in her hand. Olivia had hidden her mother's journal beside the table, pinned to the leg with her foot. She hadn't decided whether she was going to show it to Charlie yet. She wanted to see what Charlie had first.

"How are you?" Charlie asked.

"Fine," Olivia said. "You wanted to show me something?"

"You don't look fine. I wouldn't be fine knowing—"

"Knowing the woman who tried to kill you is out wandering the streets somewhere?"

Charlie nodded.

"I'm fine. I am." She sucked down cold coffee, the journal practically burning a hole through her calf. "What did you want to show me?"

Charlie slipped a few printed pages out of the book and nudged them across the table. "My sister's an investigator. Mostly due diligence for big finance firms, but she's got some skills. I asked her to find anything she could about Iris. Cost me three Christmases of being Mom's Secret Santa, but considering what she found—totally worth it."

Olivia flipped through the pages—there were only three or four, and the articles were brief—pausing when a picture caught her eye. It was a photo of a photo, the young woman in it stood next to what looked like a fireplace, but the print was too faded for her to be sure. The woman's eyes had been scribbled out, solid black.

"Iris?" Olivia asked.

"Yep. Best my sister can tell."

"Where did she get this?"

"She didn't tell me, but there's an article that goes with it. Mentions Shannon."

Charlie pulled one of the pages from the small pile and set it on top of the picture.

Recent Death of Bethany Home Woman Ruled Accidental

Olivia scanned the article until she found her mother's name.

The photo of Iris Marwood was found in the effects of a Bethany Home volunteer, Shannon MacArthur. Though she claimed no knowledge of being in possession of the photograph, or why the eyes had been blacked out with pen ink, police held her for questioning the evening following the discovery of Iris's body by the same Ms. MacArthur. Iris was found in a janitor's closet, unresponsive. Attempts were made by Bethany Home staff to revive her, but it soon became apparent that she had been deceased for some time. Despite an initial suspicion of suicide, the woman's death was ruled accidental. The police have declined to comment further.

It was all becoming too real. Olivia pushed the picture and article away, but every time she blinked she saw the black eyes.

"You think she did something to her," Olivia said. "To Iris."

"I...don't know. I think it's a very strange coincidence. Two pictures in which Iris is—" She shook her head. "And both of them tie back to Shannon."

"It's not just the pictures."

Charlie frowned. "What do you mean?"

Olivia had a feeling she was going to regret this, but she also felt like she didn't have a choice. She bent down, grabbed the journal, and set it on the table between them.

"She's been staying with my aunt," Olivia said. "I went there..."

Charlie's mouth fell open. "Did you see her?"

"No. But I took this." She nudged the journal forward. "It's hers."

Charlie didn't wait for permission. She opened the journal and pored over page after page, her eyes growing wider, her cheeks flushed. Olivia started to think maybe she'd made a mistake—this was Olivia's *life*. For Charlie, it was a thrill trip, a game of armchair detective. Olivia itched to snatch the journal back. To leave. But it felt good having someone to talk to, even if she didn't completely trust her.

Charlie paused, finally looking up. "That article—did it mention anything about a fire?"

"I don't think so." Olivia rifled through the papers until she found it again, read it through. "No. Nothing. Why?"

Charlie turned the journal around to face Olivia. "Read this."

It was an entry much further back than she'd read so far. Her eyes moved quickly over the page, devouring her mother's words.

Black eyes.

Fire.

"Iris set herself on fire?" Olivia asked. "Why would she do that?"

"I don't think she did," Charlie said carefully. "They would have mentioned it. Look, it says they tried to revive her. If she'd burned the way Shannon says, there wouldn't have been anything to revive. She'd had been a goner."

Olivia frowned. "Why would she lie? It's a journal."

"I don't know." She paused. "How much of this have you read?"

"Some." Olivia bit her lip. "It's—difficult. It's like I can't breathe after a while."

"Did you read the part about Jo?"

"Which part? She's in there a lot."

Charlie studied her face. It made Olivia want to crawl inside herself. Hide. "The part where Shannon stabbed her."

Olivia paled. "That isn't—that can't—"

Charlie flipped back a few pages. "Here. She stabbed her and put her in a cabinet."

Olivia shook her head. That couldn't be right. "You just said she lied."

"About Iris."

"But if she'd stabbed someone, they wouldn't have let her out, right? I mean, they would have put her back in prison or something."

"Unless they didn't know it was her." Charlie leaned forward, her hand close enough to Olivia's she could feel the heat. "We already know she's capable of being dangerous, right? I mean—that's why she was there in the first place. It's not out of the realm of possibility that she could have hurt someone else." She paused. "But I can talk to my sister. See if she can find anything about this Jo person. If she was another patient, especially recently, there has to be something."

Olivia nodded, but she was only half listening. She couldn't stop reading the last line of the entry. *It wasn't the first time I'd killed Jo.*

Had Charlie skipped that bit? Or ignored it? Olivia didn't want to ask. Charlie was already starting to look at her the way Kris did—part pity, part wariness.

She made an excuse about Flora and grabbed the journal before Charlie had the chance to take it from her, promising she'd let her know if she found out anything else.

"I'll let you know what my sister finds," Charlie said.

Olivia thanked her and hurried to her car, locking the doors the minute she was inside. She could feel the panic start to bubble up in her stomach, the kind of attacks she'd had when she was little, back when fear seemed to rule her life. Fear of the dark, of sounds in the walls, of the voices in her nightmares. She needed to go somewhere. Anywhere. So she drove, focusing on keeping her breath slow and steady and her eyes on the road and away from the rearview mirror where she felt someone—something—looking back at her. She didn't realize where she was going until she got off the highway, old muscle memory taking over.

Her grandparents' house hugged the corner of the block, catty-corner to a liquor store and on the edge of a wooded park where a narrow bike path wound through from one side of the town, dead-ending at a dog park that never saw any dogs. For his entire life, her grandfather boasted how his was the only property standing in the way of redevelopment of the woods—a tradition her grandmother carried on in his memory. The way her grandfather used to tell it, they bought the house back when the area was expected to bloom around them. Signs posted every mile promised strip malls and office complexes, economic injections into a town that desperately needed it. When it never happened, others moved on while the MacArthurs stubbornly clung to hope of a future that probably would never exist.

"It'll turn around someday," he used to tell her. "Just you wait."

When Olivia was a teenager, the only place to kill time was a five-screen movie theater, which, judging by the boards on the windows now, had long since gone out of business. The town did eventually get a strip mall, but only half of the storefronts were ever occupied at one time.

A small town with small minds. Olivia had been anxious to get out.

She pulled into her grandparents' long driveway, noting the large cardboard sign propped against a recycling bin—*Stop taking my cans I know who you are!!!* The lawn hadn't been mowed in what looked like at least a month—and wouldn't be, not with winter just around the corner. She parked, but didn't shut the car off, tempted to turn around. They'd had years to talk about her mother, about everything that'd happened before she was born, what happened in the weeks after. Growing up, she'd had questions but knew never to ask them. She figured when she got older, she'd be able to sort things out for herself. Grown-ups know things, she'd thought, so when she was a grown-up, she'd know things too. Laughable, really. She knew less now as an adult than she ever did as a kid.

She stuffed her backpack—journal tucked safely away—in the trunk, beneath a blanket, and locked the car before knocking on the front door. She waited a few seconds before retrieving the key from beneath the mat and letting herself in.

All of the lights were on in the living room and kitchen, and when she peered upstairs, she saw lights on up there too.

She frowned. Her grandparents had been militant about turning lights off when you didn't need them. "Hello?"

The kitchen was spotless. No breakfast dishes in the sink or coffee left in the pot. She peeked through the mudroom to the garage. Her grandmother's car was there, but that didn't mean she hadn't gotten a ride somewhere. Olivia started toward the stairs, mentally preparing herself. Uncle Patrick (mother*fucker*) always said one of them would come in and find her dead in the bathroom one day. The woman refused any help, even after the heart attack knocked her on her butt for weeks.

"If it didn't kill me then," her grandmother said, "it won't kill me now."

Olivia took out her phone, ready to call 9-1-1, but the bathroom was clear. Her grandmother's bedroom door was shut, so she knocked softly.

"Grandma?"

She strained to hear anything, but the entire floor was eerily silent. Growing up with aunts and uncles in the same house, it was easy to forget how much quiet the house could hold.

She knocked again, louder. "Grandma? Are you in there?"

Finally, she heard movement on the other side. She waited an excruciating few seconds before the mental image of her grandmother prostrate on the floor, crawling on bloody fingertips to the door, made her go in.

"Jesus Christ on the cross, Olivia." Her grandmother sat up in bed, one hand on her chest, the other midway to her nightstand where, Olivia remembered, she kept a gun. Pushing eighty and the woman was a better shot than most hunters. "You scared the hell out of me."

Maybe it was a trick of the light, or maybe Olivia's head was still stuck on the picture of Iris, but for a second, it looked like her grandmother's eyes were solid black. She blinked, and the blackness cleared.

"Right back at you," Olivia said shakily. "You know all your lights are on?"

Grandma ignored her. "What are you even doing here? Shouldn't you be at home with the baby?"

"You mean the one you haven't come to see yet?" Her voice was more confident now that they were on familiar ground. Fighting. She could do fighting.

Grandma cleared her throat. "I was going to. *Am* going to. Just—things come up. It's hard to get away."

Olivia sidestepped the lie. There were only so many she could get hit with in one day. "What are you still doing in bed? Are you sick?"

Her grandmother had always been an early riser—up before 6:00 a.m. most mornings, already through a full pot of coffee before the rest of them dragged themselves out of bed.

"I'm fine." Grandma threw the covers aside, revealing angry, red knees. She shimmied the legs of her pajama pants down. "Be better if I didn't have people busting into my house."

"I used a key."

"Well there's that, at least." She scratched her head. Ran her fingers through her short gray hair and sighed. "You want some coffee?"

The coffee shop mocha was still sitting like a rock in her gut. "Yes, please."

The kitchen somehow looked bigger and smaller than she remembered at the same time. Bigger because there weren't half a dozen people tumbling through it, snatching slices of bread out of each other's hands like hungry gulls. Smaller for the same reason. Grandma made a pot of strong coffee while Olivia sat at the table, wondering when and how to bring up her mother. She wished she and her grandmother had been closer. That words were easier.

Grandma sat a mug of black coffee in front of Olivia, already sipping her own before she sat.

"How's Flora?" she asked. Before Olivia could rearrange her face, she continued, "Don't look at me like that. I know my great-granddaughter's name."

"She's fine," Olivia said. "Good."

"Big? Healthy?"

Olivia nodded.

"Good. I'm sure people been telling you already, but get whatever sleep you can. Babies'll drain you dry."

It was on the tip of her tongue. *Just ask her.* She held the mug to her mouth, tipped the scalding coffee to her lips but didn't drink.

Grandma studied her over the rim of her mug. "Should I keep up with the small talk, or are you gonna tell me what's going on?"

Another sidestep. "Why were you still in bed?"

"I was sleeping."

"At nine a.m.?"

"I've been having a hard time falling asleep lately."

"Why?"

"Why the third degree? You want to talk about weird behavior; I can't remember the last time you came out here without me having to physically pry you out of your house. Something's going on, and if you're not gonna tell me, you might as well finish your coffee and go on with your day."

Olivia sipped the bitter coffee to give her mouth something to do. She couldn't help but notice her grandmother hadn't bothered to turn off any of the lights. "Melatonin."

Grandma frowned.

"To help you sleep."

"Right." Grandma cradled her mug in her palms. Shot weary glances out the window.

For a long time, neither of them spoke. If stubbornness was an Olympic sport, they'd have fought over the gold.

As a teenager, the topic of her mother was off limits. But Olivia was a grown-ass woman now. She had her own life, her own child who needed her to find answers.

"Did Erin tell you?" Olivia finally asked.

Grandma worked her jaw, glanced quickly down at her mug. "Tell me what?"

"Or maybe you've seen her. You have, haven't you? Paid a visit to the apartment. Maybe you're the one who helped her move in."

"I don't know what—"

"Stop." It came out fiercer than she intended, but she'd be damned if she was going to back down now. "I know she's staying with Erin."

Something like fear flickered behind her grandmother's eyes. "You're safe. Don't worry."

"I'm not worried about my safety. I'm worried about—" She bit off the last of it. Swallowed. "You should have told me. *Someone* should have told me."

"I know. I'm sorry."

"Sorry, huh. Good. Tell me this, then. When I was a baby, did I go missing?"

Grandma's face paled. "How did you—?"

"It doesn't matter. Just tell me."

"It was a long time ago, Olivia, I don't see why—"

"How long was I gone? A day? Two?"

"A day," Grandma finally said, defeated. "Not even. Eighteen hours, maybe."

"What happened?"

"Why does it matter? You're here. I told you, you're safe."

"I won't know why it matters until you tell me."

"If you're scared—"

Olivia laughed. "Scared. Scared like you, you mean?"

Grandma didn't say anything. Didn't have to.

"Tell me."

She rubbed her face. "Your mother decided she didn't want to be here any-more, so she left. She said she was going to a friend's house. And before you say anything, yes, we tried to stop her. She was bullheaded and angry with me and her dad for getting your father's parents involved. Her need for you lived in a vacuum, with no room for anyone or anything else. It made her think she could do it on her own."

"Some people believe you should be infatuated with your children."

"Some people are asking for heartbreak. The fruit of your loins, yes, but they're people too. They grow up. They leave." She swallowed the dregs of her coffee and got up for a refill. "Anyway, we told her not to go, that we would figure it out, all of us, but she was determined. I made her father slip her some cash. My mother always told me no matter how happy a marriage, every woman should have a little money set aside, for her own peace of mind. I'd been dipping into mine for years, but I made him give her the last of my stash, just in case."

"Where did she—we—go?"

Grandma shrugged. "Beats me. When her dad found her the next morning on the lawn, passed out, all she said was they went to the woods."

A chill snaked down Olivia's back. "And I was gone."

Grandma nodded. "Scariest day of my life."

"Why didn't you ever tell me?"

"Same reason I never told you about every time you scraped your knee or bonked your head as a kid. I didn't think it mattered." Then, "I told you enough. You knew enough."

"It matters. Did anyone think it had to do with her trying to—?" She couldn't say it. *With her trying to kill me.* "Did I get checked out? What if I'd hit my head? What if I had brain damage?"

"You didn't have brain damage."

Olivia didn't like the way she said it. Unsure. "I knew my mother was mentally ill. That's it. I asked you if there'd been anything else, any other *family secrets,* before we decided to get pregnant. I needed to know."

"I don't see how you getting lost once has anything to do with Flora."

Olivia picked at a cuticle hard enough to make it bleed. "Anything else you need to tell me?"

She paused a beat, then shook her head.

"You have to stop keeping things from me. You should have told me she was being released. I could have at least prepared myself."

"I know that. Okay? I understand. But there's so much you don't know about her—we couldn't risk it."

"That's your fault too though, isn't it? Keeping me in the dark?"

"She tried to kill you, Olivia. To hell with me for trying to protect you from that moment in your life."

But what if trying to protect Olivia had doomed her?

She remembered what Uncle Patrick had said on the podcast—that her grandmother knew more than she let on. That she was afraid.

Grandma continued, "I know it goes against your nature, but you have to trust me when I tell you seeing your mother won't give you the answers you want. Her mind isn't right. Never has been."

"Maybe mine isn't right either," Olivia said. "Maybe mine is just as wrong as hers."

She'd sit and stare at the cellar door...

Just as wrong as yours, she wanted to say.

Grandma sat back in her chair, studying Olivia intently. "What are you trying to say?" She clutched her mug with both hands. "Did something happen?"

"No. Nothing happened."

Grandma nodded, but the tension in her shoulders stayed. "Good."

"Why didn't you ever tell me anything about her?"

Sighing, Grandma stood. Dropped her mug in the sink with a loud clang. "It wouldn't have mattered. Not like you'd have listened. You had it in your head the minute you found out who she was, what she'd done, that she'd been wronged somehow, that it was all a big misunderstanding and if you could just figure it out everything would be roses and sunshine."

"I did not think that."

"For your tenth birthday you asked to see her police file. Patrick had been letting you stay up and watch *Unsolved Mysteries* and you figured all the answers were in it."

Olivia frowned. She couldn't remember doing that. "You should have told me. I was a smart kid. I wouldn't have romanticized what happened."

"You were always looking for somewhere to belong, honey. Your aunt and uncles were too old to relate to. Hell, I was too old to relate to. You would have clung to every detail of Shannon's sickness and then worn them like merit badges. I couldn't let you do that to yourself."

"I wouldn't."

Grandma sighed. "Give me some credit, Olivia. I raised you, didn't I? I know you better than you think."

"Do you?"

Grandma turned, arms crossed. "There's a reason we're having this talk now, and not a year ago. Or three years ago. Or five. Right? Before your daughter was even a thought in that fool head, you had better things to worry about than a past too long buried to dig up. Now Flora's here, needing you more than anyone's ever needed you, and you want to go getting your hands dirty. Why?"

Tell her.

Olivia brushed the thought away. "Because I deserve to know. I deserve to have a complete history of my life."

"No one has a complete history of their life."

Olivia shook her head. "You're all a bunch of liars. You never cared, did you? I was just a burden on you and Grandpa."

Grandma flinched, like she'd been slapped. Olivia started to take it back, an apology poised on the tip of her tongue, but Grandma waved her away, eyes glassy.

"Just promise me—no. Forget it. You want some truth? Sometimes I look at you and you're just like her. You'll do what you want and damn the consequences. Just don't come crying to me after."

Olivia pushed away from the table, wiping her eye with the heel of her palm. "Wouldn't think of it."

Back in her car, Olivia only drove far enough down the street that her grandmother wouldn't be able to see her from the window. She circled the liquor store, around the back of the property, and then followed the fence line to where it ended at the edge of the woods. Most of the trees were bare, tall birch trunks with spindly branches reaching toward the sky like fingers. Without the bulk of summer foliage, the place looked sparse. Emaciated. Hungry.

Her phone buzzed in her pocket. She pulled it out to see a text from Kris: Where are you?

She shot back a quick answer—Back soon—and headed for the trees.

CHAPTER TWENTY-THREE
OLIVIA

The tops of the birch trees swayed with the breeze, their spindly branches scraping each other. The creak of the trunks sounded like doors opening. Olivia started down the trail that wasn't really a trail but more of a worn path where the grass couldn't grow back, throwing quick glances over her shoulder. Though the leaves on the trees were long gone, the ground-level brush was thick and stubbornly green, root tendrils reaching across the path like fingers. Somewhere someone was burning garbage. The stench of the smoke as it mixed with earth and bitter greens swirled around her, the threat of a headache throbbing gently in the back of her skull.

She crossed the tree line and, every few steps, looked back. In her mother's journal, the trees seemed to close around her, but Olivia could clearly see through to the houses at the end of the grassy divide. She turned in a circle, taking in her surroundings. In every direction she could at least catch a glimpse of a clearing, a break in the trees that undoubtedly led to a yard or parking lot. It both comforted and worried her. She didn't want to admit to herself that the journal wasn't the Holy Grail she'd needed it to be. Still, she continued on. The ground was a carpet of leaves that crunched underfoot, the only sound apart from her breath.

She thought, absently, that this time of day, she should have been hearing birds. Squirrels. But the trees were abandoned, the only nest a twiggy, dried thing that dangled precariously from a low bough.

She tried to imagine how it would feel, to believe she had to escape here with Flora, and was startled to realize how it easy it was. Quiet and calm, she could imagine falling asleep curled at the base of a tree, its trunk a comforting hand on her back. Flora would sleep wrapped in a blanket of leaves stitched together with stripped bark and moss, a fairy baby.

Lost in her daydream, Olivia's toe clipped something and she tripped. She caught herself on her forearms just before her head smacked something hard and pointy. Pain shot down her arms and neck and when she rolled over, dirt and gravel clung to the scrapes along her arms. Her head started to throb. As she struggled to her feet, the hem of her jeans got caught on what looked like a rock, but on closer inspection she realized it was a brick. On her hands and knees, she brushed the leaves away and found more bricks, the edges crumbling but mostly intact. When she finally cleared most of the leaves, she froze.

The well.

It was a hard thing to look at, knowing only a few minutes difference would have meant she'd died here. Part of her wanted to run away, like it could reach out and grab her and finish what was started.

It was mostly underground, the ring of bricks barely coming up to her ankle. The mouth of it was covered with a thick, wooden plank that was partially rotted at the edges but was still too heavy for her to move. She tried using her feet to nudge it off the mouth but any pressure on her ankle sent sharp shocks of pain up her leg.

Out of breath, she sat back, studying the plank. She didn't know anything about wood, but given how damp it was out here, how much rot there already was, it couldn't have been covered long. A year. Maybe two. What happened that finally pushed someone to seal it? Olivia's grandparents weren't the only people whose homes butted up against this small, wooded area. Did some kid stumble upon it and hurt themselves? Or a beloved family dog?

Or was it another young mother, pacing her kitchen with her child at her breast, delirious with lack of sleep and food and care? Olivia leaned forward, kneeling, drawn to a sound like rushing water. She closed her eyes to better hear it and imagined she could see this young mother standing at her window, the only light coming from a refrigerator, the door left ajar. The rushing water became garbled whispers and the young woman in Olivia's mind tilted her head, listening.

In the darkness of the kitchen in Olivia's imagination, the shadows throbbed and condensed until they took the shape of the black-haired woman. She offered her hand, and the young woman, without looking at her, took it.

Come with me, a voice said.

Olivia's eyes shot open, but the image was there, burned in the back of her mind. A premonition? Or a memory? Part of her wanted to close her eyes, to let it play out. If it was a kind of memory, did that mean the young woman in her head was her mother? Would she see what happened that day?

But something told her that if she went back, if she opened her mind like that again, the black-haired woman would see her. She would *come*.

Olivia looked at the plank and realized it had been moved, barely an inch, but enough to expose the opening. Had she done it while lost in her thoughts? Or was there something beneath, something stronger than her?

She leaned forward over the opening, heart hammering and mouth dry. She remembered her mother's journal, the moment her mother peered into the well just before she fell in—

Something cracked behind her. She scrambled to her feet, tripping on a root and falling backward onto the plank. It miraculously held her weight long enough for her to slide off, but cracked down the middle as she stood. Her whole body trembled as she turned, looking for the source of the sound. Movement in the corner of her eye sent her running in the direction she hoped was out. She kept looking over her shoulder, feeling the gap in the emptiness closing. There was something after her, she could feel it, and it was gaining on her.

A scream caught in her throat like a rock and when she swallowed, she gagged.

Finally, she broke through the tree line, but didn't stop running until she reached her car. Inside, she locked the doors and watched the bend in the road, waiting for something to come around the corner.

Nothing.

Maybe she'd imagined it.

But the well was real. That much she knew.

As the adrenaline slowed, whatever she'd done to her ankle made it throb. She reached down to rub it, knocking her forehead on the steering wheel. Tears sprung as a mix of pain and frustration lodged itself like a rock inside her ribcage. Her edges were frayed, like a sweater coming unraveled.

She started the car not knowing what to do. She didn't want to go home, not yet, but the longer she sat there, the tips of the birch trees visible in the distance, the more viciously her skin crawled. Eventually she found her way to the main road just before the highway, which cut through two strip malls, one on either side. She pulled off into a mostly empty parking lot and, almost on instinct, reached for her mother's journal.

She reread the entry about the well, practically feeling the breath on the back of her neck as her mother described treading water at the bottom of the well.

I don't like the dark.

Olivia's phone buzzed. Another text from Kris. Are you okay?

Olivia had only started typing a reply when her phone rang. Kris was calling her. Immediately she thought something had happened to Flora.

When she answered, she could hear Flora crying in the background.

"What's wrong?" Olivia asked.

"I was gonna ask you the same," Kris said. "Where are you?"

"I'm fine. Why?"

"Your grandmother called. Said she was worried about you."

Olivia's face reddened. "What did she say?"

"Are you on your way home?"

Olivia didn't like the way Kris sidestepped the question. She could hear something in Kris's voice, something more than concern. She sounded scared.

What did she know?

And did Olivia want to find out?

"Yes," Olivia finally said, her voice sounding far away. "I'm on my way."

––––––––––––

Olivia expected Kris to be waiting just inside the screen door, or outside in the yard, so she didn't think twice when she saw movement beside the house, a figure in an uncomfortable crouch that slowly stood as she pulled into the driveway. She had a million excuses in her head for where she'd been and what she was doing, who she saw, and why her grandmother might have felt the need to call her wife and tell her God knew what—

But it all fell out of her head the moment she looked—really looked—at the woman standing now a foot in front of her car.

She was short, her head only a couple of feet above the hood of the car, with ashy blond hair tied back in a ponytail. She wore a burgundy hoodie with *Daytona Beach* across the chest, at least two sizes too big, which made her already thin frame seem that much smaller. Her wide eyes looked glassy, and the corners of her lips lifted in a half smile as she tangled her fingers in front of her, the same nervous habit Olivia had never been able to shake.

Her hair was different, and her face was much thinner, but Olivia recognized her immediately.

Her mother.

Olivia bit the inside of her cheek to keep focus, to keep her hands from shaking as she finally opened the car door.

"Sorry," her mother said. "I know I shouldn't—I just… Gosh, I didn't think this would be so hard." She laughed once, then wiped her nose. "When you called—I mean, it was you who called, right? I didn't want to leave it like that. Angela thinks I should let you make the first move, but—"

"So you are—" Olivia cut in. "You're her, then. My mother."

She nodded, her smile growing and then fading. "You can call me Shannon if that's easier."

"Angela told me not…"

Something flashed across her mother's eyes. "Angela said what?"

"Liv?"

Olivia looked toward the house where Kris stood in the doorway, Flora on her shoulder and her phone in her hand.

Kris nodded at Olivia's mother. "Everything okay?"

Shannon—Mom—Olivia couldn't get her head around calling her either of them—tucked a stray hair behind her ear, eyes cast downward. "I should go. This was a bad idea. I'm really sorry."

"No." It was out of Olivia's mouth before she could stop it. She looked at Kris. "I mean yes, everything's fine." To her mother, "No. Don't go. It's okay. I'll just—can you wait here? One sec?"

She nodded, but took a few steps back, putting the car between herself and Kris.

Olivia went to Kris and instinctively reached out for Flora, surprising even herself. When Kris handed Flora over, it was like being handed a sack of potatoes—limp and heavy.

"She's tired," Kris said, a half warning. She glanced over Olivia's shoulder. "Who's that?"

Olivia shifted her weight, trying to balance Flora on her shoulder without collapsing. Her legs were still shaky from the fall in the woods. "I'm pretty sure she's my mother."

"Your—" Kris's eyes went wide. "What is she doing here?"

Olivia shrugged.

"She can't be here. There's an order, isn't there?"

"I'm a grown woman," Olivia said, as if that counted for anything lately. "The order expired."

"She can't be here," Kris said again. "What about Flora?"

"What about her?"

"You can't be serious. Liv, she—"

Olivia cut her off. "I know what you're going to say, but Flora is safe. We are safe. They wouldn't have put her on outpatient care if they thought she'd hurt anyone."

She stabbed a woman. Maybe murdered another.

Kris frowned. "How do you know she's on outpatient care?"

"Erin mentioned it, I think." She fought to keep eye contact. Kris could always tell when she was lying. "I just want to talk to her."

"So talk."

Olivia's mouth set in a tight line. "Inside. Like people." Before Kris could argue anymore, she waved to her mother. "Come inside. It'll get chilly soon."

Her mother hesitated, gaze darting between Kris and Olivia before she finally nodded. When she got close, Kris grabbed Flora from Olivia, muttering something about a nap, and disappeared into the house.

Before Olivia could stammer out some sort of apology, her mother shook her head. "It's okay. I get it."

Olivia offered a weak smile. This morning she had a million questions, but now her mind was blank, her body on autopilot. Suddenly the only thing she could think about was being nine or ten and staring in the mirror, picking out features she thought matched the only picture she had of her mother. As a kid, Olivia had written journals full of fake memories, fake conversations between her and her mother, that she would pull out and read when she was feeling lonely, or after a fight with her grandmother.

Now she found herself picking apart her mother's features, wishing she had a mirror to compare. For the longest time she was convinced that the day she finally came face to face with her mother, she would feel a connection, a familiarity. Now, though, she realized how ridiculous that was. This woman was her mother, but she was a stranger. A potentially dangerous stranger.

Still, there was something in her expression, a kind of cautious knowing, that pulled Olivia in. And when her mother's gaze flicked somewhere over Olivia's shoulder, jaw clenched, eyes turned down with what looked like worry, Olivia decided.

She can see her too.

Olivia held the door open, and when her mother walked past, the side of her hand brushed Olivia's. It was like touching fire. She couldn't stop herself from flinching.

"Sorry," she muttered.

An expression flicked across her mother's face, one she couldn't quite read. "You have nothing to be sorry for."

Olivia heard Kris in the bedroom, so she steered her mother toward the living room.

"Beautiful," her mother said.

"Thanks." She gestured vaguely. "You can sit anywhere."

Her mother sat on the couch at one end. Olivia paused in front of the couch before changing her mind and sitting in the recliner. The springs in the stand were broken, so it leaned awkwardly a few inches to the left.

The silence was like thick fog. Olivia studied her mother through the corner of her eye. She didn't look how she'd imagined, though she wasn't exactly sure what it was she had imagined. Someone more intimidating, maybe. Taller. The kind of eyes that didn't look at you so much as through you.

Big black eyes.

Her mother wasn't anything like that. She was the kind of woman Olivia would ask to watch her things while she went to the bathroom at the coffee shop, the kind of woman who'd coax a toddler from a hiding place while the mother was running around the store, panicked like a headless chicken.

Olivia didn't realize how badly she'd wanted her mother to like her. How much she wanted to believe what'd happened when she was a baby was a fluke, a twist of sanity. An accident. A misunderstanding. Anything but what everyone told her. Maybe her grandmother had been right.

"She's down for the count."

Olivia looked up at Kris, wondering how long she'd been standing there. "Good. How was she while I was gone?"

"Fine."

"Fine good or fine less than good?"

"Just fine, Liv."

"She doesn't want to talk about Flora while I'm here," her mother said. "And that's fine."

My mother's funny, Olivia thought.

Kris shifted her weight. "Something we can help you with?"

"Kris—"

"No. She just shows up here—you didn't drive her, right?"

Olivia shook her head.

Kris nodded, vindicated. "Right. So she just shows up here out of nowhere— and how does she even know where we live?—after thirty some-odd years, after what she did to you... That's stalking, okay? And I'm willing to bet she knows she shouldn't be here, which makes me wonder what she wants. So." She turned to Olivia's mother, arms crossed. "What do you want?"

"I don't want anything." She caught Olivia's eye. "Except maybe to explain myself."

"Phones exist," Kris said.

Olivia must have made a face, because her mother frowned.

"You're right," her mother said. "Absolutely. I don't know what I was thinking. I'll go."

Kris said, "Thank you," and the same time Olivia said, "Don't."

They both looked at her with warring expressions—her mother hopeful, her wife incredulous.

"You're already here," Olivia added, feeling Kris's gaze boring into her skull.

"Liv, please. Can we talk about this first?"

Olivia turned to Kris, struggling to keep her tone under control. "You wouldn't understand."

"No, she's right," her mother said. "Another time."

Kris grumbled agreement.

"Are you sure?" Olivia asked.

Her mother nodded. Then, glancing just past her again, said, "Do you mind if I use the restroom, first? Getting near on rush hour and it'll be a long bus ride back."

"Of course," Olivia said, a little too loud. "I'll show you."

Her mother followed her to the hallway, with Kris watching from the living room.

"Thanks," her mother said. "Won't be two shakes."

Olivia lingered at the end of the hallway, a barrier between Kris and her mother. When her mother finally came out, she stuffed something in Olivia's hand, rushing past, her eyes on Kris.

Kris frowned, but didn't say anything, watching her move toward the door like a cat watches a mouse.

"Sorry for bothering you," her mother murmured.

Olivia hardly had time to say goodbye before Kris shut the door behind her. She caught Kris's eye, daring her to say something, to scold her for inviting her mother into her home, but Kris either decided the fight wasn't worth it, or she was saving it up for a big one later. Either way, she was grateful when Kris moved past her toward the bedroom, probably to check on Flora.

Olivia practically ran to the kitchen, opening the clump of toilet paper her mother had shoved into her hand.

It was a phone number, written in eyebrow pencil.

Text me.

Olivia slipped it into her pocket before Kris could see it.

Dinner was leftover Chinese, which they both picked at. Olivia felt Kris stare her down every few minutes, but refused to meet her eyes. She didn't want to argue about it because, at the end of the day, it was none of Kris's business. She must have said that bit out loud though, because Kris slammed her fork on the table.

"You're my wife," she said. "It's my business."

"I don't want to fight—"

"Then you shouldn't have brought a potentially dangerous stranger into our home."

"She's my mother."

"Who tried to kill you. She's never denied it, Liv. What makes you think she wouldn't do it again? If not to you, who's to say she wouldn't come after Flora?"

"Why would she do that?"

"Why would anyone? They locked her up because her mind wasn't right. Her mind still isn't right." Kris shook her head. "I don't understand why you think this is okay."

Her mind isn't right. Her grandmother's words, almost verbatim.

"You don't have to understand," Olivia said. "You haven't had to live with this legacy over your head. Look me in the eye and tell me you haven't thought about my mother every day of my pregnancy. Tell me you and the doctors weren't waiting for something to crack in my head."

Kris stiffened. Her eyes flicked somewhere behind Olivia, not quite meeting her eyes. "That's not true."

"You see? It's there. I can feel it in the way you look at me, or don't look at me. The way my doctors dismiss everything I say. This thing that happened clings to my back and the only way to get rid of it, to understand it, is to face it." Olivia sighed. "You want to know why I didn't turn her away? Because right now, she's probably the only person in the world who won't lie to me."

By the time she finished, her head was pounding.

"Flora is our priority," Kris said. "If that means—"

"I know that!" Sharp pain pinched behind her eyes. "You don't understand."

"So help me understand, Liv. Talk to me."

She couldn't think, let alone talk. Pain spread across her head and down her neck. She'd had tension headaches as a teenager, some so bad they'd leave her bedridden for a day or more.

"I need Tylenol or something," she muttered, standing. "I can't do this right now."

Before Kris could say anything else, Olivia shut herself in the bathroom and threw back four pills from the bottle of Tylenol in the cabinet, sticking her mouth under the faucet for water.

Kris knocked. Said something that sounded Very Grown-Up through the door. Olivia ignored it, sliding down the bathroom door until she sat with her legs splayed. The tile was cold through her jeans, and when she closed her eyes, she could feel them thumping against her eyelids. If she could just get this headache to go away, she could think. If she could just—

A sharp buzzing beneath her leg made her jump. She realized her phone was in her pocket, and when she pulled it out, there was a text message from Aunt Erin: She told me. Is everything okay?

She shot a text back: No. We're all dead.

That's not funny.

Who's joking?

Her phone rang—Aunt Erin—but Olivia dismissed the call and turned her phone off.

The pain was somehow getting worse. She could feel her pulse in her temples, and there was a strange flutter in her chest. A *top of the roller coaster with a broken seat belt* feeling. She tried to breathe through it, but it was like she'd come untethered from her body. Her legs felt like they were made of concrete, and her wrists were brittle twigs that cracked each time she tried to get her hands beneath her to stand. She lurched forward and fell back, hard, knocking her head on the door.

She barely felt it through the fog of pain swallowing her head.

Finally, she got her legs beneath her and stood, her million-pound head hanging, chin to chest.

She was suddenly so, so tired.

The room spun and her stomach flipped. The fluttering in her chest got worse, and she had just enough presence of mind to realize she was going to pass out.

"Don't pass out," she muttered, her lips barely moving.

She reached for the faucet, but the knobs jumped out of the way. A giggle worked its way up her throat.

What is happening?

She finally got hold of the knobs and turned, but the water trickled out the wrong color. Like piss. The light, she thought. Holding her breath, she splashed her face. Water dripped down her neck, soaking her collar and when she looked down, she saw blood. Her breath caught and she blinked once, twice—no, not blood. Red sweater. Wet.

Thoughts flicked in and out of her head, slippery as fish.

Drugged, she thought, and her whole body went hot.

Kris wouldn't have.

Except she might, if she knew what Olivia had done.

She shook her head. No, no, not drugged. Couldn't be.

Had to be.

She splashed her face again, and finally was able to lift her head.

At first it looked like she was seeing a double reflection. She squinted, forcing herself to focus.

The black-haired woman's reflection stared back, wide black eyes barely visible through the curtain of hair that covered her down to her chest.

I'm alone, Olivia thought. *I'm alone and this is wrong and there's no one behind me.*

But she could feel the black-haired woman's breath on her neck. Her hand sliding up Olivia's hip and around to her belly, beneath her sweater to the soft, wrinkly skin there. The black-haired woman's mouth split into something like a smile.

Then the smile dipped, and she laid her head on Olivia's shoulder, one eye watching through the curtain of hair, and began to hum.

"Don't worry, Mommy," she said between disjointed bars of "Rock-a-Bye Baby." "I'll take good care of her. Better than you ever could."

"You're not here," Olivia said.

A soft knock on the door. "Liv? You okay?"

"Uh oh," the black-haired woman said. "Daddy's here."

"Don't touch me," Olivia said, her breath coming in shallow bursts. She tried to wriggle out of the black-haired woman's grip, but her nails dug into the loose skin and she could almost hear it tear. She cried out. "Get off me!"

"Olivia?"

Kris banged on the door, and when Olivia lurched around to face it, the black-haired woman seemed to have disappeared.

Except Olivia could still feel here there. She turned back to the mirror and the black-haired woman was there, still clinging to Olivia's belly.

"So warm and soft," the black-haired woman murmured.

Olivia clawed at her middle, tears burning her eyes. The black-haired woman laughed. Licked the tears off her cheek.

Trembling, Olivia grabbed the heaviest object she could reach—a ceramic toothbrush holder—and hit the mirror as hard as she could. The glass spider-webbed from the center, splitting the black-haired woman's face into a hundred pieces. The black-haired woman murmured a warning, but Olivia hit it again, and again, until all she heard was the shatter of glass and the thump of her heartbeat in her ears.

"Olivia."

Olivia turned, still brandishing the toothbrush holder. Seeing Kris, she folded over on herself. Bits of glass stuck out of her arms and palms between dots of blood. Kris's lips moved, but Olivia couldn't hear any of it; it was like her ears had been stuffed with cotton. Her heart raced and her face felt cold.

"She's still here," Olivia murmured, limply swinging her pathetic weapon as Kris struggled to keep her upright. "Still here."

And then it all went black.

CHAPTER TWENTY-FOUR

SHANNON

in't dead.

Part of me wants to believe it's a cruel joke. Would Jennifer—no, that's stupid. She wouldn't. Couldn't, if I'm honest. But if I believe it's a joke, that means there's someone out there who knows what I did.

I have to know.

It's days before I can get to the kitchen during a mass smoke break. The kitchen staff are really going at it just outside the back door; the smell of cigarette smoke permeates the air, clinging to my hair and clothes. I'll need to find a way to shower or borrow one of the girls' floral body sprays. The orderlies have to fight tooth and nail for their smoke breaks, so they're not exactly gentle when they catch one of us smoking. I tried it once, didn't care for it, but that wouldn't matter once they got a whiff. Even in the Bethany Wing, smoke breaks are coveted and ruthlessly monitored. I'd have to answer questions I'm not prepared for.

Still, I pick my way through the half-dark of the unoccupied kitchen toward what should have been a zip-tied pantry. But the zip tie is on the floor, broken, and the door hangs open by an inch. I swallow the lump in my throat as I reach for the handle and pull the door open, quick, like ripping off a Band-Aid.

My neck goes hot, and I lock my knees to keep myself upright.

The bottom of the pantry is empty except for a can, the label torn off. Bet my left arm it would fit perfectly inside the label left under my pillow.

I leave the can and close the pantry, ignoring the whispers in my ear, the lips brushing the back of my neck. I should have known I couldn't get rid of Jo that easy. Should have known it was only a matter of time.

Suppose I should have mentioned—this isn't the first time I've had to kill Jo.

The evening after I found Iris, the police came to the house.

My brothers were convinced I was being arrested, practically salivating at the idea, and Erin couldn't bring herself to look at me, studying every inch of the ground, the ceiling, the mildly attractive officer's jawline.

My dad sat silently beside my mother, who leaned toward the officer with her arms crossed over her middle. She looked like she was going to puke.

"It's just procedure," the office assured me. "You're not in trouble."

That's what they always say, right before the other shoe drops.

"I told you everything," I said. "I'm not lying."

There was no fire, they said. Iris had been dead for days. Asphyxiated. They found dirt in her teeth and fingernails.

It was impossible. I saw what I saw.

"Good, that's good." His voice reached for soothing but was more like sandpaper.

I couldn't focus on anything but his cigarette-stained teeth and sour coffee breath. I kept hearing footsteps upstairs, right above our heads where I'd left the baby to sleep and fought to keep from looking up. I tried to catch Erin's eye when her gaze lingered too long on the ceiling fan, but her eyes slipped over me like a fish through wet hands.

The officer continued, "But just to make sure I got it all down right, it'd be great if you could tell me again."

"You're sure she's not in any trouble here?" Dad finally piped up. "I could get an attorney here right quick if I need."

He couldn't, but I appreciated the gesture. Wasn't anyone before or since who took my side quick as my daddy. I miss him.

"I'm sure," the officer said, a slight edge slipping into his voice. He turned back to me. "Okay, Shannon. From the top."

I pinched the underside of my thigh to give my hands something to do. I caught the officer looking, lifting his eyebrow, so I folded my hands in my lap instead. I'm a good girl.

I told him, again, about leaving the rec room, about being told to go to Marcia's office and getting lost.

"You've been a volunteer at Bethany Home for going on"—he checked his notebook like he didn't have everything I'd ever said memorized—"six months now, right?"

"Yes."

"Six months is a long time to get to know a place. Must be pretty complicated for you to get lost."

Bite him, a voice in my head said. *Bite his ear off and spit it in his mouth and make him eat it.*

It was so loud it made me jump, which earned a victorious look from the cop. He figured he had me in a corner. That I'd *confess.*

"I was upset," I said, as calmly as I could. "I'd been attacked by Laura, one of the mothers, and then finding Iris right after…" I shivered.

"Why didn't you call for help right when you found her? Especially if she was, as you said, on fire."

"I was scared! I just ran. I had the—I had Olivia with me and what was I supposed to do? Just let her sit and breathe in the fumes of a chemical fire while I screamed my head off?"

"You could have brought her to a safer place."

"So you think I should have left her in a hallway somewhere? For one of the mothers to take and do whatever they liked?"

My mother nodded once and my dad muttered a gruff, "S'right."

I'd won my parents to my side, which meant the conversation was over. The officer knew it just as well as I did, folding up his notebook.

Still, as he stood, he looked down hard on me, gray eyes through to the back of my skull. "You sure there's nothing else you want to tell me?"

There *was* a fire. Iris had burned, even if the body she'd left behind wasn't. The thing with the black eyes had taken her, the way it'd taken her baby. I wasn't sure, but when the police told me about the dirt in her teeth, I knew. It was a reminder—of her failure, of what the black-haired woman was capable of. All of Iris's efforts to keep the pieces of herself sacred did nothing. The black-haired woman had gotten Iris, her daughter. Had gotten you.

"Shannon? Is that all?"

I nodded, too afraid of what my voice would do.

The next morning, my mother woke me up out of a dead sleep by jabbing a cold finger in my armpit.

"Get up," she hissed.

It took too long for my mind to catch up with my eyes, still half-stuck in a nightmare. I'd been laying in the grass, close enough to the house I could hear my dad telling my brothers off for leaving their bikes in the yard again, but too deep into the trees for anyone to see me. Something had me by the ankles and was dragging me into the darkness, pausing every few steps to chew on my toes.

I wriggled them now, relieved to find them all attached. I turned over, felt something hard jab me in the hip.

Iris's sketchbook.

I'd found it in her room, grabbed it, and stuffed it under my shirt before Marcia found me. Gruesome pictures of goblins leering hungrily over sleeping women and children. One flashed into my mind as I saw my mother standing over me: a woman, expression calm, serene, as she knelt in front of a fireplace, arms outstretched as if in baptismal ecstasy toward a baby burning in the middle of the hearth.

"What's wrong?" I asked, unable to keep my gaze from wandering toward the baby.

"Get up," my mother said again. "We're going to church."

It was still dark outside. Erin snored softly in her bed. The only light came from the bathroom in the hallway, which flickered as my dad moved through it.

"Now?"

My mother nodded. "Don't wake your sister."

"She's not coming?"

"Just do as you're told, Shannon."

She stood over my bed, arms crossed, until I finally threw off the blankets.

"Five minutes," she said and left the room.

We hadn't been regular churchgoers since before my brothers were born. By the time they came around, dressing and corralling four kids for Sunday service was too much for my parents, who figured God would understand. I came down-stairs expecting to at least see my brothers in their pinch-neck shirts and faded khakis, but only my parents waited for me in the living room.

"Where's Olivia?" my mother asked.

"Sleeping," I said.

"For Christ's sake, Shannon." My mother pushed past me, reaching back to drag me by the arm. "You're a mother. Where you go, your child goes."

Erin had covered her head with her blanket when we barreled in, my mother opening and slamming dresser drawers until she found a clean pair of footy pajamas for the baby. She dressed her, shushing back the baby's protests, and dropped her in my arms before stuffing diapers in a bag, which she carried into the kitchen. I followed a few steps behind, the skin on my neck pinching with every breath from the baby's mouth. My mother prepared a bottle, which she shoved in the bag with the diapers.

"Let's go," she said, rushing past my dad. "We're late."

———————

The sun had just started to come up when we pulled into the half-empty parking lot. Blue-haired ladies and their teetering husbands hobbled toward the entrance, where a bronze St. Francis beckoned. Moss climbed up his legs up to the knees, and the way his mouth was twisted, it was like he was reaching out for help, but people walked past, unmoved, anxious to get to the donuts provided by the Ladies' Auxiliary before they were gone. If that wasn't a metaphor for church, I don't know what is.

My mother moved through the crowd, past the bottleneck at the community room doors where the smell of fresh coffee drifted out. She tugged on my dad's shirt cuff each time he paused to say hello. Just outside the sanctuary, tea lights in red candleholders flickered with the cough and sputter of the vent above, all beneath the watchful gaze of Mother Mary. Her blue cloak was chipped at the edges, and someone had colored in her toenails with a black marker. I remember being brought here to light a candle before my grandmother's funeral mass and thinking I heard Mary whispering in my ear, urging me to move the candle just a few inches closer to the curtains. I told the priest about it during my next confession in a rare moment of honesty and earned twenty Hail Marys and a phone call home, which got me a paddle to the ass for my trouble.

Mother Mary didn't stop talking, but I was done listening.

After my mother made a rickety descent onto her knees at Mary's feet, she stood and started toward the sanctuary, arm looped through my dad's. I started to follow, but my mother shook her head.

"Nuh uh. You and Olivia go to the mothers' room."

Dad frowned. "It'll be fine. Olivia's barely made a peep since we left the house. She's not gonna disturb anybody."

But my mother wasn't budging. "It's disrespectful."

"I hardly think—"

My mother cut him off with a look. The blue-haired ladies had had their fill of donuts and coffee and were starting toward them. My mother shifted her weight, antsy. "The mothers' room," she repeated. "You sit and you pray."

I was exhausted and starving, so rather than keeping my mouth shut, I asked, "Sure thing. Got any requests?"

If not for the blue-haired ladies, my mother would have slapped me. Instead, she tightened her grip on my dad's arm. "Pray," she said, "and hope He's listening."

She dragged my dad into the sanctuary without another word.

I knew where the mothers' room was—as a Christmas mass altar server I'd had to escort women and their broods to the room—but I took my time getting there. There hadn't been time to grab the stroller, so I carried the baby in your car seat, resisting the urge to cover her face with the thin blanket. Her face was so still and smooth it might as well have been plastic. My fingers itched with the need to touch, to reassure myself.

When I heard the bells chime, signaling the beginning of mass, I finally went into the mothers' room. I expected to find it mostly full, mothers seated with their hymnals obediently open to the opening hymn (knowing damn well they wouldn't be singing it), their kids on the floor surrounded by graham cracker crumbs and large colorful blocks.

The room was empty.

Without the colorful blocks and noise of the kids, the room felt funereal, all plain white walls and simple wooden pews. It looked bigger than I remembered, but somehow smaller at the same time. The ceiling was low and there were no windows into the hallway separating the sanctuary from the administrative offices. A small tinny speaker in the corner of the ceiling crackled to life.

"Please turn to hymn 451."

I recognized the voice of the choir director—a former amateur opera singer who drowned out even the worst of the choir.

The speaker buzzed with the opening chords from the organ.

I sat in the middle of the pew closest to the door and sat the car seat on the floor. I flipped through the hymnal and then threw it. It hit the wall with a satisfying thump.

The baby didn't react.

I only half listened as the hymn faded and the readings began—

This is a reading from the Gospel according to Luke...

—which bled into more hymns and the ceremonial ringing of bells. I took a little satisfaction in imagining my mother kneeling and standing, kneeling more, and sitting, her knees popping, a smile plastered on her face through the pain.

The priest's voice pulled me out of my thoughts, so loud it made the speaker tremble. "Jesus did not come to us to make us comfortable," he said. "Rather, He was born to set fire to the earth."

The baby wriggled in the car seat, mouth twisted in discomfort.

"Even a holy fire burns," the priest continued. "In fact, divine fire burns hotter and more brightly than the fire of man. It is not a fire of destruction; rather it is a fire that brings purity. We read in the Word of the Lord that His enemies tempt us to the flames of Hell so that the devil may dance in the ashes of our fallen souls. You may be fooled into believing this is God's attempt to trick you, to pull the rewards of Heaven further out of reach. As repentant sinners, you cannot be blamed. But such is the intelligence of God. By delivering His son to purify the world by the fire of His passion, He teaches us to not be afraid. Once we have been burned by the fire of God, the fires of Hell cannot touch us. We walk through the flames, sinners reborn, and emerge the other side worthy of the Kingdom of Heaven."

Like falling in a dream, the baby's strangled cry brought me crashing back to earth so fast I jumped in my seat. I looked down to see her clawing at the straps, her face beet red, tiny bubbles of foam forming at the corners of her mouth.

"Walk through the flames of God," the priest said. "Regain that which was lost. Burn and be reborn. Let us pray."

———————

I don't know what my mother expected to happen that day, if I was supposed to come out of that room fundamentally changed somehow. Whatever it was, it was clear I'd let her down. She didn't speak to me the rest of the afternoon.

There was a strange sort of clarity that came with accepting that you were gone. I looked at the baby in your crib and it was like the mask had fallen away, revealing this twisted, gnarled thing. Each time I looked at it, I felt the black-haired woman's breath on the back of my neck, heard her whisper in my ear.

I was a failure. A whore. This was my punishment. I would have to live the rest of my life with it. With her.

I didn't want to accept that. I couldn't. I loved you too much, needed you too much. There wasn't much I was good at, but I was determined I would be a good mother. I would do everything and anything it took to get you back. That was the difference between me and Iris. I wasn't going to give up the way she did. I wasn't too late. I could feel it.

Looking back at the sketchbook, I turned the page and found another picture I hadn't seen before because the pages had been stuck together. The same woman sat beside the now-smoldering fire, a different baby in her arms. This one's face was pink and healthy, and its arms reached up for the woman's hair, which hung playfully around its face and shoulders. Lines in the woman's face from the first drawing had smoothed, and the stiffness in her body had loosened. She looked happy. Relieved. In the remnants of the fire, a tiny skull was engulfed in ash.

I turned back to the first drawing and held it up close to the baby in your crib. "Is this you?"

She squeezed her hands into fists and her knuckles cracked like branches in a stiff wind. She opened her mouth and her tongue was gray.

Walk through the flames of God. Regain that which was lost.

Prayer was something we did over meals and under hushed breath—punch-like prayers against bad luck and worry. I closed my eyes and held the sketchbook against my chest and prayed, begging for guidance, to be shown some kind of sign.

My mother, Erin, my father...all they wanted was for me to be a good mother. To prove I was worthy of you. They didn't understand the lengths I would go, what I was willing to do, what I was willing to give up, to make sure you were safe. I would have gone to Hell and back if it meant I could bring you back with me.

So I prayed. Through dinner, as I washed the baby—still, always so still—and fed her and sang her a lullaby as Erin lingered in the doorway of the bedroom. I prayed until my lips were chapped with whispered murmurs and all meaning fell out of the words.

I laid in bed and closed my eyes, still praying.

Minutes or hours or days later, I woke up to the smell of smoke.

It was still dark, so the shallow flicker of the flames was stark against the night. A bonfire, from the look of it, abandoned but not doused. It wasn't unusual for my dad to set up a fire in the small pit, pull up a rusty lawn chair, and sip a beer alone. He called it his headspace. It was, however, unusual for the fire to be untended. His worry over the house burning down bordered on paranoia, pushing my mother outside to smoke and spraying the oven with a small extinguisher every time one of the boys' drippy pizzas started a tiny grease fire. He wouldn't have left it burning, even to go inside to pee. Better to douse it and call it a night than forget.

This, I decided, was my sign.

I didn't bother dressing. This might have been divine intervention, but even God couldn't keep my dad away forever. He'd smell it just like I did and come running. I had one chance.

I scooped the baby from the crib, balancing her on my shoulder as I slipped into Erin's audition shoes—the only shoes in the house that didn't squeak. It was as if the baby understood my intention and dug her nails into my skin. She opened her mouth, and I was hit with a dense waft of rot. Her belly rumbled as she growled, low and threatening. I thought of the lullabies that'd come from an empty room and wondered if the baby could somehow call to the black-haired woman. My body tingled as phantom teeth scraped across my bare arms and legs.

I crept downstairs and through the kitchen. It would have been safer going through the front door—it didn't groan the way the kitchen door did—but I wanted a straight shot to the fire.

By the time I reached the pit, the flames had died down to barely a flicker. I laid the baby in the grass and shoved sticks at the base of the pit where the embers still burned white hot.

"Do not fear the pit," I whispered. "Walk through the fire. Get back what was lost."

Movement came from somewhere behind me, in the trees. I froze, one hand still holding a piece of wood in the embers. The peach fuzz on my fingers singed. A soft breeze blew, bringing with it the first notes of a lullaby.

I had to move.

I looked down at the baby and my breath caught. The stiffness in her limbs and the sharpness in her eyes had faded. She smiled, and something in my stomach stirred.

What are you doing?

She wasn't my child, but she was a child, wasn't she? What kind of a person did this?

Like she could read my thoughts, the baby kicked her legs hard enough to make her scoot an inch closer.

Hold me, she seemed to say. *Love me. Care for me.*

They will twist a mother's mind, Iris had said. *They will slither through your veins to the heart of you and plant themselves there. A parasite. Make you question your own eyes. Make you question your own soul.*

Iris was ill. Logically, I knew this. And as I looked down at the baby, part of me couldn't imagine how such a small thing could wreak so much havoc on my mind. None of what'd happened to me, to Iris, to any of the women at Bethany Home, was this child's fault. I didn't want to hurt it.

Could it even feel pain?

She's a doll, I thought, *wearing my child's skin.*

Ask any mother and they'll tell you the same—if it came down to your child and someone else's, you *will* choose yours. Every time.

Knowing what I planned to do, my stomach rolled. But I knew I had to be strong. For you. For us.

I picked up the baby and kneeled, leaning toward the fire, so close I could smell my hair as it began to roast in the heat. The baby squirmed and swatted, gray tongue hanging out as she panted. It was clear to me then. She was an animal. I told myself it was a sign from God. If I could do this one horrible thing, I would have my daughter back.

I started to dangle the baby closer to the center of the fire, where it burned hottest and brightest. The flames were too close. Too hot. The hair on my arms singed, and my skin felt like it would blister. Just as I got up the nerve to lean all the way forward, someone snatched the baby out of my arms.

"Jesus. Oh, God."

My mother stood over me, frantically prodding and turning the baby in her arms.

She finally looked down at me, and I wanted to explain, but before I could form any words, she slapped me, hard, the rough edge of her wedding ring catching on my lip.

"I just—"

She raised her hand again. She had never slapped me like that before, and it caught us both by surprise. For an instant, it was just the two of us, staring at each other, the flames flickering in our eyes.

Tears blurred my vision as I sank back on my hands, the damp grass soaking through my nightgown.

"It's not her," I whispered. "It's not Olivia."

My mother clutched the baby to her chest, rocking and making shushing noises even though the baby was silent.

"It's not her," I said, louder this time. "Are you listening?"

My mother shook her head, tears dripping down her face and landing on the baby's head.

"I don't know how to save you," she said. To me or to the baby, I couldn't tell. "I tried, but I don't know how. I don't know what to do."

The fire was still burning hot. I had one chance.

I launched myself at her, clawing at her arms to try and get the baby loose, but my mother was stronger than she looked. She slung the baby onto her shoulder and easily shoved me back into the dirt. I missed the edge of the fire by a hair.

"Don't do it, Shan," my mother said. "Don't listen to her."

My face went red, and my heart skipped. "I just want Olivia back."

"She's here, honey. Look at her." She turned the baby to face me but kept a firm grip. "Look at her eyes. They're your eyes."

I looked, but all I saw were twin pools of black, framed in a slack expression. Her skin was gray and flat. An impostor.

"Help me," I begged. "Please."

"I am helping you," she said.

Without another word, she walked back toward the house, leaving me alone with the fire.

I held my hand over the flames, only pulling back when my skin started to blister.

I was sure, then, that I would never see you again.

CHAPTER TWENTY-FIVE

OLIVIA

Olivia came to with her arms wrapped in what looked like toilet paper, dotted with red. She was on the floor of the hallway, half leaning against the wall. Kris was on her hands and knees, her back half sticking out of the bathroom. She leaned back on her heels and dumped a dustpan full of glass shards in a grocery bag.

Numb from leaning against a doorjamb, Olivia struggled to sit up, but the minute she put pressure on her hands, sharp spikes of pain shot up her arms and into her neck. She whimpered, but Kris didn't seem to hear. Movement in the corner of Olivia's eye made her freeze. Was the black-haired woman still here? Had Kris seen her? And where was Flora?

"Oh, good," a voice above her said. "You're awake."

Aunt Erin stood in the opposite doorway, her expression a mix of concern and fear.

"Where's Flora?" Olivia asked.

"Sleeping," Kris said from the bathroom doorway. Her eyebrows furrowed. "Are you okay?"

"Did you see her?" Olivia tried again to sit up, hissing against the sting.

"Flora? She's okay. She's fine."

Olivia shook her head. "The woman—"

"Stop." Aunt Erin crouched next to her. "Let me help."

Olivia shrugged her off. "I'm fine." The toilet paper began to unravel, revealing shallow cuts that'd mostly stopped bleeding. She peeled the rest of it away, wincing. "See? I'm fine."

Kris stood, tying up the plastic bag filled with what was probably the remains of their bathroom mirror. "What happened, Liv? You were screaming, and when I came in, you tried to brain me with the toothbrush holder."

"I—" Her mind was a mess as she groped for an excuse. "I thought I saw a spider."

"Don't." Kris shook her head. "Don't act like nothing just happened."

Olivia let Aunt Erin help her to her feet, if only to buy her some time to think. Just because Kris hadn't seen the woman didn't mean she hadn't been there. She had been there. Olivia had felt her. Smelled her. And she'd been there for Flora.

She pushed past Aunt Erin into the bedroom where Flora lay on her stomach in the bassinet, asleep. A puddle of drool had formed in the sheet. Olivia smiled despite the pain and leaned down to kiss her head, pausing an inch above her skin.

Something was wrong.

The way cherry cough syrup only ever smelled like alcohol and bitterly sweet, Flora smelled somehow artificial. Like someone had tried to emulate that sour-sweet, warm baby scent but had ended up with something closer to sugar-soaked peat.

"Come on," Aunt Erin whispered, gently pulling on Olivia's elbow. "You'll wake her up and then we'll all be in for it."

"Have you been here the whole time?"

"Kris called me when you—"

"No. With Flora. Have you been with Flora the whole time?"

Aunt Erin's expression blanked, and the color faded out of her cheeks. "Why?"

Olivia ran a shaky finger along Flora's back. She didn't stir. "Nothing. Never mind."

"Tell me. Olivia, whatever it is, you can tell me. I swear."

"My mother was here."

"Did she—?"

"She felt terrible for just showing up. She used the bathroom and left. That was it. Kris wouldn't let her stay." Olivia remembered the note and patted her pocket, grateful to feel it was still there. "I need to lie down."

"Yes. That's a good idea." Aunt Erin glanced at Flora. "I'll just bring her into the other room."

She seemed relieved when Olivia didn't argue.

She shut the door and heard Aunt Erin tell Kris she was going to rest. She stood on the other side of the door, waiting for Kris to come in and interrogate her, but Aunt Erin must have convinced her to leave Olivia be.

Luckily, her phone was still in her pocket. There was a crack down the screen from when she fell, but it worked fine. Heart racing, knowing Kris could walk in at any second, she entered the number from the piece of paper and wrote: Hi.

The reply was almost instant: Hi. Followed by another: I'm sorry for making a problem.

She shot back: There's no problem, her face coloring with the lie.

Sweet of you to say so.

A knock on the door made Olivia almost drop the phone. She shoved it in her pocket and climbed into bed. "Yes?"

Aunt Erin poked her head in. "Sorry. I know you wanted to sleep, but—"

"But we need to talk," Kris finished, pushing past her. She softened as she studied Olivia. "How are your arms?"

Olivia pulled them out from under the blanket. "Attached."

"We should probably take you to a doctor."

"No," Aunt Erin said, a little too forcefully. "They're shallow cuts, looks like. Barely broke the skin. Some Neosporin and a few Band-Aids, and she'll be fine."

Kris didn't look too sure, but nodded. "Liv, you know I love you, right? That you and Flora mean everything to me?"

"Yes," Olivia said. And she did. Mostly.

"Me too," Aunt Erin said. "I love you like a daughter."

Almost too slow to catch on, Olivia noticed a subtle change in the atmosphere of the room. Like the heat had turned on full blast. She resisted the urge to kick the blankets off.

"Thank you?" Olivia said.

Aunt Erin smiled, but it didn't reach her eyes.

"Is that all?" Olivia asked.

"No," Aunt Erin started. "Kris thinks..." She looked to Kris, who crossed the room and sat on the edge of the bed.

"We think," Kris clarified, "that it would be a good idea for you to have someone around."

Olivia frowned. "Like a babysitter."

"Like a nanny. Someone to help with Flora."

"I can come over most days," Erin said, "for a few hours."

"But I think we need someone more...full time," Kris added.

"I thought that's what your job was."

"It is," Kris said, defensive. "I do. I am. But I can't be here all the time."

"And when you're not, I am. I don't understand." Except Olivia did understand. On some level, she'd been expecting this, but now that it was here, she couldn't believe it. "You don't trust me to be alone with Flora."

"I didn't say that."

"You didn't have to." She looked at Aunt Erin. "This doesn't feel like your idea, but I don't see you going out of your way to stop it either."

"It's not her place," Kris said before Aunt Erin could answer. "I just know it's a lot right now. Your mother showing up only added to the strain."

Olivia shook her head. That's what this was about. "Just say what you mean."

"I am."

"No. Say you want me to choose. You want me to choose between Flora and having a relationship with my mother."

She didn't deny it.

A good mother, Olivia knew, would choose her daughter. Whatever the other option, she must always choose her daughter. They didn't understand—that was exactly what she was doing. Her phone buzzed in her pocket, and she leaned back, muffling the noise in the mattress.

"We just think you should give it some time," Aunt Erin said.

"I've given it thirty-four years."

"She's dangerous." Kris ran her hands through her hair, pulling the ends. "And it's like you don't even care."

Olivia didn't respond. Nothing she said was going to change her wife's mind. She'd lied to her more in the last few weeks than she had during the rest of their marriage. She hated doing it, but what other choice did she have? Kris didn't trust Olivia to figure out what was happening with her, with Flora, but there was no one else who could. Any doctor would lock her up if she told them what she'd seen, what she felt. What she knew.

"Of course I care," Olivia said carefully. "And maybe you're right. Maybe I could use some help. I haven't been sleeping much."

Some of the tension went out of Kris' jaw. "Okay. Good."

"Do you have someone in mind?"

Kris looked from Olivia to Aunt Erin and back. "I—we could talk about it?"

"Later. I really do think I should rest. My head is killing me."

Aunt Erin left and returned with the bottle of Tylenol. She shook two out and stuck the bottle in Olivia's nightstand. "Let me get you a water."

"I—no. It's fine." Olivia tucked the pills under her tongue, pretending to dry swallow. "Give me a couple of hours?"

Kris looked like she wanted to keep talking, but Aunt Erin pulled her up by her elbow. "Of course. Let us know if you need anything."

Olivia put on her best brave face. "I will."

The second they shut the door, Olivia spit out the pills. They looked a little like Tylenol, but after the halfhearted intervention, she wouldn't leave it to chance. Kris might not have been the type to dope her, but Aunt Erin was just passive-aggressive enough to slip her a back-alley antipsychotic rather than have a hard talk. She dumped them on the floor and kicked them under her bed. Her mouth tasted bitter, the pills having partially dissolved. Whatever it was, she hoped it wasn't enough to feel the effects.

She pulled her phone out of her pocket and read the string of messages:

If you're upset with me, I understand.

I won't bother you or your family anymore, if that's what you want.

When you called, I got over excited.

I'll leave you be. I'm sorry.

She crept toward the door and pressed her ear to it, listening for footsteps or voices, but the hall sounded empty. Outside, it was already getting dark. She didn't have much time.

She sent a text: Can you meet me?

The near-instant reply: Where?

It'd been nearly fifteen years since the last time Olivia had snuck out, but muscle memory carried her silently out the window. She crawled along the side of the house, her mother's journal tucked under one arm, until she reached the hedge separating them from the neighbors. Hunched over, she ran toward the sidewalk. She didn't stop until, winded, she reached the corner. She felt her pulse in her temples and throat, so fast it was more flutter than beat.

She tried not to think about what Kris and Aunt Erin would do if they caught her.

Her phone rang on the way and for the briefest second, she knew in her gut she'd been caught. She was already thinking up excuses when she looked at the display. Charlie.

"Hello?"

"Olivia! Where are you? Can we talk?"

"Home," she lied, "I'm at home."

"Oh, good. I'm driving by your street, I'll just swing by—"

"No!" She cursed under breath. "I mean, no, I'm on my way home. Soon. We're, uh, shopping."

"Okay. Can you talk?"

"Yes."

"So, I asked my sister to look into this Jo person Shannon killed."

"Might have killed."

"Right. And let me tell you, it cost me. She's holding this over my head for the next eight Christmases, easy—"

"Charlie."

"Right. Sorry. So, she was able to get ahold of the roster of patients for the last ten years. Don't ask me how. She's a witch. Anyway, we both went over the lists—and they're short lists, no more than twenty or so women—and we found nothing. No Jo, Joanna, Josephine, Jolene, Mary-Jo, or whatever."

"That doesn't mean anything though. I mean, it could have been a nickname or a middle name. Could have been a lie."

"I thought that too. Have you looked at the Sleepy Eye website lately?"

"No."

"No roommates. None of the patients have them."

Olivia stopped walking. Frowned. "But she said—"

"She said a lot of things." Charlie paused. "Are you okay? Like, really okay?"

"I'm fine."

"Okay."

"Okay." She paused. "Thank you. For your help. I have to go."

"If you need anything—"

Olivia hung up and shoved the phone back in her pocket. She didn't know what to think anymore, or who to believe.

———————

Her mother agreed to meet her in the café of a bookstore within walking distance of Olivia's house. She was already there when Olivia arrived. Olivia spotted her at a small table in the corner, two take-out cups, a brownie, and what looked like a broccoli quiche in front of her.

Olivia hesitated just long enough for her mother to look up and spot her. Her mother gave a small wave and a smile.

There was still time to turn around. Her mother would understand.

Olivia sat, keeping the journal on her lap beneath the table.

"I don't know what you like," her mother said. "It's just black coffee. And the brownie has caramel or something in it. I don't know what that is," she nodded to the quiche, "but it looked good."

"Thanks." She didn't touch the food, but sipped the coffee to give her hands something to do.

Her mother did the same.

"You're left-handed," Olivia said.

"Wrong-handed, my dad would've said."

"Me too."

Her mother grinned. "That's something."

"Yeah."

A few seconds of silence passed. The coffee was already getting cold.

"It's a nice bookstore," her mother said. "I like a bookstore. Used to work in one, long time ago."

Was this it? The *in* she needed? "How was it?"

"Good. Lots of things to read when I was bored."

"That's good."

Her mother brushed a stray hair behind her ear. Tapped her fingers against the sides of her cup. Olivia ran her fingers along the spiral spine of the journal, digging the metal coils beneath her nail. The longer they tiptoed around each other, the less time there was before Kris discovered she was gone. Before she risked losing Flora. Risked losing herself.

She moved her coffee out of the way and set the journal on the table, one hand sitting protectively on the cover.

"Oh," her mother breathed. Something dark passed over her face, there and gone just as quickly. "I was wondering where that'd wandered off to." Her fingers twitched, like she couldn't decide whether to reach for it. "Did you read it?"

"Some of it."

Her mother nodded, anxious splotches coloring her cheeks. "You have questions."

"I had questions before I read it."

"Right. Of course. Sorry." She leaned over the table, arms crossed protectively across her middle. "I've spent years thinking about this. How it would go. Seeing you, I mean. I should never have wrote any of that." The last said with a harshness that surprised Olivia. "You hate me now, I guess."

"I don't hate you." When her mother offered a small smile, she added, "Because I don't know you. This—" She tapped the journal cover. "I need to know."

"Ask me anything," her mother said, anxious. "I'll tell you whatever you want to know."

"Is it true?"

"Is what true?"

"All of it? Any of it?"

"Depends." Olivia shot her a look. "Truth isn't as straightforward as that."

"Of course it is. Something is either true or it isn't."

"Okay, then. True or false: you love your wife."

"True," Olivia spat.

"But she doesn't know you're here. Am I right? Which means you either lied to her face or lied by omission. Lying is not an expression of love."

Olivia's face burned. "You're deflecting."

Her mother smiled. Shook her head. "You sound like Angela."

"Angela—that's your doctor, right?"

Her mother nodded.

"Earlier, you said she thought I should make the first move. When I spoke to her, she tried to warn me off altogether."

"You talked to Angela?" Her expression darkened.

"It's how I knew you were...out."

"She's just looking out for us," her mother said, almost to herself. "That's all." She sighed. Rubbed her face. Her gaze settled on the journal. "It was all true. At the time."

"What does that mean?"

"It means it's easy to mistake belief for truth. It's easy to see things that aren't there, just because you want to see them."

Olivia shook her head. She didn't need platitudes or superficial ruminations. She needed to know the truth. The real and actual. To know if what was happening to her, to Flora, could be fixed. If the black-haired woman was real. If she was losing her mind. "There's something wrong with my daughter."

"With Flora?"

"Or with me." Olivia palmed sweat off her forehead. Her whole body felt hot, but she had to clench her jaw to keep her teeth from chattering. "I don't know. But there's something—" She stroked the cover of the journal. "Someone. It's all in here. Everything. It's like you took everything out of my head and put it here. She isn't—she doesn't *smell* right. Believe me, I know how that sounds, but it's like—"

"Like someone stole your daughter and put something else in her place," her mother finished. "You don't feel the things they told you that you would when you look at her. She looks wrong and rather than feel the sort of fierce protectiveness they talk about in books and movies, all you feel is resentful."

Tears burned Olivia's eyes. God, she was going crazy, wasn't she? "Yes."

"That's normal," her mother said softly.

Olivia shook her head. "No. Listen. She hurts me. And when she looks at me...I hear things I shouldn't. And there's this woman who follows me. A black-haired woman with black, hungry eyes. I think she wants her. Wanted her. Something. I don't know."

Her mother paled. "No." She shook her head. "No. Stop. Flora is your flesh and blood. She has to be."

Olivia looked down at her arms, marred from the broken glass. Flesh and blood. She picked at a scratch that'd slightly scabbed over until a drop of blood dribbled from the wound. "I thought you would understand. I thought—" She bit off the rest of her sentence.

"I do," her mother said. "I do understand. Believe me."

She shook her head. "No. You don't." She slid the journal across the table. "You should take this back."

Her mother started to protest, but Olivia stood before she could hand it back. "I need to go."

"Already?"

"Like you said, Kris doesn't know I'm here." She smiled sadly. "She didn't understand why I wanted—needed—to see you. Knowing what you did. Tried to do. I'm risking my marriage to be here right now. Maybe more than that. Maybe everything. And you can't even tell me the truth. All I wanted was to know that I wasn't alone."

Her mother leaned over the table and grabbed her arm. "Wait. Just—" She hit her knee on the corner and winced. "You're not alone."

"No?"

Her mother lowered her voice. "They'll send me back."

Olivia's heart skipped. "I won't let them."

"Doesn't work that way."

"I'll make it that way," she growled. The woman behind the counter looked up, startled. Olivia sank back toward the chair, barely touching the seat. "I need to understand what's happening."

But her mother shook her head again. Whatever was sitting on the tip of her tongue, it was trapped behind her teeth.

"You believed this." Olivia jabbed the cover of the journal. "You believed I was wrong, the way Flora is wrong."

After a long moment, her mother nodded.

"What happened? Did you change your mind? Or did you...find me?"

A phone ringing stopped her mother from answering. She took her phone out of her jacket pocket, hanging on the back of her chair, and frowned. "It's Erin. I have to go."

Olivia blanched. Did they know she was gone? That she was with her mother?

She didn't wait to find out. Grabbing the journal, she ran out of the café and only made it a few hundred feet before she was too winded and had to slow to a walk. Her skin had gone all tingly and hot, and when she looked around, it was like her eyes were half a second ahead of her brain, her surroundings jumping into place like cuts in a film reel. She picked up the pace, despite her legs and back protesting, gulping air. Her ears started ringing like she was going to pass out, so she pinched the underside of her arm, the pain lighting up her body.

She reached the hedge and crept slowly along the edge, cursing herself for not being able to catch her breath. She imagined her neighbor's ear pressed to their walls, listening to her gasp.

But there was no one waiting for her at the door when she scrambled past, and the window was still open enough she could slip her fingers beneath and crawl inside. The room looked undisturbed. Quiet. And when she listened at the door, all she heard was the tap of Kris's computer keyboard and Aunt Erin's muffled voice.

She kicked off her shoes and jeans and slipped into bed just as it was getting dark, but there was no way she was going to rest.

They'll send me back, her mother had said.

Did that mean her mother believed her? That it was real? She couldn't tell her because she didn't trust Olivia not to run to Aunt Erin or Angela or whoever and tell them Mommy was crazy.

But her mother wasn't crazy. And neither was Olivia. Something was wrong with Flora.

Your flesh and blood.

She climbed out of bed again and, in the growing dark, rifled through her nightstand until she found what she was looking for. She crept across the room to the door and turned the handle—slowly, slowly—wincing at the creak as she pulled the door open just wide enough to see into the hallway. The only light came from a lamp in the living room, a soft glow barely penetrating the growing darkness.

Aunt Erin's voice drifted down the hallway. "...pills. Every day, like clockwork. I watch her take them myself."

Olivia heard chair legs scape against the floor. Footsteps across the creaky living room floor. Kris said, "Forgive me, but assuring me your sister is taking antipsychotics doesn't do much to instill confidence."

"It should. And anyway, people take them for all kinds of things. Some forms of depression—"

"I can't do it. I'm sorry. I have to think about my family."

"Olivia is your family. If she needs this, why stand in the way?"

Kris said something else to Aunt Erin, who responded, neither voice loud enough for Olivia to make out what was said.

Holding her breath, she tiptoed across the hall to the other bedroom, hoping they'd put Flora to bed in here. She eased the door open and slipped inside, shutting it behind her with a soft click. The only light came from a cloud-shaped night-light sitting on top of the dresser they'd filled with onesies and dresses during the last month of her pregnancy. The cloud's smile seemed to twist the longer she looked at it, becoming more menacing. She turned away from it and started toward the crib. Flora lay on her stomach, a little lump in the middle of the mattress. Her back rose and fell with soft, even breaths.

While part of her urged her to leave, to go back to bed and hope these twisted, horrible thoughts in her head went away by morning, another part knew they wouldn't. She couldn't ignore this any longer. She had to know.

Holding the nail scissors from her nightstand between her teeth, she gently eased down the neck of Flora's onesie. Her fingertips touched bare flesh and it was like every nerve lit up, on fire. Flora burned.

She's sick, Olivia thought. *A fever.*

A wave of guilt washed over her. How long had Flora been warm? Had Kris noticed? Should they call the pediatrician? Olivia stripped her down, too forcefully.

Flora jumped and started to cry. Olivia slapped her hand over Flora's mouth, muffling it, her worry over Flora doing battle with the fear of getting caught out of her room. It wouldn't matter that Flora might be sick, only that Olivia was with her unsupervised. Flora finally calmed and when Olivia pulled her hand away, something oozed out of the side of Flora's mouth. Phlegm, she thought, but when she leaned down to get a better look, she smelled pine and wet dirt.

Without thinking, she dragged her finger through the small globule and brought it to her nose.

It wasn't phlegm. It was sap.

She half stumbled back from the crib, scissors abandoned on the floor. Flora's wails shook the room. Olivia needed to get out of there. Out of the house. Away, just...away. But she couldn't find the door in the dark and her gaze passed over a shadow thicker and darker than the rest and it was like every muscle in her body contracted at once. Her head jerked back and like paint peeling from the wall, the shadow separated from the corner, becoming fuller, more substantial, until the black-haired woman stood in front of her, eyes shining.

"Do you see?" she asked. Her voice was barely above a whisper.

Olivia felt herself leaning toward it and pulled back. "Go away. Get out of my house."

The black-haired woman shook her head. "Can't do that, sweetie. Not until this is all over."

"Who are you? What do you want?"

The black-haired woman's long branch-like fingers brushed over Flora's back. Her gaze flashed to the scissors. "What were you doing to do? Your own *child*."

"She's not mine. I wouldn't. She's not *mine*."

Footsteps thundered down the hall. "Olivia?"

Olivia started for the door, but the black-haired woman blocked her way. "Uh oh," the black-haired woman said. "Daddy's coming. Better run, before she sees."

The door flung open, and all Olivia could hear was screaming.

It took a long time for her to realize it was her own.

Aunt Erin wrestled Olivia away from the crib and Kris leaned over the side—*Oh my God, oh my God*—and Aunt Erin tried to soothe her—*It's fine, she's fine*—while Olivia's body went limp and the black-haired woman watched from her shadowy corner.

"She's there," Olivia said. "She's going to hurt her. You have to—" She gulped, unable to catch her breath. "Flora's—there's something wrong with Flora."

Aunt Erin's nails dug into Olivia's skin, but she barely felt it. She shushed Olivia between tossing tepid assurances at Kris. "She's fine. It'll be okay."

Surprisingly strong, Aunt Erin dragged Olivia back across the hall to her bedroom and into bed, pinning her arms to the sides.

"We have to call someone," Kris said from the doorway. "A hospital or facility."

"No," Aunt Erin spat. "Don't you dare."

"She could have—"

"You weren't listening." She looked back at Olivia, her face marred with concern. "Sweetie, who was it? Who was there?"

"There was no one—" Kris started.

"You heard it," Aunt Erin said. "I heard it." She looked back at Olivia. "Tell me, Liv."

But Olivia's ears throbbed and her body was numb and it was like her heart was beating out of her chest. She felt cold and hot and her mouth tasted bitter.

And then a voice came from her throat, a voice that sounded like Olivia, but also not like Olivia at all. "She's coming for her. The black-haired woman. She wants her. She wants—" Her throat burned like fire. "Flora. She's gone. My baby's gone."

CHAPTER TWENTY-SIX

SHANNON

I wake up in the middle of the night gagging and pull her long black hair out of my throat. It's everywhere—in my pillow and tangled in the loose fabric of my socks and at the bottom of my coffee in the morning. She's taunting me, trying to pull me out of myself and into her games. I won't let her do it this time. This time, I'm the one in control.

Jennifer hasn't spoken to me since the apology disaster. I've tried to stay out of her way, give her the space she needs to come around, but given the way she eyes the windows of the activity room, studying the intricate locks for weaknesses, space is the last thing she needs.

I catch her right after lunch on the day I'm convinced she'll try the lock. If she doesn't make it through—and she won't—they'll only lock her up in the higher-security wing. They call it higher security, but all it means is the orderlies are paid less to do more, so are more inclined to look the other way if a patient is desperate enough (and creative enough) to get their hands on something deadly. Either way, she gets what she wants.

There are only a few minutes to go before med distribution, so I don't have long. I stand next to her at the window, close enough to feel the warmth of her skin. She doesn't move, but the corner of her mouth twitches downward. I study the window. It doesn't take long to find the broken latch, glued into place with a bit of caulking. There are scratches down the center of it, like someone had been dragging a nail through it, a little at a time. I glance down and see Jennifer's pinky nail is jagged and caked in white gunk. She's patient, I'll give her that. A desperate woman usually is. In another life, we might have been good friends.

"What if it doesn't open?" I say. "What will you do then?"

I can tell she's thinking about lying. "I don't know."

She knows. If you want it bad enough, you have a backup.

"I guess it wouldn't matter if I said something to Angela."

Anger pulses off her in waves. "I'll find another way."

"I don't doubt it."

"I can't be without Michael. I need him."

"Believe me, no one relates more than I do."

"Then why would you tell?"

"Same reason you're thinking about jumping out that window. My baby needs me."

She nods once. "What do you want?"

"They got you on risperidone, right?"

She nods again.

"Good. All I want you to do is cheek your pills for the next couple of days and hand them over to me. Easy."

"Easy?" Jennifer finally looks at me, incredulous. She starts to argue, but something in her head clicks. Either she will get caught and sent to the higher-security wing where finding her death would be all the easier, or she won't and her delusions about Michael being alive will resurface. A win-win to her. "How many days?"

"Let's say three to start."

She shifts uncomfortably. "You could just ask Angela to put you on it, if that's what you want."

And risk falling further away from release? Further from my chances of finding you? Never.

"You let me worry about me," I say. "So. How about it?"

"Fine," Jennifer says without hesitation. "But if I go down, I'm taking you with me."

I swallow. "Fair's fair."

I walk her through how to pin the tablet to the roof of her mouth, sip from the water cup and swallow the water while keeping the pill between her tongue and the roof of her mouth, but by the time the med cart comes, it's obvious I wasted my breath. She is quick, smooth, and even flashes the bored-looking orderly a wide-open, all-clear mouth before planting herself next to me on the couch. She coughs into her fist, then slides me the damp tablet.

Jo is as good as gone.

The morning after the fire, my dad took the door off mine and Erin's bedroom while Erin screeched at him from her bed.

"I still don't understand why," she whined, and then shot me a poisonous look. "I didn't do anything wrong."

"Mom wants to be able to hear the baby," my dad said.

"Then tell her the baby can sleep in her room!"

"You tell her that and see how long you live after."

Erin grumbled something under her breath.

I kept trying to catch my dad's eye as he worked. I wondered if my mother told him. What she told him. Every time I tried to corner her, to explain myself, she shook her head and practically ran from the room. That didn't mean she left me alone though. Taking the door off the hinges was only the first step.

With Erin gone, my brothers were tasked with following me from room to room, their poor attempt at playing nonchalance broken when they had to abandon their game to trail me up to the bathroom.

"Are you going to stand there the whole time?" I shouted through the door.

"Yep!" they gleefully replied.

And if it wasn't my brothers, it was my mother lingering in the hall when I brought the baby upstairs for a nap, or washing already clean dishes while I made myself a sandwich for lunch. I couldn't breathe without someone noticing, which was, of course, the point. My mother had always been (and still is, if Erin's stories are anything to go on) a head-in-the-sand kind of woman. The more she followed me, the more she sicced my brothers after me, the more confident I became that she hadn't said a word to anyone. Had probably convinced herself it was a terrible dream and was only keeping an eye on me *just in case*. I figured I only had to bide my time, keep my head low, and then I could try again and hope that you were safe somewhere until then.

Then the police came back.

One of the mothers saw me take something from the room.

No one could account for my activity on the day the medical examiner believes Iris died.

The cafeteria manager mentioned Iris and I had had altercations.

I could have *I would never*'d until I was blue in the face, and it wouldn't have made a lick of difference, so I said nothing. My mother seemed to approve, sitting beside me just as stony silent.

"You gonna charge her with something?" my dad asked.

"We're just following up," the detective said, directing his wolf-grin at me. "It'd be awful helpful if Shannon could clear up these...discrepancies."

"Only discrepancy I see is you hounding my daughter when you people already figure this for a suicide."

"I understand why you'd think that."

My dad shrunk back, an old dog bitten by the younger, stronger pup.

The detective turned back to me. "If it's alright with you, Shannon, I'd like to take a sample of your hair."

"My hair?" I asked.

"To be analyzed."

"For?" my mother yipped.

"I can't tell you that."

"Then you can't have her hair."

"All due respect, I was asking—"

"Shannon's a minor. She can't approve without my permission. I won't let her."

"Mrs. MacArthur, this isn't some *gotcha* trick." He sighed, exasperated. "We found a hair at the scene. A long black hair that isn't too far off from Shannon's length."

"I already told you I was there," I said. "Why would that rule me in or out?"

"It was twisted in the victim's fingers. Like she'd pulled it out of her attacker's head."

"My hair isn't black."

"It's dark."

"But not black."

"Even so." He sighed, his patience wearing thin. "Look, this is a good thing. If we can rule you out right away, we can stop coming here and bothering you and your family. We can stop wasting our time. I would think, as a good citizen, you would want that too."

Dad rubbed his face, looking from me to Mom and back again. "I don't get it.

We should just let them take it. Like he said, it'll rule her out right away. We can nip this in the bud."

"It's the principle," my mother said.

Principle, my ass. She wouldn't allow it because, after the fire, she didn't know what I was capable of. She didn't believe, the way my dad did, that I was good. That I wouldn't hurt anyone.

Truth be told, I don't quite believe it either.

Before my mom could argue, I yanked a couple of hairs out of my head and dropped them on the floor in front of the detective. "Oops."

He smirked, covering it before my mother could see it, and pulled a plastic baggie from his pocket, which he used like a glove over his hand to pick up the hair.

"You can't take that," my mother warned, but the bite had been taken out of her voice. He'd take it whether she wanted him to or not.

"Cauline…" My dad rubbed her knee, moving to her back when she shoved his hand away. "It'll be okay. You'll see." He smiled at me. "Our Shanny's a good girl."

My mother covered her face and cried.

That night I dreamed my bedroom had become the woods. There was wood beneath my feet, but the walls had fallen away, replaced by thick trees and the black, black sky. A hand slipped into mine and I didn't have to look to see if it was the black-haired woman. Her steps made almost no noise as we walked past the tree line, the wood floor changing to grass and prickles that stabbed the bottoms of my bare feet.

The corners of my vision started to fog, and each time I came back to sharp clarity, each time I told myself this wasn't right, that I needed to go back home, the black-haired woman's grip tightened and the fog returned.

"It's your fault," she said. "You weren't watching close enough."

I tried to argue, but my mouth wouldn't open. I nodded.

"I hear them talking—your parents—and they're so disappointed. You've ruined your life. Ruined their lives."

Her grip tightened. I nodded again.

"You're a terrible mother."

As though given permission with a look, the muscles in my jaw unlocked. "I'm a terrible mother."

"You lost your child."

"I lost my child."

"And you won't ever get her back, because you don't deserve to."

"I don't deserve to."

The black-haired woman's grip loosened, but I didn't let go. I couldn't let go. If I did, I would sink. I would die.

I woke up with my face damp and my feet muddy, and when I went into the bathroom and looked in the mirror, my eyes were solid black.

CHAPTER TWENTY-SEVEN

OLIVIA

O livia woke up to the sound of screams.

Someone was on top of her, shoving her by the shoulders into the bed. Fingers fished around her mouth and throat, gagging her. "That's good." She recognized Kris's voice. "Good. Try to puke. Come on."

Olivia flailed, knocking Kris off for a second, but couldn't get out of the way before Kris was back, sticking something else down her throat. The gagging and coughing made her woozy, made her ears hot and cotton-stuffed.

Kris' voice hitched. "No, no, no." She slapped Olivia's face. "No don't—how could you do this what were you thinking God Olivia no."

Aunt Erin's voice came from the hallway. "Ambulance is almost here."

The screaming—yes, Olivia could hear it.

She tried to ask what was happening, but Kris's nails had scraped up her throat. Just breathing hurt.

"Now I have to worry about you," Kris said, her voice all acid. "I can't do this. I can't believe you would—"

The doorbell rang and Aunt Erin bolted down the hall. She came back with a pair of EMTs pushing a gurney. Olivia tried to catch Aunt Erin's eye, but each time she looked at Olivia she covered her face.

Kris scooped Olivia out of bed, wobbling under her weight. As she was passed to the EMTs, Olivia's gaze drifted over the room. On the nightstand were half a dozen empty single-shot vodka bottles. The bottle of ibuprofen was on the floor, pills scattered like pebbles.

"What's going on?" Olivia croaked.

"Don't worry, sweetie," the male EMT said. "We'll get you right as rain."

Olivia bristled. "I'm fine. I don't need to go to the hospital."

Aunt Erin shushed her. Pointless, as the female EMT stuck an oxygen mask over Olivia's face and strapped her to the gurney. Panic buzzed up her chest. Where were they taking her? Where was Flora? She remembered the nail scissors, the sap, and her whole body went cold and still.

"That's it, sweetie," the male EMT said. "Just relax. We'll get you fixed in no time."

The black-haired woman stood over his shoulder, a sad smile splitting her face.

They shoved a tube down her throat and then stuck her in a room with an oxygen line beneath her nose and Velcro straps around her wrists and ankles.

"Just to keep you from hurting yourself," a nurse said. "I bet you're pretty woozy."

They'd given her a sedative—a strong one. Even without the Velcro, she didn't think she could lift her arms or legs. It was like they'd been packed in concrete. Kris never came into the room, but Olivia could hear her voice in the hallway. Aunt Erin's too. Low voices in serious conversation. Someone yelled, and then the door opened and the doctor came in, tired smile on his face. Olivia tried to see through to the hallway, but he shut the door quickly behind him.

Olivia groaned, remembering the last doctor who'd looked at her the way he was looking at her now—all pity and impatience.

"How are you feeling?" he asked.

She opened her mouth, but no words came out.

He nodded. "We pumped your stomach. It's normal to feel a little weak." Then, "I've ordered a psych evaluation. That'll happen tomorrow morning."

Olivia had no interest in a psych eval. "Where's my wife? Is she still here?"

"I believe she went home to tend to your daughter. There's a woman named Erin here though. Your aunt, right?"

"When am I getting discharged? She'll need to drive me home."

There it was again. That sad, impatient smile. *Stupid bitch*, it seemed to say. "You tried to hurt yourself. I wouldn't be doing my job if I let you leave without someone speaking to you."

"I didn't try to kill myself."

"Hurt yourself," he repeated. "I didn't say—"

"I didn't drink the vodka, and I didn't swallow a bunch of pills."

"If substance abuse is an issue, tomorrow you can—"

"I don't even like vodka." Talking felt like knives scraped down her throat. "Did you even bother to test whatever it was you pumped out of my stomach?"

"We don't test it, no."

"Then what gives you the right to keep me here?"

"The state's 24-hour hold." He straightened her chart and slipped it back into the pocket at the edge of the bed. "I'm not the enemy here. We only want to help."

"Then send me home."

He patted her thigh, too high up, too close to her hip. It made her skin crawl. "I'll send a nurse in with some ice chips for your throat."

He left and, just as promised, a bubbly nurse in Betty Boop scrubs brought her a cup full of ice chips with the promise of more if Olivia hit the little red Call button. She wanted to ignore the ice chips on principle, but her throat was on fire and the first few drops of icy water down her throat soothed like nothing else.

Left alone, she looked around the room, taking it in for the first time. She didn't know how much time had passed—a few hours, maybe—but it felt like seconds. She was pissed at the doctor for his pompous attitude, for his refusal to listen. Pissed at Kris and Aunt Erin for allowing this to happen in the first place by believing she would do something like death-by-painkiller. The anger helped. It cleared her head enough to notice the dry erase board directly opposite the bed. Her name was across the top in bright-pink marker. Next to it was as square with *Your Nurses* written across the top and *Allison, Britney, Shonda,* underneath.

At the center, in a big, red circle, were the words *You did this* in jagged script.

She blinked, and they were gone.

To distract herself, she tried to remember what'd happened before being brought here. She remembered seeing her mother, the coffee, how she came home and—she shook her head. Had Kris seen it already? Would she see what Olivia had? The sap and the wrongness of their daughter's face? Or was the doctor right? From the moment she'd come home with Flora, Olivia had felt like she was falling headlong off a cliff, convinced she'd been pushed. What if she'd jumped?

And if she had… If she had swallowed those pills and downed the vodka and now didn't remember, would anyone really be that surprised? Would she?

Having to be two people at once, both temptress and caregiver, wife and mother, minds are split in half. Even if somehow they didn't, if they managed to keep themselves whole, the act of mothering was torture. Breasts reduced to milk bags for animal rooting, sleep all but impossible to get, and the mind constantly twisted with wonder and worry for this helpless thing that would become no less helpless as it got older. An entire life devoted to the care and nurturing of another, always fearing, always convinced you were screwing up. Knowing deep down that whatever happened would be your fault.

The surprising thing was that more mothers *didn't* lose their minds.

She was visited no less than seven times during the night by nurses checking her vitals (and her straps). None offered food (not that Olivia was hungry) but all of them brought fresh cups of ice chips. It was a sick sort of déjà vu, ice chips between her lips and hooked up to a million monitors, except this time there was no excited anticipation, only dread. Part of her wished she could go back to that conversation with Kris and tell her how she really felt—that giving birth terrified her, that she could feel something in her mind waiting to crack, and that having a baby would finally break it open. She wished she had pushed for adoption, for Kris to carry their child, anything but this.

She didn't regret having Flora. Not for a second. But if she'd spoken up, Olivia wouldn't now be faced with two horrible thoughts: either her instinct was right and having Flora had broken something fundamentally vital to her sanity, or the child she'd been feeding, nurturing, loving, wasn't Flora at all.

The sun peeked through the blinds by the time Olivia finally fell asleep. She woke up what felt like seconds later knowing on a gut level she wasn't alone. Slowly, she opened her eyes and spotted Angela in a chair by the door, file open in her lap. Olivia's stomach sank.

As if she could feel Olivia's eyes on her, she looked up, startled, then softened into a smile. "You're awake."

"Not by choice," Olivia said. Then, thinking about how that sounded, "I just mean I didn't sleep much last night. Lots of poking and prodding."

Angela nodded. "Yeah, sometimes I think they like it."

Maybe it was the conspiratorial tone, but Olivia became immediately suspicious. Everything with shrinks was a test. Rather than say something that'd get her in deeper trouble, Olivia shrugged.

"I'm here to talk about last night," Angela said.

"But you're my mother's doctor."

She winked. "I can have more than one patient."

"Isn't that some kind of…breach of ethics though?"

"There's no rule that says I can't treat family members. It's not uncommon."

"But you're with Sleepy Eye. That's a hundred miles from here."

Angela raised an eyebrow. "And?"

Getting to the end of a thought was like slogging through waist-high mud. She was groggy and achy, and she didn't know what exactly was in the drip attached to her arm, but she bet some sort of sedative was involved.

"And," Olivia said, "why would they call you, when they could have got someone closer. There's probably someone on call, right?"

Angela's face morphed into something more serious. "In a situation like you're in, you want someone familiar. Not a stranger."

"You *are* a stranger. I don't know you at all."

"True. But I know you." Before Olivia could argue, she started to read from the file. "'Patient's wife mentioned an aversion on the part of the patient to the child. Patient's wife suspects self-harm, particularly in the breast, and suspects a motive of incapacitating herself enough that she will not have to feed the child.'"

Tears burned Olivia's eyes, and the blood seemed to drain from her face. Her skin felt cold and clammy. Kris had betrayed her. Worse, she had betrayed her to Angela, someone with the power to lock Olivia away.

Angela continued, "'Despite multiple warnings, Patient has continuously sought the company and guidance of her mother, who is herself a psychiatric patient with previously demonstrated violent tendencies.'"

"If she's so violent," Olivia shot back, "why did you people let her out?"

"Shannon is still very much under my care."

"I'm not violent. I didn't try to kill myself. I woke up and the bottles and everything were just…there."

Angela looked at her for a long minute. "Tell me about the black-haired woman."

Chills snaked down Olivia's back. "What about her?"

"How often do you see her?"

"There's no right answer to this, so there's no point in saying, right? I mean, I say I see her at all, and you say I'm hallucinating. I say I don't see her, and you say I'm in denial. I can't win."

"So what's the solution, do you think?"

"I sit here quietly until the 24-hour hold expires, then I go home to what will probably be an empty house." Olivia's voice broke at the end. She saw it with a kind of sick clarity—Kris will have left and taken Flora—the thing wearing Flora's face—with her. Olivia would be alone. She'd never know what happened to Flora. Never know if there was something she could have done.

"And then?"

For Olivia, there was no *and then.* Maybe that was the problem.

Angela dragged the chair closer to Olivia's bed, then removed the Velcro straps. "I'm assuming you won't do anything you shouldn't, right?"

Olivia hesitated a beat, then shook her head.

This time, when Angela sat, she looked at Olivia long and hard, like she was trying to see through to the heart of her. "I shouldn't, but I'm going to let you ask me about your mother. I think it's the only way I'll be able to get you to trust that I have your best interests at heart."

Olivia hardly believed that. Still, the offer was tempting. Which was, of course, the point. Finally able to sit up, she rubbed the back of her head where a dull throb had begun. *"Allow me to ask you—*does that mean you'll answer?"

Angela's eyes brightened and a smile slowly spread across her face. "You really are a lot like her." When Olivia frowned, she said, "I mean that as a compliment. Shannon is and was a lot of things, most of them in flux, but she has always been very smart and engaging. I enjoy talking to her."

"What do you talk about?"

"Without getting into specifics—you. Mostly. That was relatively recent though. Within the last year, I'd say."

"Who started it? You or her?"

"Does it matter?"

It did and it didn't, but Olivia wouldn't push. Not yet. She didn't know what Angela's limits were, how hard Olivia could go until Angela cut her off and sent her away. "And before that?"

"Mostly we'd play card games. Talk about my parents. My mother passed when I was very young. Shannon was always very empathetic. Encouraged me to talk to her about it."

"Sounds like she was the shrink, not the other way around."

"Talking about my relationship with my mother encouraged her to do the same. Your grandmother wasn't always the kindest or most patient woman. Growing up was hard on Shannon. Add to that getting pregnant at such a young age—it takes a toll."

"I don't get it. Is she dangerous or not? Am I supposed to be afraid of her or admire her intelligence and empathy?"

"Both." Angela put the file away and pulled another from the briefcase hanging from the back of the chair. Inside, a cassette was taped to the front cover. Angela peeled the tape off and rummaged in the bag. "If you tell anyone I played this for you, I'll deny it."

"Then why play it?"

"Because I think you need to hear it."

Olivia hesitated, then nodded. Trick or not, her body vibrated with need. If there were answers on that tape, she wanted them, whatever the cost.

Angela pulled a small tape player from her bag and set it on the edge of Olivia's bed. She put the tape in and hit play.

Apart from it being an actual cassette tape, Olivia knew it was old by the way the audio crackled, like the knuckles of an old man. A soft hiss cut underneath typical background noise—papers moving, a chair leg scraping against tile, a cough.

A male voice: *Today is the fifth of August 1984. One in the afternoon. Interview rescheduled from fourth of August 1984 owing to the patient's hysterical episode followed by sedation.*

"My father," Angela said.

It sounded like a door opened. More chair leg scraping. Mumbling voices she couldn't make out.

The male voice continued: *Have a seat, Shannon.*

Olivia pinched her thigh to keep from shivering.

A loud pop made her jump. Shannon flopping down on a chair.

Angela's father cleared his throat. *Good afternoon, Shannon. How are you feeling?*

Shannon's voice came through soft and timid. She sounded every bit of sixteen. Younger, even. *Is she dead?*

Olivia leaned ever so slightly toward the recorder.

Is who dead? he asked.

If she's dead I can't make the trade. I won't get her back.

A slight pause. *Let's start from the beginning. Sound good?*

Shannon didn't respond.

Another pause. The room was silent except for the hiss and crackle of the tape. Olivia almost felt like her mother was in the room with her. If she closed her eyes, she could smell her. Feel her presence in the room.

Another pause. He said, *You know, your family is quite upset. Why do you think that is?*

I'm not stupid, Shannon said.

I didn't say that.

You did. With your face.

I apologize.

No, you don't. People like you never really apologize.

People like me?

People who think they know everything.

"He hated that," Angela said, not without a little admiration.

Shannon continued, *If you knew anything at all, I wouldn't even be here. If you knew anything, you'd be helping me.*

I am helping you, he said.

She laughed. Then, something about the tape changed.

The hiss and crackled faded just long enough for a whisper to break through. *The good, good doctor helping the bad, bad mommy.*

Olivia flinched. In the corner of her eye, *Hi Mommy* appeared on the blackboard, but when she looked directly at it, it was gone. She looked at Angela to see if she would react, but she only glanced at Olivia, as though gauging *her* reaction.

Olivia settled her expression into something she hoped was neutral, her shoulders turned slightly away.

Finally, Shannon said, *You never answered my question.*

Olivia is alive, he said. *Barely a scratch on her. She was lucky.*

This time Angela looked hard at her. Olivia fought to breathe, but inside she was screaming.

When she came out of me, Shannon said, *I thought I would die. And when I saw her, I knew I would.* She paused, and Olivia imagined her picking at her nails or a loose thread on her shirtsleeve. *I think that's why she took her. I loved her too much. If I'd loved her less, she wouldn't have paid any attention to her at all.*

I don't think you can love your child too much, he said. *Someone who loves their child wouldn't—*

Wouldn't do what I did? Shannon snapped.

Indeed, he said.

You're wrong. You don't see it 'cause you can't see further than the tip of your nose.

You keep mentioning a **she.** *Who is she?*

The black-haired woman, Shannon said.

There was a long moment of silence before she continued.

You know how there's two sides of people? Good and bad?

People are more complicated than that.

Shannon huffed. *You're not listening.*

Olivia couldn't help but nod. She felt Shannon's anger in her bones. Everyone wanted to talk at her, tell her how she felt, tell her to put on a smile and muddle through, but no one could be bothered to listen. To see how much she hurt.

I think... Shannon started. *I think she's the pieces of us—of moms—that break when we do or say something we regret. Like, when you say something or do something awful, and later you think That wasn't me. I wasn't myself. I think we're right. Sort of. Us, but not us. Do it enough, and that piece of not us breaks completely away into something on its own. And because it's still, at its center, us, it feels like we do. Lives like we do. Tries to, anyway. Except it can't do it quite right, so it has to take pieces of us with it. Iris used to tell me the black-haired woman was made of vengeance. I think she was right. I think that's why I can't get rid of her. Why it all ended the way it did. Why it will always end this way.*

Shannon, he sighed. *You're not a bad mother. Your mind is—*

You're still. Not. Listening. She slapped the table with each word. *I'm not the ripped-away one. I'm not the one who can't love. She is.*

She who?

The black-haired woman. She chuckled and when she spoke again her voice had deepened. It sloshed like boots through water, mud sucking at the bottoms. *Can't keep calling her that, can I? She needs a name or I'll start to sound crazy. What was your wife's name?*

Joanne.

Jo. I like that. Shannon sighed. *Your wife saw her too, I bet. We all do. Just some of us are better at ignoring her than others.*

Angela sucked in a breath. If Olivia hadn't been deathly still, she might not have noticed.

She didn't breathe. Didn't move. She felt Angela's eyes on her, but she refused to meet her gaze.

Shannon continued, *She took Olivia and put something else in Olivia's place.*

Why would she do that?

So I would hurt the way she does. Then, almost too quiet to hear, *Because I deserve it.*

And what about Olivia?

Shannon's voice broke. *I tried. I tried so hard to get her back, but no one would listen to me. No one cared. Now she's lost forever.*

He lowered his voice, a tactic Olivia recognized from teaching. Speak softly and they have to really listen to hear you. ***Olivia hasn't gone anywhere. She's at home right now with your family.***

That's not my daughter.

Why do you say that?

Have you looked at her? Really looked? She paused, and when he didn't answer, she went on. *I guess it wouldn't matter if you did. My daughter lived inside me for nine months. I know her inside and out. I know her smell. I know how her skin feels. I know the exact way her eyes crinkle when she smiles and the noises she makes when she's happy or hungry or upset. That child is not my daughter. She's a bundle of sticks and mud and sap all rolled together to look like her.*

"Sap." Olivia hadn't realized she'd said it out loud until Angela looked up at her, frowning.

Shannon continued, *Still, it's someone's child. I didn't want to hurt it. I only wanted to get her back.*

Do you regret being a mother, Shannon?

The tone of his voice made Olivia flinch, like she'd been slapped.

Her mother must have felt the same. It was a long time before she responded.

That's not fair.

Why isn't it fair?

Everyone has regrets about things.

Motherhood is a blessing.

Are you a mother?

I'm a father.

That's different.

How?

A father is allowed to walk away.

Angela hit the Stop button on the recorder.

"Is there more?" Olivia asked.

Angela sidestepped the question and asked one of her own. "Do you regret becoming a mother?"

Olivia sank back against the pillows. "Everyone has regrets about things."

She half expected the mimicking banter to continue, but Angela said, "But you love Flora."

"I do."

"You would do anything for her."

"I would."

"But you don't believe the baby you brought home from the hospital is Flora, do you?"

Her face went hot. Angela was fishing. Looking for a reason to send her away. Part of her thought she was being stupid, that Angela was just a doctor, but then she remembered the way she'd looked at Olivia the first time they'd met. Like she was *hungry.* "I don't know what you're talking about."

She looked at Olivia for a long time before nodding. "Fair enough. I told you Shannon and I talked about my mother—do you want to know what happened to her?"

Olivia looked down. Shook her head once. Seemed like the last month of her life had been consumed by dead women.

Angela continued anyway. "When I was in sixth grade, she stopped sleeping. I'd get up to pee and find her pacing the living room. Once, she was holding a bat. Nearly killed me with it when she saw me. You know what she said?"

Olivia didn't answer.

"*I thought you were her.*" Angela paused. "Who do you think she was talking about?"

"I don't know."

"My dad figured she was stressed. Told her to rest. Gave her drugs. In the end, it didn't matter. He woke up one morning and she was missing. We found her the next day in a cupboard in the garage. She'd overdosed."

"I'm sorry to hear that."

"It was a long time ago, so the edge has dulled a little, but I think about her every day. When I met Shannon—" She stopped. Smiled. "You're not the only woman looking for answers."

She started to gather her things, putting the recorder and file back in her bag. She stood and slung the bag over her shoulder.

"What happens now?" Olivia asked. "When do I get to go home?"

"I'm going to be frank with you, because I would expect someone to do the same for me. When I leave, I'm going to file a petition to commit with the court, and if it's processed in time, you will go from here to Sleepy Eye for a few days to start. I believe you need further evaluation before I can definitively say that you won't harm yourself or others."

All of Olivia's breath left her body. "You can't do that."

"I'm trying to help you," Angela said.

Olivia shook her head, but no words would come. Staring her worst fear in the face, she thought she would be stronger. She was *supposed* to be stronger, to stand on the backs of the women whose stories she told every day in her classes, who didn't know what it meant to be weak. Instead, she shrank inward, afraid. The doctors, Kris...they didn't believe her because they weren't *listening*, the way no one listened to her mother. And now it was coming full circle. Her daughter was gone, and no one seemed to care.

"I need to talk to Kris," she said. "She'll fix this. She has to."

"You're more than welcome to call your wife, obviously, but she'll agree with me. She wants to help you as much as I do. She loves you."

Deep down, she knew Angela was right. Kris would agree. It was probably Kris's idea in the first place.

Jealousy, a small voice whispered. *Kris is jealous of your love for your child. Of your connection.*

Olivia found herself nodding along, stopping only when Angela looked at her, head tilted in observation.

"I'm going to leave those straps off," Angela said. "Prove to me I'm not wrong about you. Prove to me you want to be helped."

When Angela shut the door behind her, Olivia threw the closest thing to her—the plastic ice chip cup—at the door. It made a satisfying thwack. She only wished it had shattered.

CHAPTER TWENTY-EIGHT

SHANNON

There's something wrong with my memory.

Angela says it's a quirk of getting older—I set something down, forget I did it, or I forget the reason I walk into a room. I can't tell her I don't forget walking into rooms or putting things down.

After Jennifer gave me her pills, I went to my room to take them. I remember that.

I don't remember swallowing them, even though I know I must have. But when I look under my pillow, there they are.

Why would I do that? Why would I put them there?

The answer is simple, even if I don't want to believe it. The answer is that I didn't.

———

"What are you doing?" Erin asked.

I was in the bathroom—had been for a while—standing in front of the mirror. I turned my head left and right, half expecting the girl in the reflection to miss the action, to fall behind half a beat, but my reflection moved with me as it should.

"Looking," I said.

"Well I need to pee."

"So pee."

Erin scoffed. "Don't be gross. Just get out."

I turned, and my reflection turned with me, half a second too late.

The water was scalding hot. I hissed and shut off the tap in the kitchen sink before wrapping my hand in a dish towel. There was soap all over the counter and sink and up my arms. Wet pans sat on the Formica, water dripping on my socks and on the floor.

"This isn't right," I said.

"I'll say." My mother looked disapprovingly over my shoulder. "How long you been at this? An hour? Looks like you've barely made a dent."

"No." I studied the dishes, like the answer lay in the grease stains like Rorschach blots. "I was in the bathroom."

"For an hour?" My mother rolled her eyes. "I hope you didn't leave that water running, otherwise you're paying the bill."

"Where's Erin?"

"Out."

"Out where?"

"Why this sudden interest in your sister's whereabouts?"

Because two seconds ago she'd been in the bathroom with me, arguing about having to pee. Because I'd blinked and at least an hour had passed, and I had no memory of it.

"Curious," I said.

"Well get curious about those dishes," my mother said. "Because after that you're dusting the shelves in the living room."

I knew better than to argue. We still hadn't heard from the detective about my hair sample, and until it came back, there was an underlying understanding between us that she knew what I was capable of, that she didn't blindly believe in my goodness the way my dad did, and that she'd be happy to call the detective and tell him everything she knew if I didn't do what I was told.

I only partly believed it. My mother wasn't the kind of person to willingly invite a prying eye into our lives. But I believed enough to wash the dishes until my fingers pickled and my back ached.

I finished the dishes, then went into the living room to look in on the baby. Wherever I'd been for the last hour, she hadn't moved. Her fingers gripped the business end of a rattle, but she didn't shake it. Didn't try to shove it whole in her mouth, the way normal babies did.

"I'm not giving up," I whispered.

———————

"—this kind of news, I prefer to bring in person."

"If you're gonna arrest her, just get it over with already. I can't stand this drawn-out garbage."

"Cauline—"

"Don't. Just don't."

"Ma'am, I'm not here to arrest her. We don't like to lollygag when it comes to that sort of thing."

I came into my head just in time to catch the detective's wink.

"So she's clear, then?" my dad asked. "You ruled her out?"

Bathroom. Kitchen. Living room. It was like my body had been picked up in one time and place and plopped in another. Like dream time. I frowned, trying and failing to remember how I'd gotten from the kitchen to the living room, how much time had passed. I looked at my hands—dry, all pruny-ness gone. I glanced back at the kitchen. The sink looked empty, the floors spotless.

"Not exactly," the detective said.

"Then what's the problem?"

"Sorry—" I cut in, only partially listening. "When did you get here?"

"Don't be rude, Shannon," my mother hissed.

"There's no need to play that game." The detective laughed. "Like I said, if we were here to arrest you, we woulda done it."

"I'm not—" I rubbed my eyes. It felt like needles had pierced through my pupil straight through to the back of my head. There was something sticky on my palm, and when I looked at it, I quickly shoved my hands under my thighs. There was blood on my hand, and I had no idea where it'd come from.

"Does Shannon have siblings?" the detective asked.

"None of them would—" my mother started.

The detective put his hand up. "Ma'am. Please. I'm not accusing anyone of anything. Not yet. The test came back almost an exact match for Shannon, but the folks at the lab think it's not enough to implicate her. I won't lie and tell you I completely understand the science, but the way I figure it, either someone at the lab messed up, or they need more information for comparison."

"Why are you telling us?" I asked, thinking of the blood. "I don't know how to *cop* or whatever, but this feels like something you don't say to people you accuse of murder."

His smile was tight. "Like I said, we're not accusing anyone."

My heart was thumping near out of my chest. "Yet."

"I'd like to collect samples from all of you," he said. "It would go a long way to working through this anomaly and ruling you out definitively."

"That's what you said last time," my mother said.

"I apologize for the inconvenience, ma'am. But think of the poor woman's family. I'll be out of your life in a few days—they'll have to live with this forever."

After a long time, my mother relented. "Go get your brothers," she told me. "Erin isn't here, but you can get her brush off the dresser."

I was impressed. No one had ever out-guilted my mother.

"Thank you, ma'am. Your community appreciates good citizens like yourselves, doing what needs to be done to restore order."

My mother ripped a couple of hairs out of her head, a sad smile on her face. "You have no idea."

The next time I opened my eyes, I was in the woods. I hadn't been sleepwalking this time, I didn't think, because I was wearing the same outfit I'd been wearing all day (I was pretty sure), and though it was dark, it didn't feel late. My fingers ached, and when I studied them in the faint light, I saw torn skin and dried blood. The knees of my pants were dirt-streaked. My feet throbbed like I'd been running for miles, and my heart was only just beginning to slow.

"You all fight it, but you accept it in the end."

The voice came out of the darkness, somewhere deep in the trees, but somehow sounded like it was right in my ear. The same voice I'd heard the last time I was here.

"Accept what?"

And then I saw her, and it was like she'd always been there, if I'd only focused, if I'd only *looked*. Long ratty black hair hung to her waist, and her skin looked pale and clammy. She wore a familiar dress, the hem torn and mud-stained. Her eyes flashed as a cloud passed over the moon, and when she smiled I saw the reflection that'd been looking back at me in the bathroom mirror for days. A breeze pushed her hair forward, and I immediately thought of the hair the detective told them they'd found with Iris.

"You killed her."

"She killed herself."

"Why?"

"Because she realized she was better off in the dark. Just like you'll realize." Her eyes flickered, black coals burning red hot at the center. "You're not a mother. You don't care about your child."

"I don't care about anything else."

"Prove it."

"How?"

"A real mother, a good mother would give anything to have them back."

"I would give anything."

"Even yourself?"

I hesitated and in that hesitation, I saw what the black-haired woman saw. Unworthiness.

"You see it now," she said. "You're not a mother. Could never be a mother. Climb down into the dark with me, where you belong."

Like in my dream, my mouth opened and words came out even thought I didn't speak. "Where I belong."

CHAPTER TWENTY-NINE

OLIVIA

T he nurse approached the bed with one eye on Olivia and the other on the straps, hanging limp off the side. *Someone must have told her about the crazy lady in room 104.* Any other day, she might have found it funny—even enjoyed—the way the nurse took her temperature from as far away as possible, the way she missed the hook as she tried to hang the bag, her eyes squarely on Olivia. She'd never been intimidating, could never be the stern one, the take-no-bullshit professor who earned her students' respect the first day. She relied on jokes, self-deprecation, and giving her students enough slack to hang themselves with. But for the few seconds it took for the nurse to finish, Olivia felt powerful.

It didn't last. The second the nurse was gone, Olivia deflated, the reality of what was happening like a thousand pinpricks, a dull pain that grew and burned and felt like it would turn her inside out.

It was the kind of feeling that used to push her to the phone, to call Kris. Kris, who'd spend hours on the phone or next to her on the couch just being there, just sharing space so that it didn't feel so heavy.

Olivia was so tired of being alone.

They brought her dinner at 4:30. Olivia pushed it around the tray awhile before shoving it on the floor. Angela returned shortly after, a folder in her hand. When she saw the food on the floor, she raised an eyebrow at Olivia.

"It fell," Olivia said.

"I'll ask custodial to clean it up."

Olivia ignored her, leaning back on the pillows. She closed her eyes and wished she had taken the pills and drunk the vodka.

"There will be a car here for you tomorrow," Angela said. "I'm stopping by your house later this evening to pick up a few of your things."

No. This was fast. *Too* fast. There was no way they'd released her to Angela's care without someone talking to her. She was an adult. She had a mortgage and a degree, for God's sake. Fear and anger swirled around inside her, battling for control.

"Make sure Kris packs my vibrator. Fuck knows I'll be bored."

"Olivia—"

"How long have you been working her? How many conversations did you have with my wife before she gave in to whatever it is you're doing here?"

"I don't—"

"I'd bet money you reached out to her. Not the other way around. She would never do this to me unless she was manipulated. We're a *family*. We're—"

"*Olivia.*"

"What?" She sat up and fixed Angela with a burning gaze, tears dripping down her cheeks. "Isn't this what you want? Crazy woman finally cracks open?"

"I told you, we don't like that word."

"Which one? *Woman*?"

Maybe it was wishful thinking, but Angela looked like she'd been hit. Good.

"I understand you're upset and I'm sorry."

"You're *sorry*?"

"The truth is Kris called *me*. She was worried that maybe you'd been spending too much time thinking about your mother, that it was unearthing some repressed trauma. She said she was scared you would do something you'd regret."

Olivia's stomach dropped. "You're lying."

This couldn't be happening. There had to be someone she could talk to. Someone who could fix this. Aunt Erin? Her grandmother? What if they'd both been in on it too? She imagined Kris going to them with the idea, phone calls with Angela. It would explain why'd all been so cagey with her. Why they coddled her like she was a wild animal instead of trying to understand what she was going through.

Charlie, she thought. *Charlie would know what to do.* But how was she supposed to get ahold of her? She didn't have Charlie's number memorized, and she didn't know where her phone was, if they'd even give it to her.

"I care about you. I care about what happens to you *and* Flora."

Her voice strained as she shouted, "You're *lying!*"

"Your mother didn't believe me either. Not at first." Angela dropped the folder on the bed. "You're welcome to read the petition. I don't like to keep my patients in the dark."

"No, you like to shine a bright-yellow light into the cage."

This time, Angela didn't flinch. "See you soon, Olivia."

She didn't start crying until Angela left, the door slamming behind her.

Olivia drifted in and out of sleep, jarred awake by the urgent need to piss from all the ice chips. It was still dark when she woke up for the fourth time, her body instantly aware of a change in the air of the room. It was fuller. Denser. The light from the machines penetrated the darkness just enough that she could see to the end of her bed, but no further. She wanted to get out of bed—the light switch was only a few feet away—but childhood fears of monsters kept her legs firmly planted.

She held her breath and kept still, straining to hear anything under the blanket of darkness. The ceiling creaked and there were footsteps passing in the hallway. Hushed voices and loud voices, and underneath, she felt something there. Something watching. Waiting.

"Mommy," a voice whispered. "There she is. That good, bad mommy."

Blood rushed to her ears and her heart pounded, gaze sweeping the room, but she couldn't see anything. Shadows bent in the corners of her eyes, only to stop when she turned her head.

"It's almost over now, Mommy," the voice said. "Not long now."

In the corner—darkness blacker than black, a shadow that swallowed all the other shadows stretched upward, branches like spindly fingers.

Olivia scrambled back in bed. "What do you want?"

The shadow trembled.

"Please—" Olivia swallowed bile. "Just tell me what you want."

"Olivia? What's wrong?"

The darkness seemed to lift just enough she could see someone in the corner. Her mother. She stepped closer to the light, rubbing her eyes.

"Mo—er, Shannon?"

The corner of her mouth lifted. "I dozed off. I didn't mean to scare you. I wanted—needed—to see you, but I didn't want to wake you. You looked peaceful."

Olivia's body was still ramped up on adrenaline, her heart skipping and her legs trembling. She flung them over the side and leaned her head on her hands, taking deep breaths. "Jesus," she finally muttered. "I really am going crazy."

"No," her mother said. "You're not."

"Don't give me that chemical imbalance shit, okay? I'm not in the mood."

"Olivia." Her mother took her hands. Olivia almost pulled away. "I mean it. You're not crazy. I believe you." She glanced over her shoulder at the door. "And I know how to fix it."

"How do I know you're not lying?"

"Because when I help you get out of here, I'm all but guaranteeing they'll send me back to Sleepy Eye, and any chance I have at a normal life will be gone for good." She sighed. "But I would do anything for my daughter. Anything."

"Why now? You've been out for, what, three months? Why haven't you tried to contact me?"

"I couldn't. Erin was always watching. And my mother…" She turned slightly away and quickly rubbed at her eyes. "I just couldn't. But I wanted to. Believe me."

"We can't just walk out of here."

"We can, if you do what I say."

After a long moment, Olivia nodded. She didn't have any other choice. Once she was locked away, they'd stop listening to her. She'd be there forever. "Okay. What do we do?"

"I've been wandering around the last few hours. Watching the nurse's station."

"No one stopped you?"

"No one noticed." She stepped further into the light and Olivia realized her mother was wearing a pair of scrubs.

"Where did you get those?"

"Had 'em."

"Why?"

"Why not?" She glanced at the clock. "You're due for another round of vitals in about half an hour. When they come in, I'll already be here, checking your temperature and whatever, and they'll assume they were wrong about the rotation."

It was a flimsy plan. The more Olivia thought about it, the lower her heart sank. "And you think they'll just…go?"

"They're not exactly itching to get in here with you."

Olivia thought of the last nurse to come in and decided she was probably right. Still. "So you break me out of here and then what?"

Her mother ignored her, studying the heart monitor, the saline drip, probably making sure she could pull off looking like she knew what she was doing.

"I can't go to my house. I can't go to Erin's. Am I supposed to just...sleep on the street?"

"We'll go to my mother's house."

Olivia laughed. "She's the first person who would turn me in. Just seeing us together would be enough for her to perform some kind of citizen's arrest."

"She's not there."

"What do you mean?"

"Do you want me to help you, or not?" her mother snapped. Face reddening, she added, "Look, I can walk out of here, and you can pretend nothing happened and hope Angela is half as good to you as she should be. I know you have no reason to trust me—God knows, I wouldn't—but right now I'm the only person who can help you get Flora back."

"Like you got me back," Olivia said. "Right?"

There it was again, that flash across her eyes. After a long moment, she said, "Right."

At five on the button, a nurse gently knocked and then took two steps into the room carrying a pen in her mouth. Shannon stood over Olivia, studying the saline bag.

Shannon glanced over her shoulder. "Morning," she said brightly. "You need something?"

The nurse frowned, and when she opened her mouth, she seemed to have forgotten the pen there. It hit the tile with a gentle clatter. The noise seemed to bring her back into herself. "Who are you?"

Shannon sidestepped the question. "Helen didn't tell you about the swap, did she?"

Olivia tried to hide the panic itching its way to the surface of her face. If her mother was making this up as she went along, they were fucked.

The nurse cursed under her breath. "When?"

"Last minute, like always."

Sighing, the nurse bent over to pick up her pen. She paused halfway up and seemed to be studying Shannon's clothes intently.

We're fucked, Olivia thought. *We are so fucked.*

But whatever the nurse thought she saw, she shrugged it off. "You didn't happen to hear where they stuck me, did you?"

"Methinks it's break time," Shannon said.

The nurse's shoulders visibly loosened. "Thank God. I'm starving." She eyed Olivia. "You sure you're good here?"

Shannon nodded. "I got this. Go eat."

The nurse didn't need to be told twice. She bolted from the room without so much as a glance backward. The second her footsteps faded out of earshot, Shannon grabbed Olivia's hand. "Let's go."

Olivia was shaking too hard to argue. All she could think about were the million ways they could get caught. What would happen if they did. Then an image of Flora flashed through her mind—the Flora from the hospital, the Flora she knew was hers—and it steadied her a little. *Remember why you're doing this. Remember what's at stake if you don't.*

At the door, Shannon said, "Try to look sleepy."

Olivia almost laughed. With the amount of adrenaline pulsing through her, she doubted she'd ever sleep again. Still, when Shannon opened the door, Olivia leaned on her a little, allowed her eyelids to fall halfway closed. She breathed long slow breaths.

The hallway was deserted, save for a woman at the nurse's station. Her hair was tied up in a messy bun, with two pens sticking out of the top. There were bags under her eyes, and in the two seconds they paused, she checked her watch twice.

She looked up just as Shannon started to lead Olivia down the hall. "What are you doing?"

Shannon didn't miss a beat. "Toilet in her room's clogged. I gotta take her down the hall."

The messy-bun nurse groaned. "I'll call janitorial."

"Already did. No ETA on a fix though, and this one's had a lot of ice chips."

The messy-bun nurse waved her off, already done listening.

Olivia kept up the act as long as she could, but the further they got from her room, the harder it was to keep from trembling. It was like each step was another year tacked onto a sentence, locked away in Sleepy Eye, another crazy woman hidden from the world.

At the bathrooms, Shannon shoved her in. "There's clothes and shoes hidden in the changing table. Put them on. Quickly."

Olivia did what she was told. In the crook of the changing table were a pair of jeans, a sweatshirt, and a pair of sneakers, one of them with a hole in the bottom. They fit well enough. She studied her reflection in the mirror—she looked like hell—and tried to run her fingers through her hair, but they kept getting snagged on knots. She spotted someone's hair tie at the top of the garbage. She tied a quick knot with the broken ends and was able to get her hair up just as her mother cracked the door open.

"Finished?"

Olivia nodded. "Now what?"

"Now we walk out of here."

"But the nurse at the station—"

"Has already forgotten about us. I can guarantee she's less than an hour from finishing her shift, which means all she's thinking about is breakfast and sleep."

She slipped into the bathroom after Olivia and came out seconds later in an entirely different outfit. "Under the scrubs," she said.

Olivia figured that was what the nurse had been looking at—a second pant leg peeking out beneath the scrubs—and thanked whatever gods were watching over her for overworked nurses with more important things to worry about than fashion choices. Arm in arm, they slipped past the security station at the far end of the hall and out the double doors into the empty visitor's entrance. The woman at the desk shot them a look but didn't seem too concerned. Probably the more people who left, the better her day looked.

There was a cab idling outside. He waved when he saw Shannon.

"You know him?" Olivia asked.

"I'm paying him double for waiting. Move it."

They got in the cab and as the driver slowly pulled into traffic, Olivia looked out the back window, waiting for the other shoe to drop. Every car that changed lanes behind them was Angela or Kris chasing them down.

"Relax," her mother murmured. "Everything's fine."

Olivia turned around and closed her eyes, taking deep, measured breaths. She almost believed her.

———

They got to her grandmother's house just as the sun was coming up. Her mother didn't seem concerned, but Olivia was counting the minutes until another nurse thought to check in on her. She wondered if Angela would be the one to discover her gone when she and her boys in white came to cart her away. Would they call the police? Kris? Where would they start looking, and how long before they thought to come here? And even if her mother was sure that her grandmother wouldn't be home, how long until she came back? Every television show Olivia had ever watched told her it was only a matter of time. The police would go to relatives first. Kris, then Aunt Erin, then her grandmother. They had a few hours. Maybe a day, if they were lucky.

"You worry too much," her mother said as she started toward the door.

Olivia jogged to catch up. "They'll come looking for me here."

"Eventually. But it won't matter by then."

Using a key she pulled from her pocket, she let them inside the house.

"Where did you get that?" Olivia asked.

Shannon paused in the foyer, fingers tightening into fists at her sides. She tilted her head like she was listening, then shook it once, almost too quickly for Olivia to notice. When she finally turned to face Olivia, her expression was calm, but her eyes shone.

"If you're gonna question every step of the way, I can't help you," she said.

"I just want to know what's happening."

"What's happening is we're staying here until dark."

"And then?"

"And then we fix it. We fix everything."

Olivia wasn't hungry, but when her mother brought out a plate of buttered toast and a couple of mugs of coffee from the kitchen, she didn't refuse it. She needed something to do with her hands, to distract her from the silence. From her racing thoughts.

Where was her grandmother, the woman who never left her home if she could help it?

Had Angela already come to the hospital? Did they know she was gone?

How was her mother planning to help her get Flora back? Did it have anything to do with the switch she talked about in the tape?

As soon as her thoughts came around to the tape, all Olivia could think about was the black-haired woman. She had seen her in the hospital room, she was sure of it. Was she the same woman who'd taken her all those years ago?

"Your ears are smokin'," her mother said, offering a small smile.

"What?" Olivia asked.

"You look like you're thinking really hard about something. Hard enough to make smoke come out of your ears." She laughed. "I must be getting old. That's something my dad would've said."

Olivia nibbled a corner of the toast. Washed it down with the lukewarm coffee. "When Angela talked to me, she made me listen to a tape."

"What tape?"

"Of you."

"I see."

"He—her dad, the man in the tape—asked you about the black-haired woman."

Her mother nodded. "And you have questions about her."

"I've seen her," Olivia said. "She...touched me."

Her mother nodded again, but didn't comment. She tilted her head—listening, always listening—and sipped her coffee.

"Who is she?" Olivia asked.

"You read my journal. You know who she is."

"*What* is she, then?" She remembered what her mother had said in the tape. *Us but not us.*

Her mother studied the contents of her mug for what felt like a long time. "A friend, even when it doesn't seem like it." She sighed, a sad smile pulling at the corners of her mouth. "She helped me figure it out, all those years ago."

"How to get me back," Olivia prompted.

"Yes."

"And Flora."

"Yes."

"How?"

"The well. We'll need to—" She paused. Frowned. She set down her mug and pulled a cell phone out of her pocket. It was buzzing.

Olivia's face went hot, and it was like the bottom dropped out of her stomach. They'd already found her. "Don't answer it," she ordered.

"It's Erin."

"Don't answer it."

"She'll only keep calling."

"Please—"

Her mother accepted the call, putting it on speaker. "Hello?"

Erin's harried voice came through the line. "Where are you?"

"I'm getting coffee. You know I meet Angela on Tuesdays."

The panic in Olivia's stomach bubbled. They would both be found missing.

"Yes. I drive you."

"I took a cab. You have your hands full with Olivia and Flora. I was only trying to lighten the load." She paused, listening. "Are you okay?"

It sounded like Erin was crying. She sniffed, and when she spoke, her voice was thick. "It's Flora."

"What about her?" Her eyes met Olivia's. "Is she okay?"

"No. I don't know. She's—" Her voice hitched. "She's gone."

Olivia bit her lip to keep from shouting.

Her mother took the phone off speaker and held it to her ear. "What do you mean *gone?*"

Olivia sank low on the couch, pulling her legs up to her chest. The whole world seemed to fall away, leaving only Olivia in a darkening room with her aunt's tinny voice her only company.

She's gone.

Flora's gone.

CHAPTER THIRTY

SHANNON

There's no point in fighting her. I've always known that, but sometimes I get too big for my breeches, as my dad would say, thinking I'm smarter than I really am. She's always two steps ahead of me—too far ahead to catch, but somehow still in my ear, whispering and twisting and changing me.

After nearly a month of trying to take the pills only to find them back in the spot where I'd hidden them, edges chalky with saliva, I give up. My throat is sore from her reaching a hand inside and plucking the pill before I can swallow.

You win, Jo.

I walked back from the woods, barefoot and worried that every time I blinked I would end up hours or days ahead, with no memory of having gotten there. The black-haired woman followed behind. Close, but not too close. When I broke the tree line, she seemed to disappear, her shadow dissipating into the shadows of the trees on the ground.

Follow me into the dark.

In the darkness there is no judgment. No responsibility. Anonymity.

I would be lying if I said I wasn't tempted.

I heard yelling from the back porch and almost turned around—I'd take a manipulative poltergeist or whatever she was over my mother pissed off any day—but my mother spotted me from the window and ordered me inside.

"Shannon MacArthur, where the *hell* have you been?" she asked. There was a spaghetti sauce stain on her shirt bleeding out from an inadequate rinse, right above her breast. It looked like she'd been shot.

"Outside."

"And you figured you could just leave us to handle Olivia, right? No need to say anything to anyone or check on your daughter, for chrissake." Her face was going beet red, and her voice was hoarse before she'd even finished the sentence. "I don't know where you learned this selfish behavior from, but I swear to God if it doesn't change, there will be consequences."

"Like?"

My mother froze. Surely I wouldn't have dared.

But now that it was out, I couldn't take it back. That would have been worse. I could only push through it and hope to come out the other side alive. "What kind of consequences?" I asked. "Be specific."

It was exactly the wrong thing to say, of course. I knew that then. But it was like a small piece of the black-haired woman had clung to my hand, and when I wiped my mouth, that small piece slithered off, clinging to my lips and tongue.

My mother got in my face, whole body trembling. I could smell the coffee and whiskey on her breath, could see the remnants of lunch caught between her teeth and the black hairs growing from her lip. Her eyes were glassy and she held her arms tight at her sides, hands balled up into fists.

I almost wished she would hit me.

"You act like you're so grown, like you know everything. Doesn't even cross your fool mind that there's other people out there smarter and meaner than you. I know deep down you had something to do with that poor woman's death, even though I don't want to believe it, and I'm just as positive I wouldn't be able to prove it." She grabbed my hand so tight I felt the bones grind. "But that doesn't mean someone else, someone who didn't love you, wouldn't try."

My heart thumped in my chest and the back of my head. My eyes burned, but I willed the tears not to fall even as tears streamed down her face.

"Whatever's in there, you bury it, and you bury it deep. You're a mother now, Shannon. Like it or not, you better start acting like it." She shrank a little, spent, as the baby's cries drifted down from the bedroom. "Go upstairs. Your daughter needs you."

I moved on autopilot toward the stairs, driven by my mother's expression, by the desperation in her voice. But she didn't understand. This wasn't something I could just bury.

The black-haired woman walked backward ahead of me, her long hair tripping me up. I didn't ask how she got there. Didn't want to know.

The closer to the room I got, the louder the baby's cries became. It was like sandpaper on my nerves.

Underneath the cries was a sound like wind rushing through the gaps in a closed window—a ghostlike moan that rose and fell between hiccups.

I would follow her into the dark, I decided. And I would bring this thing with me.

I went into the room and scooped the baby up, holding her tight against my chest. She was surprisingly warm—not a worrying kind of warm, but a comforting warm. Her eyelids drooped and she curled into me, her tiny body fitting in the crook of my elbow. On the back of her neck was a trail of soft down that I couldn't help but brush gently with the backs of my fingers. Her hands curled into tiny fists and the corner of her mouth twitched upward. Tickled.

I sank down on the bed and held her for hours or minutes, studying her eyelashes and the fat wrinkles on her arms and legs. I peeked in her ear and gently pulled down her lip to look at her pink gums.

I shook my head, but there was something there. Something bothering me about the baby. For the first time, I considered that I might be wrong.

"Look at her skin," I said. "Her hair."

Fake, the black-haired woman said. *Fake.*

I leaned over and buried my nose in her hair, breathing in her scent.

"Still wrong," I said.

Look again.

This time, when I looked down, the baby's eyes were open. Her pupils were wide, nearly blocking out the whole of her ivy-green irises. The fuzz on the back of her neck stood on end and thick drool oozed from the corner of her mouth. I stood, nearly dropping her.

You ever try to hold your breath too long?

Her skin rippled, the softness giving way to sandpaper, and her pupils shrunk to pinpricks, the whites of her eyes bloodshot.

Her little body stiffened, the muscles protruding beneath her skin. I struggled to keep hold of her as she flailed with arms and legs like tree limbs until finally she went limp. Her skin shriveled around her mouth and nose and her eyes—now black—were glassy.

I spent the rest of the evening with the baby, rocking her, talking to her, feeding her. My mother walked past the room more than once, eyebrow raised as though daring me to slip up. Part of me knew that it didn't matter if I got you back, if for the rest of your life I was the perfect mother, mine would always see me as the girl in front of the fire, a murderer. Unworthy. Despite myself, I started to make plans for the after time, when I had you back and the world was set to rights. We wouldn't stay with my parents anymore. I wouldn't be able to live under my mother's thumb and threats, so I would take you somewhere north where the rent was lower and I could find a job as a waitress or a nanny. I'd meet someone kind who would help us find our roots—someone I wouldn't love immediately, but would grow to adore as time went on—and when you were older, much older, I'd tell you everything because I wouldn't be able to keep secrets from you forever.

We would have the closeness I'd always deserved, but never got, from my mother.

A fairy tale all our own.

It was gone two in the morning by the time the rest of the house fell asleep. I'd been laying in my bed listening for movement from my parents' room, from Erin's bed, for hours. The baby was fast asleep, its breath like wind through reeds, and barely stirred when I scooped her out of the bassinet. The black-haired woman was waiting at the bottom of the stairs, blending into the shadows on the walls. She smiled and, in the darkness, all I could see was her teeth.

I paused at the bottom of the stairs and waited for my mother's bedroom door to open, to hear footsteps on the landing. In my head I played out all the excuses I could use—the baby needed a bottle, the baby couldn't sleep with Erin's snoring—knowing she wouldn't believe any of them.

It didn't matter. The house was silent.

She walked behind me as I went barefoot through the back door and onto the damp grass. I eased the door shut and we waited again, but no lights came on upstairs, and there was no movement anywhere in the house.

The baby seemed to sense something was wrong. She woke up and immediately started crying. I snatched the blanket off my shoulders and wrapped it around her, face and all, to muffle the sound.

As soon as we stepped into the yard, a light came on above the back door. I couldn't remember my dad installing a floodlight, but I knew it was my mother who pushed it. She'd see the light and be out here before I could get you back.

Run.

I took off, the baby quickly growing heavy in my arms. I untangled her and dropped the blanket at the tree line, but carrying her wasn't any easier. My legs ached and I struggled for breath as I bolted between trees, already lost. It was like something inside the baby was reaching out for the ground, for the trees—each step was harder and heavier than the last.

I heard voices shouting behind me. If my mother caught me this time, there wouldn't be another chance. They'd send the baby away somewhere—or send me somewhere—and whatever hell you'd been taken to, you'd be stuck there forever. With renewed energy I pushed through the pain until finally I saw the well. The black-haired woman sat in a tree above it, her hair hanging down like moss.

Into the dark.

I couldn't bring myself to look, but I knew I had to go. I would go into the dark, but only because I knew you were there. I would live in the dark if it meant you were there with me.

The baby clawed at my shirt, at my arms, leaving bloody streaks where her nails caught skin. Her face was twisted and red, her cry broken and bleak.

Do it.

I stepped up to the well and laid the baby on the ledge, holding her down with one hand.

Throw her in. Saliva dripped from the black-haired woman's mouth into the well, her teeth bright white in the dark. *Do it. Quickly.*

There was a pop, and then searing pain ripped up my leg. My knee went out and I fell sideways, clawing the brick on the way down. I hit the ground hard, knocking the wind out of me, and when I was able to open my eyes, the black-haired woman had disappeared into the shadows among the branches.

"I got her!"

It was Erin's voice I heard first, and then I saw her scoop the baby off the ledge of the well and pull her to her chest. My dad knelt next to me, pressing one hand to my thigh. I screamed as the pain shot up through my belly.

"It's okay, Shanny," he said. "You're gonna be okay." His voice broke. "You *shot* her. I can't believe—Jesus Lord."

"I didn't mean to!" My mother stood over me, the silhouette of her night-gown ghostly against the blackness. "I only meant to stop her."

Lies.

"We need to get her to a hospital. No, Shanny, don't go to sleep. Stay awake. Stay right here."

His voice faded as my ears began to ring. My heart fluttered and I shivered. Cold.

I don't remember much after that. I don't remember going to the hospital, where they took the bullet out of my leg. I was told later I needed a blood transfusion. They told my mother I was lucky. I'm sure she loved that.

I do remember waking up later, plugged into half a dozen machines and my leg patched and swollen. I remember being visited by the detective, who tried to get me to confess to Iris's murder. I didn't say a word. I couldn't. The black-haired woman had her hand over my mouth the entire time. I was never formally charged, but it didn't matter. I was as good as guilty to anyone who could stand to look at me, of which there were surprisingly many. The day they told me I was being taken to Sleepy Eye, I made myself a promise. Next time, I wouldn't hesitate.

Next time, I would go into the dark, I would get you back, whatever it took.

CHAPTER THIRTY-ONE

OLIVIA

The only thing keeping Olivia in her skin was reminding herself that it wasn't Flora they were actually talking about. It was an impostor.

But Flora was missing.

Her mother was still on the phone, talking Erin down, trying to keep her from going to the hospital to see Olivia.

"She's fragile right now," her mother said. "All you're going to do is push her further over the edge. There's nothing she can do from the hospital except feel hopeless and angry, and neither of those things is going to make her better or bring Flora back."

She caught and held Olivia's eye. It was then that Olivia noticed how old her mother looked. How tired. The lines in her face looked like they'd been carved with a knife. She wasn't that old—barely fifty. Olivia thought it was that place that'd aged her. Staring every day at the same gray walls and the same barred windows and listening to the same soft voices tell her that the things in her head were twisting her, making her wrong. Olivia wouldn't survive a place like that. They had to finish this. Get Flora back, and then—what? Run away?

"Why would the police talk to her? She's been in the hospital."

Olivia's stomach flipped. Of course the police would be involved. It probably looked convenient as hell—the day she's told she's being committed, her baby disappears. The police wouldn't think twice about her fragility, and even if they needed Angela's permission to see her (which she doubted), they'd skirt past it anyway. They had minutes before the police discovered her missing, an hour maybe before they found their way here.

She needed help.

Finally, her mother hung up.

"What happened?" Olivia asked.

"Your wife went in Flora's bedroom to check on her before getting ready for work. The room was empty. Window open."

Something inside Olivia twisted with agony. She had to remind herself that the baby wasn't Flora. Flora had been gone for weeks. In the hospital, she'd tried to pinpoint exactly when the switch was made and decided it was the night Kris had moved Flora into the second bedroom. They'd agreed they'd keep Flora in their room for at least the first couple of months—all those middle-of-the-night black-hole dives into internet articles on SIDS had left Olivia paranoid. She'd wanted to be able to look over and see her daughter breathing.

Knowing it was Kris's fault for moving Flora was somehow comforting to Olivia.

"The police will be there soon," her mother said.

"And then they'll come here."

Her mother shook her head. "No reason to."

"If I were a cop, I'd come here."

"Then you'd be a stupid one," she snapped. "I—I'm sorry. I just need you to trust me. Okay?"

Olivia started to nod, but her mother had only ever said they would *fix* it. She didn't know what that meant.

"What happens after?" she asked.

"What do you mean?"

"I mean after. When we do whatever it is you say we have to do, when I have Flora back, what do we do? Where do we go?"

Her mother tucked the phone in her pocket. "Away."

"Away where?"

"I don't know yet."

Olivia felt sick. They were as good as caught. "We need help."

"*We* don't need anything. I know what to do."

"I have a friend. Charlie. She knows people and might be able to—"

"*No.*" The force of the word stopped Olivia midthought. Her mother pointed, inches from jabbing Olivia in the chest. "You don't tell anyone, understand? No one else gets involved. Everything is exactly how it's supposed to be. It'll work."

For the first time, her mother didn't sound so sure. It shook Olivia.

As her mother began to pace, head tilted as though listening to someone whisper in her ear, it occurred to Olivia that she'd put all her faith in a woman she didn't know. A woman who, up until three months ago, had been under care because she couldn't take care of herself.

"What do you mean," Olivia asked, "*everything is exactly how it's supposed to be?*"

Her mother only shook her head.

"Did you…abduct her?" Olivia asked.

Her mother looked at her, as though for the first time. "I didn't."

Olivia studied her, not knowing what to think. It was like her perception of reality had been twisted inside out. Nothing made sense, but if she could just keep Flora in the front of her mind, somehow, she knew everything would be okay. "What are we going to do?"

Her mother didn't look at her. "Just trust me."

"But the police—"

"The police don't see anything they don't want to. Okay? They won't give a shit that you're not in the hospital. Know why?"

Olivia shook her head.

"Because they'll be too busy looking for me." She rubbed her face. "I'm the one with a history of *violence* and *delusions*. With a history of…" She shook her head. "They'll have it in for me from the get-go, and they won't even think to look here. You know why?"

Olivia didn't answer.

"Because they'll go to Angela for hints. They'll ask her where my safe place would be, where I would be welcome to hide." Her voice rose. "And *this* house, under the thumb of *that* woman, is the last place I would go for sanctuary."

For a long time, Olivia didn't respond. It was surreal, being shouted at by her mother. "How did you know my grandma wouldn't be here?"

Her mother sighed. "If you're going to question me every step of the way, we might as well give up now. You *can't* do this without me. Understand? You *will* fail."

"Okay," Olivia said, unable to hide the tremble in her voice.

Her mother pressed her fists into her eyes and then sat next to Olivia on the couch. She squeezed Olivia's knee. "Hey. Listen. I'm sorry, okay? I'm just—I'm worried, is all. For Flora."

Olivia nodded.

"And I'm doing everything I can to fix this. I just need you to—"

"Trust you." Olivia looked hard at her. "Right?"

"Right."

"You swear you can get Flora back?"

"Cross my heart."

"Say it. Say the words."

"I swear I can get Flora back."

Part of her knew it didn't matter if they got Flora back. They could only run so far, so fast. She didn't have anything they'd need—money, connections—so it was only a matter of time before they caught her. Kris would go bankrupt trying to keep Flora when they used Olivia's insanity as an excuse to put Flora in foster care. Then they'd probably escort Olivia under armed guard to Sleepy Eye, or somewhere worse, where she'd be stuck for maybe the rest of her life, which was exactly the thing she'd been trying to avoid from the start.

Except now she knew she wasn't insane. She knew that something, someone had taken her daughter, and the only thing she wanted was to know that Flora was safe, no matter what that meant.

"Okay," Olivia said. "I believe you." Because she had no other choice.

"Good."

"When do we—?"

"Dark. It has to be dark."

"What do we do until then?"

"Hope."

When an hour passed, and then another, and the cops weren't breaking down the door, her mother spread out on the couch to take a nap while Olivia puttered around the kitchen. She wasn't hungry, but she couldn't just sit and relax either, so she found herself studying the contents of the refrigerator. It was fuller than she'd expected for a woman living alone. Then again, she didn't know her grandmother very well anymore, so it was possible she had friends who came by frequently. Or a boyfriend. The thought made her smile. Her grandmother was a hard woman, but you had to be to get anywhere in this life. The world liked soft women because they gave easily underfoot, a philosophy she didn't think her grandmother had put much stock in.

Still.

There was a roast in the refrigerator that, from a quick look at the date, looked like it was about to go off. Her grandmother was an avid shopper of sell-by meat because it was cheap, but she always stuck it in the freezer to get a couple more days out of it. If the roast was in the fridge, it meant she'd been planning on cooking it. Today.

Olivia closed the fridge and looked around at the rest of the kitchen. Their coffee mugs were in the sink, but so were a few other dishes—a pan with grease still stuck to the bottom, a plate, and silverware. Someone's dinner dishes. Her mother's? Unlikely. If she'd been here since last night, Erin would have noticed. She would have said something when she called. That meant it had to be her grandmother's, but her grandmother wouldn't have gone anywhere with dishes in the sink. Not unless she didn't have a choice.

Olivia thought of a hundred reasons why what she was seeing didn't mean anything scary—her grandmother had rushed off to help a friend in an emergency, or she'd suddenly decided she didn't give a shit about a couple of dishes.

Except that didn't sound like her grandmother at all.

She crept back toward the living room; her mother appeared to be sleeping like a rock, arms draped over her eyes. *How can she be sleeping?* Olivia thought, whose own body was thrumming with anxiety. She supposed maybe it was a skill her mother had developed at Sleepy Eye. But the longer Olivia watched her, the more she began to wonder if her mother was sleeping at all. Did she cover her eyes to keep the light out or to be able to watch Olivia undetected? Why?

In the quiet, she thought she heard movement upstairs, but as she strained to listen, the silence returned. They hadn't even bothered to check the bedrooms— how could her mother be sure they were alone? Unless she knew they weren't. Unless this was some elaborate plan to get Olivia committed to Sleepy Eye. But why break her out of the hospital, then?

There were too many questions and none of the answers sat well.

She had two choices. She could go back to the hospital where they were no doubt already looking for her and all but guarantee she would never see Flora again. Or she could choose to believe her mother.

Maybe she would just peek in upstairs, just to settle her nerves. Just to be sure they were alone.

She started up the stairs, skipping the third and fifth, remembering how they squeaked. She cast one last look toward the living room before stepping up onto the landing. The air was thicker up here, hotter, with a stale smell. All of the doors were closed, and no light shone through the gaps.

No one's home, she thought.

But she walked toward the bedroom door anyway and eased it open, wincing when the hinges creaked.

Something dragged along the bottom of the door. A scrap of paper. The edges were stained a deep rust color, and when she picked it up, unfolding it, she noticed a near-perfect thumb print near the top, just above her name.

Her stomach twisted as she began to read.

> *Olivia,*
>
> *I should call you, but I know you won't answer. I understand why you're angry, but know that I have been where you are. I've seen the black-haired woman lurking in the corners of my eyes for my entire life. My mother, my aunts, my friends…she's in all of us. I should have told you. I should have helped you. Maybe I can help you now. You can't*

The letter ended abruptly, unfinished. Olivia frantically turned the page over, searching for the end. Can't *what*? Her gaze moved away from the writing and back to the stains. She knew in her body what they were, but it was like her mind refused to acknowledge it. Letter clutched in her hand, she crossed the threshold.

Inside, the room was mostly dark, blackout curtains drawn over the windows. It smelled odd, a little like coal or something burnt, and lavender bathroom spray. Two steps into the room and she noticed the lump in the bed. She froze, remembering her grandmother asleep the last time she'd come over. But the closer she crept toward the bed, the more wrong her grandmother looked.

The blanket was pulled up to her chin, and her mouth hung just open. Olivia accidentally kneed the bed as she got closer, disturbing a fly that'd been crawling on her grandmother's teeth.

Olivia stumbled back, a scream caught in her throat. She groped for the curtains, pulling them open.

When she looked back at her grandmother, it was clear she was dead. Olivia pulled the blanket down and saw a bloodstain on her chest about the size of a fist.

"Did you know if you own a gun, you're more likely to get shot with it than use it on anyone else?"

Olivia spun around and saw the black-haired woman in the doorway. The woman held her grandmother's gun, pointed at Olivia.

She continued, "Not sure what the statistics are, exactly. I'll have to look it up."

It was like seeing two people at once. The black-haired woman sneered with crooked, yellowing teeth and hair that coiled around her like snakes... And then there was her mother. That was the face looking at her now, but it was wrong somehow. And the hair was only a shadow, but it clung in a way shadows shouldn't. Olivia resisted the urge to blink, knowing in her gut that if she closed her eyes even for a second, she was as good as dead.

"You shot her," Olivia finally said.

"Fair's fair. She shot us first." The muscles in her face slacked, expression drawn. "She wouldn't listen. She *never* listened. I had to."

"What are you talking about? You're—"

"Not Shannon." She smiled, but it looked like strings were tugging on the corners of her mouth. "Not at the moment, anyway. You're making this more complicated than it needs to be."

"I don't understand." Olivia's brain was like soup. She trudged through the memory of conversations with her mother, the journal, knowing the answer but unable to grab it with both hands. Then she remembered the tape. *Us but not us.* The worst parts of her, her regrets. The black-haired woman.

"Jo?" she said finally.

Her mother curtsied. "'Fraid I don't have any prizes for you." She gestured with the gun. "Come on. Out. It stinks in here."

Eyes on the weapon, Olivia froze. What was happening? "Is this a trick?"

"No trick. She's definitely dead. Come on."

"No. I—" She sucked in a breath, struggling to keep her composure when tears burned her eyes. Her grandmother was *dead*. And she'd tried to warn Olivia, but she'd been too stubborn to listen. Stubborn like her mother. "I thought you were going to help me."

"I said *move*."

"But my daughter…she's—"

"Enough." Her mother lunged at her, grabbing her arm hard enough to bruise, and spun her around, jabbing the gun into her spine.

With the gun at her back, Olivia wobbled down the stairs and into the living room, her mind working furiously to figure out how to get out of the house. But she was torn—was this part of the plan? Everything felt out of control, and in her gut she knew she needed to get away, to find help, but Flora… If this really was the black-haired woman manifest in her mother, could she somehow manipulate her into returning Flora? Or was she completely lost? The front door was locked—she could see the chain from here—and the few precious seconds she might get from hitting her mother would be spent trying to get the door open. There was the back door, but it was a clean shot from where they were to the back door, and Olivia didn't think her mother would miss.

Her mother dug the gun into Olivia's back. She barely felt it. Her whole body had gone numb. "Start walking."

"Where?"

She shoved Olivia forward. "The well."

"I—I thought we had to wait until dark."

"I'm tired of waiting. Move."

The sun shone without a cloud in the sky. It was almost a taunt. Olivia glanced out of the corners of her eyes for nosy neighbors, a postal worker, anyone who might see what was happening and call the police, but she knew better. Even though the yard wasn't blocked by a fence, there were enough trees around you couldn't see anything unless you were looking hard and knew what you were looking for.

But moving forced her brain to start working. This didn't make any sense. She thought they were on the same side. They were here to get Flora back. There was no reason to threaten her, unless her mother—Jo, whoever—thought she would go to the cops. She was just as at risk as her mother was. If—when—Flora was returned, it didn't matter what story she'd spin; the police, Kris, Angela, everyone would believe Olivia had taken her.

"You don't have to do that," she said when her mother jabbed the gun in her back again.

"Shut up," her mother said.

Crossing the tree line was like crossing from day into night. A chill crept across her skin as the shadows passed over her. Leaf-thick branches rustled and it sounded like rushing water. She could have run. There was a good chance between the dark and the trees she'd get away, but her mother wouldn't have been forcing her like this, keeping her afraid, if there wasn't something she wanted. Something Olivia would be unwilling to give.

"You want Flora," Olivia said.

She snorted. "Don't be stupid."

"Then why are you doing this? We were coming here anyway. Why bother with the gun and my grandmother and everything else?"

"Because you can't count on people to do what they should. Now shut up. I'm listening."

All Olivia heard was the crunch of leaves and twigs and the occasional bird.

"I don't understand. What do you want? What does Flora have to do with it?"

Her mother punched Olivia in the back of the head, driving her to the ground. Pain burst through her head, and she saw flashes of white as she fell. Her arms were too slow to catch her, so she went down face-first. Her lip caught on something sharp, and she scrambled to grab whatever it was as her mother yanked her to her knees by her hair.

"I want the same thing you do," her mother hissed in her ear. "I want my daughter back."

"I *am* your daughter. I'm right here." Her mother gripped her hair tighter, the gun pointed at her chest, keeping Olivia pinned in place. She looked her mother in the eye. "*Mom.*"

"No," her mother hissed. "Don't you dare call me that. I have worked too hard and too long for you to ruin this."

Olivia went cold. Unable to take her eyes off the gun, she spoke softly, "You used me."

"No, darling," her mother said. "You used me." She kneeled in front of Olivia. Pressed the gun to her sternum. "You used me. Jim used me. Angela used me. All of you, a bunch of leeches, taking and taking. It was torture nursing you, knowing every ounce of milk you took was stolen out of my daughter's mouth."

"Angela—"

Her mother grinned. "She tell you about her mother?"

Olivia carefully nodded.

"Did she tell you that, before her mother died, she visited Angela in her room? Tested her? Claimed the black-haired woman had accused Angela of being an impostor? She told Angela she needed a piece of her skin, just an earlobe or fingertip, that the black-haired woman said Angela was a changeling wearing Angela's skin, that if she cut it away it would shrivel and die. Not likely something a young woman is bound to forget. She looked for women like us, women who'd seen the black-haired woman with our own eyes. Didn't matter if some poor mother was living her life, protecting her child as best she knew how. Angela found her and took her. She lied and manipulated and twisted to get what she wanted. All of us little pieces in her mommy puzzle."

Olivia felt dizzy. She'd been right. Angela had been looking for her. And Olivia had been stupid enough to put herself right in Angela's path. But how would Angela even know about her unless… "She said you talked about me. For the last *year*. Why?"

"Erin mentioned you were trying to get pregnant. She got all excited, told me I was going to be a grandmother. I saw an opportunity. Jim would see the news as a trigger, but I would show him I was *healed*." She sneered. "It wasn't his attention I would need, anyway. It was Angela's. See, she was too busy pulling strings, she didn't notice hers getting tugged. We talked all about you, how I was so concerned about your future, about your baby. I thought you needed watching, just in case you succumbed to the same *illness* as me. Angela ate it up. It was only a matter of time before she agreed to let me out, not because she believed I was better, but because she knew it would bring you out of the woodwork. She could study you. Take you, if she wanted."

Tears burned Olivia's eyes. "Why do you care?"

"Because I needed you close. I needed to make sure the black-haired woman noticed you *and* your child. You would come to me for help, and then I would bring you here, and the trade I'd begun all those years ago would finally finish and I would get my baby back. *My* Olivia."

It felt like being buried. All the truth piled on top of her, all the lies, and she couldn't dig through it, couldn't figure out which was which.

"I told you," Olivia murmured through gulping sobs, "I *am* Olivia."

Her mother took a deep breath. "It's almost time. I can feel her getting close. My little girl."

Tightening her grip on Olivia's hair, she yanked and dragged until finally she released Olivia.

Olivia fell, catching herself with her fists. The sharp thing cupped in her hand cut into her palm, but she bit back the pain.

Finally, she looked up and saw the well.

"It's the dark. Can you feel it calling you?"

Olivia didn't answer, maneuvering the sharp thing—a rock shard—between her fingers. She kept her hands on the ground, hoping her mother wouldn't notice. Breath coming in shallow bursts, she studied the tree line, barely visible in the falling dark, looking for those breaks that would lead to a yard or parking lot or road. *It's not a big place*, she remembered. All she would have to do is pick a direction and run. But it had to be the right direction, or she would have to double back and risk getting caught. In the distance, she thought she saw a bouncing light. Someone's flashlight, maybe?

"Get up," her mother ordered, pointing the gun at Olivia's face.

Olivia obeyed, looking her mother in her eyes. Eye contact. That was the way to keep her from noticing. To keep her from seeing—

Her mother kicked her hand. Something cracked and she dropped the rock shard. Her stomach rolled as she looked at her finger, crooked at the middle joint. Her head swam and she bit the inside of her cheek to keep from throwing up.

"Do you hear it?"

She did hear it. She heard it with her whole body. Heard it tell her she was too late. The voices conjured images of Flora's broken body, and the agony was almost enough to kill her.

Her mother grabbed her hair again and pulled her toward the well, pushing her hard up against it, so that the stones scraped the skin where her shirt had come up.

Her mother pressed the gun to her temple. "I'm gonna need you to shimmy on down there."

Tears and snot dripped down Olivia's face. "Why?"

"Because I asked you nicely."

"I won't. Not if it means you get Flora."

"I told you. I don't want her."

"Then what do you want?"

Her mother tucked her chin into her neck. "I want my Olivia."

Olivia couldn't fight the shiver. "I am Olivia."

"No, baby. You're not."

She dragged a ragged nail down Olivia's arm, splitting the skin just enough for beads of blood to break through.

"No. Please."

Her mother clamped a clammy hand over her mouth. "Hush. Look."

The blood was too thick, the color all wrong. Like honey. Or—

Olivia gasped. "No. No, this isn't right."

"Go on, then," Jo crooned. "Mommy's waiting."

Her mother started to push her over, but Olivia clung to the side of the well, digging her nails into the ancient grout. Tears made everything blurry, but she thought she saw movement somewhere at the bottom of the well. Fingers and teeth.

"No!" Olivia screamed. "This isn't real!"

But the pain scorching through her head and across her shoulders and down her arm was real and the sickening ooze across her skin was real and the gentle cry of a baby was—

Her thoughts came sharply into focus. Flora.

"That's it," her mother whispered.

The gun hit the ground just next to her feet.

Her mother said, "You hear her?"

Olivia nodded.

"You want her back?"

Tears streamed down her face as she nodded again. Her grip on the side of the well loosened, just barely. Just enough.

Her mother kissed her cheek. Wrapped her arms around Olivia's middle. And then Olivia was lifted off the ground just enough to tip her over the side. She scrambled to grab the side the well, but the momentum was too much and her nails dragged along the cement, breaking off as she fell. But Olivia had clung to her mother, whose grip wasn't strong enough. Together, they fell.

The fall took seconds. Olivia hit the shallow water hard, her bones clanking together with a sickening crack. She gagged on floating detritus that'd shot into her mouth and up her nose. Blood or water or both dripped into her eyes and burned. She grit her teeth to keep them from chattering as she felt along the wall, trying to get her bearings.

There was nothing but the dark and the cold and the pain. When she looked up, she couldn't see the opening.

She would die down here.

The dark crooned to her and her body bent to meet it, her skin brushing the shadows. Her skin burned with the cold. Sharp pain came in waves radiating from her spine to her fingernails. She would die, but first she would suffer.

You deserve to suffer.

Damp hands crept up her body. Jagged nails dug into her thighs. She tasted blood and smelled the sweet rot of death.

Olivia nodded. Yes, she did.

She felt the black-haired woman's voice touching every part of her. Crooning, coddling, soothing. It made her skin prickle and stole the breath from her lungs. Blackness pooled at the corners of her vision, broken only by the occasional flash of brick and mold.

Something nudged her shoulder and she turned languidly to see her mother's body bobbing beside her, facedown in the water, tangles of weeds slowly wrapping around her limbs.

Fighting the pull on her body, Olivia gained just enough purchase on the wall that she could rip away the weeds and roll her mother over without sinking. Her breath caught as she looked at her mother's face, soft and painfully pale. The pieces of the black-haired woman that had lied to her, convincing her that Flora was some kind of *creature*, were gone, leaving behind this woman—her *mother*—that Olivia would never get to know. She would never be able to parse through the deception, to learn what was real and what was a story told by the black-haired woman to manipulate her. She would never know if her mother had loved her. If she was permanently broken. She would never know if her mother could have pulled herself up from the darkness, to look at Olivia with her own eyes instead of through the shroud the black-haired woman had wrapped around her. It wasn't *fair*.

There was clarity in the dark of the moment. Like a flicker of light, quick as a blink, understanding pushed through the fog and the voices and the pain. Her mother was wrong. Had always been wrong. Whatever mask, whatever evil she'd seen in Olivia was a mirage, and whatever fault she'd seen in Flora wasn't real. Flora was Olivia's daughter.

And she needed her.

Olivia grabbed for the wall, shoving her fingers in the gaps between stones, trying to pull herself up, to get high enough that she could yell for help. The nails in her thighs dug in deeper and searing pain ripped up her body. More hands emerged from the water, gray and gnarled, and they pulled at her clothes and hair. Fingers wound over her face and into her mouth, choking her as she struggled to keep above water. Crooning voices became a garbled cacophony that echoed off the walls of the well. It was deafening.

Flora, she reminded herself as her grip slipped. *She's still out there somewhere. She needs you.*

But the dark was suffocating and every breath in burned. She couldn't get purchase on the slippery wall, couldn't even see it in front of her.

If she died, Flora would still have Kris.

If she died, maybe Flora would be better off.

Yes, the voices murmured. *Yes.*

She screamed, but the sound was muffled by the hundred hands closing over her face. She couldn't breathe.

Please, she thought.

But the black-haired woman, moving like a fog through her mind, flicked it away.

She started to sink.

Just as the corners of her vision went black and the water threatened to swallow her whole, somewhere very far away, she saw a light. Flora may have had Kris, but she needed Olivia, too. More than that, Olivia needed Flora. Gritting her teeth, she peeled the hands away from her face. Blood trickled down her throat, but she shouted with the last of her breath, reaching, groping, until she heard frantic voices above her. The light brightened and she focused on it, until the fog in her mind thinned and the hands pulling her down shriveled.

She cast one last look at her mother, whose body was strangled by weeds and black sludge. Olivia's stomach rolled, wondering if her mother would become one of them now, the dead women who reached into the minds of mothers, twisting their thoughts, consuming them.

"Liv!"

Olivia couldn't see them, but she heard them calling for her—Kris and Charlie. Aunt Erin. They hadn't given up on her.

It was all she needed to find her voice. The words clawed their way from her chest, "I'm here!"

Again, louder, echoing, enveloping her.

"I'm here!"

CHAPTER THIRTY-TWO

OLIVIA

SIX YEARS LATER

I t won't be the end of the world," Kris had said.

She was right, of course. It wasn't the end of the world, but it was close.

Flora was starting kindergarten.

It wasn't the best school in the district, but it wasn't the worst either. When they toured the place, the teachers appeared to give a shit and the principal didn't talk down to Flora like she was a puppy with pigtails, so Olivia figured the place was alright enough. Flora was a smart girl. She could learn anywhere—

But not until she found her Elsa shoes.

"Aren't these the ones?" Kris held up a pair of purple sneakers.

"Those are Anna," Olivia said. "Totally different character."

Kris rolled her eyes. "Flora!" she called, "You like Anna, right?"

"No!" a distressed voice called from her bedroom. "I like Elsa!"

"I warned you," Kris said to Olivia under her breath. "That movie came directly from hell."

Olivia laughed. "Check between the washer and dryer."

Kris raised an eyebrow, but started toward the laundry room anyway. When she came back holding the Elsa shoes—pale blue, with light-up bottoms—she shook her head. "Witch," she said.

"Mom's not a witch," Flora said, appearing from the bedroom like a sprite, all pastel and glitter. "She's a superhero."

"Damn right." Kris draped an arm around Olivia's shoulders. "Don't know what we'd ever do without you."

A familiar voice slithered from somewhere in the dark corners of her mind, but Olivia shook it away before it could speak.

No, she thought. *Don't you dare.*

The bus stop was at the corner of their street, visible from their living room, but Olivia insisted she drive Flora. It was her daughter's first day of kindergarten, and she was going to soak up every last ounce of it.

"I wish I could come with you," Kris said, planting a kiss on Olivia's ear.

"You can," Olivia said. "You should. Flora would love that." She grinned. "We could get coffee after?"

Kris squeezed Olivia's shoulder, then took a half step back, hands shoved in her pockets. "I wish. You can tell us all about it tonight though. Every detail."

Us. Kris and their therapist, a soft-spoken woman named Barbara. They'd been seeing Barbara off and on for the last five years, an unspoken but vital condition to rebuilding Kris's trust in Olivia. At first, it was required by her doctors, in the beginning when she was still a signature away from being committed despite telling them everything, doing everything they'd asked of her. But then Olivia began to take comfort in those appointments with Barbara. Sometimes they talked about Flora, but most times they didn't. Sometimes Olivia spent the whole hour unloading while Kris and Barbara listened, and Olivia, after a while, began to trust that she could say almost anything without judgment. She and Kris were finding each other again, and for that she was grateful.

"You got it," Olivia said. "Can't wait."

In the car, Flora buckled herself into the booster seat—*you always do it too tight, Mom*—and Olivia started out of the driveway.

Just keep driving. Schools aren't safe. They don't care about your child. The building will collapse and she'll be trapped, and it'll be your fault because you weren't brave enough to just keep driv—

"Mom?"

Olivia blinked. Smiled in the rearview mirror. "Yes?"

"There's people honking."

Yes. She heard them, getting louder as her head cleared. She hadn't slept well last night. First day of school jitters. She was overtired. Nervous for Flora. Nervous for herself. She'd accepted another adjunct job—smaller college, more drama—and she'd already been late to class twice. If not for Kris talking her off a ledge, she would have quit.

It would be okay, she told herself. She would go to work, then she would go to Happy Hour with Charlie, where she would ignore the email that'd been staring at her from her inbox for days. Angela Tran's license had been suspended only weeks after Kris and Charlie pulled Olivia out of the well for her part in having Shannon released, knowing what she knew. They wouldn't let Olivia see the case notes, but what Shannon had been telling her that day at the well was true. Dozens of women, all guinea pigs in Angela's quest for answers about her own mother.

For six years, Angela had been reaching out to Olivia. In all that time, Olivia had deleted the emails and ignored the phone calls. In the months leading up to now, though, it'd been harder.

"Momma?"

"Sorry, sweetie," Olivia said. "Guess I had fuzz in my ears."

She finally moved through the green light just as it turned, earning more angry honks.

She turned on the radio, but it was all morning talk shows, no music. Still, it was enough to drown out the voice in her head. She'd accepted that some things that lurked in the darkness never really went away. She could only push them further into the light.

"Mommy, can you turn it down?"

Olivia nudged the volume down by a click.

"More, please."

She pretended not to hear. She could see the school at the end of the block, the place already a madhouse with cars. She managed to find a spot on the side of the street just as someone else pulled out, cutting off another car that'd been waiting. The driver—a woman with a blond ponytail and blindingly white veneers—flipped her off.

Olivia returned the gesture.

Flora giggled.

On the sidewalk, the principal waved and patted shoulders as the children moved past, actively avoiding the person in a giant panda costume. Flora adored pandas, so it took immeasurable restraint for her to sit still in her booster until Olivia gave her the okay to unbuckle.

She's a good girl, she thought.

Smart and well-behaved and kind—Flora had become everything Olivia didn't dare hope for after a group of neighbors had pulled her out of the well using an old swing rope. They'd found Flora not long after, mere feet from the well.

They pulled her mother's body out later.

At the time, Olivia didn't have to say anything, didn't have to make excuses. Between the police and Jim Tran, they came up with a story everyone could live with—Shannon had been off her medication for months. A dissociative episode combined with severe depression brought her mind back to when

Olivia was a baby, to the original trauma that, Jim said, was the reason for Shannon's mind bending in on itself. She'd taken Flora, convinced she was her daughter.

Olivia became the woman who had survived not one, but two murder attempts. A miracle, they called her. Reporters knocked on her door for a whole weekend, but she never said a word, didn't dare for fear of slipping up and saying something that could make Jim look at her the way Angela had that day in the hospital.

"Shannon was manipulating you. Angela, too, it seems," Jim had said. "I'm very sorry that I missed it."

Olivia had been all too willing to accept her temporary insanity as a combination of manipulation and undiagnosed postpartum depression.

But sometimes—

"Mommy, the panda's waving at me!" Flora laughed. "Can I go? Please?"

For months, Olivia managed to convince herself she'd left the black-haired woman in the bottom of the well. Thrust into the dark, where she belonged. But the dark is porous. It bleeds.

Flora was three when Olivia saw the black-haired woman in the mirror, eyes like jet.

Olivia had spanked Flora for purposefully spilling an entire cup of chocolate milk on the floor, and then ran to the bathroom, horrified and crying harder than Flora.

Seeing the black-haired woman, Olivia finally realized what her mother had meant in that interview with Dr. Tran. The black-haired woman *was* her. Was all of them—her mother, her grandmother, Iris, and Angela's mother... She was the darkness in their heads and the sting in their slaps. She was the moments of doubt and anger and resentment made solid. She was pain and desperation. She was a mother.

The black-haired woman looked at her now from the rearview mirror, obscuring Olivia's view of Flora.

There's only one way to keep her safe.

"Mommy?"

Only one way she'll stay your little girl forever.

Olivia broke away and turned to Flora. Flora had one hand on the buckle, gaze flickering between Olivia and the panda. One day Flora would grow up and leave her. One day, Flora would have to confront the darkness, but unlike Olivia and Shannon, she wouldn't be on her own. Olivia didn't know what it was about her family that made the black-haired woman so visceral to them, why they were so easily bent by the sound of her voice. She only knew that it was her job to make sure that if Flora decided to become a mother, and it opened a door in her mind to the darkness, Olivia would be there for her. She would believe her, and they would get through it together.

Drive away. No one will ever find you.

She would tell Flora that there was no shame in being afraid, of not trusting yourself. She would tell her that there were people willing to listen, to help, who wouldn't make her feel small or worthless as a mother because there were days—weeks—that she couldn't see anything but shadow. She would tell Flora her story—the parts that mattered—and help her find someone like Barbara, a kind ear and thoughtful heart. Because that was what had saved Olivia, in the end.

Olivia swallowed the knot in her throat and forced a smile. "Okay, sweetie. You ready for kindergarten?"

She nodded so hard her pigtails whacked her in the face.

"Do you want me to walk with you?"

She hesitated.

"It's okay if you want to be a big girl and go alone."

"I do," Flora said.

"Okay, then. Off you go."

Flora squealed, unbuckled herself from her booster, then grabbed her backpack from the floor and practically ran from the car. She didn't double back and give Olivia a kiss, probably didn't even hear her when Olivia shouted *I love you.*

Olivia waited until Flora had hugged the panda, until she waved to the principal and walked tentatively through the door, out of sight.

Then she drove, the black-haired woman still staring from the rearview mirror.

She would always be there, Olivia knew. Always beckoning. Crooning. Warning.

Olivia would not give in. Would not follow the black-haired woman into the dark. No. Instead, she would remember that small light; she would hold onto it. Not for Kris. Not even for Flora.

But for *her.*

If you can hear the call of the water,
it's already far too late.

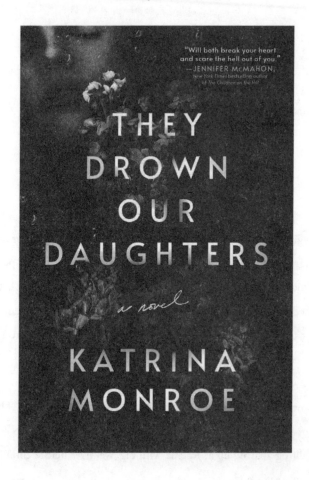

Part queer modern Gothic, part ghost story,
They Drown Our Daughters explores the depths of
motherhood, identity, and the lengths a woman will go
to hold on to both.

REGINA

R egina found Constance sprawled on the grass, her thick, graying hair tangled with purple thistles. A ring of pale blue Thalia petals surrounded her body. Her lips moved with silent words, and her fingertips twitched in the dirt. Crickets chirped, growing louder as the sun dipped slowly over the horizon. A bullfrog climbed out of Constance's apron pocket, resting on her belly.

"I don't want to kill my husband," Regina said.

Constance cracked one eye, closing it just as quickly. "Admirable." Then, "It's rude to stare while a woman communes, Gina."

The bullfrog glanced up at Regina with big, wet eyes before climbing back into Constance's pocket.

"Are you talking to me or him?" Regina asked.

Constance smirked. "Either or. It suits you both, I think."

Seemed every time Regina hiked the hill at the far end of the peninsula to see Constance, the woman had a creature hidden somewhere on her body, clinging to her as though they could absorb that essential something that softened her face and brightened her spirit while the rest of them went hard and gray.

It was resentment that made some of the people of Cape Disappointment call Constance a witch. If not for Regina's middle-class upbringing and her marriage to a man of means, she might have succumbed to the same fate.

Friends since childhood, it was Constance who Regina had gone to when she couldn't conceive. Under Constance's direction, she'd swallowed remedies. She'd danced the dances, naked around the phallic maypole. She'd burned sage and eaten enough pumpkin to turn her orange. She'd buried eggs in her hearth, under her pillow, under the bed, in the garden, beneath the steps of their front door, until her house was a veritable chicken coop, and nurtured a small ficus from seedling to leafy adult, until finally she conceived her daughter—Marina, her miracle child, who'd been born too small, her lungs struggling to take in a first breath. For days after, the doctors told Regina to expect the worst, that a child so delicate couldn't be expected to last the week. Regina had nursed Marina herself, holding and cuddling and touching until their bodies seemed to become extensions of each other. Regina never called Constance a witch, not out loud, especially after Marina took her first wobbly steps. That didn't mean others did not.

William and Grace followed Marina soon after, barely a year apart. Her husband gave his praise to the doctors who'd poked and prodded her to bruising, but Regina gave his money to Constance. Her friend was powerful in ways the doctors were not, ways Regina made a point of learning for herself.

"What's the point of the frog?" Regina asked.

"He grounds me. Keeps me tethered to the here and now."

"Sounds awful."

Constance smirked, nudging the bullfrog out of her pocket and into the grass. "If you've come for a character witness in the event of your husband's untimely demise, I'm afraid I won't do you much good."

"I don't want—"

"To kill him. So you said."

Sighing, Regina gathered her skirts between her legs and lay down next to Constance. Her hair smelled like bonfire and pine sap, and if Regina closed her eyes, she could imagine she was deep in the woods, away from the ocean and the lighthouse, the letter still crumpled in her fist.

A marriage drowned by apathy…

Women like her have teeth…

Tread carefully, my darling…

She tossed the ball of paper onto Constance's chest. Constance opened it and read silently.

"Who's Jeanie?" she asked when she'd finished.

"The daughter of one of Anthony's partners." A pause. "The woman he'd see in my place."

"Oh." She paused too. "You say you *don't* want to kill him?"

Regina smirked despite the tears welling in her eyes. "No." She sat up, snatching the letter back. "But I'd like to hurt him."

———

Dinner was a silent affair. The children, along with Anthony's niece, Liza, visiting for the summer, traded kicks beneath the table. She and Marina were both fourteen, womanhood creeping up behind them with a sack and hammer. Though Anthony shot them warning glances between bites of potato, Regina hoped they clung to their childishness. Once that line was crossed, there was no going back.

Regina pushed her food around her plate, stealing glances at her husband when she dared. He had to know the letter was gone. That she'd stolen it from his desk. Would he deny his intention to leave her? His relationship with Jeanie? Or would he approach her like a stubborn ship's captain, using honeyed words and a firm hand to convince her that his was the correct decision and never mind the rain-bloated storm clouds in the distance or the leak in the hull?

She shouldn't have been surprised. He'd had other affairs, but they were quiet and brief. Despite never meeting those women, Regina believed there was an understanding between them. They could have her husband in their bedrooms, but it was Regina who was on his arm. Regina, who'd given everything to create and maintain the kind of home and lifestyle befitting someone of his station. It was Regina who would die in the largest room of the largest house on the cape. And it was Regina's children who would inherit it all when she and Anthony were gone.

It was this understanding that helped Regina look the other way, to play the part of the blissfully ignorant wife. This time was different. This time, her husband was on the verge of throwing away all that Regina had achieved—for herself and for her children.

Dinner ended without a word. Anthony planted a dry kiss on her forehead before disappearing into his office, where he would stay until he crawled into bed in the wee hours of the morning, stinking of whiskey and cigars.

"Would it really be so bad if he left?" Constance had asked.

Yes. It would.

Because he wouldn't leave. Not after he'd spent the better part of a decade culling out a private port for his business, after dumping too much money into building a lighthouse to silence the critics calling Cape Disappointment a smugglers' port. It didn't matter how much of her own blood and sweat had been mixed into the mortar that held the lighthouse together, that it was her who made sure it was lit at night to guide sailors safely home. Regina would be made to leave behind everything she'd built, to run home with her tail between her legs or move somewhere new and be a pariah.

And her children?

He'd keep them, too, if only out of spite. And then the moment Jeanie had children of her own, they'd be pushed to the side, forgotten.

Marina laid her head on Liza's shoulder, teasing a curl out from behind Liza's ear with her little finger. Across the table, Grace slipped the last of her potatoes onto William's plate, a gentle grin on her face as he heaped them all onto his fork. When it was time for dessert, Regina knew he'd pretend to eat his entire pudding in one bite only to give it all to Grace.

She imagined the day Anthony would come to her dripping of pity and false remorse and tell her their marriage was over. In her mind's eye, she saw Jeanie waltz through the front doors, plump and ripe. She saw her children sent away to schools on the other side of the country, away from their home, away from *her*.

Regina couldn't let that happen.

She caught Marina's eye across the table and smiled.

I would do anything for you, Regina thought.

Anything.

AVAILABLE NOW

READING GROUP GUIDE

1. As the daughter of someone who exhibited signs of mental health problems, Olivia is the kind of woman who monitors herself for symptoms. Why do you think that, at the onset of what she believes to be hallucinations, Olivia decides not to seek help?

2. *Olivia did not glow.* Society often shames women who either do not choose motherhood or do not define themselves by their role as mothers. Do you think this societal shame contributed to Olivia's actions? How?

3. Would the story have unfolded differently if Olivia had sought mental health care? Or would the black-haired woman have remained a part of her life?

4. Throughout the story, Olivia laments the loss of the woman she was before she became pregnant. Does this contribute to her experiences with the black-haired woman? Why?

5. Olivia's grandmother insinuates that the black-haired woman visits all mothers, but neither she nor Olivia can determine why their experiences with the black-haired woman are more intense than what others may have experienced. Why do you think their family's visions of the black-haired woman are more visceral?

6. Shannon's point of view is presented through journal entries, later found by Olivia. Does the fact of Shannon's manipulation change the way you think about events as Shannon portrayed them?

7. If Olivia had never found Shannon's journal, would she have sought Shannon out as vehemently? What, if any, effect did the content of the journal have on Olivia's state of mind?

8. When Aunt Erin suspects Olivia might be struggling in the way Shannon had after giving birth, she warns Olivia against seeking treatment. Why do you think that is?

9. Olivia and her grandmother appear to be the only two women to see the black-haired woman and come out the other side of the experience without having succumbed to the darkness. What traits do they share that may have helped them overcome it?

10. Folklore tells us that names have power. When Shannon named the black-haired woman "Jo," do you think she gave her the power that would ultimately lead to Shannon's possession?

11. How might the story have changed if Angela had told Olivia about her own mother's experiences with the black-haired woman? Would Olivia have been more willing to speak to her? Or less?

12. At the end of the book, Olivia and Kris appear to be mending the rift in their marriage, caused by Olivia's struggles and Kris's lack of understanding. What do you think would happen if they had another child? Would history repeat itself? Would their marriage survive it?

13. Though Flora is beginning kindergarten in the final chapter, the black-haired woman still appears to Olivia despite Olivia getting treatment. This time, though, Olivia seems to have more control over her. What does this mean, if anything, about the evolution of the black-haired woman and what she represents?

ACKNOWLEDGMENTS

I gave birth for the first time at nineteen years old. I was terrified and angry and very quickly began experiencing symptoms of postpartum depression. I was lucky—my light at the end of the tunnel was bright—but that isn't true for everyone. I am extremely grateful to Julia (last name unknown), the nurse who took one look at me, a child holding a child at our first checkup, and asked me sweetly, sincerely if I was okay. Thank you, Julia, for listening to me cry for what felt like hours, for slipping me your phone number (even though I never used it), and for promising me it would get better.

Thank you to my editor, Mary, whose keen eye and encouragement have spoiled me for anyone else ever. I chose violence with this book, and it's all your fault.

To my agent, Joanna, for not blinking an eye when I abandoned a nearly completed manuscript to write this book mid-deadline. Your unflappable calm in the face of my internal chaos is a gift.

My final and deepest thank you to my wife. You know why.

ABOUT THE AUTHOR

© Bert Jones Photography

Katrina Monroe lives in Minnesota with her wife, two children, and Eddie, the ghost that haunts their bedroom closets. Follow her on twitter @authorkatm.